D0418759

TRUST NOBODY

TRUST NOBODY

JUNE HAMPSON

First published in Great Britain in 2006 by Orion,
an imprint of the Orion Publishing Group Ltd.

3 5 7 9 10 8 6 4

A CIP catalogue record for this book is available from the British Library.

ISBN-13 978-0-7528-7457-9 Hardback
ISBN-10 0-7528-7457-8 Hardback
ISBN-13 978-0-7528-7458-6 Export Trade Paperback
ISBN-10 0-7528-7458-6 Export Trade Paperback

Typeset by Deltatype Ltd, Birkenhead, Merseyside

Printed in Great Britain by Clays Ltd, St Ives plc

The Orion publishing group's policy is to use papers that are natural,
renewable and recyclable products and made from wood grown in sustainable forests.
The logging and manufacturing processes are expected to conform to the environmental
regulations of the country of origin.

The Orion Publishing Group Ltd
Orion House
5 Upper Saint Martin's Lane
London, WC2H 9EA

www.orionbooks.co.uk

For Danyel
For Rachael

I would like to thank Lucie Whitehouse who made this book possible. Also, Juliet Burton, my agent, and Jane Wood, my editor at Orion, along with her fantastic team. They have all played their parts in making my cherished dream a reality. Thank you all.

All the world's a stage,
And all the men and women merely players:
They have their exits and their entrances;
And one man in his time plays many parts.

WILLIAM SHAKESPEARE
As You Like It, Act 2, Scene 7

CHAPTER 1

5 August 1962

'What the fuck ... You planned this. Daisy, you bitch!'

She lifted the heavy hammer drill and pointed it at his head.

'Eddie, you deserve it,' she said, depressing the trigger. The machine whirred into life. The noise was deafening and the thing bucked in her hands but she was ready for it. What he'd done had sickened Daisy. Her brother-in-law kicked and strained uselessly at the nylon stockings that bound his wrists and ankles tightly to the iron bedstead. She could smell his fear and it mingled with her own.

Her heart was beating fast and as noisily as the drill. Never before had she attempted anything like this, but it was necessary. Necessary to frighten him into submission before he took charge of her life like he ran everyone else's.

His head was thrashing from side to side. Daisy could feel sweat running down her back and between her breasts as she moved the drill nearer to his temple.

'Don't fuck with me, Eddie.' He suddenly stopped writhing and looked her full in the eyes.

'You won't hurt me.'

'You don't know for sure, do you, though? Susie's fifteen. Too young for you, you bastard.' The noise and the vibration of the drill were making *her* nervous, let alone the man on the bed. What would happen if Eddie wouldn't promise? If he didn't stop making life difficult for her? She knew she couldn't go all the way with this but she daren't let him know that. Seconds ticked slowly by. Who would break first, she wondered, him or her?

'For fuck's sake put the thing down before you bloody drop it.'

Daisy pulled back, relief coursing through her.

I

'You'll leave her alone?' How she kept her voice steady was a bloody miracle. He nodded. 'This caff ain't no knockin' shop, understand?'

'I understand. Now switch the fuckin' thing off!'

She depressed the button and laid the drill down beneath the bed where she'd hidden it earlier. The minute it was out of her hands Daisy felt a whole lot better.

'Give you an inch an' you take a fuckin' yard.'

A huge sigh came from the man on the bed. 'You're clever, Daisy. I'll give you that. Luring me up here. Now untie me.'

'You didn't need much luring, Eddie Lane, an' I'll leave you for a bit longer to ponder on keeping promises.'

He laughed then. That laugh which melted women's hearts like they were ice creams on a hot day. Only it wasn't working on her. She had too much to lose, this time.

'I should be the one with a smile on my face.' She nodded towards his spread legs, his shrivelled penis. 'Not such a big man now, are you, Eddie?'

'Untie me.'

Ignoring him she looked around the bedroom. Cheap, scuffed furniture. A dressing table, double bed, wardrobe and chair. A window scanning the panorama of a grey, muddy, ship-filled Portsmouth harbour. The room smelled of stale cabbage and sweat, mixed with Jeyes fluid. Cold, unlet. A spare room. And when Daisy had cleaned it up she was going to ask if Susie would like to move in. At least she could watch over her then.

Susie was at present keeping an eye on things downstairs in the cafe and Daisy knew instinctively she could trust her. Doling out cups of tea, black like treacle, wasn't that difficult and Daisy knew the girl wouldn't dip her fingers in the till. And if she did? Then Daisy herself was to blame, not Susie.

This room was identical to Eddie's across the hall, except his housed expensive suits and smelled of cologne and had pictures of Marilyn Monroe in pin-up poses stuck over one wall. It was also a hell of a lot cleaner. Eddie didn't like mess or clutter in his life.

'There's another thing,' Daisy said.

'Something else I'm not doing right, Dais?' He was certainly back to his cheeky self.

'Bert left the management of this place to Kenny; he was Kenny's ol' mate not yours. You made sure Kenny's banged up in Winchester for two years. You're Kenny's brother, I'm his wife. So it's my job to look after this caff and its rooms, okay? Me, not you.' She jabbed her index finger first at herself then at him to underline her point. 'So you get no say in anything, okay? You want to stay here, fine. That's what Kenny wanted. But this place is my responsibility.'

A frown crossed his features, hardening his steel-blue eyes. He was a good-looking bastard – and he knew it. But there was evil in him. Her eyes flicked over his hard-muscled body.

'How could you do this to me, Dais?'

'Didn't take much persuading, did you? You thought because I slept with you once when I was feelin' really low, I'd do it again. Well, I made a mistake and that won't fuckin' happen again. From now on I'll tolerate you, but touch Susie again and believe me, if I don't fuckin' kill you when you're awake, I'll get you when you're asleep.' A look of determination bloomed in her clear eyes. 'This shithole of a caff is gonna be made into somethin' worthwhile for when my Kenny gets out. I'll make sure of that even if I nearly slog meself to death doing it. An' it's gonna be a clean place. You ain't gonna bring no scandal or coppers to this place, see?'

'I understand. You gonna untie me now, please, Dais?'

She moved to the foot of the bed and released the knot on one of his ankles. He didn't move but watched every action she took. Then he calmly flexed his foot by circling his ankle.

'Much better,' he said.

Daisy unplugged the drill and began coiling the frayed flex around it. Opening the bedroom door, she stepped into the wooden-floored hallway. Before closing the door again, she turned back to Eddie and said, 'If you can't get free now, you ain't worth shit! An' another thing.' This was going to be a cruel jab at him, knowing how much he idolised his favourite film star pin-up. So did Daisy. And it had stunned her when she'd heard the news on the wireless earlier. She flung at him, 'Marilyn Monroe was found dead in bed this morning.' She didn't wait to see his reaction to the news.

*

3

Daisy hadn't shown it, but she was still trembling when she reached the top of the stairs. Thank God she'd pulled it off. It was never going to be any good appealing to Eddie's better nature. Most of the time he never had one. He was a selfish bastard. She had to start as she meant to go on, keep the bastard in line. She pushed open the door to her room. Two large bedrooms were on this top floor, one Daisy's and one Vera's.

Vera was a prossie. But she never brought anyone back to the cafe or her room: 'This is my little nest, ducky. I conduct my business outside. This is my home. Mine and Kibbles'.'

Kibbles was the biggest tabby cat Daisy had ever seen. He seldom left Vera's room, where he had a tray to do his business in and a food dish always filled with tasty morsels. Vera left her window open and if he wanted to roam he sometimes appeared in the cafe or in Daisy's room to sleep like a furry doughnut on her bed. He was sitting on the windowsill now.

'Come on in, then,' Daisy said, pushing up the sash-corded window. Kibbles stepped daintily inside, purring loudly. 'Wish all blokes were as easygoing as you.' He jumped down from the sill to twine himself in and out of her legs as she put the drill safely away in the cupboard. If Eddie was going to come after her, it would be soon. It wouldn't take him long to free himself and the last thing he'd want was for anyone to know how she'd tricked him. Somehow she didn't think he'd bother, though. He knew which side his bread had marge on, did Eddie.

She tugged at the cotton curtains on their plastic wire. It was raining and she wanted to shut out the sight of the water running down the window panes. She could see the ferry boats in the harbour, like black beetles crawling across the stretch of water that separated Gosport from Portsmouth, the lights of Portsmouth and the Dockyard glittering through the deluge. If she'd left the window open she could have almost tasted the silt and mud oozing from the slimy Solent waters. Even on a fine day the seas were grey, not like the blue they painted them in the magazine adverts. From the cafe below came the mellow voices of The Everly Brothers, soothing her yet reminding her of Kenny.

Two fuckin' years Kenny had got. She sighed. If he'd only waited another couple of days his future would have been settled.

4

But no, they'd gone out on a job together. Him and Eddie. Some un-thought-out tinpot caper that had ended in a chase across the allotments for Kenny, and a cell for the night. And Eddie home and clear.

Breaking and entering. Two years. Another of Eddie's bright ideas that always worked for him and which left someone else to carry the fuckin' can. And while her husband was on remand, Bert goes and dies and leaves the cafe and building to be managed by Kenny. He wasn't even conscious enough beforehand to be told Kenny might not be around to do the job. The place opened early for working men's breakfasts and normally closed around seven after cooked teas. If there were still customers willing to spend money, Bert never bothered to close up on time.

Bert had liked Kenny. Well, who wouldn't? As unalike as chalk and cheese, the two brothers. Kenny soft and fair with hair that he was forever pushing back from his forehead. And he teased Bert a lot, made him laugh. Not watchful like Eddie, who reminded Daisy of a black crow. Nice to look at but ever mindful of a chance to peck at whatever he could get for his own comfort. Daisy shuddered at what she'd just accomplished. Who would have thought she, a mere woman, could put the wind up Eddie Lane?

Kibbles meowed so she picked him up, burying her face in his mackerel-coloured fur. He smelled of Californian Poppy, Vera's perfume. She smiled to herself. Vera was one of the best.

'Milk, is it?' she whispered into his warmth.

There was a bottle of sterilised on the draining board so she set Kibbles down and poured him a saucerful. 'I've got to go down and see if Suze is okay,' she said, scratching Kibbles behind one ear. The rain would make it a slow evening in the cafe.

Leaving cat and milk on the sink top, she went over to patch up her make-up.

Her reflection stared back from the mirror. Short blonde hair, blue eyes, and large even white teeth. She knew she wasn't especially pretty. Not like Susie with her doll-like features or striking like Vera, pushing forty but with a good figure. Vera was like one of them movie stars. Hedy Lamarr, perhaps? All dark hair and gypsy looks with red lips. Daisy thought herself too skinny.

5

She remembered her mum used to say she never stayed still long enough to put the weight on. Well, she was now in her middle twenties so what she saw in the mirror was what she was stuck with. She'd never be taller than her five-foot-two but she thought if she had a best feature it was her eyes. Joan Collins eyes, she'd once been told. She spat on the mascara brush and rubbed it across the block then caked it on her lashes. She was lucky they were already quite thick and dark for a blonde. She knew she had no right to moan about her looks. Or anything else, now. A place to live, money coming in, and apart from Kenny being inside for sixteen months – time off for good behaviour – she was better off than she'd ever been in her life before. Thanking her lucky stars and leaving the door ajar for Kibbles, she went out and down the stairs.

The house had five rooms in all, two at the top of the building. They were large rooms with butler sinks and gas stoves, though Daisy never cooked on hers. She didn't even know if the stoves were safe to use or not. And three rooms on the floor below, all supposedly furnished. Bert had been canny. It was easier to evict undesirable tenants from furnished accommodation. Even if the furniture consisted of only one chair and a manky bed, it was classed as furnished.

The lavatory was downstairs in the yard at the back of the cafe and used by the cafe customers as well. High on her list of priorities was to whitewash the fuckin' thing and give it a good scouring. It stank to high heaven, no matter how much Jeyes fluid she sluiced around. She must do the passageway too that ran the length of the ground floor from front to back of the place. The street door opened on to the passage which also led upstairs. No access for cafe customers but it could be reached through its kitchen this way. The double door of the cafe encompassed the corners of North Street and North Cross Street.

As she walked down the stairs she saw the room Eddie had been in was now empty.

Bert had slept in this room, but since his death and Daisy's moving in she'd slowly erased most of the old man's stuff. She'd kept a photo of him and Kenny and herself taken one day in the cafe by an enthusiastic punter with a new camera. Bert had stood that photo by his bedside. Until the heart attack claimed him. The photo was now down in the cafe on the top shelf where customers could see it – to remind everyone that Bert's Cafe would remain Bert's even though Daisy had been in residence for a couple of months now. She'd never change the name. Never. He'd been a decent bloke and well liked. And made a bloody good cuppa.

Daisy could hear muffled noises coming from Eddie's room opposite and decided to leave well alone.

At the bottom of the stairs, near the kitchen, someone had knocked over the metal mop bucket that always stood on the cracked lino and the water had swilled over the floor. The smell of disinfectant was strong. Daisy set the bucket upright, squeezed out the mop and soaked up the grey water. When she'd finished, she let herself into the cafe.

'Hi, Dais,' rang a forced cheerful voice, accompanied by a shy grin.

'All right, Suze?' Without waiting for a reply she added, 'Slow tonight?' Susie nodded. The smell of bacon frying reminded Daisy she hadn't eaten since this morning. Susie nodded towards three men lounging over by the jukebox. 'Wheel of Fortune' was playing now. An old record but it was Eddie's favourite. Kay Starr was singing her heart out.

'Just making them lot bacon sarnies.'

'Make me one?' Susie added more rashers to the pan, where they sizzled and spat enticingly.

'They're waitin' for Eddie. He said he'd meet them half an hour ago. You don't know what's 'appened to him, I suppose?' Daisy shook her head. She had the feeling Susie was glad she'd joined her. The girl was nervous around men and with good cause. She'd only agreed to be in the cafe because there was a counter between her and the customers, poor little sod, thought Daisy. Susie forked the rashers over in the pan.

'Perhaps he's been a bit tied up,' Daisy said. 'I know he's upstairs.'

Truth to tell there had hardly been any real violence in the cafe since Daisy had taken over a few months ago. This corner of the town was run down. Bomb damage had left scars, waste grounds where purple fireweed blossomed amongst the old prams and dumped mattresses. Bert had ruled the cafe with a fist of iron and Daisy hoped she was going to be able to do the same. But she did need Eddie while Kenny was inside.

The Lane brothers were well known in the area. Especially the dark one with the temper. Bastard Eddie might be but he didn't tolerate anyone shitting on him or his own.

'That's making my mouth water,' Daisy said. Susie was forking the fragrant rashers onto the marged bread.

'You want brown or tomato?' She nodded towards the sauce bottles.

'I don't expect you to wait on me, Suze,' Daisy answered. She upended the brown sauce bottle, slapped on another slice of bread and cut it crossways.

'Here you go,' Susie called out. One of the men ambled over.

'Put 'em all on one plate, ducks,' he said. He had bad skin and a dated Elvis Presley hairstyle that didn't curl properly at the front. He wore the usual uniform of leather bomber jacket and jeans. 'No sauces.'

Without a word Susie complied and he slouched back to his mates, clutching the plate. Daisy felt Susie freeze beside her as the kitchen door opened and Eddie came in.

'Evening, girls,' he grinned. His eyes found Daisy's. She always forgot how tall he was until he stood near her.

'Some mates of yours here,' she said. 'I was going to tell 'em you was tied up but you're here now.'

'Bitch,' he muttered, picking up one of her sandwiches and taking a large bite. Then he put it back on her plate. 'Mmm, nice that, Dais.' He then glared at the men.

'C'mon, let's get outa here.'

'Aw, Eddie, I only just started eating,' said the youngest-looking of the three.

'Fuckin' bring it or leave it. I ain't waiting.'

'You look nice tonight, Eddie,' Daisy said. And meant it. He had on a dark navy suit, new, and it fitted perfectly across his broad shoulders. 'Shame such a good-looking bloke can be such a shit.'

He grinned. It was to Eddie's credit that he never bore a grudge.

He usually paid back a grievance straight away. Then forgot about it. He never even glanced at Susie.

Eddie swept past Daisy and opened the street door. One of the blokes, the auburn-haired, good-looking one, said, 'Goodbye, Mrs Lane.'

'Get a move on, Bri,' Eddie snarled at him. 'You too, Cal.' They followed him into the rain, and Daisy turned to Susie who looked uneasy.

'It's going to be all right,' Daisy told her. 'I had a bit of a word with him. He won't touch you again. I promise.' Susie looked like she didn't believe her.

'I want you to come and live here with me, Suze. I don't want to think of you sleeping on the moored-up ferry boats, understand?' Susie gave a half smile at Daisy which never reached her light blue eyes. The cut on her lip had stopped bleeding but it was still swollen. Daisy guessed that had come from the gold signet ring Eddie always wore. Tomorrow the swelling would be more pronounced. The bruises on her upper arms and legs which she'd reluctantly showed Daisy earlier would still be there in the morning too. She was just a fuckin' kid, for Christ's sake. Daisy walked over to the cafe door and slipped the top and bottom bolts into place, then she turned the red cardboard sign round to 'Closed'.

'No arguments, Suze. I'll make us a nice cup of tea and you can tell me all about it.'

CHAPTER 2

'I didn't encourage him, Dais, honest.' She wanted Daisy to believe her.

'I don't think for one minute you did. That bugger doesn't need encouragement. Are you a runaway?'

Susie's heart plummeted. She grabbed hold of Daisy's wrist.

'Don't tell the coppers. I can't go back.'

'I wasn't going to turn you over to them. But you must be honest with me.' Daisy extricated her hand.

Susie wanted to tell Daisy about her mother who had shacked up with a sleazeball. There had been plenty of men in Doreen's life but Ray had to be the worst.

'Mum could never cope on her own,' she said, as Daisy set a mug of strong tea in front of her. Susie stared hard at her. This woman was a really nice person and she wanted to confide in her, but what if Daisy blamed her?

'Go on,' said Daisy.

'I thought when we got the council flat in St Mary's Street in Southampton everything would change. Mum promised it would. She said she'd stop looking at problems through the bottom of a glass of gin. Well, we moved in this flat and it was real nice. Just me an' her. Mum got a job cleaning on the liners at the docks. You know where I mean?'

'Sure I do.' Southampton Docks was one of the biggest employers in that area. 'Go on, I'm listening.' Susie could see she had Daisy's full attention. That was another nice thing about Daisy, she listened. Really listened. She didn't chime in and try for a bit of one-upmanship like some people who, if you had a black cat they had a blacker one, and liked the sound of their own voices.

'There was only the two of us. Mum was "between fellers". I didn't mind rushing 'ome from school to get the dinner on and keep the place looking nice. We went out together on Saturdays and got bits and bobs from Kingsland Market and the flat got really nice.'

Aware of the silence, punctuated only by the driving rain on the windows, Susie got up from the stool she'd been sitting on. Lifting the wooden counter flap, she went round and started collecting fag-filled ashtrays. She wasn't going to let Daisy see her cry. Not again. She'd done a lot of crying lately and some of the worst was when Daisy had found her huddled on the stairs with her blouse torn open.

'Leave that. We can do it in a minute.'

Susie piled some of the ashtrays on the counter but, instead of going back to where Daisy was sitting with her feet up on the rungs of a chair, she went and slumped on a seat facing the rain-spattered window, and began talking again.

'That's where she met Ray. The market. He was doing house clearances, collecting the stuff during the week and flogging it at the market at weekends. Couldn't bloody lose. He charged to shift the stuff from the houses then charged the punters to buy it. So he 'ad a bit of money to flash about.' A huge sigh escaped her. 'He took Mum out a few times and then he moved in.' Susie turned her head towards Daisy who was watching her thoughtfully. 'I didn't expect Mum to live the life of a saint, without a bloke in her life, but even I could see he was scum. That's 'ow it started. Him pressing himself up against me when he had to get past me. Then making excuses to be alone with me. You know the sort of thing. "Why don't I walk up and meet Susie from school, Doreen? So you know she gets 'ome safely? Don't want her hanging around with any boys, do we?" Well, at first I thought, give him the benefit of the doubt, perhaps he don't realise what he's doing. But he knew all right.' She felt the anger rising and tried to hide it from Daisy by asking nervously, 'D'you think I could have another cuppa?'

''Course.' Susie made to get up. She wasn't used to anyone

waiting on her, but Daisy was already on her feet and waved her away with, 'I'll do it. You carry on. That's if you want to, of course, I don't want you to upset yourself.'

'I want to tell you,' she said, watching Daisy refill the kettle. 'In fact, Daisy, it's a relief to talk to someone who don't think I'm a slag.' Alarm rushed through her body as she felt a sudden rush of panic. She ran her fingers through her tangle of hair. 'You don't think that, do you?'

''Course not! Do I seem the kind of person who'd judge you?'

Susie looked at her and smiled. No, she could imagine Daisy would find some good, even in a killer. A small woman who, because she was slim, looked more like a girl. Her cropped blonde hair framed a face that sometimes seemed sad and yet, when Daisy smiled, it was like a dark room that had an electric light suddenly switched on. She was sort of illuminated from within, yeah, that's the word, illuminated, thought Susie. But you knew you could trust her. Because she had the kind of eyes that never wavered when they looked at you. Large sincere eyes that saw right inside a person. Susie realised, if you had Daisy for a friend you were all right. And she'd give you the benefit of the doubt. But if Daisy made an enemy – well she wouldn't like to be Daisy's enemy. That could be scary.

'What about your mum? Didn't she twig . . .'

'The first time 'e came into my bedroom was when Mum was cleaning cruise ships, working nights. I was thirteen. He said if I didn't let him, he'd leave Mum. Well, she was happier than she'd ever been and still off the sauce, though she was using from time to time. He'd started her on that. But I 'ad some silly notion that if she didn't have a bottle of gin to 'and everything would be all right. I didn't know what he meant by "let him". But he said lots of dads "cuddled" their daughters. I'd never 'ad a proper dad, so I didn't know about that but I did know that Aisha, my friend, she came from a big family and they was always cuddling each other and laughing and larking about.'

'So that's how it started?'

Just then the whistle blew on the small kettle and Susie jumped to her feet.

'Stay still. I said I'd do it.'

Susie sat down again and examined her bitten nails. She watched Daisy's quick body movements as she bustled with the brown earthenware teapot and produced Bourbon biscuits from a high cupboard and shook them onto a plate. Presently she brought the whole lot on a tray round to where Susie sat near the window.

'Don't get the idea I liked it. Or him.' Susie watched for the telltale look of disgust to form in Daisy's eyes. But nothing happened. All she could see was genuine concern.

'Go on,' Daisy said softly.

'He said it would be our little secret and that I was helping to keep Mum happy. An' how could little cuddles hurt anyone? But I got so I was scared to go to bed when Mum wasn't there. At first that was all it was, the cuddling. Then 'e wanted to get under the covers with me. I hated the smell of him, Daisy. The hairs on his body. And then 'e made me touch him. You know, down there. Until, in the end 'e was doing things to me that I know now only married people should do and it hurt. It hurt me so much.' Susie couldn't help herself, she started to cry.

Daisy let her sob until the girl wiped her nose along the sleeve of her pink, grubby cardigan and said, 'I stopped going to school. This was a few months back. I thought all the kids could see inside my heart and know the filth in there that had been going on for so long.' She felt her lower lip tremble again, but she carried on. 'He said if I didn't go back to school he'd tell Mum it was me who started it all. If Ray did that, Mum would start drinking again. And the heroin was bad enough as she was spending a lot of time on the nod and taking time off from work. I couldn't go to school where Aisha and the others were droolin' over boys because I felt so sick about them behavin' like silly kids. I had to get away from Ray. So I ran. No clothes, no money, but he won't make me touch him ever again because I won't go back.' She'd made her mind up about that. No, she'd never go back. Never. Daisy pushed tea towards her. 'You know, nobody's waited on me since Mum did when I was small and had the measles,' Susie whispered.

'Better make the most of it then, Suze,' Daisy said with kindness. 'If you take the room I'm offering, it goes with a job. Helping in the caff can be monotonous and hard. And the smell of fry-ups gets into your clothes something terrible. Anyway, I think you should still be at school.' A frown had crossed Daisy's face.

'Please . . . ? Let me stay here. I'll work hard. I promise.'

Daisy said nothing for a few moments. She pushed the plate of biscuits across the table, then answered, 'I can't afford to get in trouble with the authorities.'

'In a few months I'll be sixteen.' Susie could see Daisy was having problems coming to grips with this. Trying to work out dates in her head, probably, she thought. And who could blame her? But Susie had told her the truth. 'I don't have to go to school,' she insisted. 'Fifteen's the leaving age. And if you turn me over to the cops they'll take me back home to Ray and what 'e's got lined up for me. Or they'll put me in a children's home until I can get a job. And I've been in a couple of 'omes when Mum's been on the bottle before and believe me you learn more stuff in them places than ever you do on the streets—'

'Okay, okay,' Daisy cut in. 'You can stay.'

'Oh, Daisy, you won't regret it, I promise you. Anyway, they'd be sure to put me in care for a while. Now that Mum's pregnant.'

'Oh, you poor kid!'

'Don't feel sorry for me. I don't want nobody's pity. It's Mum as deserves pity. Losing 'er proper job was on the cards before I left. Ray started her in on the heroin, gave her the habit so he could put her on the game. Most of the time she don't know where she is or who she's with now.'

'Have you—?'

'Don't be stupid. I 'ad enough trouble keeping out of the way of Ray. In the end there was so many blokes coming and going in the flat in St Mary's Street that I couldn't 'andle it no more.'

'Did you tell your mum?'

'At last I had to. I came home one afternoon an' there was this old bloke sitting in 'is underwear in my room. I knew what 'e wanted all right. But he wasn't getting it from me. But Ray? He denied he knew anything about it. Said the bloke was pissed and just went for a lie-down. Then 'e dangled a fix in front of her and told her I was trying to split them up. She can't help 'erself. Can't see no further than the next fix.'

'So she believed him?'

'Yeah, and that hurt like hell. I knew then it was her or me, though I didn't want to leave 'er, specially not with the little one coming. But I knew it wouldn't be long before . . . He's a fuckin' shithouse, that Ray!'

'So you ran away and came down here?'

'Got a lift with a lorry driver at Bargate in Southampton. He was deliverin' roofing tiles to a Gosport contractor. I wasn't bothered where I went as long as it was away from Ray and his wandering 'ands. Nice old bloke the driver was . . .'

'. . . Then you fell into Eddie's clutches?'

Susie nodded at Daisy. Her forehead was creased into a frown and she was looking tired, very tired. She'd dipped a biscuit into her tea and it had broken off, falling into the cup. Daisy tried to fish it out with a spoon and gave up.

'I was kipping on the moored-up ferry boat 'cause I was skint. He saw me coming off to go to the public convenience near the ferry. I thought he was a good-looking bloke who really wanted to be nice. He bought me a meal in that Dive caff on the ferry terminus. When he said 'e could get me a more comfortable bed for the night with no strings attached, I believed him.'

'Yes, well,' said Daisy. 'He can charm the fuckin' birds out of the trees, that one.'

'You'd 'ave thought I'd learned a lesson or two already, wouldn't you?'

Daisy shrugged. 'Eddie can be nice when he wants to.'

'Yeah, well, I know that an' all now, don' I? He told me he owned a caff further up in the town. I thought it was a bit funny he didn't take me there straight away 'stead of buying me a meal in another caff first. He said there was some rooms above his place and I could 'ave one.'

'Oh, he did, did 'e? Well, he doesn't have a say in how this place is run.'

'And I know that, now, as well.'

'So he eventually sneaks you in here?'

Susie nodded. 'I guessed I'd have to pay somehow and he *is* good-looking. All I wanted to do, Daisy, was have a bit of a wash and go to sleep in a proper bed . . .' She paused.

'Get on with it.'

'He got rough. I couldn't let him.' She started to cry. 'I'm not a slag . . .'

Daisy got up and gathered her in her arms.

'There, there . . .'

'Don't let 'im touch me again. I'll work here but don't let him near me again, please, Daisy? I don't want any man ever to touch me again.'

'Suze!' Daisy was shaking her, trying to stop her outpouring. 'Look, you are under age. Get it? Underage for sex. Sex with your stepfather, sex with fuckin' Eddie. I understand you don't want to go back to Southampton and maybe into care. But what about Eddie? Do you want me to report him for what 'e tried to do?'

Susie stopped sobbing, sniffed, and said quietly, 'No.' She shook her head. 'I don't want no coppers involved. If you get them buggers round I'll 'ave to tell them everything. I can't do that. It was hard enough telling you.'

'Okay, then. What if I said I can promise Eddie will leave you alone?'

'How?'

'Ask me no questions an' I'll tell you no lies.'

'Promise?'

'It's a promise. You'll be safe with me.' Daisy stared out at the rain. Susie could see that the shadows beneath her eyes had almost completed a full circle in the small pale face.

She sat thinking about Daisy's words. About her kindness. About the trust this woman was offering to a complete stranger. After a while she got up and took the tray back to the counter. She lifted the flap and said, 'I'd better earn my keep.' It was as though some unspoken agreement had been reached between them and Susie had decided to take the initiative.

'I wouldn't ask you to do nothing I wouldn't do myself,' Daisy said.

She showed her how she liked the stairs and floors mopped down every night with disinfectant. How she cleaned the surfaces of the tables, chairs and counter tops, wiping them with diluted bleach to kill the germs. How all the rubbish had to be wrapped up in newspaper and taken out the back to the big metal dustbins to keep away rats and mice.

'I can't abide dirt. There's enough cockroaches in this place without encouraging them.'

Susie was tired out but she worked with a will. She thought Daisy must have had a hard life to understand what other people went through. She wondered what her husband was like. Was he like Eddie? She didn't think so. She'd studied the photograph of him in the cafe. He looked a good laugh, easygoing.

Later they had another cup of tea and then Daisy produced clean sheets and blankets.

'These'll do for tonight. Tomorrow we'll get the room sorted properly. The room next door to yours is empty, I'm going to use it for bed and breakfasts. Eddie is across the hall.' Susie must have frowned for Daisy snapped, 'Don't look like that. It will be all right. Trust me.'

When Susie finally climbed into bed she honestly thought she'd worry herself sick about Eddie. But she'd slipped the bolt on the inside of the door and dragged a chair and propped the back of it beneath the door knob and felt a little better after that. Before she slept she thought about how Daisy had taken a chance on her and promised herself she was going to prove she was worth the risk.

CHAPTER 3

12 October 1962

Kenny Lane opened his eyes. Shit, he thought, I'm still alive.

He hurt like hell. His body felt as though it had been repeatedly slammed against a brick wall. And in a way, it had. The fuckin' wall had been Big Eric, and what that fucker wanted he got. He'd wanted Kenny. And he'd had him.

He tried lifting his head from the block of prison concrete that masqueraded as a pillow. A groan involuntarily escaped.

'You all right, mate?'

Bill Hammond, aka Casanova and in for bigamy, peered down at him from the top bunk.

'What you fuckin' think?' He felt sick and the smell of piss and farts in the cell was making him gag. He tried to shut out the memory of what had taken place last night before lockdown. But he knew it was going to stay with him long after his body had healed. He remembered clearly every terrifying detail. It had started in the showers.

'Ain't you the pretty one?'

Big Eric had stepped up close to him just as he was soaping himself. Kenny had glanced towards the doorway where two of Eric's men stood guard. Kenny's heart dropped like a stone. He'd tried to laugh off rumours that Big Eric fancied him, that Eric had even started calling him Golden Boy to his mates. All he wanted to do was keep his head down and do his bird and get out of the fuckin' place without any trouble.

'C'mon, make yourself nice and slippery, you're gonna need it.'

'Get away from me, cunt.' Already Eric had a massive hard-on.

'Don't be like that, sweetie. You got two choices, Kenny. Either you give in and take it like a man. Or you struggle. An' I like a bit of spirit. Makes no fuckin' odds. I always gets what I fuckin' wants.'

Eric's fist had come from nowhere straight into Kenny's gut. While he was doubled up, gasping as the breath left his body, Eric had twisted him around and slammed him from the shower stall to the nearby sink and rammed into him. Kenny had screamed with pain but Eric's huge hand had found his mouth, practically cutting off his air supply. He'd struggled, but that had excited Eric and while Eric grunted, humiliated and ripped into him, his cronies had kept one eye on the scene before them and one eye on the corridor outside for screws.

Afterwards when Kenny lay huddled back in the shower stall, bleeding and sobbing with the water running down over him, Eric had said, 'Now you know why they call me Big Eric. Don't worry, you'll get to like it, Golden Boy.'

For what had seemed a lifetime, Kenny had crouched there, huddled on the cracked white tiles. He knew the water was never going to wash away the filth. He'd been invaded. Degraded. The mental anguish hurt just as much as the pain from his body. He was still crying when Casanova had furtively crept in looking for him.

'You can't stay in here.'

Kenny didn't give a fuck. But Casanova turned off the shower and dragged him to his feet.

'If the screws find you in here there'll be questions asked, and if you give any answers, right or wrong, you'll get done over by just about everyone. Nobody tolerates a fuckin' grass. Can you walk?'

Casanova had miraculously got him back to the cell with no one being any the wiser. As Kenny had collapsed onto the bunk he'd asked Casanova just one question.

'Why?'

'Because Big Eric can. An' you ain't the first. Shouldn't be so good-looking, mate. Though he ain't never fancied me!'

Kenny had blessed the fact that it was time for lockdown for the night. Had even grunted as the screw did his nightly pilgrimage checking cells along the corridor. But it had taken him a long time to drop off for a few troubled hours of sleep. Now he was awake again and thanked God it would be a while before the buzzer sounded for the day to start properly.

'Thanks,' he said gruffly. Casanova's dark curls lay sweatily flat against his forehead and his brown eyes showed concern.

'Forget it,' he flung back at Kenny and disappeared from view.

Kenny stared at the wall. He had one photograph. It wasn't framed. They weren't allowed glass frames. It was a copy of him, Daisy and Bert in the cafe. Daisy and Bert were smiling down at him. He wished he was home.

Up beside Casanova's bunk there was hardly room for the green paint to show through. He liked women. That's why he kept marrying them. Only thing was, he forgot to bother with divorces first. Casanova wasn't even that good-looking but he was a nice bloke and he certainly had the charm. He'd confided to Kenny, 'I takes a bird out for a drink, whispers a few sweet nothings in her pretty ears and before you knows it her knickers are in 'er 'andbag before we leaves the pub.'

Usually of a morning Casanova was chirpy. But today he was quiet and Kenny respected him for it. He felt as though he never wanted to laugh or make idle conversation ever again. He thought of what there was to look forward to after slop-out and again thanked God he worked in the kitchen and that Big Eric worked in the machine shop. He felt tears rise and forced them away.

He liked working in the kitchen. Repetitive work, and done on a grand scale because the prison was overflowing with cons and screws. He didn't mind scraping carrots or peeling spuds, or even washing mountains of dirty plates and greasy dishes. He just didn't think about it. He let his mind wander instead. Oh, they could lock him up all right but they couldn't lock his mind up. His body was the prisoner, wasn't it? Not his mind.

He wondered if he'd have liked working in the library? Casanova had told him he was a fool to turn that job down when it had been offered to him as it was a prized job. Said it was a doddle there. But what did Kenny want with books? He'd never read one right through in his life, and at twenty-five he thought he might not want to bother to start now. He wanted to do things, not read about them. Anyway, that was Daisy's department. She always had her nose in a book from the library. Bloody Eddie as well. But Daisy was always scribbling things down. One day he'd asked her what she was writing and she'd told him her hopes and dreams. She passed the notebook over for him to read but he declined. Told her they were her own private thoughts. She'd liked him for that. Kissed him and told him he was a 'sweet' man. Well he didn't feel fuckin' sweet this morning.

He felt used. He could smell the bastard all over him. Even though he knew he was clean, the water had run over him for so long, the bastard's smell wouldn't go. And he certainly wouldn't tell anyone. This was his secret, what happened with Big Eric. Casanova wouldn't talk. And Eric's cronies? Well, he had to take his chances on them opening their big gobs, didn't he?

As for Daisy, it was one secret he wasn't going to share with her. She had enough on her plate running that cafe and keeping an eye on Eddie and his demanding ways. He knew Daisy was never sure about Eddie. She said at times he could be cruel, but Kenny knew Eddie cared about Daisy a lot more than he ever let on. Was he worried about this? No, not really. Because Eddie was a good man to have about when things weren't too hot. And with Eddie living in the cafe at least he knew no harm would come to Daisy.

When Kenny was small Eddie, who was two years older, had often taken the blame and the beatings that Pappy had regularly doled out. Pappy was Eddie's dad. Thought he was Kenny's too, but Kenny didn't think so. Why, he didn't look a bit like him. Kenny didn't know who his dad really was. Not that he cared. Portsmouth and Gosport being naval places with moving populations meant that many kids never knew who their true fathers were, especially after the war when the Poles, Americans, Italians and Turks went back to their own countries. So many different nationalities had been billeted in the area to swell the army and navy and the air force. The word bastard was used regularly when Pappy was knocking their mum about. And Kenny distinctly remembered one particularly violent fight when Pappy had knocked his mother down the stairs and she couldn't move because her leg was all twisted underneath her. Pappy was mouthing off about three bastard boys. But he must have made a mistake because there was only him and Eddie.

He didn't remember much about his mum, except she smelled nice. Of clean clothes. And she'd been warm and soft. But that had been a long time ago. Eddie had looked after Kenny, always been there for him. What did Kenny care about real fathers? Maybe he was Pappy's kid but perhaps Pappy just never liked him. After all, it was possible, wasn't it, to have a child and not like it? Pappy, in his own way, had much preferred Eddie. Kenny had seen it in the man's eyes. But Pappy had a funny way of showing it. When Pappy wasn't sober Eddie got twice as many beatings as Kenny, probably because Eddie always stuck up for his little brother. Eddie looked just like Pappy, with his gypsy dark looks and smooth-talking ways. Eddie had once told Kenny that because he looked so much like his father Pappy needed to beat it out of him. But the times Eddie won his father's approval mattered even more to Eddie, and he swore one day he'd have Pappy beholden to him for a change. One day Eddie had vowed to him he'd have the upper hand. Kenny had laughed and said, 'You really love the old bastard, don't you?'

Eddie had blushed like a little kid and said, 'Yeah. He's my dad, ain't he?'

But it was himself that Daisy had gone for. Even if he wasn't as broad-shouldered or as tall, or as smart with his reading and writing as Eddie, Daisy loved him. And he loved her. And he liked to make her laugh.

And soon he was due a visit because he'd sent her a visiting order.

The buzzer sounded. Another short day had officially begun. Short because the cons rose early and went to bed early. But it was going to be a long and painful day for him after last night.

'C'mon, mate, move yerself,' said Casanova.

CHAPTER 4

14 October 1962

Daisy gave a final spray with the hair lacquer. She needed to look good for her Kenny. Last night had been the ordeal of peroxiding her roots and now she stood back to survey the result of her endeavours. She'd put some pan stick make-up on to disguise the shadows beneath her eyes. The hard cafe work was beginning to take its toll. On her feet from morning 'til night, peeling spuds, washing pots, and all the while keeping a smile on her face for the customers, it wasn't easy. Best of a bad job she reckoned, wrinkling her nose at her reflection in the mirror.

On a wire hanger on the back of the bedroom door hung her new red slub-weave two piece, bought in the market off Big Al's stall.

'You'll catch your bleedin' death in that.'

Susie had wandered in and was nosing around. She was more at ease with herself these days, thought Daisy, and had gained a bit of weight and a bloom to her cheeks. Her short black skirt and white top looked good on her. She kept out of Eddie's way when he was around, which wasn't often these days. 'Business afield', he called it. Daisy didn't know where he was and didn't much care. After that time in the bedroom back in August when she'd dared to get the better of him, he seemed less sure of himself. And on odd occasions she'd catch him looking thoughtfully at her. One thing was certain, he would be up to no good wherever he was.

'I want Kenny to be proud of me an' it's not raining,' Daisy told her.

'But it's freezing out there.'

Outside, the sky was blue, clear and it was cold. In the mornings you could feel that first nip of winter in the air and the trees were well into shedding their red and gold leaves. Autumn smells different, crisp and of bonfires, Daisy thought. Not that there were many bonfires in the town. No proper sodding gardens for a start. Daisy hated the winter. Hated being cold, despised the dark mornings and short days. The summer was her time, when perhaps she could take a walk down Stokes Bay beach. Maybe paddle in the Solent waters. She liked to think that the scent of the salty air had been blown in from lands of spice and colour. Kenny had said it was only Smith's crisp factory she could smell. But life seemed easier in the summer.

She slipped on a white blouse, then took the skirt from the hanger and wriggled it up over her hips. She loved the smell of new clothes.

'You'll look so good that the other cons'll ogle you an' Kenny'll get jealous.'

'Kenny's not like that. You're thinking 'e's like Eddie and that's not fair,' said Daisy.

'Ain't you putting a coat on?'

'No, just this jacket.' She pointed to the short jacket, picked it up and slipped it on to survey the result. That'll have to do, she thought. She grabbed her new white clutch bag and stepped into new white stiletto-heeled shoes. 'I think I've got everything I need. Money, visiting order, make-up, compact, hankie . . .'

'You takin' him something?'

'Yes, sweets and ciggies.'

'You goin' across on the ferry to catch the train at the Harbour Station?'

'What are you, a bloody policeman with all these questions?' Susie's face fell. In fact it looked like a smacked arse.

'I was only askin',' she mumbled.

'An' I was only jokin', you silly cow!' Susie's face immediately brightened.

'Well, I like to know everything is taken care of,' she said.

'I know you do. An' I also know you'll be able to cope today on your own.'

It wasn't the work, or the customers, that worried Susie, it was Eddie. Daisy realised this. If he was around she was like a bleedin' jelly on a plate. 'Eddie's gone to the race course, Goodwood.

Somethin' special going on there today, he said. He won't be back 'til late tonight, if at all. An' I'll be home around six.' Daisy watched Susie's face brighten.

'Okay,' she said. Daisy could see she was glad she'd shared that bit of information with her. Eddie was out of the way. If it wasn't for Kenny, Daisy wouldn't have given him house room.

'I'm walking down to the ferry, catching the bus to Fareham then the train. When I get to Winchester I'll get a bus to the 'ospital 'cause it's at the top of the hill opposite the prison. It sounds better to ask for a ticket to the 'ospital than the prison, doesn't it?' Susie nodded vigorously and her blonde curls bounced around her pretty face despite the clip which was supposed to hold them in place.

So far no one had been bothered by her sudden appearance behind the counter. Customers liked her. Daisy had casually mentioned she had a cousin down for a while and let the white lie, and the gossip, take its course. She knew Eddie would never mention anything about Susie appearing in the cafe. Suze was a godsend. She was someone she could bounce ideas off, almost like a younger sister. And Daisy had never had a sister. And the poor kid had been through such a lot she had an old head on young shoulders. She hoped Suze would stay around for a long time.

The cafe wasn't doing such great business that she could afford to pay huge wages but Susie seemed satisfied with room and board and money in her pocket. She'd got herself a few clothes, mostly rose-flowered dresses, which she looked good in, and tops and skirts for wearing in the cafe. She'd also had a go at back-combing her hair in the latest bouffant style but the curls wouldn't let it stay where she wanted, not even with loads of hair lacquer.

Susie was now straightening Daisy's bed.

'You don't have to do that,' Daisy said.

'You can make mine while you're about it, ducky.' Daisy glanced towards the voice. Vera was poised in the doorway.

'I've come on the borrow, Dais.'

Californian Poppy wafted into the room along with Vera, who was clad in a black silken dressing gown, cinched in tightly and showing off her neat waist.

'I need your curling tongs. I'll bring 'em straight back when they're cold. I left mine too long on the bleedin' gas ring and when I went to use them they was so 'ot I dropped them an' they come away at the 'andles. Got a fuckin' great 'ole in me new Persian rug from Charlie the carpet man as well. I wasn't 'alf cross.' Vera's vermilion mouth cracked into a big smile. The cat was at her ankles. 'An' you don't have to come chasin' after me, Kibbles. Just because you want some milk.' She bent down and picked up the daft big lump and the cat started purring. The sound filled the room.

Daisy looked over towards the draining board.

'No problem,' she said. 'And there's milk over there. I know you've only just got up an' there won't be any in your room.' Though she seldom used the ancient gas stove that stood near the sink she did like to keep tea-making facilities handy. Nothing better than a nice cup of tea when you fancied it.

'Thanks, Dais,' Vera said. 'I'll use yours an' get some more later. I 'ad the last of mine for a cuppa before I went to bed.'

'How many times do I have to tell you there's always milk in the cafe you can use.'

'I know my place.' Vera's face took on a haughty look. She was so bloody independent, was Vera. Sometimes she couldn't see how she hurt other people by declining offers of help. 'I wouldn't take without asking, you know that.' She sniffed the top of the bottle then took a saucer from the top cupboard, filled it and set Kibbles on the draining board where he began lapping noisily.

'Best thing about cats,' she said, folding her arms across her breasts in their pointed bra, 'is that they're more dependable than men. A cat stays out at nights and treats the place like a bloody 'otel, so what do we women want men for?'

'Well, I'm sure if you don't know, then I can't help you,' Daisy said, giving Susie a wink.

'Good answer, Dais. Though cats don't 'ave any money, do they?' She looked down at Daisy's shoes. 'They new?'

'Yeah. I'm off to see Kenny.'

'Thought you looked especially nice.'

Vera stared at Susie, who was busy trying to make hospital corners with the candlewick bedspread.

'If you could just spare a bit of bread for some toast?' Vera looked again at Susie who never raised her head from her task.

''Course,' said Daisy, giving Vera an old-fashioned look. 'Come on downstairs.' She picked up her bag. ''Bye, Suze,' she called, giving herself a final glance in the fly-specked mirror before walking out onto the stairs. Vera followed closely, the tongs clutched in one hand, her wedge-heeled fluffy mules click-clacking down the stairs behind Daisy.

'Love the nail varnish,' Daisy said, nodding towards Vera's red toenails when they stood together in the kitchen. She lifted the lid off the big enamelled bread bin but Vera laid a red-tipped hand on her arm.

'Bugger the toenails an' I don't want no bleedin' bread. You should know by now I don't eat breakfast. I just want to talk to you.'

'Oh?'

Vera was speaking softly and looking towards the stairs as though willing Susie to stay away.

'Come on then, what's the matter?'

'It's your Eddie.'

'He ain't my soddin' Eddie. What's 'e done now?'

'That's just it. We don't know.'

'Who's "we"?'

'The girls, the local toms.'

'I thought if they saw him coming they ran a mile?'

'That's true,' said Vera. 'He's a cruel bastard an' no one wants to take him on. It's only when a naive new young girl goes with him … an' you know he can charm the birds off the bleedin' trees.'

'So? We all know he likes them young, Vera.'

'That's as maybe, but he was in the Albert during the week and whispered something to the landlord as made old Bill Tanner nearly shit himself with fear.'

'What?'

'Dunno. But he was too scared to have Eddie thrown out. Well, he'd most probably have had the place trashed if he did that. He kept giving Eddie black looks, an' it looked like Eddie was just waiting, biding his time. Well, you know Eddie don't 'ardly touch the drink, so why did 'e spend so long in the Albert? All I'm

27

saying, ducks, an' you never 'eard it from me, is that he's up to something an' I don't want anything to come back on you or this place. I know how 'ard you works.'

'When ain't he up to something?' Daisy said wearily. She put her arms around Vera and hugged her, the familiar poppy scent comforting her as usual. 'Between you and me, eh?' she asked, looking up the stairs where they could hear Susie singing tunelessly. They smiled at each other.

'She's all right, ain't she, that Suze? I'll 'ang around today in case the girl needs any 'elp,' Vera said, opening the street door and pushing Daisy through, out into the cold. Daisy shivered. 'An' you should 'ave a coat on. It's enough to freeze your bloody drawers off out there.' She slammed the door.

Daisy walked down to the ferry and caught the bus, shivering all the way. At the station she saw the woman on the opposite platform just as her train drew in. She was not much older than Daisy and reed thin. She was real class. She wore a white wide-brimmed hat over immaculately permed blonde hair. Her finely arched brows and dark eyes were set off with lips red as holly berries. A white swagger coat, patent high heels and a black clutch bag completed the effect. It was unusual to see such a mystifying creature on Fareham Station, someone who'd have been perfectly at home shopping in a high-class London store.

Daisy had felt the bees' knees back at the cafe in her new suit, but this woman here made her look dowdy. Why couldn't she have that same self-assured elegance? She glanced along the platform. Everyone was looking at the vision, especially the men. Leering and licking their lips, knowing she was way out of their reach but wanting her anyway. She obviously didn't have to run a cafe, keep an eye on a brother-in-law who worked the wrong side of the law, and have a husband who was in the nick, Daisy consoled herself. She looked down at her ankles and breathed a sigh of relief. At least they weren't swollen today like they usually were from standing for hours behind a counter serving teas. Be grateful for small mercies, Dais, she told herself.

As she boarded the train she saw the woman hurrying along

before disappearing from view across the bridge that connected the platforms.

Daisy liked sitting and watching the fields and villages pass by. There was an elderly gentleman in the carriage immersed in his newspaper and, though he didn't light up, she could smell the pipe tobacco clinging to him. A harassed young woman in a thick jumper and jeans had the whole of the opposite seats to herself and her two very small and boisterous children who were attempting to run her ragged. The packet of digestive biscuits she was using to bribe them to silence wasn't working. The carriage smelled of dog ends and was none too clean. But it was a train ride and a day out for Daisy and her high spirits weren't to be dampened.

She thought about Kenny and what they would talk about. He was funny, her Kenny, she thought. Like a child really. Not too great in the brainbox department but his heart was in the right place. And that was what counted with Daisy. But if only Kenny didn't idolise Eddie so much. That was his trouble, really. He wanted to be like Eddie, couldn't see Eddie was a shit. Daisy sighed. Why on earth was she thinking about Eddie Lane when she was out on the loose for the day? And she hated to admit it but she was cold. There was practically no heating in the compartment. When she got back she'd give both Suze and Vera the satisfaction of being able to say, 'We told you so.' As she left the station and began the walk to the bus, a black taxi overtook her with the glamour girl sitting in the back.

Winchester Prison was not as forbidding as some prisons Daisy had seen. She knocked on the small gate set in the larger wooden one and showed her V.O. After she'd passed through identification and had Kenny's gifts taken off her she was shown into a clinical waiting room. The place had a dead smell about it. And the other people already sitting on benches possessed a zombie-like quality, almost as if this was a place that dared anyone to laugh, talk or smile. And all the time, somewhere, she heard the sound of doors clanging.

Eventually her name was called and she was shown into a large room with a parquet floor, full of tables with chairs set across from them. Other visitors were sitting quietly waiting. She didn't recognise them from being in the same waiting room where she'd been. Two guards were in the room, where she sat and waited for Kenny to be brought in. An eerie atmosphere of resignation seemed to seep from the cream and green-painted walls. The whole place was chilling and uninviting. It reminded her of a castle she had once visited on the Isle of Wight with her mum when she was a small child. She'd thought then that place was Dracula's castle. She was scared. And though she wasn't scared now, she knew that she could never be locked up. She would rather die first.

They unlocked the door, led Kenny and a line of prisoners in. He came straight over and kissed her.

'Wotcha, Dais,' he said. He smelled of carbolic soap.

'They've cut your hair again.' His hair had darkened almost to an ash blond. Not being able to go out in the fresh air, she thought. 'You all right?' She wanted to hold him some more but the guard was frowning at them. So she sat and held his hands across the table instead.

''Course I am. Don't I look it?'

'Yes,' she lied. She told the lie to protect his feelings. In truth he looked bloody awful. Sunken eyes, sallow skin and, strangely, he'd put on weight. Stodgy food, she supposed. She could always tell when Kenny was worried about something because he had a small nerve at the top corner of his mouth and it flickered involuntarily. It was doing a fuckin' war dance now.

'Gotta keep my looks, Dais. Don't want you leaving me for someone else.'

Sod the guard, she thought. She got up and went round and kissed Kenny. Long enough to show him he was being a silly sod but not so long for the guard to come over and start complaining. Daisy gripped Kenny's hand hard.

'Listen,' she said, surprised at the depth of her feelings. 'I ain't going nowhere, see?'

The smile that creased his face didn't reach his eyes, but she knew he was feeling more relaxed for he took his hand away and leaned back in his chair. Trying to look at ease with his surroundings.

'Did you bring anything?'

'Left it with the guards.'

'You don't 'alf look nice.'

'Clothes and shoes care of Gosport Market. Easier to shop now I'm living in town. Better than that 'ole in Henry Street.' Oh, God, she thought. How easy it is to say the wrong thing in here. But now she'd started she couldn't stop. 'Only another couple of weeks and you needn't have been in here. You needn't have gone on the rob with Eddie. You could have been on easy street, thanks to Bert.'

'Don't go on, Dais,' he said wearily. 'I keep on saying the same thing to meself, you know. It ain't no fuckin' picnic in 'ere. How was I to know that Bert had left the management of the caff to me?'

Daisy shrugged. Other prisoners and visitors had swelled the noise and children were in the room as well. She heard sounds of scraping chairs, and caught the smell of unwashed bodies.

'Just a couple of weeks an' everything would have been different.'

'One good thing, Dais, you got a roof over your head. And money in your pocket now. That's more than I've ever been able to give you regular.'

'Have I ever complained? An' it's not the same without you.'

'Do you mean that?'

''Course.' There was an ominous silence and, almost like a premonition, she knew what was coming next. Her heart beat fast.

'You've slept with Eddie, 'aven't you?' His statement, though expected, still took her breath away. She stared at him without answering, not knowing how to reply.

'It's all right,' he said. 'He's took every one of the girls I ever 'ad. I expected it to 'appen.' The nerve flickered wildly. Daisy tried to reach towards him but he was leaning further away and his chair was tilted so it was balanced on the two back legs. So she sat perfectly still.

'So you're just guessing?' she said.

He sighed. 'I don't blame you. And he can't 'elp it. Like he's frightened I'll 'ave somethin' he won't get. For all his smart talkin' he's very insecure, Dais.'

'I can't believe we're 'aving this conversation,' she said. 'If you really thought I'd slept with your brother surely you'd kill me? Or 'im?'

31

He shrugged. 'Dais, I'm in here. I can't do nothin'. But if you say you love me then I believe you. Why? 'Cause I've never known you to tell a proper out-and-out lie. So if you say you're going to build the caff up into somethin' to be proud of for the both of us then I believe you—' Daisy started to say something but he waved her away. 'Let me finish. I don't want to know the ins and outs. An' it's not even important if it happens again...'

'It bloody well is to me,' Daisy snapped. 'An' you'll hear why. The night you was taken into custody I was absolutely distraught. I didn't know what was 'appening to you, to me or what was going on. The fuckin' coppers wouldn't tell me nothin'. Eddie came to the flat. He was doing his comforting bit but I wouldn't be calmed. I don't know how I let it happen. An' afterwards I 'ated him. You don't know how much I 'ated him. Because he'd used me just like he uses everyone. An' I'd fallen for it. I 'ate the bugger. An' now you won't even let me give him his marchin' orders from the caff...'

'Dais, calm down. Or they'll cut the visit.' She was shaking. She looked towards the nearest guard who was studying them, almost as though the bloke could lip read or something and was real interested in what was going to happen next. Daisy took a deep breath and folded her hands in her lap. Though she supposed the guard had witnessed similar scenes many times and was only interested in stopping anything violent before it got out of hand. Composed now, expecting Kenny to be angry at the confession, she waited. But he wasn't angry. Instead, hurt shone out of his eyes. And something else. Fear. But whether it was for Daisy, or him, or even Eddie, she had no idea. He was trembling. Daisy stood up and leaned across and pulled him, and the chair, nearer the table.

'C'mere, you,' she said.

She thought he'd resist, but he didn't. She took his hands in hers; his palms were damp with sweat. His eyes seemed to bore into her as he said, 'Eddie has to stay with you. I'd worry more if you was on your own with just them two females for company. Eddie won't let any 'arm come to you. Trust him, Dais. Will you come and visit me again?' She took her hands away and wiped her eyes with her fingers, where tears had formed wetly on her lower lids. Didn't want her mascara to run.

'How can you ask me that when I've just said I love you?' And for the first time he gave her a proper Kenny smile.

'Just testin', Dais, just testin'.' He shifted in his seat. 'How's the new girl?' She was relieved he didn't want to talk about her any more.

She'd written and told him about Susie, that she'd hired a young girl to help in the cafe. She knew all the letters in and out of prison were censored, so she'd been economical with the truth. Didn't he have enough on his plate to worry about, being in there, without knowing how Susie came to be living with her?

'She's okay,' she said. 'And I'm keeping her away from Eddie.' He laughed.

'We got a big name on remand in 'ere.'

'Who?'

'Roy Kemp.'

Daisy gave a sharp intake of breath. Roy Kemp kept the London toe-rags well and truly in order. It was rumoured the police had an easier time leaving him, the Krays and the Richardsons to sort out the real villains. Mafia connections had also been mentioned in the newspapers.

'He's a celebrity, ain't he? Have you met him?'

'Nah. He keeps 'is head down. But he's got respect in 'ere. An' not just with the cons.'

Although he was smiling, and even laughed a few times trying to put her at her ease, it was his eyes that worried Daisy the most. They were as dead as cod's eyes on a fishmonger's slab.

'Remember when we met, Kenny?' She was trying to ease the pressure a bit by talking about happier times. 'My mum was alive then.'

'Yeah, and she told me to take care of you when she was ill and knew she wasn't goin' to get better. Well, I haven't done a very good job, have I, Dais?'

'When we first started goin' out together you was honest with me, Kenny. Told me you'd been in trouble with the police and was on probation. I remember you sat me down in the Dive cafe with a cup of tea and a currant bun and held my hand and told me all

33

about your family bein' locals an' you bein' born 'ere, same as me, and Eddie bein' in the army then goin' inside and goin' to live in Hull when he came out. You told me Eddie had kicked a night watchman unconscious when the two of you burgled a warehouse an' how you bein' younger had got off more lightly. But those days you 'ad a job on the building site an' you was stickin' to it. I was proud of you for that an' proud because you didn't try to hide anything.'

He smiled. 'We've had a funny old time of it, Dais. An' you've never complained.'

'What's to complain about? I chose you and you chose me. An' Bert chose you to manage the caff. Ever wondered why?'

'Not really. We went in regular an' he was always nice to us. He was a funny old sod.'

'That's as maybe, but until his will is sorted out properly I think I owe it to Bert to make a success of what he's given us. A new start.' Just then the buzzer sounded. The guard stepped from his corner, motioning the prisoners to rise, and in dribs and drabs goodbyes were said. Daisy clung to Kenny, trying to capture the smell of him so she could remember it when she was home and lonely again. Tears rose unbidden and she couldn't watch him being led away. She crocodiled with the other visitors until she was let out of the metal gate, then the wooden one, and into the blessed cold, fresh air. Then the tears came hot and fast as she practically ran down the hill into the crowded town. There was a bitter taste in her mouth and a blister on her heel.

Daisy hurried on until the pain made her swear. She stopped and held up her heel to examine it. She wasn't wearing stockings so it was easy to see the blister was bleeding and had stained the white shoe leather. It wasn't going to hurt less until she did something about it. Her eyes searched through the throng of noisy people towards the shops. Ahead was a Woolworth's. She could buy plasters in there. She pushed open the glass door, felt the warmth inside the store hit her and collided with a woman.

'I'm sorry.' They spoke simultaneously. 'But it really was my .

fault,' Daisy insisted. She laughed. It was the vision from the platform.

'No damage.' The woman looked Daisy up and down. Daisy showed her the blistered heel. 'Did I do that?' she asked.

'Oh, no. I was just coming in here to buy plasters. New shoes,' she explained.

'Don't waste your money.' The woman snapped open her bag and thrust two cellophane-covered strips into Daisy's hands. 'Are they enough?' She had a London twang to her voice. Not really cockney but not posh either. Well modulated. Her expensive perfume wafted over Daisy as the two women stood aside to let an old woman pass through the door with a multitude of bulky shopping bags.

'Just the job. Thanks ever so much,' Daisy said. 'Now all I need is somewhere to sit down so I can sort me heel out.'

'How about the bus station?' Daisy thought she must have looked a bit stupid for the woman added, 'They do a good cup of tea in the cafeteria. We've plenty of time if you're catching the next train back to Fareham. I saw you at the station.' She took Daisy's arm and gently propelled her along the pavement towards the bus depot. It wasn't far to hobble. Daisy sat down gratefully on a plastic chair while her new friend cut through the other seated customers to buy tea. She returned shortly with two strong teas in mugs.

'I always end up in here after seeing Roy. Prisons are such gloomy places.'

Never would Daisy have guessed they were going to the same place when the woman's taxi disappeared while Daisy was walking towards the bus.

'We're lucky they give us a private room to talk in. Maximum security and all that.' Daisy nodded. It hadn't taken her long to put two and two together – the smart woman was visiting the high-profile prisoner Kenny had mentioned. They sipped their tea and Daisy thanked God she could move her foot about without the shoe rubbing. Cigarette smoke hung like fog in the cafeteria. The elderly waitress wore carpet slippers with holes slit in the sides for her bunions to poke through. She came and wiped the table with a dirty cloth.

'Moira's my name. What's yours?'

'Daisy. Daisy Lane.' Moira told Daisy she lived in London.

'But you came from Fareham?' It was the opposite direction. Moira frowned, tapped her red-tipped nails on the formica table top, then put her hand to her forehead as though willing the answer to come.

'Of course. I've been staying in Titchfield. Do you know it?' Titchfield was a sleepy, pretty village some way outside of Fareham, made up of ancient timbered houses and with farmland at its outskirts.

Daisy nodded. 'I'm near the ferry at Gosport.'

'I know Portsmouth well, that's across the ferry from Gosport, isn't it? Roy owns a club and has some other bits and bobs going on down there.' Daisy didn't ask any questions though she was as curious as hell. Mum always told her that people will tell you what they want you to know, so it was useless to pry and get called nosy for your trouble. She reckoned that was a good rule to live by. They chatted about silly stuff, like two old friends. Then Daisy noticed the clock on the wall. Moira saw her frown.

'Don't worry. The London train goes just before yours and I've booked the taxi to pick me up from here. We can share it, if you like.'

'Only if you let me pay my half.'

'I don't think so.' She waved her hand as though brushing Daisy's offer aside. 'My treat. Actually, it's nice to be able to talk to someone who understands what it's like when their man's in prison. What's your . . .'

'Husband,' Daisy finished for her. 'Two years. Sixteen months if he's lucky. Housebreaking.' She watched as Moira digested these facts.

'Roy's on remand. But they won't sentence him. They can't have anything that'll stick on him. We've got a brilliant solicitor so it's just a case of wait and see.'

They chatted all the way back in the taxi and only separated when they discovered they had to go to different platforms. Before she left, Moira said, 'I think we could be friends, you and I, Daisy. I don't really have many friends. Since my mum committed suicide when I was young I tended to keep apart from people. Until I met Roy. And he became my whole life.'

Daisy's mouth must have dropped open at this.

'It's all right, Daisy. I have to talk about it. I spent too many years before I met Roy letting it take over my life. Then a few years ago Mum's best friend Ruth died in awful circumstances and as I'd sort of looked up to her, even copied the way she dressed and looked, if it hadn't been for Roy I don't know how I'd have coped. 'Course, I wasn't married to him then.'

'You've not had a very good time of things so far, have you?' Daisy was appalled tragedy could strike so easily and in such a short time to someone as elegant and obviously so caring as Moira.

'My mum and Ruth were both born in Rhyl. Ruth Ellis, you know?' Of course Daisy knew. She nodded. 'Ruth's dad Arthur Hornby was a cellist and my dad – so I was told, because he didn't stick around long enough for me to find out – played the violin. He was much older than my mum and he disappeared after getting a job with Ruth's dad on a liner bound for the Atlantic. Good riddance to bad rubbish, I say.' Though Daisy didn't think she really meant what she said, her eyes clouded with tears as she said it. Must have been really hard for Moira to have lost so many people from her short life, she thought.

Moira and Daisy swapped phone numbers and addresses and promised to meet. For once in her life, Daisy felt quite important actually possessing a phone number, even if it did belong to the cafe. She folded Moira's address and tucked it inside her purse. When they said goodbye, Daisy knew she'd met someone she really liked, even though beneath the expensive perfume and classic clothes the woman had an aura of sadness that hung around her like a shroud.

CHAPTER 5

13 November 1962

Piece of piss, thought Eddie. He patted the roll of banknotes snug in his Crombie's inside pocket. How easy it had been to enter the Victory Inn on the foggy hard and tell them they needed protection.

'Pay me and you'll get no sailors making trouble with the regulars in here.'

'But we don't see the skates fighting much in here. It's too near the Dockyard and the M.P.s patrol regularly. 'Sides, we already got protection.' The bloke had smirked at Eddie.

Eddie's blood had boiled but he stayed very calm. He stared at the row of optics in front of the mirrored shelf at the rear of the smoke-filled bar. Pat, Bri and Cal were watching his reflection, waiting for a sign.

'You could have a nasty fight on yer hands at any time. Now supposing those three men over there decided they didn't like this place?' He nodded towards the ever biddable Cal.

As the three men overturned tables and chairs and smashed glasses, Cal threw a pint glass and it hit the mirror with a loud crack which shattered the glass, showering it everywhere. The place emptied of the few customers it had quicker than the blink of an eyelid, and the landlord and his plump barmaid were left cowering in a corner. Bri slipped the bolt on the front doors. The place stank of old wet fags and a mixture of spilled beer and spirits. Silence reigned once more.

'Okay, okay,' came the voice of the landlord.

Eddie had already emptied the till. Poor pickings there, he thought, and bent and picked up a bottle of Brickwoods brown ale as it rolled off the shelf towards him. He'd stood and watched the preceding violence with a calm smile on his face before walking to the rear of the bar.

'It seems we've cleared the place, lads. What a shame.' With his hand on the neck of the bottle, he cracked it on the metal edge of the sink. It broke, leaving a jagged edge and brown liquid gushing and frothing into the dirty washing-up water. He swaggered around to the customers' side of the bar where his two victims crouched, shivering with terror. 'Get the fuck up,' he said quietly. The landlord stayed down. Eddie could see the sweat glistening on the man's forehead. The woman rose hesitantly, then she started to scream. Eddie grabbed her with his left hand and threw her across the room to where the boys were. 'Shut 'er up,' he said. Pat grabbed her and, as she sagged against him, he clamped her mouth with his hand then threw her on the floor. Eddie watched dispassionately as she lay there in a crumpled heap. He turned to the landlord.

'If you ain't going to get up you'll have to learn a lesson down there.'

Eddie laughed as he saw the dark stain spread over the man's trousers. The smell of piss rose and hit him. He leaned down and drew the broken bottle across the man's cheek. The man tried to slap the glass away and in jerking his head it caught the corner of his mouth. The blood spurted.

'He's a bleeder.' Eddie smiled at his pun. 'Sorry about the mess.' He threw the bottle onto the floor where it shattered. 'But see how easy it is for trouble to start. Now if you was to go upstairs and get the money to pay for the first instalment on your new damage protection insurance, it won't happen again. Unless you forgets to pay a premium, of course.' He threw the man a bar cloth proclaiming Brickwoods Best, then watched as, sobbing, the landlord pressed the dirty cloth to his face and then rose shakily to his feet. 'Cal's going to go with you to make sure you don't do anything silly, like try to telephone anyone.' He nodded towards Cal, who followed the man out through the beaded curtain at the back of the bar. Already blood was showing through the towel. Eddie chucked another one at the retreating figure. 'Better take this, mate, or you'll make a nice mess.'

He ambled over the broken glass to Bri. The woman was crying softly, hunched on the floor.

'Don't cut me,' she cried.

'I ain't gonna touch you. Wouldn't soil my hands. But you got to have something to remember us by or you won't remind your boss to put the premiums by.' He aimed a sharp kick at her. As he moved, the glass crunched beneath his shoes. She cried out in pain and tried to curl further into herself.

The landlord and Cal returned with a blue drawstring bank bag. Eddie pulled it open.

'That'll do for now.'

The landlord bent down to the woman and touched her face. She flinched. He looked up at Eddie, most of his face obscured by the blood-soaked cloth held tightly in place by his other hand.

'When will you come back?' His voice was shaking, muffled by the cloth.

'Whenever I want. You won't forget me, will you?'

'No, I won't forget,' mumbled the man. Eddie shoved the bag into his pocket and made to leave. He got to the door and Cal pulled up the bolt. Then Eddie turned, the glass crackling beneath his feet.

'Get this place cleaned up,' he said. 'How do you expect customers to drink in filth like this? Oh, and by the way. I'd much prefer it if you called me "sir" when I come in again. And don't think of involving any of the boys in blue in our little transaction. Wouldn't like to think of any of your nearest and dearest coming to any harm, would we?' He stared at the two of them, her lying on the floor and him bleeding, trying to comfort her. Then he'd walked away.

Four pubs they'd done. Sweet as a nut. He wondered why the protection racket had never occurred to him before. After all, he'd heard it was how the Kray twins got started. And look at them, Kings of the Smoke, hobnobbing with the famous in their clubs. Protection was money for old rope.

He'd sent Cal, Bri and Pat home with fair wads in their pockets. Cal lived at Clayhall, just outside Gosport town and approached via Haslar bridge over the creek. Cal was staying with his young nephew in a prefab. His sister had died of cancer the year before and Cal had moved in to look after the lad, a gangly youth of about sixteen with bum-fluff on his face. Cal wanted him to stay on at school. And do better than he ever did. Cal had ended up working in a baker's until he'd chucked it for better pickings with Eddie. Of the three, Eddie was closest to Cal. Not that he ever confided in anyone, much.

Pat had a touch of the Irish in him with his dark curly hair that he fancied was like Elvis's and a honeyed, lilting brogue to his voice. He was okay as long as he didn't get sidetracked by the booze. He'd been off the sauce for a good long time now. Eddie knew how hard it was for him. He wasn't too bright but he was a big brawny bugger and could hold his own in any rough stuff. He sure knew his way around cars though. He was shacked up with some ugly bitch down Old Road. Ancient enough to be Pat's mother, Eddie reckoned. But she was keeping him on the straight and narrow as far as the booze was concerned, so who Pat was shagging was nothing to do with Eddie. Bri lodged with them.

He was a bit of a mystery: he'd tagged on to Eddie when the fair was down in Walpole Park, told him he'd got fed up with wandering from place to place. He was a good-looking bloke, magnificent chestnut-coloured hair. One time he'd been a market trader, educated, too. You could hold a decent conversation with Bri that didn't involve swearing. It wasn't that Eddie didn't exactly trust Bri, in fact just the opposite. After all, Bri always seemed to be the one ready to protect him. Not that Eddie couldn't look after himself. Far from it. But he couldn't get his head round why a feller like Bri would have chucked his lot in with the travellers in the first place. Still, Bri was quiet and quick and kept his head when there was trouble. Most importantly, he did what Eddie told him. But he preferred not to hurt people if he could figure a better way to get them to do what Eddie wanted. Eddie smiled to himself.

Anyone who lived down Old Road had to keep their eyes open and their mouths shut. He remembered a barney a few months back which had started over some slag sleeping around. Eventually some wisearse had called in the police because people were getting hurt left, right and centre. Proper carnage night it was. When the coppers did arrive they stayed in their patrol cars until the worst was over. Then calmly cleared up afterwards. It was said that the coppers walked round in pairs down there, with another pair behind them to watch out for the first pair. Eddie laughed and kicked at a coke bottle. It slid along the pavement and rolled into the gutter to lie with some wet sweet-wrappers.

Eddie wanted a kingdom of his own, and he was determined no one would stand in his way. And he wasn't going back inside for no bugger, that one time had done it for him. All that slopping out and kow-towing to other cons and the screws just to keep your sanity. It was another world in there. He'd told Kenny to keep his head down. And he hoped he could. Silly young fucker.

All that dripping and moaning about not having any money for the rent. If Eddie had had money then he'd have given it willingly to Kenny. But he'd been skint as well. The best thing they could come up with was a spot of housebreaking. And how was he to know the stupid cunt of a woman was in bed asleep when Kenny climbed in through the transom window that Eddie had flipped up with a screwdriver?

Kenny had gone straight to the front door and made sure it was locked fast before he'd let Eddie in through the kitchen door. That way, no one would be able to get in the front way with a key. Eddie had heard the old girl coming down the stairs. Daft fucker, thought Eddie, what was the use of wearing dark clothing, gloves and a balaclava if Kenny had insisted his had itched his face and taken it off? The woman had come into the kitchen and switched on the light. The daft old bat had screamed, then had been stupid enough to try to pick up the telephone on the wall. Kenny had knocked it out of her hand and she'd stumbled to the floor. A dog had started barking but by this time both of them were away, out the garden and on to the allotments. Lights and noise were coming from all over the place. Eddie ran and kept on running. Kenny had split from him and was running towards Ann's Hill.

Eddie hid for a while in some runner bean plants. He took off his sweater, gloves and balaclava and dug them beneath some rhubarb. He reckoned by then the Criterion Cinema would be emptying for the night, so he walked casually out of the allotments and through the alley until he reached the back of the cinema. He'd timed it just right. Then he'd sauntered into the toilets of the

Queen Charlotte pub opposite and washed his hands and combed his hair, then stood at the bar with half a pint of bitter in front of him moaning to the barman about the film, which luckily he'd already seen.

Kenny hadn't been so lucky. Caught, identified and charged. He'd ended up in Winchester nick.

Eddie didn't have to worry that Kenny would split on him. That was one thing he'd never do. Never. And Eddie would never go on the rob again, not unless it was a big job. A bloody big one. And after tonight he was on the way up, wasn't he? Definitely.

The night Kenny had been caught and before he was charged, Eddie had rolled a sailor heading for the bus station off the last ferry. There'd been enough cash on the bloke, who'd been left with nothing more serious than a few cracked ribs, to pay Kenny's fuckin' rent. After that came the news about the management of the cafe. So if they'd only waited, everything would have turned out fine and Kenny wouldn't be inside now.

He crossed the road by Burtons, the men's outfitters. Maybe he'd buy himself a new suit tomorrow. He liked nice clothes. It had started to drizzle. The kind of damp that gets right inside you. He turned up the collar of his coat and turned his hat brim down low, and his eyes scanned to the corner near the Dive cafe. It was still open. Closed when it wanted to, that place. That cow Vera was standing by the taxi rank.

'What's new, Vera?' She looked freezing cold.

'Nothin', Eddie. Only bloke I talked to in the past half hour was that copper, Vinnie, the one you went to school with, remember? Business is slow tonight.'

Eddie nodded. How could he forget his one-time mate? But he didn't want to think about Vinnie. Too many bad memories there. He stared at Vera. He could feel her fear. He liked that. Fear was power. But he had no axe to grind with her. She did her share around the cafe and Daisy was fond of her. God, he could smell her from here. Bloody perfume she chucked on like holy water. It was enough to put a bloke right off, not give 'em the come-on. Still, he had to admit, Vera had her head screwed on right. Must have, to have lasted so long on the game. And she still had bait left to catch a few more fish.

'I'm fed up. Think I'll take meself off home. No sense in catching me death, is there?'

Eddie realised the drizzle had turned to spears of slanting rain, hurling itself against the tarmac. He also knew that if he hadn't appeared Vera would probably have stayed there, waiting for punters. The clock on Holy Trinity church struck ten o'clock, echoing in the cold night. The lights of Portsmouth twinkled distortedly through the rain.

'Ten,' he said. 'Time all good boys and girls were tucked up in bed.'

'See you later,' Vera said. The sound of her heels clattered on the cobbles as she walked down North Street. Eddie watched until she went from his sight. From the back, with her neat arse swinging from side to side and her shapely legs made longer with the aid of her black high heels, she looked young. It wasn't until you got close up you could see she'd had a rough life.

'One more slag off the streets for tonight,' he whispered to himself. 'An early night might do her some good.' Where to now? Too early for him to go home, and where was home anyway? He patted his inside pocket. The money felt reassuring. Home was wherever he wanted it to be, tonight. It was definitely too early to go back to Daisy's for some kip, even though the town seemed devoid of people.

Daisy. He smiled. Now there was a plucky bitch. The only woman who'd got his measure and dared to stand up to him. And the only woman who could have got away with it. He thought of how she'd conned him into removing his clothes and he'd let her tie him down to the bed. His cheeks felt hot now, remembering. He laughed as he walked along, deep in his own thoughts. And the drill! Where on earth had she got the idea for that? One of those bloody books she always had her nose in, he supposed. But then, he liked a good read himself from time to time. Still, it had frightened the shit out of him. God, she'd looked fierce, like a young lioness protecting her cubs. Well, Susie was now one of her cubs. He'd made a mistake there, all right. Still, he wouldn't go near that again. Not if it meant that much to Daisy.

He thought again about the night Kenny had got caught. Not that he'd known then that Kenny was in custody. He'd gone round to their flat in Henry Street. Poky one-room place. He didn't know Daisy very well then. They'd got married when Eddie was inside and then he'd been away up in Hull after coming out of prison. He'd kept away for Kenny's sake.

'I'm glad you've come,' she'd said. 'The police have been round an' searched the place.' She had been crying and looked like a lost kid. 'Was Kenny with you? When he went out, he said he'd be back with the rest of the rent money we owed. But he wouldn't tell me where he was going. The coppers said there was two men.' Then she'd burst into tears again. She had a coat on over a long flannelette nightie that went down to her ankles and her feet were bare. He remembered how small her feet were, and how vulnerable she looked. She must have been lying on the bed sobbing her heart out for she had pillow creases all down one side of her face. Well, he couldn't leave her like that so he pulled her towards him and she cried into his shirt. She didn't smell of perfume but clean, like a pile of fresh ironing. And she was small. Barely up to his chin. Her blonde hair was sticking out all over the place and her nose had started running.

'Get into bed,' he'd told her. Then he'd made her some tea using the gas stove on the landing outside and shared by the other residents. He put into the cup a good dollop from the quarter-bottle of brandy that he'd bought in the Queen Charlotte, in case he couldn't sleep himself that night after the run-in with the law. He didn't normally take alcohol. He liked to be in control at all times and he knew just how daft some people could get with a few bevvies inside them.

'D'you think the coppers'll come back?' she'd asked. He didn't think so, but he said, 'They might.'

'They frightened me.'

'Do you want me to stay for a while?'

'All right,' she'd said, but not until she'd thought about it. He gave her some more tea, held her while she cried for Kenny. Then he lay on the bed beside her, cuddling her. After that, it happened.

At first he wanted her because she wasn't his. Afterwards, as she slept, he watched her and was convinced he'd been gentle with her because it was impossible for him to hurt her. And yet he had. By

45

fucking her. He realised that when she woke she'd hate him because he'd made her let her guard down.

He'd got dressed, left the dingy room and crept downstairs and out into the night. He'd rolled the sailor as he'd reeled off the last ferry; singing his fuckin' head off the skate was. Well, he wasn't singing when Eddie kicked him. And Eddie knew then he'd always look out for Daisy, whether she wanted it or not . . .

'Stranger on the Shore' was playing on the jukebox. It was drifting out from the Nelson Arms. The rain was getting to him now and he decided a half a pint of shandy in the dry and warm might just do the trick. He pushed open the brass and glass door and went inside. The noise he'd heard from outside was not just from the music but from the foreign sailors. He looked at their hatbands. Dutch probably. Then he saw the girl.

She was pulling on the sleeve of a young skate who wanted nothing to do with her and kept shrugging her off. She was slightly overweight with stringy blonde hair, scruffy and very drunk. She had a scar on her neck that ran diagonally from her collarbone to her chin. It looked quite recent.

'Half of bitter shandy,' he said. The barman served him without a word, the liquid slopping on the sticky wooden bar top. His eyes scanned the room to see where the girl was now. She'd given up on the sailor and was chatting to the landlord who beckoned towards a beaded hanging curtain at the back of the grubby saloon. The girl pushed her way unsteadily through the noisy mob of drinkers and picked up a holdall from under a corner table. Then she made her way back, lifted the bar top and disappeared through the jangling curtain. Eddie guessed she was a bed and breakfast. There were about seventy pubs around the town. Alcohol and seaports went together, along with casual lodgings. And tarts. And Eddie knew a slag when he saw one. He could also feel a headache coming on.

That was the last thing he needed, one of his headaches. Sometimes they were so bad it was like a black blanket had been thrown over his head. He couldn't think straight or act rationally. The sickness made him want to scream and the depression caused him to say and do things he knew days later he would be horrified

46

at. Yet even when those things were happening and he knew he should stop, he couldn't. They'd started on his tenth birthday, the headaches.

Kenny had wanted to buy Eddie a birthday present, so Kenny had stolen coppers out of Pappy's trouser pockets while Pappy was sleeping off the drink. When Pappy woke and saw Eddie eating liquorice strips he'd asked him where he'd got the money to buy them. Eddie hadn't answered, guessing immediately what Kenny had done. Eddie told him he'd taken the money, defying Kenny to say a word. Pappy went into one of his rages and knocked ten bales of shit out of Eddie. He'd discovered three things that day. One, if you steal, don't get caught and don't admit to a thing; two, trust nobody, and three, the beating, mainly about the head, had resulted in these blinding depression headaches that came without warning.

He looked at his barely touched drink in its greasy glass. His stomach heaved. He decided an early night might be a better option than staying in this filthy, noisy hole. He could also smell the stench coming from the nearby Gents. A bloody dump, this, he thought.

'Have you got a light?'

It was the girl. He pushed her away.

'Well!' she said in a loud aggrieved tone. Two sailors glanced at her. Then Eddie turned and moved towards the door. He heard it slam behind him. Gulping great lungfuls of air that smelled of salt and mud, he turned towards Beach Street. Not wanting to pass the Dive cafe or go up through the High Street, he walked instead through the darkened boatyards, lit only by the odd street lamp that scarcely illuminated the bomb sites covered in brambles, old prams and railway sleepers. It would take him less than five or six minutes to walk up South Street and cross the High Street to Bert's. The rain had eased. He heard footsteps behind him. It was the girl again.

'Have you got a light? I don't give up that easy.'

She was breathless. Her eyes were very bright, the pupils enlarged. She was on something. All the kids were these days, probably that new stuff, that party drug, MDMA. Hadn't he done a nice little deal himself on that? Not for him, of course, he didn't believe in choking back the profits. But the punters loved it. It was coming over by the boatload from Germany. The girl put her hand on his arm. She didn't look clean, and he shook her away without answering. But she wouldn't take the hint. Her hand was on his Crombie sleeve again.

'If you don't smoke, I bet there's something else you'd like.' He looked at her then. She was pretty in an unkempt, unmade-bed sort of way. 'A lovely man like you shouldn't be out here on your own. We could go and find somewhere quiet.'

She was about sixteen. Been around the block a few times and then some, Eddie thought.

The cobbles shone in the lamplight near the floating bridge.

'Fuck off,' said Eddie. 'I'm not interested.'

'But I could make you interested,' she said. Her hand snaked beneath his Crombie coat and found his fly. He felt himself respond to her touch and hated himself for it.

'Mustn't lie, Big Boy,' she said. Her hand was massaging him.

He groaned, wanting to move away yet pinned by her hand.

'Let's find somewhere more private,' she said. She slipped her arm through his and walked him down towards Simmonds' Boatyard and the darkness.

'What's your name?'

'Al,' he lied.

'Mine's Adele. I got here today from Plymouth.' The gateway was open to the boatyard and she led him in, stumbling over planks of wood and stones. He saw shapes of sawing horses and the tall outlines of boats under construction. He could also smell fibreglass in the air. He felt the hard wooden hull of a boat at his back and the scent of wet sawdust was in his nostrils. His cock was throbbing, tight against the material of his trousers. Opening his fly she let him out. She sank to her knees and took him in her mouth. He let her do it and watched as her mouth took in the full, thick length of him. Then her head moved backwards and forwards almost in a rocking motion. The heat and softness of her flickering tongue as she sucked and licked him was exquisite. He put his hands on her shoulders and thrust into her, feeling her face hard against his belly. One of her hands found and cupped his balls then she ran her fingers over his thrusting buttocks until she found his arsehole.

'No, let me inside you,' he gasped.

She pulled away, stood up, and put her hands on her hips. She was silently mocking him and the way he'd let his cock rule his head. He felt his erection flag and anger surface. He made a grab for her but she side-stepped him.

'How much do I get?' Her voice was hard. Eddie's teeth clenched together. She knew he wanted it. The bitch had the upper hand, or thought she did. He realised this was the way she worked her punters and his anger rose even more.

'Fuckin' bitch,' he cried, 'I don't pay for it.' His hand connected with her face with a loud thwack and she almost whirled on the spot before falling back heavily amongst the wet woodchips and bits of sawn planking. Eddie fell beside her and tore at her underclothes. She gave no resistance as the thin garments were yanked aside. He was kneeling astride her now and pulled her legs apart so he could enter her. Her body was warm and pliable. He ripped into her, thrusting, withdrawing and thrusting again.

'Who's got the fuckin' power now, cunt?' he groaned. When he'd spent himself inside her he had to stifle his own sounds. He lay for a moment. Then shuddered as the final spasm shook his body. God, how he hated her for making him lose control.

Then he realised she hadn't moved, nor made a single sound the whole time he was fucking her. He eased himself from her and knelt up, adjusting his clothing, then he stood. She lay in the same position, and quite still, her clothes wet and crumpled and spread about her. The only difference now was the darkness oozing from the back of her head into the lightness of the sawdust. Bending down he tried to lift her head but it didn't want to move, not without heaving up the solid plank of wood she'd fallen on. The plank was fastened tight to the back of her skull, speared by a large nail that must have been sticking out of it.

The church clock chimed quarter to eleven. Eddie was shivering. He rose slowly, ran his fingers through his wet hair. The rain had started up again, washing the wet sawdust and blood from the girl's hair as she lay amongst the rubbish. She looked so young, thought Eddie. So fuckin' young.

He bent down and felt her neck for a pulse. Nothing. He closed her eyelids with his thumb, then whispered,

'I'm sorry. So fuckin' sorry.' He picked up his hat and shook the droplets from it before putting it on and then he looked about him. He heard only the sharp staccato sounds of the rain beating on the multitude of surfaces. Then in the harbour he caught the jangling sound of a buoy. Satisfied there was still no one about, he made his way back through the rows of half-finished craft and stepped out onto the road. He walked swiftly up into South Street then turned right into South Cross.

Eddie let himself in the street door. The house was silent apart from the usual night creaks that the old building made. He climbed the stairs. Susie's door was closed. He opened the door to his own room. His wet Crombie he hung on a hanger and put it on the picture rail near the window. He dusted his hat with a handkerchief and put it on the top of the wardrobe, then changed his trousers and took off his shirt, leaving his white tee-shirt on. He counted his money and stashed it away with the rest in a secret place he'd devised. Then he sat on the edge of the bed and put his head in his hands. After a while he got up and, closing the door behind him, went downstairs. He needed a drink, him, Eddie Lane, who didn't drink.

In the kitchen he lit the gas under the kettle. Surprisingly, his headache was passing off. Then he began slapping marge on bread. He didn't really want to eat but he was going for normality, going through the motions. He heard the street door open.

Vera was wet through and brought in not only the rain but the cold night air as well. She looked thoroughly miserable. She took off her jacket, beneath which was a red crepe blouse that was wet at the front and the collar.

'All right?' he asked.

'Do I look as if I'm all right?'

'If you will stay out in the rain.'

'Yeah, well. I did a favour for someone. Now I wish I'd 'ad the sense you did an' come 'ome earlier.' For a moment her words didn't sink in. When they did, he realised she thought he had come straight home after their meeting at the taxi rank. Home and dry,

Eddie boy, he thought. If anyone came round asking questions, with a bit of luck she'd be his alibi. His spirits lifted.

'Just making a cuppa. Couldn't sleep. Want one?'

'Do I fuckin' just,' she said, kicking off her sodden shoes and collapsing onto a wooden stool. She picked up a cotton tea towel and started rubbing her wet hair. 'Me fuckin' feet are killin' me.'

'Where've you been, while I've been trying to kip?' he asked for emphasis.

'Nel, my mate, 'ad the flu and sent a girl down to ask if I'd do her john she 'ad lined up. I went along to Mumby Road, did him. Took her 'alf the money back to 'er place and got caught in the fuckin' rain.' She stuck out one leg and examined it. 'An' I got a fuckin' run in me stocking for me trouble.'

'Never rains but it pours, does it, Vera?' He laughed. 'I'm making a sandwich, how about you?'

'Why, Eddie Lane, you can be a real darlin' when you wants. A real darlin'.'

CHAPTER 6

5 December 1962

'Damn.' Susie picked at her broken nail. 'Just when I was getting to like you long.' She flexed her hand with the five fingers spread wide. She was proud of the way she'd stopped biting her nails. Now they were long enough to put a bit of varnish on.

'No red,' Daisy had warned. 'Punters don't like red. It puts 'em off their eggs and bacon. Pink or clear. Take yer pick.'

'Did you say something?'

Si Leadbetter was standing by the counter. He was the delivery boy for The World's Stores in the High Street where Daisy bought her groceries for the cafe. They sold everything in there, from broken biscuits to sugar by the pound in blue bags, and meatstuffs of every description. Susie thought The World's Stores was pushing it a bit as a name. Did they really have branches in Africa and Outer Mongolia as well as Gosport High Street? Still, fair's fair, she thought. They gave good service and value for money and the delivery boy made her feel funny. A nice sort of funny.

'Just broke a nail,' she said. Si leaned across and grabbed her hand.

'Let's have a look.'

'Don't be silly,' she said, pulling away. 'It's only a nail.' Then she flicked at him with the tea towel. 'Thought you was helping to collect ashtrays?'

He made a mock salute. 'Right, ma'am, left, ma'am. Right now, Boss Lady.'

Susie laughed at his antics. He was always making her laugh. He'd started coming into Bert's a few weeks back. Then he'd surprised her by inviting her to the pictures. She'd been wary at first, not wanting to be alone with a male, for a start. But Si was different. He wasn't pushy.

The picture was *Lawrence of Arabia* with Peter O'Toole. Lots of desert and motorbikes. They sat in the front row. Not the back row for a quick fumble like most fellas on the make. She admired him for this. And he'd bought her a choc ice in the interval and brought her straight home, then thanked her at the street door for going out with him.

So far he hadn't attempted to kiss her. To tell the truth she was a bit cross about this because she wanted to be kissed by him. But she wasn't going to make the first move. She didn't want him to think she was fast. She really liked him. From his face, which was covered in freckles so that there was hardly a space between them, to his hair, which was pale ginger, almost golden, like the colour of the setting sun, to his feet, probably a size nine, she thought. About five-foot-ten he was, with green eyes and fair lashes that seemed almost invisible until you were close up and saw how long they really were.

Si had also been helping Daisy tart the cafe up a bit. They'd painted the smoke-stained ceiling brilliant white, standing on tables and using wide brushes tied to broom handles. Daisy had bought the stuff from Murphy's, the hardware shop opposite.

'If you can't get it in Murphy's it ain't worth 'aving,' she'd said. Susie thought she was probably right. Murphy's sold everything from nails to tin baths, which hung on huge hooks outside the shop.

Daisy had also got hold of a brand-new jukebox. A Wurlitzer hi-fi stereo with two hundred selections. But she'd still insisted they leave some old favourites on it, including Eddie's beloved 'Wheel of Fortune', as well as 'You Belong To Me' by the Duprees; 'Big Girls Don't Cry' by the Four Seasons; 'I Can't Stop Loving You' by Ray Charles; 'Sealed With a Kiss' by Brian Hyland and, of course, a couple of Elvis tunes, 'Return To Sender' and 'Good Luck Charm'. The punters loved the jukebox. It stood, elegant and gleaming, just inside the main doors.

'Daisy's turned this place right round, hasn't she?' said Si.

'Yes, it's better now we're cooking proper full breakfasts as well. We catch people on their way to work. Some come in for mid-morning fry-ups, because it's good value for money. Lunch-times are good, too. Anything you like, with chips.'

'Is it better that all the main cooking is over and done with by two o'clock?'

'I should say so,' said Susie. 'But a few people still come in for a cooked tea. And there's the cakes and doughnuts and that special bread pudding that Daisy makes. The customers love that. It's full of spice and fruit. She says she won't give me the recipe because it belonged to her mum and it means a lot to her.' She laughed. 'Says she'll leave it to me in her will.'

'What, the bread pudding? Won't it be all mouldy?'

'The recipe, you daft ape! Anyway, anytime she makes it, it don't last long on the counter. An' that's a fact.'

'Do you think changing the hours of the caff is an improvement?'

'Yes. Very early in the morning for fried breakfasts 'til the evening at seven or so is much better. Daisy says we can stay open later if we feel like it though. But by closing earlier we've lost the pub turn-outs an' that's when trouble used to start. We've been doing well. So well that Daisy's upped me wages.'

'And what about the rooms upstairs, they sorted?'

'One spare room, an' it's used for bed and breakfasts.'

'I think you like it here,' said Si.

Susie thought for a moment. 'Too right I do,' she said. 'Daisy's a lovely boss.' She didn't add that she was still scared to leave her door unlocked at nights. Though she saw little of Eddie nowadays. When he was around he simply acknowledged her for Daisy's sake, then ignored her. And it suited Susie just fine.

Si smoothed down his wiry hair but it immediately bounced back up again. He wasn't particularly handsome but he was nice looking and, besides, she thought it wasn't the wrapping on the present that counted, it was what was inside.

'Sometimes the customers leave me tips,' she said. 'Daisy lets me keep everything. Many of the customers are really poor but they are lovely, some of them.'

'And what about me? Am I lovely?' asked Si. 'Do you like me, an' all?'

Susie went very quiet. She could feel herself blushing.

'You know I do,' she said, looking into his green eyes. But it was Si who went bright red and had to lower his gaze.

Inside her there was a great battle going on. Si believed she was Daisy's cousin. She didn't want to lie to him. Lies had an awful habit of growing out of control. Yet how could she explain about her mother, her awful life in Southampton and the disastrous meeting with Eddie? She wanted to be completely honest with Si, but what if he turned away from her in disgust? She didn't think she could cope with that.

Si cleared his throat. He was running his index finger around the top of a glass.

'Suze,' he said. He didn't look up from his task.

'What?'

He cleared his throat again.

'Would you like to come and spend Christmas over at our house? I asked me mum and she said it would be fine.' It all came out in a rush. Susie could see he'd been terrified of asking her.

''Ang on, Si,' she said, 'catch your breath.' He stopped playing with the glass and stared at her expectantly.

Susie put out her hand and lightly touched his arm.

'Please say you will . . .' He looked like a kicked puppy.

'I'd love to.'

'I didn't think you would. You will?'

She nodded. 'It's been a long time since I experienced a proper family Christmas. Will there be chicken?'

The ecstatic smile dropped from his face. His eyes were downcast.

'We're having a duck, courtesy of The World's Stores,' he said sorrowfully. 'Though I could buy a chicken and ask Mum to cook it if you really . . .'

'Duck? Oh, Si, how exciting!' She'd never eaten a duck before. How posh was that?

'You'll come? You'll really come?'

She nodded, but was forced to stop when he suddenly leaned across the counter and kissed her full on the mouth. Susie felt she had died and gone to heaven. That kiss was all the better for her having to wait. But there was still the nagging thought that honesty was the best policy. Later, she thought, she'd talk to Daisy. Daisy, her saviour, the one person in her life she could truly trust. Daisy would know what to do.

CHAPTER 7

17 December 1962

'Want a hand with that, Dais?'

Why did she always think Eddie had an ulterior motive when he offered to help?

'Get a bit of winter sunshine and it shows up all the dirt and dust in the place,' she said, looking down at him from her lofty perch on the top of the rickety wooden stepladder. 'I've washed these nets' – she shook out the bunched-up curtains – 'and soaked them in Reckitts Blue but if there's one thing I hate doing it's threading the bloody wires through again.'

Eddie was looking up at her. She could smell the fresh, clean scent of Imperial Leather soap on him. He had a wry smile on his face, like he was laughing at her discomfort on the top of the ladder. His white shirtsleeves were rolled up and the shirt was hanging outside of his well-fitting jeans. She saw afresh why women's eyes followed his every move.

'Looking good up there, Dais. Specially in those tight pants.'

She had on a pair of black capri pants and a black sweater that was tight at the waist and had batwing sleeves and a low rolled neckline.

'Stop looking at my bottom,' Daisy snapped. 'And bloody help.'

He was in a good mood and so was she. Perhaps it was because Christmas was approaching, or perhaps it was the mild sunshine, but whatever it was it was pleasant.

'I just asked you if you wanted any help.'

'Well I do. For your cheek you can bloody well finish stringing these.'

'Why not? I ain't got nothing else to do at the moment.'

You could have swept Daisy off that ladder with a feather. She never thought Eddie Lane would agree to string nets. It was a quarter to seven in the morning and everything was ready for opening up the cafe except the curtains.

'You're in a happy mood today,' she said. 'You're not usually up this early.' He put up his hand and she held on to it while she descended. He lifted her bodily from the last three steps, holding her close as he did so. Maybe it was the clean smell of the soap or maybe it was his maleness but it wasn't un-nice, she thought. 'Stop that,' she insisted, pushing the nets into his hands.

Somehow Eddie and Daisy had reached a kind of truce. He certainly seemed to have forgotten the drill incident and Kenny had been right: with Eddie around not many people seemed willing to take advantage of a woman running a cafe. He'd certainly proved his worth recently.

'Thank you for what you did the other night,' she said.

'You've already thanked me.'

'Yeah, well, it was really quite somethin' you standing up to those three drunks like that. I really thought they was going to do some damage.'

'They were just three lads, pissed at seven in the evening after celebrating a mate's wedding,' he said.

'But I was proud of the way you protected me and Suze, it could have got nasty.'

'It would have got even nastier if they'd laid a hand on you,' he said.

'Thanks anyway.' The meaning of his words didn't escape her.

Eddie had landed a punch on the lad who had grabbed hold of Susie. Then he'd bundled the three of them out of the cafe in a flash. A couple of chairs had been turned over but that was the only damage. Luckily, there had been few customers in since they were about to close and no one had got hurt. Except Suze, who had been shaken by the experience, but told Daisy later not to worry, she was fine.

'That was simply three lads who'd had a bevvy too many and tried to throw their weight around, but I want you to promise me that if anyone comes in demanding money and I'm not around, for God's sake give 'em the fuckin' money. With a bit of luck they'll go and you'll come to no harm. We don't want you getting hurt, do we?' Daisy shook her head. She could see the logic in this, but she was working hard for the money going into that till. He could sense her hesitation.

'Promise me?' His face was grim. She nodded.

Eddie pressed the metal hook over the eye screwed in the window frame and jumped down from the ladder. She'd needed to stand on the very top rung to reach the curtain rail but he was only on the third step. She was struck by how tall he was and how kind he could be when he wanted. But then she remembered there was a dark demon inside him and she mustn't forget it. He moved the steps along and tried to pull the curtains into some kind of straight line.

'I ain't messin' about trying to straighten these,' he said, giving up and jumping down again. 'An' I know what you women are like. However straight I gets 'em they won't be straight enough and you'd only change it.'

'Probably,' Daisy said, and laughed, because he was right.

'When you seeing Kenny again?'

'I'm waitin' on a visiting order,' she said. He moved aside so she could climb up to sort the curtains. He held on to the ladder, steadying it.

'Wouldn't you like to see him?' she asked.

'The authorities don't think much of ex-cons visiting cons. Any more than he'd care to see my ugly mug when he could have your pretty face staring at him across the table. Is he all right?'

'I dunno, Eddie. He says 'e is. But I don't believe him. He don't look or act right to me.'

She patted the last flounce into place and climbed down. She went to lift and fold the steps to return them to their place in the hallway.

'Let me do that.' Eddie took them from her and carried them through as though they were feather-light. 'Daisy, bein' inside can do things to a bloke. There's all kinds of pressures in there. From the cons as well as the screws. He still in the kitchens?'

'Yes.' She'd followed him through into the hallway.

'Well, then, at least you know he should be eating all right. An' he ain't going to gob into his own food, is he?'

'What on earth do you mean?'

'Well, that's what happens if someone takes a dislike to you.'

'Can't they tell the guards?'

'Dais, you're priceless. Where do you think Kenny is? Fuckin' Pontin's Holiday Camp?'

'That's awful.'

'That's nothin'. I saw a con piss into the biscuit mixture. We 'ad a good laugh later when a new boy said they were the best biscuits he'd ever tasted, better even than his mum used to bake.'

Eddie put his hand on her shoulder. This time she didn't move away.

'You and me told him to keep 'is head down. An' Kenny ain't stupid. He's a survivor. He'll be all right, you'll see.'

Just then Susie came clattering down the stairs in a rose-flowered skirt and red sweater.

''Scuse me,' she said, squeezing past so that Daisy had to lean into Eddie's warmth. 'Some of us 'ave work to do.' She smelled of 4711 Eau de Cologne. Heavily. Eddie wrinkled his nose. As she went through to open up, Daisy put her finger to her lips, daring Eddie to say a word. She frowned at him to disguise her grin, and moved towards the stairs.

'I still haven't forgotten it was probably your fault Kenny's banged up,' she said.

He grabbed hold of her arm as she was about to climb the first step.

'What good would it have done if we were both inside?' There was anger in his voice now. 'Have you forgotten he wanted money for the rent on that poxy place?'

'I didn't know he was going to fuckin' steal it.' She stared at him. Everything he was saying made sense. It was Eddie who had sorted the rent. Eddie who had stopped the lads from damaging the cafe. Daisy needed him. She felt the heat rise to her face. She didn't want to be beholden to Eddie, yet she was.

'Another few weeks and we'd 'ave been sorted in this place,' she said.

He released her arm.

'Yeah, well. You didn't know that at the time, did you? So that's the way the cookie crumbles, Dais. Ain't it?'

'So I just have to make the best of it?'

60

'That's right.' He turned away and went back into the cafe. Instead of going upstairs, Daisy went out to the backyard, needing to think.

Surrounded by clay flower pots and three tall chimney pots that Daisy had planted with rose bushes, Vera was sitting on an orange box. She was muffled against the cold but still wearing her fluffy mules, stockingless, her face turned up towards the fragile sun. Her back was against the wall, her feet propped up on an oil drum. A romantic fiction book, its cover depicting an impossibly good-looking man kissing an improbably beautiful girl, lay on the ground beside her.

'God, look at Lady Muck,' Daisy said.

'Ain't me what's mucky. It's that bloody lav. I've swilled enough disinfectant down it to drown meself, but still it stinks somethin' rotten.'

'What did you use?' Daisy sniffed noisily. Vera was right. The smell was awful.

'Zoflora Honeysuckle.'

'You're 'aving me on,' Daisy said. 'Anyway, who said you had to sit next to the bleedin' lavatory?'

'I needs a bit of fresh air.'

'Well this air ain't fresh, is it? Jesus, ain't you out on street corners enough?'

'Ain't the same,' Vera said. 'Anyway, I might get a bit of a tan.'

'It's fuckin' December, you daft cow.'

'Well, I tans quickly. Because me 'air's so dark, you see.'

'We both know that comes out of a bottle,' Daisy said.

'What's the matter with you? You're in a right mood.'

Daisy stomped off to the back scullery. She picked up a milk pan she'd got off the catalogue as a free gift and filled it halfway with water. Footsteps on the lino behind her and the acrid smell of cologne told her Susie had arrived.

'There you are,' the girl said. 'Nets look nice in the caff. Why don't you stay out here and 'ave a bit of a chat with Vera?' Daisy could see a gleam in her eye. 'I could bring you both a nice cuppa tea.'

'Wouldn't 'ave anything to do with a delivery I'm expecting from The World's Stores, would it?' Susie blushed as red as the roses on her skirt. Daisy flicked a drop of the water at her. 'So that's why you smell like a fuckin' knockin' shop.'

'Aw, Daisy.'

'Well, at least you smell better than the toilet out back,' said Daisy. She heard Vera laughing in the yard. She could hear a pin drop, that one.

'Leave 'er alone. You was once all dewy-eyed like that,' Vera shouted. Daisy looked at Susie standing there expectantly waiting for her answer.

'S'pose I was, once,' she said. 'Oh, go on then. If you can't manage, give us a shout.' The girl left in a flurry of petticoats and scent.

Daisy took the pan of water outside and dribbled a little on the dirt in the parched flower pots. It hadn't rained for a while and the earth was quite dry.

'Don't you know you don't water in the winter? The plants is all dormant.'

'Who are you? Percy fuckin' Thrower?'

'I'm just sayin', that's all.' Daisy set down the pan, pushed Vera's feet off the drum and rolled it to the wall beside her. Then she sat down next to Vera.

'Sorry I snapped,' she said. 'It's Eddie. He winds me up.'

'Take no notice of 'im. He don't mean 'alf of what he says. Take 'im with a pinch of salt, that's what I says.'

'I'll take 'im the right way one of these days,' Daisy said. 'By the bloody throat!'

Vera sighed. 'What you 'aven't twigged is that he's got a bit of a thing for you.'

Daisy looked at her as though she'd suddenly sprouted an extra ear. 'Don't be stupid.'

'Have it yer own way, Miss Knowall. But I'm tellin' you the truth.'

'Has 'e said anything?'

'Doesn't 'ave to.'

'Well,' Daisy said. 'I don't believe you and I don't want to hear any more about it. I love Kenny. I always have . . .'

'Perhaps that's the trouble, Dais. You was a kid when you met him. So was he. You've grown up. Bloody fast. You've 'ad to. Eddie's different. He's got a bit of savvy.'

'Too right he has. I've heard about things—'

'Believe what you see, not what you hear. Eddie does what 'e has to do to survive. Believe me, I know all about that. But that's his business. An' you got to give 'im credit, Dais, 'e leaves 'is business at that street door. 'E don't bring it 'ome and lay it at your feet, does 'e?' They were both quiet, Daisy pondering Vera's words. Both had their faces turned towards the sun, Daisy imagining it was ten times hotter, and that it wasn't a poxy town backyard but a sun-kissed beach abroad.

''Ere you are.' It was Susie. Two mugs of tea slopped onto the tray and two chocolate Wagon Wheels were narrowly escaping the spreading wet patch.

'Thanks, Suze. Fall over that bit of lino again, did yer?' Susie looked at Daisy in surprise.

'How did you know?' Daisy shook her head but Susie had already gone, back to the cafe and Si. Daisy passed a mug of tea to Vera.

'What's new in the town?' Daisy asked, biting into the thick, creamy chocolate of the Wagon Wheel.

'Coppers was in the Dive, again.'

'What for?'

'They still ain't got nobody for that poor cow as was found in the boatyard.'

Daisy thought back to that afternoon a while back when a plain-clothes dick and a uniformed copper had come waltzing through the door. The afternoon was quiet. Susie was shopping in the market, and Vera and her were sitting down for five minutes in between customers.

Eddie was clearing some of the junk off one of the top shelves for Daisy, grease-encrusted ornaments full of plastic roses that she wanted to get shot of.

'Hey up, it's the law,' said Eddie, and continued with his mission of stuffing rubbish in a brown paper carrier bag. Two men had walked through the door.

'Just the bloke we need to see,' said the taller of the two, turning the sign on the door to Closed.

Eddie smiled and shook his head. He wasn't looking at the constable who was doing the talking but at the other man. He was even-featured, with curling, short dark hair escaping from a trilby set rakishly back from his forehead. A fawn-coloured gaberdine raincoat left unbelted covered his navy suit. He was every bit as tall and broad as Eddie.

But Daisy was drawn to the man's eyes. Long lashes, well-delineated eyebrows defining irises of different but complementary colours. One eye was brown, dark as plain chocolate, the other was the colour of amber. A sprinkling of freckles fanned the top of his cheekbones and the bridge of his aquiline nose. Far from detracting from the man's looks, his unusual eyes enhanced them. When he smiled, which he did, first at her, there was something about him that made her grin right back at him. And when he grinned wryly at Eddie, Eddie laughed.

'What 'ave I done now, Vinnie?' he asked.

'You tell me, Eddie. Not worried I've come around asking a few questions, are you?'

Eddie jumped down from the stool he'd been standing on, put the bag of rubbish on the counter and walked towards the two men. Daisy thought he had lost a little of his swaggering confidence.

'I know 'im. That's the copper who's in charge of the murder hunt,' said Vera, chiming in. 'You know, that girl in the boatyard.' She rose from her stool. 'We read about it in the papers, didn't we, Eddie? Terrible thing to 'appen in Gosport. Me an' Daisy said—'

The young policeman cut her off with, 'Perhaps you can tell us where you were the night the girl was murdered at the boatyard, sir?'

He plucked a notebook from nowhere and waited. His superior continued his friendly gaze at Eddie, allowing the constable to take the lead.

'When was it?' Eddie frowned at the young copper.

'Don't tell me you've let a murder slip your mind. November thirteenth. Where were you, Eddie Lane? Just answer the fuckin' question.'

64

'DS Vinnie Endersby, is that the way you allow this constable to interview me?' Eddie pushed his face as close to the DS's as he could get without touching him. Vinnie Endersby neither flinched nor moved.

'No time to waste, Eddie, old mate,' he said unperturbed. 'Where were you?'

'He was in 'ere,' shouted Vera. 'He was 'ome before I was. An'—'

'Vera, you don't need to tell me old mucker Vinnie nothin'.' Vera tutted and looked away.

Vinnie Endersby sighed before saying, 'You were about the town that night, Eddie. You were seen by me at the ferry.'

Eddie lifted his hands in a gesture of resignation. He grinned cheekily. Moved back then shrugged his shoulders. For some reason the attitudes of the two men reminded Daisy of a time when she was a small child and her mother had taken her to Victoria Park in Queen Street in Portsmouth. Daisy had been mesmerised by two brightly feathered male peacocks. Tails majestically swaying, glittering in the sunlight, they paraded themselves before a dull brown female. Daisy and her mum had giggled as the two had swaggered and staggered, posing on skinny wrinkled legs beneath their heavy plumage.

'Typical of men,' her mum had laughed. 'Always need to show off before a woman.'

'You know me, Vin.' Eddie winked at the man.

'Too well, Eddie,' the DS replied.

'Better tell the truth, then, hadn't I? I come back from Pompey. Ain't got a fuckin' clue what time that was. 'Ad a chat with our Vera by the taxi rank—'

'Ten o'clock. The Trinity Church was chimin'. Then he came 'ome . . .'

Eddie and the detective turned to Vera who shut up immediately.

'Vera left an' I wandered over to the Nelson. It was full of foreign sailors. To tell the truth I wasn't feelin'—'

'You never went in that pub—'

'Vera, shut up,' Daisy said.

'Carry on,' said DS Endersby.

'I 'ad a rotten 'eadache. I ordered an 'alf. But I didn't 'ave but a mouthful before I left an' came 'ome.'

'Did you talk to anyone in there?'

'Talk? You couldn't 'ear yerself think, let alone talk.'

'You must have spoken to someone.'

Eddie thought for a moment. Then ran his fingers through his hair.

'The barman. This girl. I shouted at a girl who was going round accosting the skates. I might even have told 'er to fuck off when she started on me. I don't remember too clearly what I said but she was touting for custom. I remember thinking she probably 'adn't washed herself for months.' Eddie closed his eyes and grimaced. 'Can't abide dirt and filth. Present company included, of course.'

'What then?' Vinnie Endersby ignored his sarcastic remark.

'Nothing. I left. And came 'ome.'

'Leave the pub with anyone?'

'Do me a favour! I ain't a fuckin' fruit so I didn't leave with a sailor, did I?'

'What about the girl?'

'Not my type, Vinnie.' Vinnie smiled, showing strong white teeth. 'You knows my type, Vinnie, don't you?'

Daisy, watching the body language between the two men, the goading, the posturing, came to the conclusion there was a history between them.

'No one on the force knows you better than I do. And one day you'll pay for every sin you've committed. It's called Karma. What goes around, comes around. But, Eddie Lane, for once in your life you might be telling the truth.'

'Whatever do yer mean, Vin?'

'We know she was still in the bar when you left and the rest of what you've told me so far checks out, even to the fact that you never finished your drink before you went. I don't suppose you've heard anything—'

'Do me a favour, Vin. You really think I'm gonna run over to the cop shop? Turn nark for you? Fuck off.' He turned away.

The detective shook his head, sighed, then turned to Daisy.

'We're simply checking things out,' he said. Daisy felt his eyes rake over her. She hated herself for the beginnings of a blush she knew would rise and tint her cheeks bright red. 'Asking if anyone saw or heard anything unusual.'

Daisy nodded. Amazingly, Vera never opened her mouth.

'Don't mind if we come back to have a chat to your customers?' the constable asked. Daisy shook her head, glad to look away from Vinnie Endersby's probing stare.

'Anyone else living here?'

She nodded. 'But she's not in.'

Just then, as though to prove her a liar, Susie came swinging through the door, her arms full of market bags. Daisy pointed towards her. 'Suze,' she said, 'these gentlemen are tryin' to find out if we know anything about the girl found in the boatyard.'

'Oh?' Susie said. 'If I can 'elp, I will. Just going to put these in me room.'

Eddie had asked amiably whether the coppers wanted cuppas, but they declined. After putting a few questions to Susie they turned to go. Eddie walked to the door with them, turned the sign back to Open and saw them off the premises.

Daisy was brought back to the present by Vera's voice.

'I told 'em again there was a lot of foreign sailors about that night.' She bent and picked the spoon up and stirred her tea. 'S'pose it could 'ave been one of them. They've gone back to sea now. I told the coppers again we was all tucked up that night early. I was the last one in and that was about eleven.' Daisy stopped chewing her mouthful of biscuit, swallowed, and asked, 'What about fingerprints?'

Vera sipped her tea, the spoon still in the mug, before saying, 'They're 'ardly going to take me into their confidence about that, are they?'

'But they always find fingerprints in films.'

'This is real life, ducky. She was found in a boatyard with all that crap about, sawdust and whatnot, and it 'ad been rainin' all night. A bloke was walking 'is dog early in the morning an' the dog ran in the yard. Gave 'im a nasty fright. The man, not the dog. Well it would, wouldn't it?'

'Why do they keep askin' the same things?'

Vera shrugged. 'Dunno. But that Vin Endersby is like a dog with a bone, he won't never let go of nothin'. You know, 'is missus 'as messed 'im about somethin' awful an' he won't let go of 'er neither. Anyway, I told 'im you and Susie was asleep. Eddie was making tea and a sandwich. An' he was in ages before me. I even told 'em Eddie fixed *me* a cheese sandwich.'

'He *what*?' Daisy nearly choked on the chocolate.

'Don't look like that. 'E can make tea and sarnies, you know.'

'Wonders will never cease,' Daisy said. Well, perhaps he really had turned over a new leaf. Was he going to become Mr Nice Man?

'I keep tellin' you. 'E's all right. But best not ask what 'e gets up to until the law starts pounding on the bleeding door. Until then, it ain't nothin' to do with you, Daisy girl.'

'You're right.'

It was pleasant sitting there, Daisy decided. She even managed to ignore the lavatory pong. That tiny bit of warmth from the sun made everything seem better. She finished her tea then sat back, resting her head against the brick wall. Vera had her eyes closed. She looked at peace with herself. How lovely it was, Daisy thought, to be in someone's company and not have to worry about making small talk. Daisy and Vera were at ease with each other. Daisy wondered how long Vera had lived at the cafe. Forever it seemed. Bert had, it was rumoured, been good to her. She'd been left some money, apparently, but until the will was sorted out properly . . .

Daisy closed her eyes and dozed.

'Dais, it's the telephone. No peace for the wicked,' sighed Vera.

'Wonder who it is?' Daisy scrambled up. Running down the hallway she nearly collided with Kibbles, padding down the passage in search of his mistress.

'Well, you'll soon know,' shouted Vera, to have the last word. But she didn't because Daisy yelled back, 'Visitor for you, Vera, a man in a grey coat.' She laughed, imagining Vera having a fit, because no-one ever called at the cafe for her, certainly never a feller, and she didn't have her warpaint or glad rags on.

Daisy picked up the phone. It was Moira Kemp. She had telephoned Daisy several times since that first meeting back in October. Her husband wasn't at Winchester Prison any more.

She'd been right. The case against him had been dropped, like she said it would.

'Dais, can you come to London?' Her voice had a trembling, dazed quality to it.

Daisy thought for a moment. It would be difficult, especially now.

'I don't know, Moira. So near Christmas we get busy. I can't expect Susie to run the cafe on her own.'

'Not now. No, not right now. 'Course you can't. I wish you could, but ... How about for the New Year?'

Oh God, she thought. What would she do in a place like London over New Year? But she was more concerned about Moira. She'd taken to phoning at very odd times, not that Daisy minded, but sometimes at two or three in the morning.

'I don't know.' Daisy was flustered. She could afford the train fare all right but it would cost real money to keep up with Moira. She'd watched her spend cash that day in Winchester. Daisy couldn't afford luxuries like taxis and such.

'Please?' That one word held so much intensity that it was difficult for her to refuse. 'You've already helped me so much by being my friend.'

'I've done nothing,' Daisy said quietly.

'Dais, you have helped me. Please come. You can meet Violet.' Violet was Moira's mother-in-law. Daisy wondered why it was suddenly important that she meet her. Moira carried on, 'I can pay for someone to help out in the cafe.'

'That won't be necessary,' Daisy said. She didn't want her to think she was a charity case, even if she did have to look after the pennies. With Suze, Si and Vera around, and Eddie in a good mood, she decided to take a chance. 'All right.'

She could almost feel the relief in Moira's voice as she said, 'I'll come down in the car and pick you up at lunchtime on New Year's Eve.' Then without another word, she hung up.

Daisy looked at the silent receiver. That Moira was a funny one and no mistake, she thought. There was something brittle about her, like she might break. Before replacing the receiver on the cradle she dialled Moira's number.

When Moira answered, Daisy said, 'Why don't you come here

and see me before the New Year? We won't 'ave much time together but we could go out and 'ave tea and cakes somewhere. And a girly chat of course.'

Almost before she'd finished speaking, Moira was shouting her thanks down the phone.

'I can't come tomorrow or the day after but I'll come on the twentieth. Oh Daisy, you're a true friend to me. Thank you, thank you, thank you. I'll come in the afternoon. Isn't it exciting . . .'

Daisy eventually managed to stem the flood long enough to utter goodbye. She walked down the passage and poked her head inside the cafe door. There were four people eating. Si was lifting bags and packages which Susie was ticking off on the invoice as he was reading her the contents. Two lads were standing by the jukebox and Elvis Presley's sexy voice was crooning.

'All right?' Susie asked, looking up, pencil poised.

'Mmm. You're going to Si's for Christmas, aren't you?' Susie nodded. 'Will you be back before the New Year?'

'Yes, why?'

'Thought I'd spend the New Year with Moira. Is that okay?'

Si looked at Susie and then at Daisy and smiled. No, more than a smile, a grin which lit his face.

'I'm off work until Jan fourth. If you like I could come round and help out.' He suddenly went bright red and stammered, 'Not . . . not to stay. I'll ride round each day on my bike.' Daisy wanted to laugh but didn't dare.

'Well, thank you for that lovely offer, Si. I only expect to be away for the one night.'

Daisy left them to it and went back into the yard and found Vera dozing, Kibbles sprawled over her lap, asleep. Daisy watched the contented rise and fall of the fat cat's belly as he slept. Vera had hardly moved.

'Look like a pair of bloody angels, don't they?'

She whirled around. The whispered voice had come from Eddie. She stepped back into the scullery,

'Why do you always have to creep up on me?'

'You are so paranoid, Dais,' he said, reaching his hand towards her face. She shrank back. He'd changed out of his jeans and casual shirt into a dark blue suit.

'I'm off to the dog track,' he said. 'Bit of business over Portsmouth.' He touched her cheek. 'It's only a smudge on your face, Dais.' He had some sort of cologne on that smelled like oranges.

'Oh,' she said, feeling foolish. 'Anyway, why are you telling me where you're going? You don't usually.'

'Just thought you might be worried about me?'

'Hmm! You can think on, then.' He turned to go but not before Daisy had seen his smug grin. Then he shifted back.

'Dais? Have you got a passport?' She looked at him as though he'd gone mad.

'What would I need a fuckin' passport for? I've never been further than the poxy Isle of Wight in my life.'

He laughed. 'You ought to get yourself one, girly. You never know when it might come in useful.'

'Why?'

'Because I'm off to Greece next week on a bit of business, just before Christmas, and you could have come with me.' Daisy looked at him as though he'd said they could fly to the moon next week. Then she collected her wits about her.

'Think a lot of yourself if you think I'd go anywhere alone with you.'

'If that's the only thing stopping you, you could have brought someone else as well.'

She thought of her and Vera shopping for cheap knick-knacks down cobbled alleyways. And wasn't the weather kinder in Greece at this time of the year?

'You're fuckin' serious, aren't you?'

His guard dropped and he looked hurt.

'Yes. And before you say anything else, you know damn well Kenny would 'ave said, "If you got the chance to go, Dais, you fill your boots."'

Daisy began to laugh. Because that's exactly what Kenny would have said. But he'd have added, 'You'll be all right wiv Eddie. 'E won't let any 'arm come to you.'

She sighed. 'I can't go. But if you're back by the New Year, I would really appreciate you keeping an eye on things here.'

'Because you're in London with Moira.'

'How do you know?'

'I overheard.'

'Should 'ave known you don't miss a thing.'

He ran his fingers through his glossy hair. Then he shrugged and walked away. She watched his broad shoulders until he opened the street door and went out.

CHAPTER 8

Vera came in from the yard. 'I'd 'ave gone, like a shot,' she said, as she filled the small kettle at the sink. 'You should do as 'e says and get a passport. Want a cuppa?' Daisy nodded.

'Oh, so I suppose you heard all that?'

''Course,' she said. She'd wrapped a turban around her head, but it had slipped while she'd been asleep and was lopsided. She lit the gas beneath the kettle. It burst into life with a loud popping sound. 'Told you 'e likes you.'

Daisy glared at her. In the cold light of a winter's day Vera looked tired and suddenly showed her age. Daisy's heart softened.

'Go out and keep the seats warm,' she said. 'I'll make the tea. And keep that flea-bitten moggie off my seat.'

She could hear Vera outside cooing to Kibbles as she busied herself with the tray. Truth be told, Daisy loved the cat almost as much as Vera did. She carried the tray out so they could catch the last rays of the sun.

'Ever wish your life had been different, Vera?'

Vera thought for a moment before answering.

'What's brought all this on? An offer of a trip abroad? Well, me answer is, no. I've 'ad some really awful lows in me life, but I've 'ad some terrific 'ighs too. Anyway,' she said, 'it's all a learning curve, innit?'

'What do you mean?'

'Well, the person you are today depends on whatever you learnt yesterday.'

'That's a bit deep for me,' Daisy said.

'No, it's not. Would you change your life?'

73

Daisy thought for a while, warming her hands around the hot mug.

'Prob'ly not, but I'm hoping I've got a lot more to look forward to than hard work and visiting my old man in the nick. But I see what you mean. I can't change it. But I can learn from it.'

'Exactly. Now you're going to say, "Surely, Vera, you didn't decide to be a prossie? And if you did, how come you never wanted nothing more?" '

Daisy looked at her. She wasn't going to ask her any such question. But perhaps there comes a time when friends need to talk, need to let others in on what makes them tick.

'Well, did you? Want anything more?'

Vera shrugged. 'I've learnt not to want anything that I can't grab for meself. This is between you and me. When I was fourteen I 'ad a baby. I loved his dad but 'e was married. At that age you know sod-all about fuckin' life. My mum and dad chucked me out. Said I brought shame on their good name.' She was talking in short, clipped sentences, almost as though she was doing nothing more than relating the story of a film she'd seen. Daisy couldn't begin to understand the pain that was hidden in those words. Her heart went out to Vera. Vera's face was expressionless.

'What did you do?'

'The father of my baby got me into an 'ome for wayward girls. That's what it was called, a home for wayward girls, can you imagine? A big grey building like something out of a Dracula film. Way out in the country it was. It was run by the nuns. Told me 'is wife didn't know about me and that she was ill. Mind you, that was the first I'd 'eard of any illness.' Her eyes grew wistful. 'Oh, Dais, 'e was a lovely man at first. I'd dream of what it would be like when all the things come true that 'e was promising me. Even the smell of 'im made me go weak at the knees. I know that I learned a lot from 'im, especially that men can be fuckin' bastards. Hush, Vera, don't be cynical,' she chided herself. 'Anyway, as soon as I was safely in the nuns' care, 'im and 'is wife buggered off to Australia. I only found that out from one of the nuns. And then I was left 'olding the baby, so to speak. You know I nearly called my baby Clyde because 'e was born on May the twenty-third and it was the same day them two gangsters was shot in America,

74

Bonnie and Clyde. But well, who'd want to saddle a kiddie with a name that had such shame attached?' She tried to smile, to make a joke of it, but Daisy saw tears in her eyes and the smile became a sort of resigned grimace. She put out a hand and touched Vera's arm.

At the movement, Kibbles yawned, his pink mouth opening wide then closing so he could start up his purring again.

'They don't make any demands, do they, cats? Not like men?' Vera bent her head and buried her face into his mackerel-coloured fur. The noise he was making grew more ragged. Then she sniffed and sat back up again, quite straight, leaning her head once more against the red brick of the wall. 'Anyway, the deal was that I would sign the child away for adoption as soon as it was born. I 'ad the baby and the same nun as told me my man 'ad hopped it to Australia must 'ave felt sorry for me and made the mistake, or perhaps it wasn't such a mistake, of letting me 'old me child instead of whipping 'im away at once. Well, I knew then I couldn't let 'im go. 'E was a tiny little scrap but 'e didn't look like Albert and 'e didn't look like me. But 'e was mine. The only fuckin' thing in this world that did belong to me and 'e needed me and was I going to give 'im away? No, I fuckin' wasn't. I felt this overwhelming love for 'im. You'll see, Dais, one day when you 'ave kids, you'll know how that feels. I'm not talking down to you or anything. Just saying that loving a kid ain't like loving a man, or a friend. It was like nothin' I'd ever experienced before. That his father was a shit, I could 'andle. That wasn't nothin' to do with my baby. No one was going to take him away. But I knew they would. Unless . . .'

She paused and picked up her tea and took a good long pull.

'You sure you wanna hear this? It's all in the past now, Dais.' Daisy couldn't speak but she nodded. Vera took a deep breath. 'I got my stuff together in the night, weren't much, and I stole along to the nursery and took 'im. James, I called 'im. But only in my mind. I'd seen a film with James Stewart in and just liked the name. The nuns weren't expecting anyone to escape so I walked out of that place as sweet as a nut.' Vera dabbed at her eyes with a corner of her blouse. 'I was nearly fifteen, no money and a baby wrapped in a stolen blanket. I also knew no bugger was gonna 'elp me unless I 'elped meself. I got a lift to just outside of Portsmouth with a lorry driver. He dropped me at Horndean after buying me a fry-up in a pull-in cafe. He was nice, 'ad kids of his own, all grown up. Kind, 'e was. I didn't tell him nothin'. Didn't 'ave to. 'E could see I was only a kid meself and in trouble. 'E gave me ten shillin'. I didn't find the note until I unwrapped the baby, tucked inside 'is covers.'

'Go on,' Daisy said. She wanted her to continue. All the time she was talking she wasn't crying and Daisy could see that now she'd set in motion her memories she needed to unburden herself. Vera shook her head from side to side and sighed. Her long gold drop earrings jingled softly against her cheeks. Vera had loads of jewellery. Most of it eye-catching, most of it cheap. But the earrings were gold and Daisy never saw her without them.

'It was morning. We'd driven through the night, see. I remember it was a clear, cold day and I walked along this road towards a place called Hambledon. I didn't know nothin' about the area. Never 'eard of Portsmouth. My milk 'ad come in and I fed the baby. Funny, I didn't know nothin' about babies but it was like it was already programmed inside me to keep 'im warm an' dry an' fed. Natural mother's feelin's I suppose.' She looked wistful. 'I was tired. I 'adn't slept in the lorry. But I kept walking and the sun came out and dried up the dew an' it got warmer. The baby wasn't heavy but my arms ached. And I didn't feel so good. Kind of shivery. Anyway, there was a farm and some cows in a field. I knocked on the door to ask for a glass of water but there wasn't anyone there. So I drank water from a tap outside and walked about hoping to find someone. Thought they might be able to give me a job. I didn't want to get in trouble for being where I wasn't supposed to be so I walked on a bit further and there was a field where they 'ad cut the corn and it was all in these stooks.' Vera made a sort of bunching shape with her two hands. Kibbles lifted his head, stretched but settled again.

'Anyway, I made a sort of bed out of one of them bundles of corn, near a hedge, and went to sleep in the sun. When I woke up it was dark. James was crying so I fed 'im but I was really poorly. It was like a bad dose of flu. Somehow we snuggled down together, though I was terrified of rolling on top of 'is little body.

That was the last I knew until I woke up in a vardo. That's a caravan. My baby was in a wicker basket at the bottom of the bunk I was in, asleep. And there was this woman with long gold earrings and a wrinkled face, wiping my 'ead with a cloth she was wringin' out in a bowl. She was singin' to me, an' I didn't understand a word of it. She stopped singing and told me I'd 'ad milk fever. Her hair was long and all coiled about her 'ead. She had really kind eyes. She said 'er son had found me and the baby and carried us to the caravan. Two days I'd been there in that van an' didn't know a fuckin' thing about it. She'd been feedin' my baby with milk from another woman who had a year-old baby who was still on the breast.

'I think that was when I realised what a selfish cow I was to 'ave exposed James to danger. This woman, Rose, had watched over me, fed me stuff and looked after James. I know now if it hadn't been for 'er I could have died. Three caravans there were. And they, the travellers, were meeting up on Hambledon Common with relatives who was taking fairground equipment over to Gosport for the Michaelmas fair. Rose told fortunes. Well, she'd saved my life, I reckon. No-one asked me questions, just accepted the fact I was there. I didn't go out sellin', they wouldn't let me. But they fed me and let me an' James go on sleeping in the van 'til I was properly well. She said I 'adn't taken enough care of myself after childbirth. She gave me these earrings. I'll keep 'em on 'til I die. Rose did more for me in that couple of weeks than me own mother did in her lifetime.' Vera ran her fingers through Kibbles' fur. 'Me mum and dad were strict churchgoers. But charity didn't begin at home for me.' She laughed bitterly. 'Make what you will of that, Dais.'

'How come you ended up here?' The sun was fading fast now and in a while it would disappear, blotted out by the wall at the back of the lavatory. Then the bitter cold would set in. Daisy was nervous that if they had to move indoors and break the bond that had grown between them, Vera might not want to carry on with her story.

'We came to Walpole Park for the fair. It was understood I was to leave. They hired on local blokes to help set up the rides on the green, but travellers stuck with their own kind. Rose looked after James and I went lookin' for a job. I got one in The Fox.'

'The pub next door?'

She nodded. 'Live in. Serving behind the bar. The baby was no problem as 'e slept most of the time and so I thought everything was going to work out fine. This was before the Haytors.' She named the present landlord and his wife. 'It was all right for a few weeks. Then the old man – Haytor's dad – started coming into my room. Seemed to think because I 'ad a baby, I was fair game. One night after we was closed and everyone had gone 'ome he got 'old of me. Big bloke 'e was. I was that frightened. I ran down to the bar an' he followed me. Tore me clothes. Broke me fuckin' arm he did. But not before I'd walloped him wiv as many bottles of spirits as I could throw at 'im. I was screaming blue murder and managed to escape into the street wiv 'im running after me. 'Im in his shirt, no trousers either. And who d'ya think was coming out the caff to see what all the fuss was about? Bert. Quick as a flash 'e sized up the situation. Well 'e knew what the dirty old bugger was like, didn't 'e?' She waved towards the open back door. 'I sat in that very scullery there, 'olding my shattered arm and snivelling.

'It was nineteen thirty-five and I remember it as though it was fuckin' yesterday. I couldn't stop crying. Bert went and got my baby and brought 'im back to me. You know, the little tyke 'ad slept through the bleedin' lot. Then Bert said, "You ain't goin' back in there no more." That was after 'e'd laid out the dirty old fucker cold, in 'is own bar. It took six weeks for the plaster of Paris to come off me arm and during that time Bert changed and fed James and looked after me. After that I served in the caff and looked after the baby until I realised I'd have done better to 'ave let the poor little sod go for adoption. After all, what kind of life was he 'avin'?'

'But you wasn't on the game then?'

'No,' she laughed. 'I wouldn't let no one near me. Bert was like a father to me.' She saw Daisy frown. 'Don't you disbelieve me. 'E really was. 'E only 'ad eyes for one person in them days and it wasn't me. But 'e was a kind man. A good man. He'd been a bit of a lad in his younger days and made some money in his murky past. That's how come 'e bought this place. Anyway, we 'ad a customer, a woman, always dressed to the nines, she was. Very smart. She used to talk to me. Always smelled nice. Wore a lovely red fox fur. Its eyes used to shine and seemed to follow you. Never without it, she wasn't. Her name was Lily. Same as the scent she always wore.'

'She was a prostitute?'

Vera nodded, and her eyes grew shadowy. Daisy could see how glamorous this Lily must have seemed to an impressionable young girl.

''Course, I didn't know nothin' about that then. Bert put me right. But I realised that moppin' floors and serving teas wasn't going to get me much outta life. An' it wasn't doing James much good neither being stuck behind the counter where I was afeared 'e'd get boiling tea or worse spilled on 'im, or else 'e 'ad to stay upstairs. And I'm telling you, twenty-odd years ago, upstairs was nothin' to write 'ome about.' She laughed, showing her white teeth. Vera always looked after herself, Daisy thought. Very clean. Hair, body, teeth, all scrubbed and gleaming.

'Lily said she didn't let no one near 'er without wearing a johnnie, a rubber. And she 'ad regular check-ups with a doctor. She'd built up a select few "friends", she called them, who trusted her and she had faith in them. She was going to retire when she was forty and buy a pub in Alverstoke. Which is where she is today.'

Daisy looked at Vera, who smiled and said, 'But that's another story. I 'ad a better idea. I told Bert what I wanted to do an' he was 'orrified. He said the caff was a clean place and no slags plied their trade there. I told 'im I wanted to be like Lily. Bert knew the score. An' he was all for it when I told 'im why. I asked him to 'elp me find a couple who would look after James. I would pay this couple if they looked after 'im proper and I would pay for James to 'ave the best possible education. On the one condition that they brought James up as their own child and never told 'im who I was or where the money 'ad come from.'

'How did Bert feel about that?'

Vera smiled. 'By this time, he'd got used to me being around. 'E was a rock. I think in the twenties he'd been a bit of a gangster 'cause 'e knew all kinds of weird and wonderful people. Been involved in some trial at Ilford where a bloke had tried to kill the husband of 'is lover. Anyway, Bert 'ad a bit of clout in them days. 'E wasn't the sad old man all his life that people thought 'e was. 'E found a middle-aged couple who 'ad no kids of their own. Round in Beach Street, they was. It broke my 'eart but when I used to see them with 'im in the pram I could tell 'e was loved. The deal was I gave up all rights as a mother. In return for statin' how I wanted his future mapped out until 'e was of an age to go 'is own way, I was to keep away, yet settle a stated amount each month for schoolin'. He'd 'ave a better start in life than I ever did. And of course 'e was never to know his real mother was me.'

Daisy couldn't believe a woman could give up her child like that, yet still live in the same town. Trying to guess the pain it must have caused her was impossible. As if tuning in to her thoughts, Vera put her hand on Daisy's and said, 'You got to remember, Dais, in those days between the wars it was really 'ard. Us women never 'ad any of the rights we 'ave now. Everyone was livin' 'and to mouth, then. But I was livin' life high off the hog's back, doing clients with money and bein' 'andsomely paid. I even 'ad a couple of posh rooms near the ferry and a sort of maid. I say sort of maid, because Em was really my cleaning lady, eighty if she was a day. But she would take the fellers' 'ats and coats an' put on a la-di-dah accent which didn't fool nobody. Cared a lot about me, she did.' Her eyes dimmed at the memory. 'You know there was only two of us at 'er funeral. Me and Bert. An' I paid to put 'er in the ground. Anyways, the Williamses got the son they always wanted and, 'cause I knew 'e would go to university, make something of his life, and never know he wasn't their child, I got the satisfaction of seein' my son was loved and cherished and would never know 'is mother was a prossie.'

'But you knew where he was?'

'Yes.'

'And you didn't contact him?'

'No. A promise is a promise.'

'God, you were some strong lady,' Daisy said.

'Not at all. As the years passed I was more sure than ever that I'd done the right thing. Bert was a sort of go-between. So I knew all there was to know without the involvement. And no one was more proud than me when James won a place at King Alfred's College in Winchester. 'E's a solicitor now. Lives in London and is engaged to a very pretty girl from the 'untin' and shootin' set.'

'And he knows nothing?'

Vera shook her head. 'What good would it do now? The Williamses live in a cottage in the country near Amesbury. They're proud of their son and 'e loves them. I did what I could for 'im. Sometimes the best parents ain't necessarily the birth parents. Remember what you asked me earlier? Do I wish my life had been different? My son – *my son* – is a well-respected man. That gives me a lotta satisfaction. Along the way I've 'ad a lot of laughs. Made good friends. Had a good life, so far...'

Daisy looked at her. Did she really mean what she was saying?

'Daisy,' she said. 'Don't look at me like that.' She pushed Kibbles from her lap and twisted around on her makeshift seat. She got hold of Daisy's hands and held them. Her touch was warm and Daisy could feel the chill leaving her fingers. She hadn't realised until then just how cold it had become. 'When you get up in the mornin' you got two choices how to face the day. With a smile. With a frown. See what I mean? I chose, well I 'ope I did, to smile. I also thanked God for the way Bert looked after me.'

'What do you mean?'

'I don't mean he was a pimp or anything like that, but because of his connections I was able to go on working without anyone wanting a cut of my earnings. Neither did I get beat up by the johns like some of the girls. Which is why, now Bert's gone, I'm shuttin' up shop.'

She said it as though she had taken a while to reach this decision and was sure it was the right one.

'I've got a bit of money put by. And because I looked after meself, like Lily showed me, I've got me 'ealth. Between you and me, Dais, I hope to go into the retail business next year. Negotiating on a property in the High Street as we talk.' She let go of one of Daisy's hands and gripped her arm. 'This is between you and me, okay?' Daisy nodded. 'Only there's some people in this town as might put the block on things if it gets out. So keep your fingers crossed for me. Nothing is certain 'til the lease has been signed and contracts exchanged. Do you know 'ow cold you are, girl?'

Daisy was shivering. She nodded her head. Vera got up and stretched, reminding Daisy of the way Kibbles unfolded himself from sleep, putting his heart and soul into it as he extended his supple joints. Then she bent down and gathered the mugs, clattering them on the tray. Daisy caught a whiff of Californian Poppy. Forever after, Daisy knew that perfume would remind her of Vera, the bravest woman she had ever known. Vera went over and scooped up Kibbles who was sitting on one of Daisy's flower pots, washing behind his ears. Together, the three of them went indoors.

'I think I might 'ave a go at whitewashing and scrubbing that lavatory soon,' Daisy said. 'You're right, it stinks.'

CHAPTER 9

19 December 1962

'Vera, you awake?'

'If I wasn't, I am now.' He heard her padding towards the bedroom door. She opened it just wide enough for her tousled head to show through and stared at him. 'What d'you want?' She still had her make-up on, including her false eyelashes.

He put his fingers to his lips and motioned her to come out and down the stairs.

When she'd gone back in to put on a dressing gown, he checked his watch. It was ten to three. He moved to Daisy's door and listened. Silence. Satisfied, and as quietly as the creaking boards would allow, he crept downstairs again to the kitchen. After lighting the gas under the kettle he waited for Vera.

'D'you know what the time is?' She had on her usual black silk wrap but had dispensed with the mules, probably because they would waken the dead as she clip-clopped down the stairs.

''Course I do. Which is why I don't want to wake Dais or Susie.'

She eyed the kettle. 'Making tea?' He nodded. 'You didn't get me up in the middle of the night to make me a cuppa, surely?' Of course he didn't but he was not sure how to approach her. He didn't want her laughing at him. Oh, no, he wouldn't be able to stand that. But would she laugh? Her and Dais were pretty pally, perhaps she might understand.

'What you doing about Christmas?' he asked.

Fuckin' hell, he thought, she was standing there with her mouth open. He suddenly thought that if he'd asked her to marry him, she wouldn't have been any more surprised.

'What do you mean?' Her tone was wary. Fuck it, he thought. Here goes.

'It's Daisy's first Christmas without Kenny, right?' The relief on Vera's face was noticeable. 'I ain't gonna be 'ere. Suze ain't gonna be 'ere. What about you?'

'Well, I usually spend the day in the New Forest at a quiet little hotel with . . .'

'Spare me the gory details. If I pay you double what you'd get from 'im, would you make sure Dais isn't alone?' After her initial amazement, he could see her working out the pros and cons.

'I could I suppose, yes.' The whistle had started up on the kettle. Speedily she turned off the gas so that it wound down sadly. She poured the water into the brown teapot and stirred it. ''Ow many did you put in 'ere?'

'Three.'

'Thank Christ for that. Can't abide gnat's piss. You don't 'ave to give me money. I'll be glad to do it.' She put the lid on the pot and the knitted cosy over the top of it. He'd already set out mugs and put the sugar and milk on the side. He saw her studying him.

'Why?' Her eyes had narrowed.

'Why what?' He knew what she meant all right but he wasn't about to discuss his innermost feelings with her.

'Don't piss me about, Eddie Lane. Why?'

Here it comes, he thought. The fuckin' cross-examination.

'She's my brother's wife and I don't want 'er on her own.'

'I don't think that's the real reason, but since I ain't gonna get a better one out of you . . .'

'Take this.' He pushed a wad of money into her hand from his inside Crombie pocket. 'Buy a bird, some nuts. Or better still, take 'er out somewhere.'

'You know she won't leave this place.'

'Buy 'er somethin'.'

'Can't you?'

'She won't take anything off me. She's made that plain. If she could, she'd 'ave me out of this place like a shot.' He was getting bored with the conversation. All he wanted was to make sure that Daisy was all right while he was away. 'You gonna do this or not?'

Vera tucked the money into her dressing gown pocket, then

poured out the tea. Replacing the pot on the table, she slid a mug towards him.

'Put yer own fuckin' milk in. You know I'll not leave 'er on 'er own at Christmas.'

He ran a hand through his hair. It was still wet. Droplets of rain clung to his coat. 'I don't want 'er to know,' he said.

'Perhaps she should. Might make 'er change 'er mind about you.'

He glared at her. Poured in milk straight from the bottle. Stirred the contents of the mug, then drank it back as though his life depended on it. He dropped the empty mug in the red plastic washing-up bowl in the sink, ran some water over it, turned off the tap, wiped his hands on a tea towel, left the kitchen and went upstairs to bed.

In his room, after chucking his Crombie on the chair and slipping off his wet shoes, he stared at a particularly modest picture of Marilyn on the wall, still pouting, from the film *Niagara*. Poor bitch, he thought. He didn't believe for one moment that she'd taken an overdose to end her life. He knew women. Hadn't she bought a new house? Lost weight? Women didn't go to all that trouble when they were thinking of ending it all. He couldn't believe she'd do that, any more than he could believe that one day Daisy wouldn't understand the depth of his feelings for her.

Well, he would wait, however long it took, he would wait.

He heard Vera on the stairs. Opening his door, he beckoned her over.

'Thanks, Vera,' he whispered. 'And goodnight.'

Vera looked at him, puzzled.

''Night, Eddie.'

CHAPTER 10

'It's goin' to be a cold enough Christmas to shrivel a dog's bollocks off,' said Vera.

'You say the nicest things,' Daisy said, pushing a plate of breakfast toast across the table towards her. She looked at the clock to check the hands had moved since the last time she'd looked, five minutes ago at six thirty. 'Moira's due around two this afternoon. Will you be 'ere?'

'Don't fret. I said I would, didn't I?'

Daisy didn't answer. She was separating bacon strips for the breakfast rush. She'd begun opening the cafe earlier in the mornings to catch the workers for breakfasts. It was going really well too. The harder she worked, the more money she could bank for when Kenny came home. Only thing was, she was on her feet even more now. She knew she was pushing herself beyond her limits and she was losing weight. It wasn't that she wasn't eating but she never seemed to have a minute to herself these days. And there was all the lugging of stuff about the place. Dragging wooden tables to mop underneath them, the stairs and landings to wash daily, bed and breakfasts to cater for. The trade with the B and Bs had tripled. Cleaning, cleaning, always bloody cleaning. Cooking fry-ups where the grease seemed to cling to her clothes, her hair. Even after a good wash-down she felt certain she still smelled rank. But she wanted Kenny to be proud of her. Needed him to have a fresh start in life, with money, so he'd never need the cheap thrill of stealing ever again.

'... An' it's fuckin' dustbin day today an' Eddie forgot to put 'em out. He should've dragged them four heavy metal buggers through from the backyard for me ...'

'Stop it, Dais.'

Daisy stared at Vera. She knew she was behaving badly. She was tired all the time, yet when she went to bed, she couldn't sleep. Now she was losing her sense of humour.

'I'm sorry, Vera.'

'You're doin' too much. No wonder you're nervy and tired. If you're gonna do these early breakfasts, you 'ave to shut the fuckin' caff up sooner at nights.'

'But the money ... I need to make things work for Kenny.'

'You ain't gonna be no use to Kenny in a fuckin' coffin, are you? All the money in the world ain't gonna make up for you bein' a total wreck. For fuck's sake sit down and have a cuppa and a bit of this toast.'

Vera got up and came towards Daisy, who allowed herself to be sat at the table. Vera picked up a piece of the toast and forced Daisy to take it.

As she ate she thought about the coming visit to London. She was looking forward to it so much, excited at leaving the cafe for a while.

Then she remembered the dustbins. She put the half-eaten toast back on the plate and rose from the stool.

'Now where you goin'?'

'Dustbins. The men arrive earlier near Christmas. Just in case they got any Christmas boxes to come.' She looked at the clock again. 'They could be 'ere any time now. I don't want 'em to miss me.'

'Oh, for fuck's sake,' said Vera. 'Sit fuckin' still, will yer! I'll put the bleeders out!'

'They're heavy.'

'I ain't fuckin' fragile!' She plonked down a mug of steaming brown tea so hard in front of Daisy that the liquid slopped on to the formica tabletop. 'Drink this. Eat the bloody toast. And don't fuckin' move!'

Daisy heard her high heels snapping on the brittle lino of the passage floor. She heard the back scullery door creak open, felt the rush of freezing air as it sent icy fingers probing down the hallway and into the cafe.

'OW! Fuckin' 'ell!' Daisy heard a funny sliding noise, then

silence. She rose so fast from the table that the stool she'd been sitting on clattered over on to the floor behind her.

'Vera! Vera, what's the matter?'

Every step Daisy took nearer the backyard the air became colder. She shivered. She had two jumpers on and she was still cold. The wireless had said the whole country was due a winter it had not experienced for years. The new year was promising to have snow on the ground without a sign of a thaw until well into February.

Daisy gasped. Vera was on her knees on the frosty ground. The winter whiteness enabled Daisy to see clearly though it was still dark.

'You all right? Speak to me, Vera.' Ice was shining like diamond grains on the earth. Daisy fell to her knees beside her friend. Whatever would she do if something bad had happened to Vera?

Vera's mouth was set in an angry line. Daisy looked into her friend's eyes. Somehow both of Vera's false eyelashes were hanging down, giving the impression of two hairy caterpillars crawling up her cheeks.

'Help me up,' hissed Vera. Daisy could almost feel the waves of indignation issuing from Vera's small frame. Daisy put her arms beneath her friend's armpits and hoisted her upright until they were both in a standing position, arms locked about each other.

Vera's eyes were fierce. She was breathing through her nose as though she might explode.

'Get off me. That's enough of that.'

She brushed Daisy away, took a step back and began frantically massaging her behind.

'Are you hurt?' Daisy was scared.

''Course I ain't fuckin' hurt. But my arse is gonna 'ave one helluva bruise on it. I slid on the fuckin' ice, didn't I? Now I've frozen all me assets.'

Daisy was so overcome with happiness that no permanent damage had been done that she threw her arms round Vera again and began sobbing.

'I thought you was hurt,' she wailed. 'I thought you was hurt.'

Vera sniffed. Then extricated herself anew from Daisy's embrace.

'C'mon, let's get these fuckin' bins out before my tits freeze.'

The chore done and Daisy eating fresh toast, Vera poured out yet another cup of tea and said, 'I went to a bit of a party last night. Guess who was there?'

Daisy shivered. All the heat had left the cafe.

'Dunno. Shall we light the oven and leave the door open so it warms this place up a bit? I'm freezing; don't know about you.'

'I'll do it.' Vera took a box of Swan Vestas and opened the enamelled door, bending down and lighting the jets after turning on the gas tap. After the initial loud pop it didn't take a moment for the greasy, gassy smell to burn itself off and the flames from the oven to turn orange and blue and hiss contentedly.

'That's better,' said Daisy. She could feel the warmth already. 'Turn it up high. C'mon, tell me about the party.'

'Well, it was a man who asked about you.'

'About me?'

'A nice-looking man.'

'Nice looking?'

'Tall and well dressed.'

'Well dressed?'

'For fuck's sake. I'm talking to a bleedin' parrot now.'

Daisy looked up to see Vera smiling.

'Who was it then?'

'That old school friend of Eddie's That copper, Vinnie Enders-by.'

'What did 'e say?'

'Just asked 'ow you was. If you ask me, I think he fancies you.'

'Don't be so daft. You think every man who comes in 'ere fancies me. He don't know me.'

'He don't 'ave to. Not to fancy you. That's 'ow it all starts.'

'You're always tryin' to pair me off with someone. First it's Eddie.'

'You'd be all right with Eddie. Haven't I told you so before?'

'I'm not listening. How do you know this Vinnie went to school with Eddie?'

'Vinnie's dad told me.'

'I suppose he's an old friend of yours?'

'Used to be. Until he married that Isabel Carter. Vinnie, 'is boy, 'ad a terrible time when 'e was a kid. Them eyes might make him look a bit of all right now, but when 'e was young 'e used to get some stick from the bullies.'

'Eddie?'

'No. It was Eddie as used to stick up for 'im and wallop the bigger kids. Always been a battler, 'as Eddie Lane. Well, he 'ad to be. With 'is dad he 'ad to be on his toes all the time. So if he wasn't keepin' an eye on Kenny, he was lookin' out for Vinnie – an' 'imself of course.'

'I don't know nothing about this.' Daisy shrugged her shoulders. 'Why didn't Kenny tell me Eddie's mate was a policeman?'

'Because they ain't mates no more.'

'It don't make sense.' Daisy looked confused.

'I'll tell you if you promise you never 'eard it from me?'

'You know I don't say nothin'.' She looked at the clock. There was still time for a bit of gossip before she had to open up. Besides, she was just warming up nicely, wasn't she? She shuffled her stool nearer to the open oven door.

'Don't take all the 'eat,' said Vera. 'Make room for me.'

Daisy inched over and Vera put her seat next to Daisy's.

'What about Eddie and this Vinnie Endersby then?'

'Well, Vinnie got given this mongrel pup that had been ill-treated. It was really in a bad way, so I 'eard. He took it 'ome but his mother wouldn't let 'im keep it. She suffered with terrible asthma, knew the animal was in the house before she even saw it 'cause it brought on a real bad attack of 'er breathin'. Vinnie took it round to Eddie. Poor little Eddie. He'd always 'ankered after a proper pet of his own. Couldn't 'ave one because after the drink his dad consumed there was barely money for food, let alone to feed an animal.'

'Scraps,' said Daisy. 'Mum fed our Fluff on kitchen scraps. Didn't do the cat any harm. She lived to twenty-one, our Fluff.'

'Their dad was such a bastard, if he fed the boys scraps it was a good day.' Vera sighed. 'If they 'ad fish and chips it was like Christmas and birthdays rolled into one. 'E was an awful man. Yet Eddie tried so many ways to make the bastard love him.'

'Did 'e let Eddie keep the puppy?'

'Eddie didn't ask. The old sod never usually rolled 'ome until the early hours. Eddie went down the corner shop an' stole a tin of Spam. He fed the dog and slept with that puppy in his bed. Of course he couldn't take it to school so he left it shut in the bedroom with a dish of fresh water. Vinnie told his dad that Eddie had threatened to cut Kenny's tongue out with the kitchen knife if he breathed a word about Eddie's pet. The brothers shared a room and the bed, see? Kenny wouldn't do nothin' that might bring harm to his 'ero.'

Daisy nodded, waited for Vera to have a sip of tea and begin again.

'Vinnie and Eddie walked home together, well Eddie ran to see his pet. Kenny was laggin' behind. Scared in case his dad had found the puppy. But Eddie was excited. He nearly shit himself when he pulled the key on the string through the letter box and went indoors. But the place was empty, as usual. There was a note on the table from Pappy telling him to heat up some chips he'd left in the oven for their tea. Eddie lit the gas oven. Left it on low so the newspaper wouldn't burn. Kenny was still out. Eddie went upstairs but the puppy was nowhere to be seen. They searched the house and the garden, 'im and Vinnie. Didn't find 'ide nor 'air of it, though. Eddie was distraught.

'After a while Kenny came home and Vinnie and Eddie set the table with plates an' salt an' vinegar. Eddie took out the heated-up chips and carried the newspaper parcel to the table. When he opened the wrappin', there weren't any chips lying on the paper. There was a puppy, though. Warm from the oven. Its poor little head flat as a pancake where someone had stamped on it. And Eddie's dad looking through the kitchen window at 'em. Laughing.'

'Fuckin' 'ell,' shuddered Daisy. 'That's sick.'

'Too right,' agreed Vera. 'But young Eddie still 'ad the presence of mind to knock Kenny flying out of the way before 'e could see the mess inside the newspaper.

'Apparently, Eddie never uttered a word. Just stared at his father. Vinnie ran from the house screaming. He was only a kid, after all. His mum an' dad tried 'ard to bring their family up decent. They didn't play no sick mind games with their kids. But great as Eddie's and Vinnie's friendship 'ad been before that, Eddie never spoke to Vinnie again. Eddie was ashamed, you see. At least that was what Vinnie's dad reckoned. Ashamed that the first friend 'e'd ever had, apart from his kid brother, had 'ad to witness such a terrible thing.'

Daisy was silent for a long time.

'That's going to haunt me.' The tears began to prickle the backs of her eyes. Vera let her cry. Then took a hanky from her pocket and handed it to her.

'Imagine what Eddie went through. Don't judge Eddie by what 'e does. Judge him by what 'e's 'ad done to him, Daisy. Like I said, all 'e ever craved was the love of 'is old man.'

After a while Daisy wiped her eyes on the handkerchief.

'So the DS and Eddie certainly do have a history together and the measure of each other?'

'Measure for measure, Daisy. Measure for measure.' The two women sat in silence for a moment.

'Any tea in that pot?'

Vera jumped. 'You gave me a start,' she said to Susie, who'd come in. Vera clutched her heart, making mock gasping noises. Susie had come down ready for work in a pair of tight black ski pants with elastic on the insteps. A fake mohair red sweater brought colour to her cheeks. She reeked of 4711 cologne.

'What you doin' up?' Daisy asked.

'I told you I was going to 'elp with the early mornings.'

Daisy frowned. Had she? She had so much going through her mind just lately. 'I don't know whether I'm comin' or goin',' she said, shaking her head.

'Well, why don't you go on upstairs and 'ave a bit of a kip. You look all in.'

Daisy looked at Susie, then at Vera.

'I'll wake you at one o'clock so you can prettify yourself for your rich friend,' said Vera. She leaned towards the stove and turned the gas tap off.

Daisy got up and walked towards the door. Then she turned.

'Vera?'

'Yes?'

'The puppy?'

'While young Kenny sobbed on the floor, wondering why his idol had knocked him flying, Eddie calmly took the bundle out through the scullery, past his drunken, laughing lout of a father, and buried it deep in the garden beneath a privet bush.'

Moira handed Daisy a small packet.

'What's this?' Daisy was fingering it, trying to work out what it contained.

'You don't have to keep it 'til Christmas. You can open it now. Then if you don't like it I'll change it.'

'If it's a Christmas present you'll make me feel really guilty because I 'aven't bought you one,' said Daisy.

Moira beckoned to the girl in the black skirt and white blouse. 'Over here, please,' she said. The girl slouched to the table and took a notepad and pencil from the pocket of her frilled apron. She sighed and said the well-worn line, 'What would you like?'

Moira raised her eyes enquiringly at Daisy. 'Tea?'

Daisy nodded. The waitress licked the lead of her pencil. 'Pot of strong tea and a plate of fancies, please,' Moira ordered.

The girl's lips moved as she scribbled on her pad and then walked away. Daisy saw she had on black seamed stockings with the new fashionable pointed heels. The girl had stared at Moira nonstop since they had entered the tea room. Moira seemed oblivious to this, but Daisy remembered the first time she'd spotted Moira on Fareham Railway Station. And today she was enough to make anyone – woman or man – drool. She had on black trousers tucked into soft black leather boots, a black polo neck sweater, and the whole outfit topped by an ocelot fur coat with a matching ocelot pillbox hat. To crown it all, her blonde hair was immaculate and her nails perfectly painted red.

Moira reminded Daisy of someone. But however hard she tried she couldn't think who it was. Maybe her mind was playing tricks on her. Tiredness often makes you think irrationally. She decided not to worry about it. After all, she was having a little treat sitting here, away from work, with her friend.

So instead Daisy thought about the fancy cakes baked on the

Black Cat premises. The warm tea room was filled with the scents of vanilla and ginger. She hoped the waitress would bring some of the shortcake shells with the cream filling. She began tearing at the paper wrapping on the gift.

'Do you like it?'

''Ang on, let me get the box open.'

Daisy gasped. Nestling on the black velvet inside the box was a brooch, a small raised glass oval, containing an image of a tabby cat.

'It's like Kibbles,' Daisy exclaimed. 'It's lovely.'

'You do really like it?'

'I love it!' said Daisy. She was deeply touched by Moira's thoughtfulness and generosity. And she would have to keep it away from Vera who would be bound to have her eye on it. 'Thank you.'

'I like buying gifts.'

'I like being bought gifts.' Daisy took the brooch and, snapping it open, fastened it to her belted red woollen coat. She looked down at her chest then thrust her shoulder forward displaying it to Moira, all the while smiling broadly. 'Only now Kenny's inside I don't get any presents. Not until today, that is.'

The waitress returned. She set the plate of fancy cakes down first. There was a shortcake shell. Daisy hoped Moira wouldn't choose that one. Then she felt mean for thinking such an awful thing. There were green jam tarts, doughnuts oozing with cream and jam, and two iced fancies topped with glace cherries. The girl finished putting out the cups and saucers and the pot of hot water to top up the small teapot.

'I used to buy presents for Roy every time I went out,' said Moira. The tone of sadness in her voice didn't escape Daisy.

Moira lifted the teapot lid and began stirring. 'Sometimes, Daisy, I feel as though my brain is all scrambled up. Do you ever feel like that?'

'Only when I'm tired.' She remembered the early morning and how crabby she'd been. A couple of hours' exhausted sleep had given her a lift and she felt fine now.

'When we were first together, Roy wanted a child. So did I.' She put out her hand and stilled Daisy's fingers as Daisy spooned sugar into a cup. 'You don't mind me talking frankly to you, Daisy? Only I feel as though we are going to become real friends. And friends can share anything, can't they?'

Daisy smiled at her. 'I suppose so,' she said. After all, she thought, didn't she share almost all her innermost thoughts with Vera? *Almost.*

'Do you want children, Daisy?'

'I hadn't thought about it, what with Kenny not being around. When 'e comes out of prison, until we get properly on our feet, I might go on the pill. Or even have one of those new coil things fitted.'

'Roy doesn't make love to me as often as he used to.' Daisy gulped at her tea. 'I don't think I'm the only love of his life, you see?' This was going to be a tough conversation, Daisy thought. There was sharing secrets and sharing secrets. She thought of Vera's frankness about all matters sexual. But then, Vera had a wise attitude to life and what made people, men in particular, tick. And she treated sex like a happy necessity. It was easy to laugh at Vera's stories of her escapades, but Moira? Daisy wasn't sure she was ready for her most intimate details.

'I think I'm becoming a nuisance to him. An embarrassment—'

'Surely not,' broke in Daisy. She wanted to steer the conversation away from Moira's marital problems. After all, it seemed disloyal to Moira's husband. But the best reply she could come up with was, 'I wish I knew who you remind me of. You're so like . . .'

'Ruth Ellis?'

Daisy's heart felt like it had suddenly been dipped in the icy waters off the ferry landing stage. Of course, the murderess Ruth Ellis. The last woman to be hanged in England. Back in the mid-fifties, it was, because she shot her lover David Blakely dead when she became an embarrassment to him and he no longer wanted her. But why would anyone want to dress like a dead woman? Why wear dated clothing? Why, when the fashions of today were vibrant and exciting? There was no accounting for people's tastes. But the more Daisy thought about it, the more it distressed her.

Then she remembered Moira telling her about her mother and

her friend. The friend Moira idolised who died in awful circumstances. Ruth Ellis. Moira had told her all about her.

Daisy stared at her friend with concern. Was Moira suffering under some kind of delusion? She'd had a terrible childhood, with every person she loved taken from her, her father abandoning her, her mother committing suicide. Was Moira identifying with Ruth Ellis because in her tortured mind she could see herself acting out some similar future fantasy?

And what of Roy Kemp? Was he really having a bit on the side with another woman? Whatever the answers were, the most important question was, was Moira losing control? Daisy stared at her.

Moira hadn't eaten a thing. She kept on stirring her untouched tea. The spoon scraping round and round the china cup. Daisy reached out her hand and stilled Moira's fingers, shaking her head as she did so. Then she took hold of the shortcake shell, lifting it to her lips and biting into its buttery freshness. It gave her the courage to ask, 'Why do you dress like her? Copy her hairstyle?'

'She was the bravest person, ever. I wish I'd been able to talk to her at the end because I can totally sympathise with her feelings. I know what she went through. How she felt. The desolation, the pain she endured. Do you know, she was glad when her lover was dead? Happy that he could never hurt her again. Sometimes I feel she speaks to me from her grave.'

'Perhaps her mind was so disturbed she couldn't help herself?' Daisy said. 'Jealousy can be dangerous.'

Moira sipped her tea daintily. 'Perhaps. She loved the seaside, you know. Mum and her went on holiday to Cornwall. Ruth wasn't blonde then. She began peroxiding her hair later.'

She put down the china cup on its delicate saucer and opened her handbag. Bringing out a small brass and enamelled tin, she flipped open the lid and picked out a pale-coloured pill. She swallowed it with another mouthful of tea.

'You should eat something,' Daisy said. Moira was busy putting the enamelled box back into her handbag. Daisy pushed the plate of cakes towards her and she chose an iced fancy. She watched Moira nibble the smooth pink icing then set the cake down on the rose-painted plate.

'I'm so looking forward to the party on New Year's Eve,' Moira said.

Daisy nodded. Her head was reeling. What if she went to London and Moira decided to do something silly? Shoot her husband?

For fuck's sake, she thought, snap out of it, Daisy, before you go round the bleedin' bend. But she couldn't help asking.

'Moira, you haven't got a gun, have you?'

Moira laughed. 'Don't be silly.'

Daisy rationalised things. After all, she knew Eddie had a flick knife, didn't she? And once, a long while ago, Kenny had come home with a shotgun. Which Eddie had promptly disposed of for him. And Moira's old man was a villain, wasn't he? So of course he'd have a gun. Didn't all gangsters have weapons? The Kray twins? The Richardsons?

'But you wouldn't . . .'

'Of course not. I'd hurt him where it would cause the most pain, though.'

'What would you do?' Daisy had to force herself to keep her voice steady. Moira was scaring the shit out of her.

'I'd destroy the thing he wanted most,' she said with a smile.

'Which is?'

'That would be telling, Daisy Lane. That would be telling.' And then she surprised Daisy even more by taking the largest doughnut from the plate and biting into it hungrily. From the kitchens Daisy could hear Frank Ifield plaintively singing 'I Remember You'.

Oh yes, thought Daisy. I'll remember you, Moira Kemp. All my life, I'll remember you.

CHAPTER 11

New Year's Eve 1962

'You look pretty snazzy in that gear,' said Vera. 'Specially the white boots and the fluffy white hat. Keep the snow off you, they will.' It had started snowing on Boxing Day and continued freezing and snowing. Daisy hated it. The cold got into her bones and made her miserable.

'Do you think it's a bit much with this green suit?' Daisy stared at her reflection in the mirror. The fake fur hat was the latest fashion, even if it had come at a knockdown price from the market. 'Does it show where Kibbles pulled at the fur with his claws?' She bent her head towards Vera.

'Serves you right for leavin' it on the bed, silly cow.' Vera peered at Daisy. Her eyes narrowed almost to slits. 'No. And 'ow many more times you gonna fuckin' ask me? You look lovely.'

'I can't compete with Moira and her classic clothes.'

'You don't 'ave to. She wants you to be with her because she likes you. Not 'cause of what you're wearin'. 'Ave you got everything? Money? Spare pair of knickers?' Daisy laughed. On the floor was a small holdall, on top of the bag a very large bunch of flowers, mostly forced daffs and greenery. It was the best Jacky on the market could offer at this time of the year. But it made a sweet-smelling and colourful show and Daisy was hoping that Moira's mother-in-law would like her gift.

'I'm a bit worried I won't know how to behave in someone else's house.'

'For fuck's sake, shut up,' said Vera. 'You're gettin' on my tits now. You are goin' out so you won't be in their house for very long. How can you say you won't know how to behave? What you gonna do? Tear their place up?'

'Don't be daft.'

'Just be natural. Be yourself. What you wearing tonight?' Vera was studying herself in Daisy's mirror now and pulling faces as she checked the skin around her eyes and neck. 'I'm gettin' a right ol' bag, ain't I?'

'Who's paranoid now?'

Vera looked at Daisy and smiled, then went over and squeezed her arm.

'You'll be all right, girl.'

'My black dress.'

'Oh.'

'What do you mean, oh?'

'Well, it's not very ... very ...'

'Fancy?' She nodded. Daisy sighed. 'I can't go on spendin' money on myself, even if it is cheap gear I buy. I need to put by as much as I can for when Kenny comes out. In fact I was thinkin' of keepin' the cafe open later at nights and maybe get in a few live acts so the kids can sit and drink coffee and maybe listen to music, dance. You know, local rock 'n' roll bands. Skiffle sounds and lads who set the girls sighin' and screamin'. I'll need to apply for a licence for that. Coffee bars are all the rage—'

'Whoa,' Vera said. 'One thing at a time, Dais. You'll kill yourself if you ain't careful. Workin' so 'ard. I only 'ope your Kenny knows what a treasure 'e 'as.'

Daisy ignored her.

'It all costs money, Vera. To make money you 'ave to spend a bit. If my black dress won't do then I'll ask Moira if I can borrow somethin' of hers. We're almost the same shape. If you look at us with your eyes closed.'

'You're funny, you are, Dais.' Vera grew thoughtful. 'We 'ad a good Christmas together, didn't we?'

Daisy smiled at her. 'The best. There I was, worried that I'd be on my own and you made it all so good for me. Never thought I'd go to church on Christmas Eve, mind you.'

'Why ever not? I go regularly. Well, I go every Christmas Eve.' Vera never was a good liar.

'Not me, Vera. Been a long time since I was in church. I even got married in the registry office. But Christmas opened my eyes.

Those little kids singing their hearts out in the choir and St John's Church done up so nice to welcome everyone. You've got hidden depths, you 'ave, Vera. Then to come back 'ere to mulled wine and mince pies. That was a surprise. Didn't we laugh when we got tiddly?'

'Worse in the morning, wasn't it, when we started on the bleedin' sherry. Took us all day to get the fuckin' dinner on, didn't it?'

Daisy started to giggle again at the memory. 'In the end we never did cook those sprouts, did we?'

'No, but we did listen to the Queen's Speech.'

'You fell asleep, Vera, you know you did.'

'Well, you was so pissed when I woke up an' asked you what she said, you just looked at me with them big Joannie Collins eyes of yours an' said seriously, "I don't know. Let's 'ave a drop more sherry."'

'Anyway,' Daisy said, giving her a hug, 'thanks, Vera, you're one in a million.'

'Yeah, well . . . Listen to that noise!'

A car was tooting out in the snow-covered street. Daisy hurried to the window and looked down.

'Look at that, Vera!'

'Fuckin' 'ell, you better not keep 'er waitin'. Bloody 'ell, a chauffeur as well.' Daisy snatched the holdall, flowers and clutch bag and ran from the room, almost colliding with Eddie who was coming out of his bedroom. She dropped the flowers.

'Shit!'

He bent down and picked them up. Luckily they'd not spilled from their paper wrapper.

'What's all the fuss?' he asked as he handed them to her.

'You know very well. See you when I get back. The car's 'ere waitin' for me.'

''Ave a good time, Dais,' he said. But he wasn't smiling. Eddie had got back last night and Daisy hadn't had time to ask whether his business in Greece had gone to his satisfaction. Not that he'd tell her anything without prompting, she thought.

'Will you make sure there's no bother . . .'

'Don't worry. We'll shut up well before the seasonal drunks

come out causing trouble.' He smiled then and his whole face softened. She felt a warm rush of gratitude towards him. So much so that she reached up and kissed him on the cheek. Then continued her flight downstairs, throwing open the street door and almost running into the arms of a burly man dressed in a grey monkey suit.

'Hold on, missy,' he said, catching her before she tripped. He smelled of peppermints and fags. Moira was sliding out of the open rear door of the biggest car she'd ever seen. She ran gingerly towards Daisy on high heels, making indentations in the frozen snow, and grabbed her in a bear hug that nearly squeezed the breath out of her. The flunky was standing to attention awaiting Moira's orders, his peaked hat slightly crooked where he'd bent to grab Daisy. For some reason she wanted to laugh. And all her fears about going to London and meeting Moira's family dissolved like ice-cream on a hot summer's day. Just like Vera said they would.

'It's so lovely to see you again, Dais.' Moira tucked her arm through Daisy's. 'Take her bag, Charles.' Charles smiled at Daisy and she handed him her pathetic holdall. It looked small in his great hands. She noticed the thick gold signet ring on his pinky finger. He opened the front passenger door and put the bag, along with the flowers, in the foot-well.

The car was a silver-grey Humber, huge, shining and the chrome glistening so brightly you could see your face in it. Charles stood to attention while the women climbed inside the spacious interior. It smelled of polished leather. Daisy slid in first, then Moira sat next to her and Charles shut the door. Daisy looked out through the gleaming glass. Both Vera and Susie had their noses squashed to the window watching every move they made. She waved and they waved. Snow was heaped on the window sills. Vera had Kibbles in her arms and she held on to his paw and shook it so it looked like he was waving too, even if he did look totally bored with the whole business. A lump came into Daisy's throat. She was only staying overnight but you'd have thought she was going away from her loved ones for a sodding world cruise or something. But they were a family now, weren't they?

Daisy's eyes travelled up to the window of the bed and

breakfast room. Eddie nodded down at her. His face was unreadable.

Charles got in the driver's side and started the engine. They purred down North Street, past the ironmonger and the pet shop and the fire station. Daisy felt like she was a queen on a state visit. Curtains twitched as they passed. Excitement welled up inside her. She swivelled round on the squashy seat and looked at Moira. She had on the ocelot coat. It wasn't fake fur like the ones in the market, but the real thing. Underneath she wore a black wool dress, much classier than the one Daisy had brought for the evening. She decided she wouldn't even take her dress from the holdall but come right out and ask Moira if she could have a borrow of something of hers.

'Isn't this lovely, Dais?' Daisy nodded, too full to even speak properly. They glided along Mumby Road and into Forton Road then past Brockhurst and towards Fareham. 'Want a drink?' Moira asked. She was like a little girl, excitable. She pressed a button and, hey bloody presto, a drinks cabinet complete with bottles of booze and glasses swung into view. In the rear-view mirror Daisy caught sight of Charles. He was watching Moira's every move.

'Not this early,' Daisy said. Was it her imagination but did Moira look cross she'd refused?

'Then I won't either.' She depressed the button and the cabinet disappeared back into the shiny woodwork. Daisy caught the stress on the word 'won't' and it jarred. Was Moira used to drinking this early in the day? One thing for sure, she was animated, edgy even. Daisy decided Moira was over-excited at seeing her again. Daisy squeezed her hand and Moira grinned back at her.

'How long will it take to get there?' Daisy asked.

'Not too long.' Charles smiled at her in the mirror. 'As long it hasn't snowed again and iced up even more.' Charles was very clean and scrubbed looking.

'Don't talk too loudly,' whispered Moira. 'Charles can hear every word we say to each other.' Daisy couldn't see how that was possible unless they shouted as there was a heavy glass screen between the front and the passenger bench seat. But she nodded anyway, wondering what she was getting herself into.

'I'm going to take you somewhere special, first. Aren't I, Charles?' Charles nodded and again Daisy's eyes were held by his in the rear-view mirror. She began to feel that perhaps Charles was not simply Moira's chauffeur but maybe her minder as well.

Moira prattled on about this and that and Daisy was content to let her talk. She spoke of films she'd seen, shows she'd been to, clubs and the people she'd met there. She was name-dropping. But not, Daisy realised, for effect. Either she really did know these characters or else it was all pure fantasy. Daisy decided, as the car certainly cost more than a fiver, that she was for real. After all, it was clear Roy Kemp had money to burn. But money wasn't making Moira happy, that was a dead cert.

'It don't feel as if we're moving,' Daisy said. 'Even with the bad weather this is such a smooth ride.' The landscape had given way to white snow-filled fields with the trees shot with frost. They stood about like naked, white-skinned scarecrows. Inside the car it was warm as toast. Soon the countryside disappeared and they were into the suburbs.

'We're almost there.'

Daisy craned her neck and tried to guess where. All she saw were scruffy houses like the ones they'd left behind in Gosport, a grey street with a railway and viaduct, dirty gutters and crisp packets blowing against iced-over wire-netting fences, dog shit on the snowy pavements and very little for Moira to get excited about. Daisy might as well have been back home, she thought.

'Here we are. See the pub?'

They'd rounded a corner and climbed a slight incline in the road.

'Where are we?'

'Where else but Hampstead? The Magdala Tavern.' This came from Charles. The resignation in his voice sent a slight shiver down Daisy's spine.

'Stop here,' Moira demanded in a loud voice. Charles obeyed. It was an ordinary pub, Charrington's Wines and Spirits emblazoned on its exterior. Yet almost before the car had drawn to a halt Moira was out of the door and round to Daisy's side. 'Come and see.'

Daisy got out, but stood, wondering what she was supposed to be looking at. She pulled her suit collar up. Despite her fluffy hat she was freezing. Moira grabbed hold of her and pulled her towards the wall of the tavern. 'Put your fingers here,' she commanded. Daisy let her grab her hand and raise it to the cold stone, where she felt indentations. Something, she didn't know what, something dark like a premonition ran through her body. She pulled her hand away as though the wall had bitten her.

'She shot him here, you know. Those are the bullet holes. He deserved it. The fuckin' bastard.' This was said with such vehemence Moira's body shook. Moira's words and the way she spat them out chilled Daisy. She didn't like the way she was feeling or the way Moira was behaving.

'This is 'orrible,' Daisy said. 'Like when people rush to the scene of an accident. They're fuckin' ghouls.' Moira stared at her. There was an icy wind and it was trying to ruffle her hair. But the firm hold of the lacquer kept it practically immobile.

'No. It's not horrible. He deserved it.' Moira stared across the road. 'He was coming out of the pub when Ruth shot him. She couldn't stand what he was putting her through. It was driving her round the bend. I know just how she must have felt.'

'You're frightening me, Moira,' Daisy said. She had a sudden urge to shake her out of this ... this admiration for something so very unhealthy. There were tears in Moira's eyes now and Daisy didn't want to be on this street outside the pub any more. The car's engine was still running and Charles, immobile in the car, was staring at Daisy. Then he got out and went to Moira. Gently he took her arm and led her back and sat her inside. Daisy got in the car as well.

'That's enough, Miss Moira.' Charles' voice was firm as he returned once more to the driving seat. Daisy heard the click of door locks. She tried the handle but the car door wouldn't open. 'Precautionary measure,' Charles advised, though he said it with tenderness.

Daisy couldn't wait to get away.

Moira sat slumped as though all the stuffing had been knocked out of her. The platinum hair, permed and set in that lacquered fifties style, the red lips, the heavy eye make-up and the tailored clothes. A carbon copy of Ruth Ellis. Daisy looked in the mirror and saw Charles staring at her. He gave a little nod imperceptibly, and seemed relieved that she understood. Moira was a very frail lady indeed.

Charles turned the steering wheel of the car and they moved off, back the way they had come.

'Why don't you try to sleep, Miss Moira?' And taking heed of his words Moira snuggled against Daisy, her feet up on the leather seat, her shoes kicked to the carpet.

'Thirteenth of July, nineteen fifty-five. I know exactly how she felt.'

'Go to sleep,' Daisy said. Putting her arms around Moira, she felt her breathing grow shallow as she sagged against Daisy and then slept.

Moira had taken her to The Magdala like it was some kind of treat. It meant a lot to her, that place. She seemed to think the killing was justified. But why? One thing Daisy knew, the happy Moira she had met at Winchester had been replaced with this sad clone of a killer. Something was very wrong indeed.

CHAPTER 12

Kenny sat in his cell, his head in his hands. For once he was alone and it would be a while yet before the buzzer went for work duty. It had been another long night, with Casanova farting and snoring away like a fucking good'un. He thought he was going mad.

He could never do as Eddie had told him, 'keep yer head down'. Not because he didn't want to, but the bleeders in here wouldn't let him. And it was eating away at him like a fucking maggot in an apple.

And that cunt Eric wouldn't let him be. Going around like he owned the place. And the screws not bothering because Big fucking Eric kept order among the inmates, making it plain sailing for the screws. No trouble on the report sheets. Why? Because Big fucking Eric sorted it before trouble got that far. And if other cons got hurt? Who cared? 'I fell over, sir.' 'I slipped, sir'. Those were the bog-standard replies when someone got done over. Fucking clumsy lot, cons. And everyone was happy with the seemingly peaceful atmosphere. Except Kenny.

He was bloody terrified and he didn't know what to do about it.

Terrified to be in the showers. Terrified in the canteen listening to the sniggering from the cons at what Eric was putting him through.

He hated the smell of the man, the touch of his hands on his flesh and the way his skin crawled when the bastard used him then finally left him, alone and snivelling.

Eric's currency was tobacco, fags, money-changing. He gave out fags, drugs or coinage in exchange for paper money slipped to prisoners during visits. Blow was easy. So were amyl nitrate poppers, but orange sunshine was favourite. Coke and heroin were easier to get inside than out, decided Kenny. Not that he was interested. He didn't know what half the drugs were or how they made you feel. He'd asked Casanova, he knew everything.

Casanova was like Daisy, reading books like they were going out of fashion. Daisy liked all kinds of books, especially ones about other people's lives. But Casanova read a lot of what he called 'instructive reading'. Kenny said he preferred to do things, not read about them. But the truth was he wasn't very good at reading. He had to concentrate a long time on the words and sometimes by the time he got to the bottom of the page he'd forgotten what the beginning was about. He liked books with pictures in best. But he did spend a long time figuring out what to write to Daisy and, even though his letters were very short and his spelling wasn't too good, he knew Daisy didn't mind. Her handwriting was very clear and she didn't go on and on about stuff he didn't care about so he liked to get letters from her.

When he'd asked Casanova about the different kinds of drugs, Casanova said some of the so-called 'new' drugs weren't really new at all but had been around in different ways from as early as the First World War. Some had been used as slimming aids and truth drugs by the bleeding American Army. Now even the kids on the outside were starting to use them. Eric liked the poppers best of all because they gave him a better hard-on.

Kenny felt the resentment and the anger grow inside him at how he was being used. Like a fucking rag doll. The trouble was he was never going to get any peace. He couldn't bear to think about it. Just wanted it all to end. He'd started to cry again. He did that a lot these days. Sometimes he didn't even know he was crying.

But he did know Big Eric would go on hurting him. Unless he could do something to stop him. But what?

What would Eddie do? He'd never have got in this situation in the first place. He'd have been the fucking aggressor, would Eddie. He wished Eddie were with him. Not because he wanted Eddie inside, but ... Eddie always knew how to deal with things.

Kenny wiped his eyes on his blue shirt tail. His hands were shaking. Sometimes he found he was clenching his fists tight. So tight that his nails dug into the palms of his hands and drew blood.

It bloody well hurt. Yet he didn't know he was doing it. Until he felt the pain.

He was glad Eddie was keeping an eye on Daisy. That was a turn-up for the books, Bert asking him to run the cafe. He didn't really know the old duffer all that well. Not until him and Daisy started going in Bert's as somewhere they could spend a bit of time together out of the rain or the cold weather. They'd sit for ages over a couple of cups of tea. Bert never seemed to mind. Sometimes he'd make them a sandwich and tell them it was 'on the house'. Bert was kind. Kenny thought he might have been lonely. He'd once asked Kenny how his mum was. Told him he'd known her a long time ago. When Kenny told him his mum was dead, the old man had cried. Daisy made the old feller go through to the back. Sat him down and made him a cup of tea for once instead of him making teas for everyone else. Then Daisy and Kenny had stood behind the counter and served until it was time to close up. Bert had come back later and stood in the kitchen doorway, watching them, with a sort of half smile on his face. Nice old fart, though. Daisy'd run that place better than Bert ever had. His heart beat faster thinking about Daisy. She'd looked so pretty when she'd visited him last month. He didn't want her visiting every month like she was allowed because he felt so miserable inside. Not at all happy like he used to be before. If she wanted to see him, he'd send her a visiting order. Then he'd work himself up into a mood wondering how the visit would be.

He could see all the other cons in the visiting room staring. He'd felt proud. Jealous at the same time, though it wasn't like him to be jealous. And the funny thing was she didn't even know she was beautiful. Not an obvious tarty-looking prettiness like Jayne Mansfield or some of them other Hollywood stars, but that quiet bloom of beauty English starlets had. Like that, that – why couldn't he think of her name? – Carol White. Yes, that was it, Carol White. That's who Daisy reminded him of. And he'd sent her away from the prison in tears.

A real shit he'd been to her. After she'd come to visit him and brought him stuff. But he couldn't seem to help himself. He looked forward to visits, then when she was here, he said awful things to her. She didn't deserve it.

It was proper that Eddie stayed at the cafe and kept an eye on things. There had been a right lot of turds in that place in the past. Bert had sorted them but Daisy could get caught in a lot of flak on her own. Eddie would take care of her. Hadn't he seen it in Eddie's eyes? That look? Eddie had always taken Kenny's girls. Not because he wanted them. No, just because he could. But Kenny understood. He sighed.

Eddie had to be the best.

Girls liked Kenny. He didn't know why. Sure, he didn't look too bad – but it was as if girls felt safe with him. Like he was their little brother or something. When Eddie was about it was a different kettle of fish. Eddie could have any girl he wanted. He was like a magnet where they were concerned. But one fuck and he threw them over. It was a kind of torment inside Eddie. To be the best, to take what he wanted. To keep on proving he could accomplish whatever he set his mind to. Not just to other people but himself as well. Kenny sometimes wondered if it was still Pappy he wanted approval from.

And Eddie wouldn't be crossed. He'd seen and known him do awful things. Especially when he was in a rage.

Like when they were at school together. Of course, Eddie being older was in a higher class, but he'd always wait for Kenny so they could walk home together. This boy, Colin Wilson, had scarf-whipped Kenny in the bogs. Frightened him so much he was scared shitless and wouldn't come out.

Eddie finally found him cowering, covered in his own shit and piss, behind a bolted door. Got him home and washed him gently all over, like he was a baby. Then cleaned his cuts and put iodine that stung like fucking hell on bruises and scraped knuckles where he'd tried to protect his face.

The next day Colin Wilson never got to school.

When he came back two months later, he had a livid scar running from beneath one eye to his mouth that made his top lip all crooked. He kept away from Eddie and Kenny. Never did tell anyone what had happened. Was really quiet after that. But Kenny knew all right. It was like Eddie was saying, 'You mess with my brother, you mess with me.'

And Eddie and Daisy?

Well, Kenny was in here. And if Daisy really fell for Eddie? That was something he didn't want to think about, not now. One thing he was certain of, they both cared about him. And Eddie and Daisy? They were his world.

What he had to work out before he went round the fucking twist was how to stop that wanker Eric from coming on to him. It was a new year tomorrow and he had to put an end to this misery before it finished him.

Why was it always Eddie looking after him and not the other way around?

What would Eddie do?

CHAPTER 13

New Year's Day 1963

What the fuck is she up to? Eddie slammed his coffee cup down on the counter so sharply that the remains of the drink splashed over the rim. Stomping over to the jukebox and bending aggressively, he pulled the plug so that the Everly Brothers never had time to 'Wake Up Little Susie'.

Daisy had asked him to keep an eye on things and he had. Doling out teas and bacon sarnies like he was some bloody gofer to fucking has-beens and wannabes with nothing better to do at the beginning of a brand-new year 'cept sit in some poxy back-street fuckin' cafe. He'd left the street door open to get rid of the stench of fags; now he kicked it closed and slid the bolts into place.

You've been had, boy, his brain was telling him. But he still wiped down the counter to get rid of the offending coffee spill.

And there was bloody Vera swanning about like fuckin' Lady Muck, watching him so he didn't get too pally with that Susie. As if he'd want to after her divvy boyfriend had been there. True, he'd once had plans about setting Suze up in the spare room. Wouldn't have done much about it though, not with Vinnie hanging about and her being underage. Was he already on to him? Who'd have thought Vinnie'd end up in the force? Always was as sharp as a tack, that one, even as a kid. And he'd seen the way his eyes had lingered on Daisy, the bastard. He kicked a chair into place. Picked up an overflowing ashtray and dumped its contents into the tin container kept for collecting rubbish from the tables. Would have made a nice little earner, Susie would. And what had he done about that? Fuck all, because he didn't want to hurt Daisy and the fucking reputation of the cafe that was so dear to her heart.

'Yeah, you've certainly been taken for a ride,' he said aloud. 'All because you really care about that cow your brother married.'

Hadn't he watched her leave yesterday in that fuckin' great Humber with that monkey opening doors for the blonde bit to greet her like a bosom buddy? An' she was on something that one was. Eyes like piss 'oles in the snow. Well, there was money enough there to keep her in her habit. He'd find out what Daisy was up to. She wouldn't make a fool out of him in a hurry again.

And what had happened when she'd got in earlier today?

Put a fuckin' biscuit tin on the counter and asked him if he wanted a bit of cake. He caught sight of himself in the reflection from the window, face scowling, dark brows almost in a straight line – foot tapping angrily as he stood remembering the past twenty-four hours.

He was jealous. Of course he was fuckin' jealous.

Eddie looked at his watch. Ten past three. He couldn't go to bed. Couldn't sleep, not now. Perhaps it was time to put plan number three into action. Being as plans one and two were functioning well and the money was rolling in. First he'd muscled in on the old insurance game, then got into the drug scene, and there was more for him to follow up on both those plans. And for now, didn't the early bird always catch the worm?

Ten minutes later he was walking along North Cross Street, feet barely making a sound on the ice-brushed pavements, and into Mumby Road. The air was biting cold. He could smell the silt from Forton Creek, acrid, stinging the back of his throat with its pungency despite the frost. Get January and February out of the way and soon it would be summer. If only the cold would give way a bit and a proper thaw take over. Daisy liked the sun and so did he. The weather was a farce, he told himself. There was even a chilling mist at the water's edge. Thank God it was off the sea and usually cleared away with the day's light. Not like that shit they had in London. Sixty people killed by the smog in December in three days, so the paper had said. Must be fucking awful to live in that place, he thought. P'raps that's why they called it 'The Smoke'?

Along Forton Road he stopped outside a large Georgian house set back from the main road. There was an antique shop next door called The Cellar, its windows crammed full of interesting bits and pieces. Might have a proper decko in there one of these days. It was run by a bent-up little crone with a heart of gold. She'd lived in Gosport all her life, so she'd once told him. He wondered if she knew Pappy? They'd be about the same age. Gosport was full of two sorts of people. Transients like the skates from Collingwood, St Vincent; and soldiers and marines in St George's Barracks or blokes off the airfield at Gomer. And families living practically in the same run-down streets where their ancestors had been born. He could walk through the town market on any Saturday and nod to blokes he'd been to school with and old blokes who'd sat round the house when he'd been a kid, Pappy's cronies. But now their venue was changed. They'd be sitting in the ferry gardens on the wooden benches, dressed like scarecrows and then shuffling about with sticks to prop 'em up. Once upon a time they'd been as handy with their fucking feet and fists as Pappy had been.

He thought about the last time he'd gone to The Cedars.

Cost a fucking bomb to keep him in there, an' the daft old bugger didn't even know who he was half the time. Kenny couldn't have cared less about Pappy. He thought Pappy was in a council home somewhere. When Eddie had shown him the paperwork about The Cedars he'd barely glanced at the documents, just said, 'The bastard's done nuffink for me. Let the state look after him, I don't wanna know. Don't ever mention his name to me again.' Eddie had respected Kenny's wishes.

The rest home was in Alverstoke – a nice place, as them places go, of course. Stank of piss and God knows what else, which got to you as soon as you was let in the place. But what else did you expect with the old folks mostly incontinent? One thing, they served bloody good food in there. Pappy had always liked his food. 'Course the pretty nurses had to feed him now and Eddie suspected Pappy didn't know what he was eating from one day to the next. But that's what Eddie was paying for, wasn't it? Nurses to tend to his every need. To keep his father alive. For despite the beatings and psychological cruelty he'd endured as a kid, he knew his father cared more for him than Kenny. And whatever Pappy had doled out to Eddie, he'd never give in like Kenny and forget about the old bastard. Perhaps to spite the old man he wouldn't give up on him. Ever.

Kenny would laugh at him if he ever found out Eddie was doing all this for a man who'd professed to hate his guts. So it was another secret he'd keep close. And he'd go on finding the money until the old bastard was finally pushing up daisies.

It was either The Cedars or some state institution where the daft sod would be left to dribble his feeble life away. He'd been at the nursing home for a few years now. Eddie had gone to see him just before Christmas.

'Come in, you're just in time for carols,' said a helper, after unlocking the big oak front doors. They had to lock them in else some of the old fogies would go walkabout.

'Your father's in here.'

Eddie had been shown into the main guest room where about ten old dears sat about in wheelchairs waiting for death, knees covered in brightly coloured crocheted blankets. His dad hadn't recognised him. Nothing changes, thought Eddie. He'd never noticed him when he was a kid, neither. His father's hands were blue veined and paper thin, the knuckles swollen. He'd seen those knuckles swollen many times, usually after they'd landed heavily round a much younger Eddie's head.

'Can't do it no more, can you, Pappy?' he'd said, but without malice. How could he be angry about the past when all he'd ever wanted was for the old bastard to love him?

Besides the captive audience in their wheelchairs, Eddie and a middle-aged woman visiting her mother were the only guests. Four nurses and two cleaning staff came in to watch, standing by favoured patients and holding their hands and talking to them as though they were kids.

Eddie liked the carols, sung by a jolly group of assorted men and women dressed in Christmassy red and green with glittery tinsel scarves. Who cared if they hit a few wrong notes and forgot words, they smiled and belted out the carols with gusto. One woman, a middle-aged blowsy blonde with an infectious grin and too much cheap perfume, clasped Pappy's hand and sang 'Scarlet Ribbons' in a not too tuneful voice, producing a cheap scarlet ribbon and laying it gently about Pappy's neck. Afterwards, when the music had died away, she'd kissed Pappy on his old grey head. Eddie had seen the tears in Pappy's eyes, heard him croak the familiar chorus, saw the blank look descend on his face again after she'd walked away. And he marvelled how memories could be jogged, songs remembered and sung, when Pappy didn't know what day it was or even that his son had come to visit.

He brought his thoughts back to where he was now and, lifting the catch on the tall gate that flanked the main road, slipped into the garden of Chestnut House. A long path led to the steps of the once fine Georgian residence. Originally built for a local victualler, a Gosport man of substance, it was now a brothel.

An iced-over fish pond, without fish but containing a cast-iron bedstead, lay next to an enormous chestnut tree, bare of leaves now but magnificent with tall creamy cones of flowers in May. And in the autumn glossy red conker fruit lay about the garden until it was trodden into the concrete paving by men's boots.

Eddie climbed the short flight of steps and banged on the door.

He knew some of the girls living in the house, but like most Gosport whorehouses the place needed organisation and Eddie knew he was just the person to do it. The women on the game lived their separate lives in the many rooms the old house provided. It was about time he took these fucking freelancers in hand. It was going to be his new year resolution, helping others to reach their full potential.

He had to bang a couple of times on the paint-peeling door before a top window was thrown open.

'What d'you want?' A tousled red-haired woman stared blearily down at Eddie. She was clutching a bright red silken dressing gown around her. 'It's a bit early, ain't it?'

'C'mon, darlin'.' Eddie knew she wouldn't refuse him. 'If you don't want to oblige, find someone who will.' He rubbed his hand over his crotch. He saw the woman eyeing his expensive wool Crombie and new trilby hat. She could see money, the crafty cow.

''Ang on.' She disappeared and he heard the window close before the sound of footsteps clattered down uncarpeted stairs. The door swung open and a shaft of gamy air nearly knocked Eddie back. 'Got a new year's present for me, 'ave you?' She put out her hand and made a snaking grab for Eddie's penis. She had the most God-awful bad teeth Eddie had ever seen on anyone. He hated himself for getting an instant hard-on the moment she touched him. 'My, there's a big boy,' she said. 'Tell Mama what yer wants?'

Eddie slapped her hand away. The surprise on her face made him want to laugh.

'Go an' wake yer slag pals up an' get 'em all down 'ere.'

He was now standing in a room filled with cheap furniture. Three standard lamps, each hung with a different coloured chiffon scarf, attempted to make the room look glamorous, as did the beaded shawls slung across the horsehair sofa. Pity the wallpaper was hanging off in places, with patches of damp mould beneath showing green and black.

'Why should I?' the cheeky cow said. She'd tied up her wrap and was standing with her hands on her skinny hips. He reached across and pulled on the sash. Her dressing gown fell open to reveal a snatch of black hair that was nothing like the colour of her vibrant head. Her breasts were full, with large honey-coloured nipples. His large hand gripped one of them, tightened and twisted.

'Oww,' she squealed.

'Because I fuckin' told yer to,' he said, releasing his grip on her. 'And in case any of you cunts think of trying any funny business, I 'ave a little persuader 'ere.' From inside his Crombie pocket he brought out his flick knife and depressed the button so that the long, sharp blade snapped out. The look on her face told him she'd rather deal with him with the others around than try her luck on her own. She fled up the stairs and he heard muffled voices and doors banging, then feet pounding on bare wood floors.

He moved to the fireplace, stood with his back to it. It was a good vantage point, with a view through the rear window to the back gate and the front window showing the path he'd just walked up. If there was going to be trouble from any johns in the house or from outside he was ready for it. But since he'd already sussed out the girls here and their boyfriends, he felt confident. No, he told himself, more than confident. It was going to be a piece of piss. After all, wasn't he Eddie Lane? The Eddie Lane who was goin' places fast? He flicked the blade back into place and put it away in his pocket.

The protection racket was going like a bat out of hell. He didn't make the collections himself, not any more. Just a word from one of his boys and the dosh was handed over, sweet as a nut. Cal was the crazy one. One look at Cal and the hands were reaching in the tills quicker than a fart through a colander.

Seven women now stood in the living room in varying states of undress.

'Fuckin' 'ell, all your clients must be drunk or blind if they fancy any of you lot. I 'ope you tarts yourselves up a bit for the johns. If you did, likely there'd be more sleep-overs, especially today as it's the first day of nineteen sixty-three. I know a lot of blokes like to fuck the new year in.'

He'd never seen so much smeared make-up and grubby nightwear. Body odour permeated the room. A thought flashed through his mind that Vera, with her scrubbed sweetness and fuckin' Californian Poppy, really knew how to present herself.

'Okay, now what?' asked the mouthy red-head. She seemed to have made herself the spokeswoman.

'Well, Bella. I'm your new boss.'

''Ow d'you know me fuckin' name?'

Eddie tapped the side of his nose. 'That's fer me to know an' you to find out.'

'An' what d'you mean, "boss"? We already pays our way 'ere. An' it costs us enough to live in bloody peace.'

Eddie stepped back as far as he was able, until his back was touching the mantelpiece. Bella had moved closer and her breath stank worse than the lavatory at the back of the cafe. He studied the women. Four were attractive enough. One was older than Bella, she looked to be in her late thirties. She had enormous tits. Nothing else going for her, but some blokes liked a good faceful.

The last one was small, fine-boned. Looked about fourteen, with badly bleached hair that stuck up at the back.

'Well, you'll all have to shag a bit fuckin' harder, won't you, girls?' Bella frowned. Eddie raised his hand and she flinched as though expecting him to hit her. But he merely pushed her away from him. 'Get out of my face. I'm putting you in charge,

Mouthy,' he said to Bella. 'And for fuck's sake clean your teeth. I can't abide people who don't look after themselves. Don't you know cleanliness is next to godliness?' He walked towards the girl and in a quiet voice asked,

'How old are you?'

'Eighteen.'

'An' I'm Father Christmas.' He lifted her chin. Defiantly she stared back at him. 'Don't be shy of Eddie. How old are you?' His hand left her chin and rested on her bird-like shoulder. Then he gripped it, hard, pulling her towards him. She tried to twist away but couldn't. She barely reached his shoulder, just like Daisy.

'Sixteen,' she said. 'My name's Liz.' She had small, even teeth and a creamy tint to her skin. She hadn't been on the game long, he was certain of that.

'Well, girlies . . .' he said, reaching once more into his pocket with his free hand and withdrawing the knife. He snapped it open and drew the long, thin point down the side of the girl's nose. Looking directly into her eyes, he spoke to all the women. 'I know you won't do anything stupid.'

Perspiration blossomed on the girl's upper lip. Her breathing was ragged and shallow. No one in the room moved.

'Good thinking,' he said. 'Didn't take long to make my point, did it?' Then he laughed. 'Make my point. See?' No one laughed. Eddie took it in his stride and said, 'Liz here will be my special girl for today. She's going to come for a little walk. The rest of you can go back to bed, make tea or do whatever it is you do in the mornings. You could even clean this shithole up. And wash yourselves. But in the meantime you can ponder on ways to make a bit more money in case I need to up my incomings.'

And all this time Liz stood frozen as a statue, too terrified to move.

'Now, the way things is gonna work is this. I know Bella collects your rents every Friday and the money goes to a post office box number in Clapham. Your punctual payments impress me. So it shouldn't be any bother for Bella to collect, not exactly rent, but let's say, sixty per cent of your earnings. Now I think I'm bein' very fair 'cause I know pimps that take a much bigger screw. But I ain't no fuckin' pimp so we'll call it a maintenance charge. To be collected and sent to a local box number. All right?' No one moved. No one answered him.

Eddie rotated the knife to the base of the girl's nostril. Two of the women screamed. Although tears rose in Liz's green eyes she didn't attempt to pull away.

'Good girl,' he said. 'Now, I'll ask you all again. Is it going to be all right?'

Heads nodded. He threw Liz away from him and she fell in a crumpled heap on the stained carpet.

'What 'appens if we don't want to pay?' This from the woman with the tits.

'Don't want is made to want.' He bent down and grabbed hold of Liz yet again. Now he could smell her fear. All the fight seemed knocked out of her as she allowed him to hold her limply as a broken toy. She put up her hands to shield her face just as the tip of the knife caught the back of her hand.

'Please, please, leave me,' she cried.

'Shut the fuck up, Kath,' shouted Bella to Tits, then to Eddie, 'You'll get the money all right.'

Eddie watched the thin trickle of blood slide off the back of the girl's hand. At the sound of the blade clicking back into the knife's handle, Liz slumped against him, holding on to him for support.

'I'm glad we all see eye to eye,' Eddie said. Without waiting for a further reply, he grabbed hold of Liz and pulled her towards the front door.

'Where are we goin'? My room's upstairs.'

'I'm an outdoors man at heart. Even in this weather.' Her flip-flop mules clicked across the steps as he half pushed her down the frosted concrete path and out of the front gate.

Across the road he shoved her through a hole in the broken railings of St Vincent's playing field and across the wet, snow-laden grass. When they reached the sports pavilion he pushed her against the wall.

'Didn't think I was goin' to fuck you in that house, did you? A knife in my shoulder blades would 'ave been a good start to the new year, wouldn't it? What makes you think I come up the fuckin' Solent in a bucket?'

'I'm cold,' she said. 'My feet is fuckin' frozen.'

'Don't worry. I'll soon warm you up.'

He pulled her thin housecoat apart and the buttons popped. She let him do what he wanted, without any resistance at all. He knew she was frightened and her fear sent the adrenalin buzzing through his body. He nudged her legs apart and unzipping himself, burst out and upwards. She was a small, slight girl.

'Put your legs around me.'

Then he began ramming into her.

One hand he used against the wall for support; with the other he clamped one of her arms against the brickwork. She was powerless. And he loved it.

'Daisy,' he breathed, 'Daisy.' Then he shuddered. And shuddered again. Withdrawing, he let her go and she used him to steady herself. She rubbed at the wrist he'd jammed against the wall, a sullen look on her face.

'You fuckin' 'urt me,' she said. He could smell her muskiness on him and now it sickened him.

She gathered her torn garments around her as best she could. She looked across the field to where a dog was barking at the frozen snow on the grass. Eddie followed her gaze. A man was walking his dog. She searched for her sodden mules.

'You 'urt me,' she repeated.

'If I 'ad, you'd have known it.' Eddie tidied himself, tucked in his shirt, got out a comb and began running it through his thick hair.

'An' me name's not fuckin' Daisy, it's . . .' She got no further for he slapped her face hard.

'Your name is any fuckin' thing I want it to be.' Then he shoved her in the direction of the house. 'Now get to fuckin' work.'

Without looking at her again he turned and walked in the direction of the bloke with the dog.

'Mornin', mate,' he said. The old man leaned on his stick and eyed Eddie warily. The black mongrel dropped the ball from his wet jaws. He yelped playfully at Eddie then eyed the ball, flattening his paws either side of it on the grass.

'Want to play?' asked Eddie. He picked up the soggy ball and threw it. Excitedly, the dog ran. Eddie looked up at the sky.

'Gonna be a nice day, mate.' He began walking away, then turned back.

'An' a happy new year to you,' he said.

CHAPTER 14

March 1963

'I know why Vera loves you so much,' Daisy sniffled into the softness of Kibbles' fur. 'I love you, too. You don't hurt nobody, do you?' The cat smelled of Vera. His purring grew and filled her room. He was stretched out on her bed as though he owned the place. 'You've not got a care in the world, 'ave you?'

'An' I suppose you 'ave?' Vera stood in the doorway, in her fur coat, a steaming mug in her hand. 'Self-pity ain't gonna get you nowhere. Drink this. I made it strong. Caffeine gives yer a lift, did yer know that? God almighty, your face looks fuckin' 'orrible.'

'An' thank you for those few kind words,' Daisy said, sitting up and taking the mug of coffee that looked like mud and was going to taste like it. She put it on the bedside table. 'I could probably use that to varnish the counter downstairs.'

'See?' Vera said. 'You ain't even tasted it an' already you're brightening up. Bad visit?' The mattress springs squeaked as she plonked herself down. Kibbles rubbed his head against the back of her hand and idly she played with his ears. Daisy turned and pulled a feather pillow upright so she could sit more comfortably against the headboard.

'You off out?'

Vera's black fur coat had a high collar on which a diamante cat brooch winked in the electric light. A cheeky red felt hat with a veil and an enormous feather was pulled down on one side of her shining hair. Daisy always wondered how she managed to get the pencilled lines of her brows so even.

'Only a quickie. Ol' Donald out at Alverstoke. Been doin' 'im for years, ever since 'is wife died the day before the Coronation. Well, before that an' all if the real truth be known. But officially since then. Can't 'ave any real impropriety where magistrates are concerned, can we?'

Daisy giggled.

'There,' Vera said. 'Glad to see my job gives you a laugh. Want another laugh?' Daisy nodded.

Vera got up from the bed and unhooked the clasp of her coat collar. Taking the lapels, one in each hand, she swung open the fur and posed. A tiny frilled white apron with an embroidered bib was all that encompassed her top half. The bottom half was barely covered by a black shortie skirt beneath which black silk suspenders held up fishnet stockings. Red, impossibly high-heeled shoes with silly little bows on the front completed her outfit.

'You ain't got no knickers on,' Daisy gasped. Vera's flesh was creamy white between the tops of her stockings and her suspenders.

'Yes I 'ave. Only they're crotchless. 'E likes me like this.' She flicked her coat back into position and Daisy sat there stunned. 'Well, come on, 'ave another laugh.'

With the fur tucked around her again she looked the epitome of propriety.

'You're never going out like that?'

'He'll pick me up in 'is flash Bentley from the taxi rank. An' drop me back there later when we've played our little game of "master an' servant" at his posh home.'

Daisy had this sudden vision of the wind blowing the coat open and a taxi driver happily dying of shock.

'But before I gets brought 'ome 'e always treats me to a lovely meal 'e's cooked. Loves cooking 'e does. All this new cordon blue stuff, French wine and bread sticks. That's when we change roles, see. An' I tell him 'e ain't washed up properly an' I 'its 'im with this.' She turned, and from outside Daisy's bedroom door picked up a long cane feather duster. Each feather a different bright colour. Vera took her shocked expression as concern. 'It don't 'urt, Dais. It's a bit of fun. Go on. 'Ave a laugh. Take yer mind off Kenny an' 'is moody ways.'

Daisy got off the bed, disturbing Kibbles who rolled sideways but resettled himself, ignoring them. Putting her arms around Vera, she began to sniff.

'You're a tonic, you are. Don't know what I'd do without yer.'

'Well,' Vera said, disentangling herself. 'One thing you can do is to stay up 'ere an' get a bit of rest.'

'The caff?'

'Fuck the caff tonight. Suze is down there an' that's what you pay 'er for. Si's 'elping 'er out like 'e's a lovesick eight-year-old. They can cope. I'll be back 'ere about ten-thirty. An' if there's any clearin' up left I'll do it.' Daisy sniffed again and looked her in the eye.

'Not dressed like that, though, eh, Vera?'

She stared at Daisy for a few seconds.

'Silly cow,' she said. And clattered down the stairs on her daft heels.

Daisy closed the door on the sound of Ray Charles professing undying love on the jukebox, and the rest of the cafe noises. It had been the jukebox – well, actually, the choice of music played on the machine – that had started the silly row in the prison.

Kenny appeared not to have slept. His skin had what Daisy supposed was prison pallor, grey and dough-like. He was already seated in the scruffy visiting room when she was shown in. And he'd lost even more weight. His hands were shaking, though he was trying not to let her see because he had them clasped tightly in front of him on the formica table. Daisy scraped back the chair and sat down.

'Ain't they feeding you?' she asked. Which was the wrong thing to say and straightaway he gives her 'that' look. The one that tells Daisy she's in for a rough ride, that sets her on edge, having to be careful of everything she tells him.

'Ain't you got nothin' sensible to say?' Daisy knows she's missed the moment to kiss him. So she tries to take his hands in hers but he whips his off the table so she can't touch him. Her heart's thumping. She doesn't know what to say, what to do. So she tries again. Anything to get that sullen look off his face.

'They treatin' you all right?'

'Fuckin' 'ell,' he snaps. 'That all you got to ask? I'm in prison, for Chrissake.'

Daisy sighs. 'That new jukebox is popular,' she says brightly.

He looks at her and for a moment she thinks she can see the barriers coming down. Perhaps it's gonna be all right after all.

'What records you got on it?' So she goes through the new list: 'Wake Up Little Susie', 'Wheel of Fortune', 'Cathy's Clown', 'Wooden Heart'. He's nodding and listening, then he snaps.

'What you still got them ol' things on there for?'

''Cause the punters like 'em.'

'Bollocks! Well, I fuckin' don't.' And then he's ranting an' raving about how she doesn't know what she's doing and just when she's thinking she can't stand it no longer, he gets up and says, 'This visit's over.' So there she is sitting there like a spare part, and watching him stomp off with the prison warder fast on his heels. She looks around and all the room's gone quiet because everyone's looking at her like she's got three heads. So that was that. Her visit to her husband.

All the way home on the train she kept crying and trying to work out what she'd done wrong, so she could avoid doing it the next time. If there was a next time. Supposing he never sends her another visiting order? He's in there and she's out here and it's impossible to talk properly in that God-awful room. She misses him. 'Where's my lovely Kenny gone?' she moans.

Kibbles makes a bleating noise, just to let her know he's still there. He's lying on his back with his paws in the air. Daisy runs her hand over the paler, grey-coloured fur on his belly. He stays quite still, purring, watching her. Then he rolls over on to the *Evening News*, making it crackle.

'Forget it, eh, Kibbles? Otherwise it'll drive me round the twist, eh?' Since that seems to be the obvious answer, she undresses and gets into bed properly. After pulling up the white candlewick bedspread she leans over and picks up Vera's coffee. One sip and she's wired.

'Your mum might be a genius with men but she can't make soddin' coffee.'

She manages a couple of mouthfuls, sets it down again and glances at the newspaper. It's full of the Profumo and Keeler affair. Only they're still looking for Christine Keeler. Profumo's wife, the

British actress Valerie Hobson, is saying she'll stick by him because she believes he's done no wrong. John Profumo, the Minister of War, is saying he'll not hesitate to issue writs against anyone who libels or slanders him.

'Everyone's got their problems, cat. I can't be readin' this. There's enough trouble about, ain't there?' Daisy says.

She snuggles down with the soothing sound of Kibbles and the muffled music from below, overlaid now with rain battering against the windows. At last the winter is over and the snow has gone. She thinks about the telephone call from Moira earlier. Moira's got problems to end all problems, not that she was making a lot of sense. Daisy can't decide whether the shit she swallows gives her the problems or she takes it to forget the problems. Like New Year.

When Charles stopped the car outside a terraced house in a very ordinary London street, Daisy thought they'd arrived at the wrong place. But almost immediately the front door was opened by a grey-haired motherly type in a wrap-around pinny. Charles got out of the car and went straight up and kissed her on the cheek, then opened Daisy's door on the pavement side. As she climbed out he opened the nearside front car door and put the flowers into her hands.

'They for me? Well, thank you, love. How thoughtful.'

'Hello,' Daisy said, trying to pass her the flowers, but instead of taking them she enveloped Daisy in a hug.

'Hello, dear, I'm Violet. I expect you could do with a nice cup of tea. The kettle's on.' From the open doorway smells of baking assailed Daisy's nostrils and she realised she was starving.

Violet was peering into the back of the car where Moira lay curled on the seat.

'Gone off, has she?' She turned to Charles, who'd taken off his peaked cap and thrown it on the seat. Already he'd placed Daisy's holdall just inside the front door of the house. 'You know what to do, Charles, there's a good boy.'

Over six feet tall and built like a brick shithouse, a boy he was not, thought Daisy. But he didn't seem to mind her calling him that. He picked up Moira as though she was a doll and carried her into the house and up some stairs just inside the front door. Moira opened her eyes, saw where she was, then closed them again. But not before she'd looked for Daisy.

'You won't go, will you, Dais?' Daisy shook her head.

'Come along in,' said Violet. But Daisy was worried about Moira.

'She ain't well,' she said, following Violet down the hall to the kitchen. There was a scrubbed table with chairs around it and a dresser with willow-pattern dishes, cups and saucers. A butler sink gleamed white as driven snow with a curtain around the bottom of it, and a gas cooker was producing the heavenly smell.

'We know that, love,' Violet said. She took the flowers and set them on the draining board, then bent down and produced a glass vase from underneath the sink. After filling the vase with water and settling the flowers, she placed them in the centre of the table. 'Don't they look nice?' She stood facing Daisy and put her hands on her hips. 'Why, you're only a little slip of a thing, aren't you?' Daisy could smell violets. She saw Daisy sniff. 'Scones in the oven. And that's my perfume. To match my name. And yours is Daisy, so we're two pretty flowers together, aren't we?' She laughed. She wore no jewellery apart from her wedding ring. On her feet were comfortable brown-checked slippers with red pom-poms. She pulled out a chair. 'Take your lovely white hat off, dearie, and your green jacket, else you'll feel the cold later. Sit down and talk to me while I finish the baking. We're all worried about Moira, and that's a fact.'

A large tray was laid with five cups and saucers. Violet filled a milk jug and set it next to the sugar bowl. She started opening freshly made scones from a wire cooling tray. Inside each she dabbed cream, then raspberry jam that looked home made. She piled the scones on a large willow-pattern plate and put that on the tray. On the stove the kettle started to hum. She removed the whistle, letting the kettle steam, then went out into the hall.

'Tea's ready,' she called. Coming back she made two pots of tea. The first in a large brown earthenware pot. Then she filled a smaller one, hand-painted with violets. 'My Roy bought me this,' she told Daisy. 'Just let me get them their tea and then we'll have a nice chat. Hungry?' Daisy nodded. 'There's more scones in the oven,' she said. 'Boys like their sweet things, don't they? They get hungry when they're upstairs discussing business.'

Daisy heard steps on the stair carpet. A tall, well-built man came into the kitchen. He was very smart in a dark pinstriped suit and shiny black shoes, his hair Brylcreemed back from his forehead. For a fleeting moment he reminded Daisy of Bri, Eddie's mate. Then she realised she was being silly. Same build, same type of gypsy looks, but Bri's hair was the colour of conkers. This man was dark and practically filled the kitchen. He nodded politely to Daisy and she smiled in return.

'This the tray, Mum?'

'Yes, Roy. Be careful now. This is Moira's friend Daisy.' He smiled again. 'Tell the boys there's more cake if they want.' He lifted the tray with ease.

'You don't 'alf look after us.'

'Get away with you, you're all my boys, aren't you? Except you are my favourite because you're my very, very own.' He gave her a cheeky grin and went out. Violet bustled at the oven then produced another tray of scones, steaming with the heat, golden brown and risen beautifully.

'I could do with some of those in the caff,' Daisy said.

'I'll give you the recipe,' Violet answered, putting the baking tray on the draining board. After transferring the scones to the wire tray to cool, she poured the tea and put jam and cream on scones for Daisy. She was just like one of those old-fashioned mums they had in the films.

'Shall I take up somethin' for Moira?'

'God bless you, no. She won't want anything. She'll sleep for ages. And sleep's more good than tea, isn't it?'

Daisy nodded. On the window sill were cheap plaster of Paris figures, like the ones kids make at school or the type of ornaments you win at fairs.

'Roy got me those,' Violet said proudly. 'Took him just three darts to win the little elephant. The space ship he made in the infants' class.' There was also a framed photo of three men and two women, dressed for an evening out. Two men, alike as peas in a pod, in suits, with their arms about a middle-aged woman. The men looked familiar to Daisy. Next to them was the man she had just met, also suited, with one arm about Violet's shoulder.

'Two shy Violets with their boys. The twins and Roy at the opening of their new club, The Kentucky, in Stepney. The twins spent a lot of money on that place. A couple of thousand pounds on carpets and such. And do you know, it's going to be used for a new film being made called *Sparrows Can't Sing* with that lovely girl Barbara in it – you know, Barbara Windsor? You got kiddies?'

'No, not yet. One day, I 'ope.'

'Of course, with your Kenny away, you're not likely to have any yet, are you, dear?'

Daisy shook her head and bit into a scone. It tasted wonderful.

'What's wrong with Moira?' she asked, through a mouthful of crumbs.

'Nerves.' She treated Daisy to a warm smile, then said, 'I won't beat about the bush, dear. Moira's been phoning you a lot, hasn't she?'

'Is that why I was brought 'ere? So you could find out what she's been telling me?' That stopped Violet for a moment but she soon regained her composure.

'No flies on you, is there, love? So what *has* she been telling you?'

'I 'ave to be honest with you, Violet. I like Moira and I like you. But Moira says a lot, stuff I don't understand an' don't want to know. Do I make myself plain?'

Violet stared at her for a few moments. Then her eyes narrowed and her forehead creased as though she was making a decision.

'We understand each other perfectly, Daisy. Now, how about another cup of tea?' Daisy smiled. Interrogation over, for a while, she thought. Violet got up from the chair and said without warning,

'What do you want most from life, Daisy?'

Without hesitation, Daisy answered, 'Peace. The cafe doesn't belong to me. Kenny was left to manage it. Until the owner's will has been sorted out, I need to make a go of it. It's not posh, just a working man's place that I want kept trouble free.'

'Good sentiments, dear. Keep the police happy and they'll let you alone. If you can't keep them happy, make them leave you alone.' Daisy wasn't sure she understood her. Then Violet asked, 'Anyone else living there apart from you, Kenny and your brother-in-law?' Since Daisy hadn't mentioned Eddie, she guessed someone had done their homework on her background.

'One permanent lodger and a girl living in who 'elps me in the caff. And one room, spare, which I keep for bed an' breakfasts.' Violet nodded her head. There was little point in keeping the truth from her as Violet seemed to know all about her.

'So you're alone, apart from them?'

Daisy nodded. 'Me mum died.'

'You poor dear.' She'd brought the teapot back to the table. 'We'll let it stand, shall we?'

'She 'ad a tumour, ill for quite a while. She was glad I had Kenny. She said he wasn't the sharpest knife in the drawer but he wouldn't cut me deep, neither. She was right. Sums my Kenny up.'

'Want to talk about her?'

'Not much to say, really. She loved me. I never knew me dad. She said 'e was killed in the war. Said 'e was a kind man. We was poor. 'Ad to stuff me shoes with cardboard when it rained, to stop the wet gettin' in.'

'Didn't we all?' Daisy knew then Violet had had it rough as well. She could see by her eyes she was thinking about things she didn't want to remember.

'You remind me of her.'

'Do I?' Violet's eyebrows had risen in surprise. 'I'd have liked a girly. Only ever had the one boy, you see.' Daisy heard a chair scrape against lino upstairs. She looked expectantly at Violet.

'Only the boys. Tell me some more.' She poured out tea and Daisy put in milk and stirred it with a spoon. A small silver apostle spoon. Daisy withdrew it from the cup and studied it. 'Set of six, belonged to my mum,' Violet said. 'I'll give them to you, as a present.' Daisy shook her head.

'You're a good girl. An honest girl. I feel it in my bones.'

'Thanks, Violet. I miss me mum. It was difficult to believe she'd died. She was in remission. Kenny an' me was movin' into the flat in Henry Street. We knew she didn't have long. I'd got 'er settled in the front room downstairs in 'er house, I was with 'er nearly all the time. Mrs Lovell, the next door neighbour, used to sit with 'er sometimes.' After all this time the pain was still just as acute as the day it happened. Tears stung Daisy's eyes. Violet searched in her pinny pocket and came out with a neatly ironed hanky.

'Mum got me an' Kenny together an' told us she didn't 'ave anything much to show for 'er life. Kenny butted in an' said all 'e ever wanted was me, that I'd made a big difference to 'im. Mum said she 'ad a bit of jewellery, made Kenny go to the sideboard an' get out a tiny black lacquered box. Inside was two brooches. I'd never taken no notice of these brooches 'cause I'd seen 'er wearin' them almost every day. One was a gold-coloured bar with a gold leaf design and an ivory rose. The other one was a small half-moon shape with marcasites. She said my dad had given them to her, an' when her an' Dad had no money they'd always managed without selling them. The 'alf-moon diamond brooch had belonged to Dad's mother, the ivory one was Dad's wedding gift to her. I told her we could sort all that stuff out later. I never wanted to face up to the fact she was goin' to die.'

Violet was silent, waiting for her to continue. Daisy marvelled that she was opening her heart to a woman she'd only just met, talking and thinking about things that had lain dormant for years.

'The next morning the doctor an' the nurse came. Mum was perky. She'd even had a bit of breakfast, only porridge, but it was somethin'. That afternoon Kenny said his brother had found out they was takin' blokes on at the buildin' site in the town, he was out of work, as usual. An' would I go with him as it would be a good time to meet 'is brother who'd just returned from up north. Before that he'd been in the nick. Eddie was after a job as well an' they was going to meet up.'

'Did he get the job?' asked Violet.

'That was the funny thing. There wasn't no jobs going after all. Kenny was furious. We waited in Bert's caff an' Eddie was late. He 'adn't been to the building site so we did 'im a good turn an' told 'im the bad news. It was that day me mum died.'

'Oh, Daisy.' Violet got up and came across and put her arms around her. 'What a terrible thing, dear.'

'Someone started knockin' on Mrs Lovell's back door. Off she goes to see who it is. She 'as to go out our front door an' round the alley to get to her back door 'cause she always kept 'er front door bolted. When she eventually gets round the back, there's no one there. She reckoned it was kids, well you know what little buggers they can be. Anyway, when she gets back to our house, Mum's lying on the bleedin' floor. Doctor reckons she tried to get out of bed an' it was too much for 'er.'

'Death comes when we least expect it, love. Did you give her a nice send-off?'

'Best I could, Violet. She 'ad no insurance so I got a Provi cheque out for most of it an' Kenny's brother Eddie chipped in, which was really good of him as he didn't hardly know me an' he'd never even met Mum.'

'What about the brooches? Couldn't you have sold one of them? That would have saved you going into debt, wouldn't it?'

Daisy sighed. 'Many times I've wished I'd kept that little lacquered box instead of it going back in the drawer. 'Cause when we went to look it wasn't nowhere to be found.'

'How strange? Do you think Mrs Love—?'

'No way, Violet. Mrs Lovell 'ad known about those brooches for years. She could have 'ad them any time she wanted. She was Mum's friend. No, I think Mum put that box somewhere else. But where?'

'They've not turned up?' Daisy shook her head. Her cup of tea had gone cold. To hide her tears from Violet, she started clearing the table. As she was running hot water into the sink to wash up, the kitchen door swung open. A man stood there with the tray.

'Just in time, I see.' He put the tray on the draining board. He was very softly spoken, with a smooth London accent. 'You must be Daisy?' He held out his hand, but Daisy's were all wet. She quickly dried them on a tea towel and shook his hand. It was warm, firm.

'This is Ron Kray,' said Violet.

'You didn't 'ave to tell me. I recognise 'im from the photo.' Daisy gestured towards the photo frame. She rolled up the sleeves of her white blouse where the cuffs were damp, just for something to do, because she didn't know what else to say to him. He spoke to Violet but she couldn't catch what he said.

'Goodbye, Daisy. I'm sure we'll meet again,' he said softly, before closing the kitchen door behind him. Her knees were trembling. I've just met Ron Kray, she kept thinking. I've just met a real live London gangster. Then the kitchen door opened again and Roy came back in.

He smiled. His strong white teeth showed just a tiny chip in front, a flaw that made him all the more attractive. Fucking hell, Daisy could see why Moira had grabbed him and married him. Daisy could see kindness in his slate-grey eyes, yet she caught cruelty hidden there too. Not a man to be crossed. Her mum used to say that eyes are the windows of the soul. Daisy reckoned she was right.

'The lads said thanks, Mum. I'll just see them off.'

'All right, Roy. Tell Jack I'll see his dad next week at the hospital.' He left the kitchen and Daisy heard voices and footsteps and then car engines starting up. The front door slammed and Roy came in again.

'You really did us proud, Mum.' Turning to Daisy, he said, 'I think she deserves a cuddle, don't you?' Without waiting for an answer he grabbed Violet and whirled her around.

'Get off, you daft lump,' she squealed. But she was loving every minute, Daisy could see that. She turned back to the washing up in the sink. Violet stopped her.

'That's enough chores. Why don't you go upstairs and see if Moira's awake? You're in the small bedroom at the back. She's going to be a good friend to your wife,' she added, for Roy's benefit.

In the hall Roy picked up Daisy's bag. She noticed his heavy gold ring with the large black 'R', the thick chunky gold cufflinks at his wrist. She wondered why they all lived together in such a small house when there was obvious wealth.

'Mum put you in the small room. Moira and I are in the front. Mum sleeps downstairs. Her legs are not what they were.' From that she guessed the men's meeting had taken place in the other upstairs room. 'Mum was born in this house. Says she'll only leave it in a box.'

'She's nice, your mum,' Daisy said. He swung the door open to a room that was all chintz and frills, spotless. He put the bag on the bed then he sat down as well. His long legs stretched out in front of him.

'I would like Moira to be your friend,' he said.

'I wouldn't be here if she wasn't already.'

'If she could phone you from time to time?'

'She already does.'

'I'm aware of that. I'd be very *grateful* . . .' he stressed the word, 'if she could go on doing it.'

'Not a problem,' Daisy said, but she wondered what she was getting herself into, and what was behind his words.

'She has no friends of her own. None that are good for her. I could make it worth your while.'

'If I didn't like you, I could be insulted by that remark.' He looked taken aback at that, but then he smiled.

'Gutsy. I like that. And if her imaginings become – how shall we say – wilder?'

'Listen Roy Kemp, I don't need no fuckin' monetary gain for bein' a friend.'

'Good answer. But I run a family firm, and debts are always paid and collected. In full. So, I'll owe you, for now. Got business down your way too – Portsmouth, Southampton. By the way, what's your star sign?' What on earth had birth dates got to do with anything, Daisy wondered.

'November. I'm a Scorpio.'

'Excellent. You know how to keep secrets then, don't you?'

'Yes. An' don't forget the sting in me tail neither!'

'Well, I'm a Pisces so we're two water signs together.' He was about to say more when a voice called,

'Daisy? Is that you?'

Moira put her head round the door. 'I woke up and thought you'd gone.' Her face was pillow creased.

'But it's New Year's Eve an' we're goin' out,' Daisy said.

Moira looked confused then said brightly, as though she'd suddenly remembered, 'Of course we are.' She stared at Roy. 'Why are you in here with Daisy?' He moved towards her and, putting his arms around her, kissed her lightly on her forehead. Daisy noticed how small Moira was against him in her stockinged feet.

'I was showing Daisy her room, sweetheart.' She seemed relieved.

'I want Daisy to come and choose something to wear.' She stepped towards Daisy and took one of her hands. With a gentle squeeze to Moira's shoulder he went downstairs. 'I want all my girls dolled up to the nines,' he shouted back, as Moira led Daisy to her and Roy's bedroom.

'Pick something out. Anything you like. I'm going to have a shower.' Moira swung open the door to a mirror-fronted wardrobe running the length of one wall. The rest of the room was all satin and frills. Daisy couldn't imagine Roy in it.

A shower? Daisy could hardly contain herself. That meant she could use the shower too! She began sifting through Moira's clothes. Expensive perfume wafted all over her. There was so much choice! Glittery stuff? Not really me, she thought. Long evening clothes? No. On the bed was a plastic-wrapped, frilly-skirted, white long-sleeved dress with a fitted strapless top. Daisy guessed that was Moira's outfit. She noted the style and decided she ought to wear something similar. She didn't want to look out of place. Then she remembered Moira had the strange habit of copying a dead woman's clothing, so she opted for a dark green, fitted, sleeveless little number with a hem that just rested on her knees. It would also go well with the black bag and shoes she'd brought with her.

Moira came back into the bedroom, her hair in a shower cap with big floppy flowers on it and a white towel the size of a sheet wrapped round her.

'That's what I'd like to wear.' Daisy held out the green dress for inspection.

'Fine. The bathroom's yours.' Wish it was, Daisy thought. One day – one day, Daisy girl – you'll have a bathroom, she promised herself.

Thank God Moira'd left the water running. Daisy looked at the shower handle with its red and blue symbols and decided she'd have made a right bollocks of it if she'd had to switch the thing on herself.

For ten minutes she was in bloody heaven, hot water running all over her and chasing Moira's expensive soap. Back home, Daisy sometimes went to the public baths, where, for a few coppers, you could have a bath in a green-painted wooden cubicle with really hot water. You had to take your own towels and soap but it was worth it for the lovely fresh feeling you got afterwards. Most days though she made do with standing in a bowl of hot water and having a good wash.

She came out of the bathroom smelling like Vera on a Saturday night. She must have had a squirt of every smelly thing she could lay her hands on.

As she was getting dressed Daisy noticed the cause of some of Moira's mood swings.

'What's them marks on your arms?' Daisy knew what they were, all right, but she wanted Moira to tell her. Immediately Moira tried to hide the tell-tale tracks. Daisy realised she always had her arms covered. She grabbed hold of Moira. 'Does Roy and Violet know about this?'

Moira nodded. 'I'm clean now.' Daisy didn't believe her for one minute. Moira's voice fell to a whisper. 'Well, I only take a few poppers now. Perhaps a few lines of coke sometimes. Don't tell on me. I can let you 'ave some.' Daisy pushed her away so hard she had to make a grab for her before she spun into the mirrored doors.

'Seen too many brains turn to mush with that crap. You're a fuckin' fool. Why are you doin' it?'

Moira looked frightened. 'He wants a kiddie.'

'You should be pleased about that. Seems a reasonable request to me.'

'He's got someone else.'

Here we go again, Daisy thought. She had watched Roy's behaviour towards Moira. Was this really how a bloke with a bit on the side behaved? Then again, he must have quite a few women giving him the eye. And Moira? If she carried on like fuckin' Dopey Dora, who could blame Roy?

'An' pumpin' yourself full of that shit is goin' to solve things?'

'Don't tell him.'

'I thought you said 'e knew?'

'He sent me away to get clean.'

'Didn't work then, did it?'

'Up until I found out about Elaine, it did.'

'Are you sure this ... this Elaine is his girlfriend?'

She nodded. 'I think so.'

Daisy shook her head. Moira was making her brain hurt. What if this was another of her fantasies? Daisy looked at the bedside clock. They had about fifteen minutes left to finish getting ready.

'If I thought I was going to have his kid, I'd kill it.'

'Don't talk wild like that. You love 'im.'

'Of course. But I'd do it to spite him because he's killing me inside by even touching another woman.'

'Good thing you ain't 'avin' a kiddie, then,' Daisy said flippantly, but inside she was shitting herself listening to Moira's ramblings. 'Look,' she said, 'we'll talk about this when we get back tonight. In the meantime, it sticks out a fuckin' mile he loves you. So let's go, enjoy tonight, eh?'

Daisy gave her a quick hug, smiled at her in the mirror and handed her a plastic box containing false eyelashes she'd spotted on the dressing table.

'Put these on. They'll give you a lift.' Moira's eyes brightened immediately and she grinned at Daisy.

'One thing you don't need is false lashes, Daisy. You've got lovely eyes. Reminds me of someone . . .'

'Joan Collins!' they both said together and laughed.

Violet was dressed in blue glitter and Roy in a dark suit and pointed leather shoes. Daisy reckoned they were Italian. She felt like the Queen as they drove through London. They even had a drink of champagne in the car, served in long glasses, not Babycham ones. She was giggling like a kid, Moira too.

The Rainbow Club lived up to its name, with its coloured twinkling lights. Roy and Moira knew everybody and introduced Daisy to so many people she forgot their names as soon as she heard them. There was dancing, and food like she'd never eaten before, and she lost count of how many glasses of champagne she sank. Some faces were familiar, then Daisy realised they were only familiar because she'd seen them at the pictures. The little busty blonde, and the other glamorous blonde with the long page-boy hairstyle, in a dress that sparkled like diamonds, who told Daisy that her mother-in-law had lived in Gosport. And then they were all kissing each other because Big Ben said it was New Year's Day.

*

It had all passed in a rainbow-coloured haze, but it was more a muddy brown when Daisy was woken up by Violet in the morning with a cup of tea. Her mouth tasted like Kibbles' litter tray.

'Breakfast in ten minutes,' Violet told her. She looked all bright-eyed and bushy-tailed.

'Don't want any, thanks. Just gimme that lovely tea.'

When Daisy got downstairs, feeling like she'd been run over by a truck, Charles was already waiting outside in the car, suited and booted.

'Roy's out on business. Moira's still asleep. Here's the sponge cake, dear.' Violet handed Daisy a large biscuit tin and a slip of paper. 'And here's the scone recipe.' Then she produced a dress bag. 'Hope you won't be offended, but you looked so lovely in this dress last night, Moira decided you should have it.' Daisy didn't know what to say, she was so choked up. She put her arms around Violet and kissed her pink, violet-scented cheek.

Daisy fell asleep on the way home. When they arrived back in Gosport she'd no idea whether it was morning, afternoon or night. She asked Charles to drop her off at the fire station at the end of the road. When she walked into the cafe Eddie was the first person she saw.

'Hallo, Dais,' he said, in that lovely easy way he had of talking, as though she was the only person who mattered to him in the whole wide world. 'I was worried about you.'

Daisy put the biscuit tin on the counter top.

'No need to worry. Want a bit of cake?'

Since then Moira had been phoning and phoning but Daisy hadn't been up to see her again.

Now the rain had stopped, and there was Kibbles, curled up like a furry doughnut beside her.

CHAPTER 15

1 May 1963

Eddie heard the telephone before he reached the street door. It continued ringing until he lifted the receiver.

'Dais,' he shouted up the stairway. 'It's that woman for you.'

After a few seconds she came padding down, wrapped in her old blue coat. Her hair was sticking up like harvested corn, mascara smudged around her eyes. As she neared him, he caught the scent of talcum powder. She'd obviously been woken from sleep

He went up to his room where he changed into a black tee-shirt and jeans, exchanging his black shoes for a pair of grey leather slip-ons. His suit, after brushing, he hung in the wardrobe. He leaned forward and stared in the dressing table mirror, pulling a face as he checked his teeth, his skin, his reflection. He decided he liked what he saw. Then he combed his dark hair straight back and flicked the front forward until it suited him, just right.

As he was descending the stairs he heard Daisy talking.

'Moira, I'm sure he really loves you. No, I'm not cross you phoned. Honestly.'

He saw Daisy move her slight weight from one foot to the other, then run her fingers through her hair which made it stick up even more. He smiled to himself. Clearly Daisy was trying to pacify the woman on the other end of the line. She was like that, he thought. An eternal fuckin' peacemaker.

'I will come up. I promise. But we're busy here at this time of the year. Holiday makers an' weekend sailors with their boats moored at the boatyards. Yes, of course. Yes.'

He heard her say goodbye and the phone click back on its cradle. He walked towards her.

'Cuppa?'

'God, yes.'

'You don't 'ave to call me God. It's Eddie, remember?' She gave him a weak smile. She looked tired. 'Is everythin' all right?'

She nodded. 'That was Moira.'

The bitch was always phoning, morning, noon and night. Didn't seem to care what time, neither. Didn't the cow realise how hard Dais worked? She looked awful, her flesh showing sharp angles where once it had been rounded. Of course Daisy had always been slight, but now ... He looked her up and down.

'Ain't you got a proper dressing gown?'

She seemed puzzled at first by his remark.

'Me? No. I 'ad a grey flannel one when I was a little dot, an' wore it till the arms reached me elbows and the bottom came up to me middle. This ol' coat serves me just fine.'

She'd look good in a bloody sack, thought Eddie. He went into the kitchen and busied himself making tea and setting out cups. Everything was spotless from the previous night. Daisy had followed him in and was now staring through the window across the way at Murphy's sales assistant, setting out pots and pans on hooks outside the ironmonger's, ready for the new day. An array of flower pots, compost, flowering climbers and bedding plants lined the pavement, making a bright splash of colour in the dingy street.

'Didn't realise it was so late. I didn't sleep so well last night.' She looked up at the sky. 'Gonna be a scorcher today, Eddie.' She turned to him. 'You just come in, or just goin' out?'

'Dunno. When I'm with you I don't know whether I'm comin' or goin'.'

He watched her reaction. It was a second or two before the meaning of his words hit her.

'Oh, shut up.' But he could see she didn't mean it. Her smile told him that.

'Goin' up to see Moira?'

Daisy shrugged her shoulders. He tried again. 'You 'ad a good time at New Year, didn't you?' She turned to face him and nodded. 'You can't work all the time, girl. You need to get out of 'ere sometimes.'

She'd never let on to him about what she'd got up to in London, same as she'd never admit to being worn out. Daisy could be as tight as a duck's arse when she wanted. But he liked that about her. Most women were too gabby.

'I wish,' she said.

'Kenny would want you to enjoy yourself. You know he would. Just because he's banged up, he won't expect you to do fuckin' time an' all.'

He slid her tea towards her. Daisy sat down on a high stool, the counter between them.

'Glad you think so.'

He leaned across so that he was mere inches from her. He took a deep breath to give him courage.

'I could take you out, if you wanted? We could have a day in the country. See that new James Bond film with Sean Connery, *From Russia With Love*. Go for a meal? To the races?' His heart was beating fast. He'd done it, finally asked her.

'What? Sort of keep it in the family, like?'

'Daisy, I never meant . . .'

He didn't know what to say. Obviously she'd thought he wanted a shag. He wished he'd kept his fuckin' big mouth shut.

'I know what you meant, Eddie Lane.'

It was a waste of time explaining he really would like to take her out, be nice to her, get rid of some of that tiredness beneath her eyes, make her laugh. It had been a long time since he'd seen her smile, really smile. It was gonna take forever to get on the right side of Daisy again. Trouble was, she didn't know what he was feeling inside, didn't know he was really sorry for taking advantage of her that time in Henry Street. And she could cut him to shreds with a single careless remark. She was looking at him, staring at him with those big eyes of hers. Later, he knew he would think of all those witty quips he could have spat back at her, but right now he didn't have a thing to say. Not a thing. And now he could feel one of his infernal headaches starting up.

Desolation flooded his heart. He was as powerless now as when he'd been a kid and Pappy would shut him in the coal hole, that awful cupboard beneath the stairs. Hours he'd be in there, trying to see through the pitch black, his nose stuffed with the rank smell of coal dust and droppings from the scrabbling creatures that lived in the cavity walls. He always tried not to cry when he was in there, because his tears made channels of dirt down his face and he would get a thrashing afterwards for 'rolling around in there', as Pappy claimed. Even when he kept quite, quite still, barely breathing, the dust seemed to drift towards him. That was why he didn't like dirt and muck now, he supposed.

Any little thing could upset Pappy, and he'd lose it. Eddie would be shut in the coal hole when Pappy was sober, and when he was drunk. Once he'd been in there all night because Pappy had had a right skinful, then fallen asleep. He'd got so cold, so very cold. He could smell it now, the cold and the dust, remember the fear pounding away inside him. He pulled himself back from the past. It didn't do to dwell on stuff like that. Gave him headaches, it did, remembering that shit. What goes around, comes around, thought Eddie. He had the upper hand now. Wasn't Pappy now in his own special cold, dark place? And he, Eddie Lane, was . . .

'I might just do that.'

What was Daisy saying? That she would let him take her out? No. She didn't mean it. She was having him on, just trying to keep him sweet while she kept him at arm's length.

Well, two could play at that game. He'd show her he didn't care one way or the other.

'Anythin' you say, Daisy. Anythin' you say.'

And he gave her a wink before going back upstairs to his room.

Susie watched Eddie chatting to his three henchmen, as she called them. She wouldn't trust any of them further than she could fuckin' throw 'em. But she had to admit with Eddie around it was peaceful enough in the cafe. And he didn't scare her so much neither, these days. In fact he didn't come near her nor speak to her hardly, unless he had to.

There was quite a few different customers using the cafe now. Daisy said it was a working man's cafe. Only in the beginning they never seemed to get anyone in who actually had a bleedin' job.

It had been mostly yobs, users, pushers and drunks then, but the drunks had started going down to the Dive now. Eddie had also had a quiet word around town. Almost overnight most of the pushers and the druggies had stopped coming in. Daisy said all customers was welcome, even the layabouts, as long as they didn't linger too long over one cuppa. And the prossies was well liked by Daisy because they didn't try to pick up casuals in there. Daisy said they was working women an' if they was working the streets they deserved a bit of warmth an' a cuppa.

Actually the cafe was getting to be a nice place, much better than when Bert was running it, so she'd heard regulars say. Breakfast time was well busy, men was coming in at lunchtimes for proper food. In the afternoons young women brought in their mums and their kiddies, and in the evenings all sorts came. The jukebox played nonstop then. The girls with their bouffant hair and the lads chatting an' laughing an' scooters parked outside belonging to the fluffy-hooded parka crowd.

The food was good too, mostly fry-ups with chips. Pies, sausages, eggs, chicken bits and that new stuff – quiche, Daisy called it. But you couldn't fool Susie, she knew it was really only egg and bacon flan.

Daisy had a lot of home-made stuff on the menu too, scones, and her famous bread pudding, and a sponge cake that melted in your mouth. She'd brought that recipe back from London.

Susie had asked her about London. She'd wanted to know what the dresses was like at the New Year's bash. Whether she'd danced. All sorts of things like that. Because London was, well, sort of special, wasn't it? Not like this dreary ol' backwater. But Daisy had just smiled and said, 'It was great. I 'ad a lovely time.' Like trying to get blood out of a stone, it was, when Daisy didn't want to tell you something. Not that Susie was complaining. She knew she could rely on Daisy never to talk about her own past with its dark secrets.

She worshipped Daisy, never minded any extra work Daisy might want doing. An' she loved being in the cafe. It was a warm, happy place. And for the first time in her life she had money in her pocket to buy nice things.

Most of all now she wasn't frightened when she went to bed. Not like when she lived with Mum. In fact she was happy, really happy. Except for one thing. Si.

'Why won't you let me, Suze? You know I love you.'

They'd been to a dance at Lee Tower Ballroom. Lee on the Solent was a tiny seaside place about four miles from Gosport. It wasn't a busy area but it did boast a sand and shingle beach, a few shops and a good dance hall right by the sea.

The place was jam-packed. There was girls in tight skirts, girls in flared dresses, blondes, brunettes and redheads. An' fellers giving them the eye and propping up the bar until near the end of the evening when it would be time to make their choices an' try their luck. It had been a really good night out, with an excellent band that played the latest tunes, and a silver ball thing on the ceiling that glittered as it spun slowly round.

The evening was warm, and afterwards they'd eaten ice-creams bought from the kiosk outside the dance hall. Then they'd walked along the shoreline, holding hands. The waves had splashed over the pebbles, clean and salty smelling, not like the mudbath at the ferry in Gosport. A warm breeze and the scent of the flowers in the hanging baskets along the side of the main road made Susie feel as though she was on some tropical island, like the ones she'd seen in films.

They'd lain on the beach on Si's coat so Suze wouldn't get tar on her new taffeta skirt. She'd snuggled into him. He smelled of beer and peppermints and himself, which was comforting.

'I really care about you, Suze,' he'd whispered, his mouth close to her ear.

'I really like you too, Si.'

He'd pulled her close and kissed her. She liked him kissing her. It was slow, lazy and gentle and she never wanted it to stop. Then he pushed his tongue into her mouth.

She was shocked by that, and a little scared. No one had ever kissed her like that. It was nice, though, like exploring new boundaries, but lightly, softly, sweetly. And she wasn't being forced to do things, not like before.

After kissing for a while he tentatively put a hand on one of her breasts. She'd been expecting this. After all, men liked women's breasts, didn't they? She didn't like it much but for Si's sake she pretended she did. Even when he'd pulled up her new pink angora sweater and lifted her white cotton bra over her breasts so he could bend his head down and fill his mouth with one.

Then it happened. He was nuzzling her and teasing her nipple with his tongue and teeth. And then his other hand, which had been mostly around her waist when it wasn't pulling up clothing, started to creep up her stockinged leg. Her heart was beating very fast. She let him run the flat of his hand across her nylon stocking. He was gentle, so gentle, not tearing and grabbing and hurting. His fingers continued exploring, past the soft white skin between her stocking tops and suspenders, then to her white cotton panties. He touched her fanny lightly then began massaging it. She lay quite still. She liked what he was doing. It was giving her a funny feeling down there, between her legs, that she had never experienced before. It was like a flower becoming moist and opening up with the warmth and gentleness of his fingers.

Because they were lying so close she could feel the heat, through the thin grey cloth of his trousers, of his penis, big and iron hard, its engorged head pushing against her.

Then his fingers pulled the cotton of her panties aside and she almost gasped as he touched, oh so tenderly, inside the cotton to her very private place where ...

'No!' She pushed him away and jumped up, scattering sand and stones and making him roll from her with a look of such astonishment on his face that she was scared. It was only Si, but she was terrified.

She ran as though her life depended on it, pulling her clothes in place as she went. Finally she collapsed against a wooden breakwater, and the tears came as she remembered the pain, the degradation, the shame of before, of her mother's boyfriend and his callused hands on her skin. Men ... She felt like she had been swallowed whole and spat out.

Si reached her.

'What's the matter, Susie?' He was out of breath, his eyes full of concern. He tried to pull her towards him.

'No, don't.'

'What is it? Did I frighten you? Wasn't I doing it right?' He stood there, with the wind ruffling his beautiful red hair, his eyes downcast. 'I've never done it before,' he whispered. 'It's what men and women do, ain't it?'

She took a deep breath, pushed her hair away from her face and put her arms around him, feeling the warmth of his body against the chill of her skin, experiencing the comfort that was hers for the taking, and wanting to ease his confusion.

'I know,' she said. And of course she did, too well.

But Si didn't know about the abuse she had endured in the past. He didn't know and she couldn't tell him.

'It's your first time,' he said. 'You're bound to be scared.' He was holding her tightly, stroking her hair, her neck, her back. She should have said something then, but the moment passed. The fear came back that if she told the truth, her beloved Si would think she was a slag, that it was all her own fault.

She couldn't risk losing him.

In that moment she knew she loved him.

In virtual silence they caught the bus home.

At the street door of the cafe he gave her a chaste kiss on the cheek.

'I won't hurt you,' he said. 'But one step at a time, eh, Suze?' Then he left her. But the pain gnawed away inside her. She had to be honest with him, had to tell him the truth, even if it meant losing him.

Vera was furious. She was also freezing cold. Although the weather had turned and it was warmer at nights, it had rained. It had stopped now but the dampness was eating into her. She never heeded the warning 'Ne'er cast a clout 'til May be out.' She didn't know what a fuckin' clout was but it had to be warmer than the sleeveless dress with buttons down the front that she was wearing.

'Fuckin' Rufus. Late again,' she mumbled to herself. Vera named him Rufus because he'd never told her his proper name. She'd called him Rufus the Red one night because of his ginger hair, and the name had stuck. She had no doubt that he'd turn up tonight. He hadn't missed a Thursday in four years. If he wasn't such a nice guy, she'd go home, maybe find a clout an' put it on to keep warm. 'Stop it, Vera, you been on the game so long it's turning you fuckin' doo-lally.' She laughed to herself. 'Well, Rufus, me old cock, you'll have to cough up a bit extra for me discomfort, that's all.'

'Still waitin' for him, Vera?' It was Elsie, her friend, looking a bit ragged tonight. Elsie specialised in sailors. She could tell you the name of every naval ship due in port for the next month. Looked 'em up in the *Evening News*, she did. Elsie's patch was sacred. She'd earned the right to that choice piece of Gosport an' she had the scars to prove it.

'Hallo, duck,' Vera said. 'He's me last punter for today. Won't take long, 'e never does. I'm planning on washing me hair tonight.' But Elsie wanted to confide.

'You know that cow Bella, from Forton Road, has pinched one of my clients?'

'No!' Bella wasn't a town tom and Vera was surprised. Elsie worked the patch in the middle of the High Street near the Star and Garter, a matelots' pub.

'I goes into the Star to find Tommy an' I sees 'im sittin' in the corner. 'E tells me I'm late. 'E's already been done. He points to the bar where the slag 'as her arms round Vonnie Wright, the coalman from Albert Street, an' says, 'er – she said you was 'aving a day off. Well, I goes over to slagface an' pulls 'er away from the bar. I grabs 'er gin an' sloshes it all over 'er an' I'm thinkin', that'll make you smell a bit sweeter. Then 'cause I 'ave respect for Andy at the Star, I drags 'er outside and down Hobbs Alley. Andy don't want no more bother in his pub, not after that big fight last week, does 'e?' Vera shook her head. It was a bad do, that fight. Broken bottles in faces, knives drawn, blood everywhere, all started by some coked-up yob. The *Evening News* was full of it.

'I'm all ready to paste 'er against the windows of Dewhurst's the butchers when she starts cryin'. Says she can't manage, she's got overheads.'

'Can't manage? She can manage the whole fuckin' Navy at once.'

'Yeah, but she says they all 'as to pay twice as much minder's money now. There's this new guy.'

'Why pay 'im as well?'

''Cause they'll get cut, beat up an' worse if they don't. There's only a few girls like yerself, Vera, who ain't accountable to some fuckin' pimp, charging extortionate prices for looking after 'em. An' we all know lookin' after means takin' our money and doin' fuck all except knock us about an' get us a few snorts now an' then, which we pays for anyway. Am I right or am I right?'

'You're right.' Vera wished Elsie would hurry up and get to the punchline because she could see Rufus's car coming along Mumby Road.

'This new guy is screwing all the toms, left, right and fuckin' centre,' Elsie went on. 'An' not just around 'ere. It's the same bloke who's takin' a cut from them new sex shops in Southsea and Pompey.'

'So who's the fuckin' new bloke, then?' Vera asked impatiently, waving madly at Rufus.

'That fuckin' Eddie Lane. An' no one's gonna say no to that bastard, are they?'

Vera walked thoughtfully towards the car. Her mind was in a whirl. She knows Eddie's a law unto himself an' he ain't no worse nor no better than other scum. As long as he keeps looking after Daisy, what 'e does is his own affair, she thinks. Main thing was Daisy mustn't get hurt. She didn't need to know all the ins an' outs, but then she won't, will she? Eddie'll take care of that. Now she'd better keep her mind on her own work.

'Rufus is late!' she snaps as the door opens for her. 'Nana's cross. Very, very cross.'

'I couldn't get away,' Rufus mumbles. Vera notices he's had a hair cut, regulation short back and sides. His ginger hair will be quite wiry until it grows back again. 'The wife's mother has come down for a few days. I had to go to the station to pick her—'

'Not interested. Nana doesn't care. Rufus is a very bad boy. He won't get Nana's bubbies if he's late.' She watches as his eyes fill with tears. His hands shake on the steering wheel.

They will drive to a secluded place. He will play with her breasts and suckle her, curled up on the back bench seat like a child. Vera will continue to talk to him as though he is a baby, a grown man who doesn't want to grow up, who needs his Nana to comfort him. When the time is right and the slobbering is done, Vera will pull him off.

Vera wonders about his wife. It takes so little to please Rufus. Why doesn't she pleasure him? Vera gives a long sigh. But then, she thinks, if she did, I'd be out of a job, wouldn't I?

*

'Vera?'

'Yes, ducky?' Vera was tonging her hair. It sizzled and smelled like singed pork as she grabbed a tongful and attempted to wind it to her scalp. 'Ouch!' she said as the burning tongs touched her head.

She allowed the tongs to slide out from the hair and a perfectly formed sausage appeared. She aimed for another headful while there was still enough heat left in the tongs. If they'd cooled, she'd have to lie them across the gas flames until they glowed red again.

'I'm gonna buy you some electric ones,' said Daisy.

'Don't want none. I don't want to electrocute myself.'

'No, you'd rather stink the place out, wouldn't you?' Daisy sat down and studied Vera, who grinned back at her in the mirror. She had no make-up on and looked ten years younger.

'What do you want, Kitten?' asked Vera. At the word kitten a huge tabby lump landed in Daisy's lap and tried to push his face into her neck. 'Take no notice of him,' said Vera. 'Like all men he wants you to know he's here.'

Daisy kissed Kibbles' wet nose.

'Yuk! You don't want to be doin' that. He licks 'is bum.'

'Dare say that's a lot cleaner than some of the things you lick.'

'You cheeky young bugger,' said Vera. But Daisy knew she wasn't offended.

'I been wonderin', do you reckon Bert would 'ave approved of the changes to the caff?'

Vera looked taken aback, then said, ''Course he would, Bert weren't always a tired ol' man, you know.'

'Tell me more about him.'

'What do you want to know about that ol' bugger for?'

'I just do.'

'What can I say? He was a bloke like any other.'

'I know that. Kenny used to bring me in the caff, remember? We'd smooch to the old jukebox. But I never paid any attention to Bert.'

'Bert sort of faded into the background. He didn't let on about 'is past and 'e never spoke about the future. He was 'ere, then 'e wasn't. Just Bert who ran the caff.'

149

'But what's the connection with Kenny? Why did 'e want 'im to run things?'

The tongs had given up their heat now. Vera moved to the gas stove and propped them carefully over the flames.

'Probably because 'e was a nice old bloke who wanted to give Kenny a start in life.'

'But life ain't like that, Vera. You should know that. No one gets somethin' for nothin'.' Vera sighed, her eyes judging the heat of the metal in the flames.

'Did you sleep with Bert?'

Vera put on a look of mock horror.

'He was an ol' man!'

'Did you?'

'Yes.'

'Then why didn't he leave you in charge?'

'Because I'm not kin to him.' Vera gave a little gasp and put her hand over her mouth.

'What d'you mean? And don't give me any of your ol' flannel.'

'Okay. But you mustn't let it go any further. It'll come out when the time's right.' Vera took up the tongs and spat on them. They sizzled. 'I slept with Bert one night, crawled in beside 'im when I'd 'ad a bad night and I was lonely.' Daisy raised her eyebrows. 'Oh yes, madam. I get lonely at times. We got to talkin'. They say "the 'ead that shares the pillow shares the secrets", don't they? I asked 'im if he'd ever been married.'

'What did 'e say?'

'He said there 'ad only ever been one girl for him an' that was Queenie Smith. Only she wasn't Queenie Smith no more. She was the reason he'd come back to Gosport after bein' away for years. He'd never forgot 'er. Even though 'e was fourteen years older. She'd married a local villain. Had a little boy, only things wasn't going too well for 'er. Her ol' man used to knock 'er about, the kid too. But Bert kept an eye on her, an' an ear open in case she needed 'im. Sure enough one day she comes knockin' on his door.'

'That's the trouble, ain't it, Vera? We always go for the wrong blokes. We says we want nice fellas but we don't really go for 'em, do we?'

'Are you listenin' or not?' There were only a few sections of Vera's head not yet covered with dark sausage-like curls.

'Sorry.'

'She's been knocked about bad. She's got 'er kiddie in 'er arms. What can Bert do? Nothing, except take 'er in. Which of course he does, because 'e loves 'er.'

'What 'appens then?'

'What d'you think 'appens?'

'She stays?'

'God 'elp me. She stays long enough for 'im to wash 'er cuts an' bruises. See to the little one . . .'

'Like 'e did for you as well, didn't 'e, Vera?'

'I told you 'e was a lovely bloke. Anyway, Bert's got the girl of 'is dreams in 'is bed. An' don't forget she was the reason 'e come back to this shithole. But when the mornin' comes, she's gone back to 'er own house. Where 'er old man gives 'er another thumping for bein' out all night.'

'Did she tell him where she spent the night?'

''Course not. She tells 'im she spent the night in an open beach hut at Stokes Bay. Cryin' an' thinkin'.'

'He believes her?'

Vera nods. 'What's not to believe when she daren't disobey 'im? Nine months later she 'as a little boy.'

'You know, I 'ave sometimes wondered if they got different dads. Do they know?'

'There's no flies on Eddie. But even if 'e knows the truth, he'd never hurt Kenny. So if Kenny hasn't twigged, you don't say nothin' until the time's right. Okay?' Daisy nodded. Vera smiled at her then said, 'If you do, I'll knock your fuckin' block off!'

Vera put the now cooling tongs back on top of the oven grill. She sat down on the edge of her bed, then lifted her slippered feet onto the candlewick bedspread, tidying her wrap about herself.

'Now give me back the one true love of me life.'

CHAPTER 16

20 May 1963

Casanova dumped a pile of library books on Kenny's bed.

'I got that book on Spitfires I was after. They bought it for the library specially 'cause I put an order in. Want to 'ave a decko after me?'

'Na,' said Kenny as the book, smelling of new print and crisp pages, was thrust open in front of him on the blanket. Casanova never let up on trying to cheer him up. Kenny appreciated it, even if it didn't help. 'I got other things on me mind.'

'What things?' He stood over Kenny, leaning his arm on the metal side of the bunk.

'Big Eric. I can't take no more. I'm gonna get even. An' you're gonna help.' He looked up into the other man's face.

'You got no fuckin' 'ope in 'ell an' I ain't lifting a finger. I value my life too much. You better forget you even told me this. We got work in ten minutes so get your arse into gear.' Casanova turned his back on Kenny.

'This plan'll work an' there won't be no comebacks.'

He saw by the way his friend had turned round and was now watching him that he was wavering, not really wanting to know Kenny's great idea, but not wanting to ignore his plea for help either.

'I'll give you me snout ration.' Kenny knew that would get him going. Casanova smoked like a fuckin' chimney.

'I don't know. He's one mean bastard an' I'm due out before you. I don't want to lose no remission.'

'Snout for three weeks?' Kenny could see him weakening. Casanova ran a hand through his dark hair.

'No fallbacks?' Kenny shook his head.

'Four weeks?'

'Done! Here's what you do...' Kenny outlined his plan, his heart beating nineteen to the dozen.

Casanova listened intently. 'So I yells fire when I gets back to the library after lunch break. The screw what minds his business between the kitchen and the library sorts it. An' you sorts Big Eric in the kitchen?'

'Yeah.'

Kenny knew he wouldn't ask how he was going to sort out Big Eric. Casanova was only interested in the part he had to play.

'I ain't got to start no fire? I just yells it?'

'You don't even 'ave to raise your voice,' soothed Kenny. 'One mention of fire an' it'll start a fuckin' stampede. You know what it's like in 'ere. News of a blaze in a small area where cons are locked in? Pandemonium in ten seconds flat. The screws will think they've a fuckin' riot on their hands. No-one'll even remember who first whispered the word.'

'If they do, I get Big fuckin' Eric as a bonus present?'

'Won't 'appen.'

'Four weeks' snout then?'

Kenny nodded. He had him now. Wonderful what a little persuasion could do. He felt the excitement rush through his body.

'You gotta watch the clock in the library.'

'Right.'

Kenny was scared shitless. The canteen echoed with its usual clamour. Cons sat on benches at tables laid out in rows. There was supposed to be relative silence, but toleration was the key word.

Kenny worked in the kitchen but he didn't serve the food. He ate with the rest of them. Could he pull this off? Did he really have the guts?

He waited in line, moving slowly along amidst the smells of overcooked vegetables and body odour. He'd never get used to prison ways, never. Only for now, he knew he had to. Today it was mash, greens, peas, and something that looked like corned beef cooked in gravy. He remembered the glutinous mess that had emerged from the huge round tins. He'd scooped it into aluminium containers and helped prepare pastry crusts to cover it. He took an apple for pudding. He didn't eat apples but he knew who did.

His legs felt like lumps of lead but he forced himself to walk normally. Carrying the tray and breathing with small shallow breaths, he threaded his way through the tables. His heart was hammering against his chest as he neared Big Eric's group.

'Move it,' he said to the bloke sitting next to Eric. He put his tray on the table. At first Kenny thought the bloke was going to cause a ruck, but when he saw who it was he shifted himself and his tray along to make room. Eric stared at him with a bemused expression.

'Well, well, well,' he said. 'Look who's joined me for lunch. My Golden Boy.' Titters arose from the blokes at the table but Eric silenced them with one look. Kenny looked at the hairs on the back of Eric's hand as he forked the meat mixture into his mouth. Eric chewed methodically and Kenny almost puked. But he knew he mustn't fuck up his plan so he took a deep breath.

'I changed me mind.' His voice was low, so as not to be overheard. 'I ain't fighting you no more. I want you to look after me.'

Eric stared at him. Under the table he found Eric's groin and began to knead it. Eric's cock swelled alarmingly at his touch. Kenny thought of the black bombers and amyl nitrates that Eric swallowed to enhance his sexual performance and he was disgusted with himself. But this was a necessary chore.

'Well,' said Eric, putting down his knife and fork and moving closer to Kenny so he could feel the benefit of his efforts. Kenny could smell his fetid breath. 'I told you, you could either have it soft or hard but I see you wants it both ways. You've taken matters into your own hands, Golden Boy.' Then he laughed at his own joke.

Eddie would go through with this, he told himself. Eddie wouldn't let himself be beaten by a fuckin' scumbag like Eric.

'Will you look after me?'

'I said you should come to me of your own free will, boy, better than me takin' what I want. And now you 'ave.' Kenny nodded. Eric's brown eyes were like pools of shit, he thought, fathomless ponds of filth. 'It's about time you let me love you up good, the easy way.' He's fuckin' bought it, thought Kenny. The prick's swallowed me performance. So far, so good.

'We can't do nothin' in 'ere.' He removed his hand and brought it to his lips and kissed it. Eric's eyes betrayed him with the torment of deferred pleasure. 'Come to the kitchen at four. The others will 'ave just left for Recreation. There'll be about fifteen minutes before the kitchen is locked an' I'll be waitin'. It'll be just the two of us.'

'Glad my Golden Boy is seein' sense at last. I can do a lot for you, you know.' Kenny forced himself to give Eric a significant smile.

Eric squeezed his knee. The heat of his big mauler through his dungarees brought bile to Kenny's throat. He was sweating, his shirt sticking to his back. But the fucker was falling for it. Kenny felt elation rise. Eric really thought he wanted him. He couldn't see further than his own dick.

'Can I stay 'ere with you?' Kenny asked. He had to go through the motions. His fuckin' life depended on it.

'From now on this is your rightful place.'

Thank God Eric's brawn was mightier than his brain. Kenny tried to force down a few mouthfuls of food, every swallow reminding him of Eric's cock jammed in his throat. When he felt he couldn't go on with the farce any longer he rose, put his hand on Eric's shoulder and shifted his apple to Eric's plate.

'For you,' he whispered. No one took any notice of them. No one dared interfere with Big Eric about his business. Kenny left the table and joined the gaggle of prisoners leaving the canteen. He left his tray at the designated area and proceeded to the washroom. When he was safe inside a cubicle he shut the door and sagged against the cold wall. Then he fell on his knees on the urine-soaked tiles and vomited into the shit-stained pan.

Kenny had a few minutes alone in the cell before he started work. He sat down on his bunk, letting the tension flow from his body, focussing on the job ahead. God, he hoped it was going to work. If it didn't he was a fuckin' dead man.

He thought of his brother. Never had he done anything without Eddie goading him. Now was the time to prove to himself he could be every bit as clever and cruel as Eddie. No, better than Eddie. Because Eddie would have wanted the monetary gain from Eric's business empire. Kenny wasn't interested. Eric could keep all that shit – the money laundering, the baccy market, the drugs, down to every last fuckin' purple heart. All Kenny wanted was peace, for Eric to leave him alone so he could do his bird and get out.

After looking around the walls of the cell, he rested his head in his hands. When he was locked in and he knew Eric was locked in his cell was the only time he could relax. He shuddered.

'Come on, dickhead,' said Casanova. Kenny could smell tobacco on him. He'd just had a roll-up. Casanova rolled the thinnest fags Kenny had ever seen, said it made the snout go further. Casanova had two books in his big hands.

'Where you goin' with them?'

'Got to make it look good, ain't I? After all, I works in the fuckin' library.'

'Good thinkin'.'

The few hours of work in the kitchen seemed interminable.

'Keep moving,' said the screw. 'What's the fuckin' matter with you? Those carrots ain't gonna shed their own skins. Get a move on.'

Kenny looked at the guard. He was thickset and hard-eyed, another screw fed up with the system. Kenny decided the screws, spending each day inside, were prisoners every bit as much as the cons.

A stew was being prepared for the evening meal. The kitchen echoed with the sounds of metal pans clanging and the smell of food lingering and in preparation. It was warm and pleasant and Kenny knew just the right places to hide utensils that could be brought out later. He couldn't get nothing out of the kitchen past the other cons or screws. Everything was checked and counted, then locked away. Couldn't have everyone murderin' each other with the kitchen knives, could they? Course not.

When the work was winding down in preparation for the afternoon's relaxation period, Kenny was behind with his chores.

The kitchen crew were getting agitated, watching Kenny, looking from the screw to the big round wooden clock on the wall, then back to Kenny.

The buzzer sounded. Kenny, with the others, stood to attention. Kenny could sense the screw's anger. He was fed up, wanted a cup of tea like the rest of them.

'Right, file out. Not you, Lane.' The cons started to move in an orderly line. The kitchen surfaces shone. Every utensil had been counted.

Nothing to worry about, thought Kenny, except his own area where today he hadn't been as slick as the others.

'You finish cleaning that—'

The screw's orders were interrupted by running feet and raised voices outside in the corridor. The guard turned and on cue left Kenny to it and raced towards the door. And why shouldn't he leave Kenny alone in the kitchen? Kenny had always shown he could be trusted. And afterwards when the screw would remember that Kenny had been left in the kitchen? Well, it would be Kenny's word against the screw's. And without backup from another single person they couldn't do fuck all about it.

'What's the matter, sir?' asked Kenny innocently, as the guard rushed off down the corridor.

'Never you mind, finish up, then clear off out.' He slung the words over his shoulder as he ran.

Kenny had about three minutes until Big Eric came looking for his jollies. Big Eric wouldn't be put off by some fire commotion down by the library.

Kenny swiped at the table top. Must clear away as he'd been told.

He dragged a heavy stool across the kitchen and put it behind the door where it wouldn't be seen by someone entering the kitchen. Then he lifted the weapon and climbed on the stool.

What would he do if it wasn't Eric coming in? Well, he'd be fucked, but they'd still have to prove it was him. And if the cons thought they knew? Then that old chant of, 'I didn't see nothing, sir', 'I don't know what you're talkin' about, sir' could be relied on to ensure a similar accident wouldn't happen to anyone who grassed him up. The guards? They were a different matter but they'd still have to prove it. His mouth was dry, his hands sweaty. He wiped them on his overalls. With the noise coming from outside it might be difficult to hear the sound of Eric's measured footsteps.

He looked at the clock. Just coming up to four.

From the corner of his eye he glimpsed the familiar blue shirt. With both his arms in a curving motion he swung the heavy-duty metal meat tenderiser downwards. As the weapon came towards Eric, his eyes and mouth opened wide. It hit Big Eric full in the face. Kenny heard the crunch of bone as Eric sagged to the floor. He jumped from the stool and lifted the tenderiser, taking careful aim.

'Go for it, Kenny,' he said beneath his breath as he brought the weapon down again. The tenderiser dropped from his hand and clunked on the tiles. Dragging Eric's heavy and inert body inside, he kicked the metal kitchen door shut. Eric was making gurgling noises. 'Shut the fuck up, moron,' Kenny said, kicking him in the side of his head. He grabbed the stool and carried it back across the kitchen. Then, ignoring the man bleeding profusely on the floor, he picked up his weapon and took it to the sink.

Fresh blood smells metallic, he thought, as he rinsed and turned the weighty object beneath the spray of hot water. Bits of skin and pulp were caught on the metal points. Almost gagging, he picked at the bloodied bits with his fingers, watching pieces of Eric's face float away with the jets of water. When he was convinced the implement was clean enough, he wiped it on a rag and stacked it back on the kitchen top. He checked the sink was wiped clean. The clock told him he had very little time before the screw remembered he was still in the kitchen.

He surveyed the pulpy area where Eric's nose had been. Eric was out of it, but still breathing, a sort of throaty, gargling sound. His face was torn to buggery. Kenny looked down at his own overalls. Not a fuckin' speck of blood on him. He felt the surge of elation. He had done it. He had shown Eric who was the boss.

'Not so fuckin' big now, are you?' With careful aim he kicked Eric in the bollocks, watching the involuntary twitch of the man's body. Satisfied justice had been done, Kenny carefully prised open the metal door, peeked out into the hallway, and squeezed through, pulling the door closed after him. He walked briskly towards the library to see what all the fuss was about, whistling the song from *Snow White and the Seven Dwarfs*: 'Hey ho, hey ho, it's off to work I go'. Daisy said he never could carry a tune properly. But he'd made a fuckin' good job of messing up Eric. That should put him out of action for quite a while.

When Eric got out of hospital, he'd be gunning for Kenny, but Kenny had wrecked him once and he could do it again, couldn't he?

CHAPTER 17

30 May 1963

Now Daisy knew the brothers had different fathers, she understood why they were so dissimilar. Yet there was that extremely close bond between them. Their mother, Queenie, had by all accounts been a gentle person, cowed by life and the brute of a man she loved. She'd had no control over her love. The wrong man he might have been, but love isn't turned on and off like a tap, thought Daisy.

Eddie came and went. Daisy had begun to believe he wasn't as bad as he was painted. Well, not to her, or Vera, or Suze. He'd also kept to his promise of not bringing his business interests inside the cafe. What he got up to elsewhere was nothing to do with Daisy.

Moira rang her up constantly. Her stories seemed to get wilder. But Daisy had witnessed the kindness of Violet towards her and the consideration of Roy, so she guessed a lot of her anguish was caused by drugs. She had no idea how bad Moira's habit was now. Or even how she'd be able to hide anything from her husband in a house that small, with the eagle-eyed Violet watching her every move. All Daisy could do was be there for her. She reckoned Violet knew the score.

Daisy was constantly tired, but actually life was good. She felt wanted, and wasn't she achieving a better life for Kenny?

But first she had to sort out Susie. Here she was, at six o'clock in the morning, sitting on a stool in the kitchen crying her eyes out. Dressed in one of her rose-patterned bouffant skirts and a plain white top, Susie looked like a lost little girl. Daisy's heart went out to her.

'What's the matter with you? There's only an hour left before we open an' everythin's gone pear shaped.'

'You wouldn't understand.' Susie's blue eyes were glittering with tears.

Daisy knew she didn't mean that. She was waiting for her to ask her again. Well, she wouldn't.

'Don't tell me, then. Just shift your arse to the fridge and separate the bacon strips so they're ready when I need 'em. Start to look like you're a bit 'appy else you'll put the customers off their breakfasts.'

At this Susie started to cry even more. Daisy took a piece of kitchen roll and shoved it under her nose.

'Wipe yer nose. I can't be 'avin' this, Suze, ducks. What's the matter?' Susie looked at her through her tears and took the soft paper, blowing her nose heartily. Daisy saw the real distress in her eyes.

'I love Si,' she sniffed.

Daisy was happy for her. She liked Si. And it was obvious he thought the world of Suze.

'So?'

'Don't you understand? I really *love* 'im.'

'Bully for you. He's a lovely lad.'

'He thinks I'm a virgin.'

'Fuckin' 'ell. What are you goin' to do?' Susie was an honest girl. Daisy knew she wouldn't want to keep secrets from the man she loved.

'I don't know. I 'oped you'd be able to tell me.' Daisy thought carefully. How would I feel, if I was Si? Would I want to know about my girl's past? I would, if sometime in the future I expected to marry her and have children, she decided.

'You can't start a life together on dishonesty. You 'ave to tell 'im.'

'I can't. He won't want me if he believes I've been used by all an' sundry. An' you should meet his family. They're so nice.'

'His family 'ave nothin' to do with it. It's Si you 'ave to please, not them.' Daisy thought for a moment. 'Do you want me to 'ave a word with 'im?'

Susie's eyes lit up, then faded again.

'No. Wouldn't do no good. He'll hate me even more for gettin' you to do me dirty work.' She was absolutely right.

'What if Eddie took 'im to one side, man to man? Then Eddie could stress how you ain't never looked at anybody until he came along, which is only the bloody truth anyway. He looks up to Eddie, don't 'e? Si wouldn't be much of a feller if 'e didn't understand. And if that was so, you'd be better off without 'im anyway. But somehow I don't think your past'll make a blind bit of difference.' Daisy grabbed Susie's shoulder and forced her to look into her eyes. 'It ain't your fault. Don't you ever think you got anythin' to be ashamed of.' She let her go. 'Anyway, Si thinks the sun shines out of your arse'ole. Shall I talk to Eddie?'

Susie had at least stopped snivelling now, and Daisy could see she was thinking about the offer.

'Would Eddie do that? For me?'

'Sure,' Daisy said without hesitation. She pulled up a stool and sat beside her. 'Look, love, you got to stop thinkin' you're to blame for any of this. You're the victim 'ere. The fuckin' bloke what started this wants 'is dick cut off, that he does. I've watched you blossom an' flower into a lovely girl. So don't tell me 'ow nice Si's family is. You are nice. Better than anyone I know.' Then Daisy stressed, 'You're a survivor.'

'Am I really?'

Daisy nodded. 'And you're also my friend.'

Susie beamed through her tears. Daisy resolved to talk to Eddie at the earliest opportunity.

Later, as Daisy was reading in bed, there was a gentle tap on her door. The clock said two-fifteen a.m.

'Come in,' she called quietly. Vera had gone to bed hours ago so she knew it wasn't her.

Eddie hadn't been in long. Although he'd discarded his coat, his damp hair was a dead giveaway. He held a mug of coffee in his hand which he put on her bedside table. He made better coffee than Vera. Under his arm he carried a large bag.

'You owe me, Daisy Lane.' He sat down on the edge of the bed, and tried to hide the bag behind him.

'What d'you mean, I owe you?' She nodded towards the coffee. 'I could just do with that. Thanks.'

'Everythin's goin' to be all right with Suze an' Si.'

'How on earth 'ave you managed that so quickly? I only asked for your 'elp at lunchtime.'

'Anything for you, Dais. I got hold of 'im at work. On his own. Told 'im the truth. That we don't all have good families. That she's a smashin' kid an' deserves to be loved by someone who can really appreciate her. And that if he wasn't man enough . . .'

'You never said that!' He shook his head and treated Daisy to a lovely smile.

'Oh, you,' she said. 'What'd 'e say?'

'It wasn't what he said. It was what 'e did.'

'What?'

'Cried his fuckin' eyes out. I can't abide to see a grown man cry. Made me want to weep with 'im. He loves her. They'll end up wed. Mark my words.' Daisy sighed with relief for the pair of them.

'Thanks.' There was a lot more she could have said, but she was near to tears herself. 'You can be so lovely when you wants.'

'Take this then.' He brought out the brown paper bag and shoved it towards her. Outside, the wind blew rain across the windows, making the frames rattle. Daisy could see Eddie was embarrassed at giving her a present.

'I don't take gifts from you,' she said. His face dropped. Immediately she was sorry, hated herself for being thoughtless. 'What is it?' she asked. It had been a while since anyone had given her a gift, not since the beautiful cat brooch that Moira had presented her with. She peeked in the bag, then slowly drew out a soft white garment.

The terry-towelling dressing gown slid over her hands. It was soft as Egyptian cotton, long enough to reach her ankles. Once more a lump rose in her throat. She looked up into his worried face.

'I love it,' Daisy said. 'Thank you.'

He looked relieved, even managed another smile.

'You will wear it?'

She nodded. ''Course I will.'

She loved Kenny, but she was lonely.

He wasn't there. And Eddie was. So when he asked her to even up the account between them, she agreed.

'No strings?' She made him promise.

Susie and Vera told her to go and have a good time.

'Don't think we can't manage. We can, can't we, Vera?' Susie was a different girl now. Daisy had never seen her so happy. All day long she sang and hummed stupid lovey-dovey songs that got right up Vera and Daisy's nose. But they didn't have the heart to tell her to shut up.

Daisy was waiting for Eddie outside the cafe. He'd told her he wouldn't be long. He had to collect some transport. She couldn't believe her eyes when he came round the corner in a red MG that had wire wheels and chrome bumpers.

The top was down and he was smiling broadly as he pulled up. Vera and Susie were gawping through the windows at them.

'Whose is it?' Daisy asked. She ran her hands over the sleek bonnet.

'Whose d'you think?'

'It's never yours!' Two seats and a small space for luggage. Daisy fell in love with it at once.

''Course.'

He got out and opened the door for her. She slipped in, sliding her legs into the deep well at the front of the car. Black leather surrounded her. She loved the smell. He got back in.

'I'm impressed, Eddie. Where you been hiding this little darlin'?'

'I keep 'er garaged in Seahorse Street. Couldn't leave it outside the cafe. Someone would damage it. Do you really like it?'

'Do I ever! Where'd it come from?' Daisy had always wanted to learn to drive. 'I could imagine me flying about in somethin' like this.'

'Ask more questions than a bloody detective, don't you? I got it as payment for a debt.' He ran his fingers through his dark hair. He was wearing a dark blue suit with a lighter blue shirt. He had on some new cologne. Really nice, Daisy thought. She waved to the two nosy parkers still watching from the cafe window.

He turned the key and the deep-throated growl of the MG's engine was music to Daisy's ears. The breeze blew her hair and the sun was on her face as they drove through the High Street. She kept hoping she'd see someone she knew so she could wave to them and show off. She looked at Eddie's profile and thought, he's not such a bad bloke. Bloody tasty, really.

They drove to Fareham, then past Portsmouth and Chichester, through the countryside to the special sporting event at Goodwood. The fields about them were green with growing crops. Sweetness from scented flowers and early roses in cottage gardens wafted their way in the warm wind. There was an air of expectancy in the heat of the sun. A promise of good things to come.

'I've never been to a racecourse before,' Daisy said.

Goodwood was packed. She saw women in pretty dresses, men in bowler hats, kiosks where you put money on the horses. There were places to buy alcohol and teas. Daisy liked best the enclosure where the horses paraded before each race, their coats shining with health.

'They're bloody huge close up, aren't they?' Eddie laughed at her. She wondered how many other women he'd taken there.

'It's not always as glamorous as people think,' he said. 'Some of the punters get addicted. Lose everything. Cheat, steal, lie. Anything to get that high that comes when the nag is running. Some say it's worse than heroin.'

'How do you feel about gamblin'? Can you take it or leave it?'

He nodded. She'd guessed so. He was a very strong-willed man.

'It's like the casinos,' Eddie said. 'No one wins except the bosses. Treat gambling as a bit of fun and don't let it get to you. There's a lot of wannabes and could-'ave-beens 'ere. The only innocents are the horses.'

Daisy liked the smell of the place, the excitement, the atmosphere. She jumped up and down when she thought her horse was going to win, and tore up her betting slip and swore when it didn't.

They had champagne, Eddie sipping at his but not finishing it. Daisy ended up drinking it for him.

'I've never seen you drunk,' she said.

'And you never will,' he told her darkly. 'Seen too much of that when I was a kid.' She remembered Vera telling her about Eddie's dad – the way he drank, and knocked him and his mum and Kenny about. She thought of that terrible, terrible incident with the puppy. Daisy looked up at him. He didn't know what was going through her mind, but he grinned down at her protectively. 'All right?' Daisy nodded. She was. She really was. In fact she felt bloody marvellous.

After the races they went to Littlehampton, where her mum had taken her when she was a kiddie. She remembered a fair on the green and she'd gone on a roundabout in a miniature helicopter. She couldn't have been more than five years old at the time.

Eddie left the car near the park. After putting the tonneau on in case it rained, they walked across the grass towards the sea.

The tide was out and Daisy asked, 'Can we walk right down to the sea?'

He laughed. 'If you want. You'll 'ave to take your shoes off.'

'So will you,' she said. The sand stretched for miles. At least that's what it seemed. There were people sunbathing on the beach and kiddies building sand castles and throwing pebbles. Mums with young families had picnics set out on blankets. Daisy could feel the heat of the sun, smell the candyfloss and chips. All of it was different, wonderful. Even the smell of diesel fumes from the little sightseeing tram that took passengers up and down the front filled her with a sense of well-being.

'Don't the sand feel squishy when it seeps between your toes?' she said. Eddie had his suit jacket over his arm and his socks stuffed in his shoes, their laces tied around his neck. His trousers were rolled up. She'd never seen him so relaxed. He threw seaweed at her. She ran. With her shoes in one hand and her clutch bag in the other, she ran like the wind. The warm water splashed against her bare legs and, with the breeze and sun on her skin, she felt like one of the racehorses they'd just left, running as though their lives depended on winning the race. Breathing deeply of the clean salty air, taking in great lungfuls, cleaning away the dirt and grime of the cafe and the problems she'd left behind. Eddie caught her up and grabbed her. Laughing, she fell to the stones of the pebble beach. They lay there, exhausted, their shoes and accessories on the beach around them. Daisy lay back on the shingle with her eyes closed, listening to the sounds of the gulls whirling and crying overhead, and the far-off splash of the waves. She felt a shadow blot out the sun. When she opened her eyes Eddie's face was just inches away. It seemed the most natural thing in the world to let him kiss her.

That kiss was all she had ever wanted a kiss to be. She'd never tasted a kiss like that from Kenny. Tender, yet the passion welling up inside her every bit as forceful and dangerous as those waves could be. She put her hands on Eddie's shoulders and pushed him gently away.

'I'm sorry,' she said. He was still leaning over her, his breath sweet on her cheek. He didn't look at all sorry.

'Why? Don't be. You don't know how long I've wanted that to happen.' He was tenderly smoothing strands of hair away from her face. 'You must know I fuckin' love you?' They stared at each other. Well, she thought, there wasn't anything to say to that, was there?

Then he lay back on the pebbles with one arm beneath her shoulders, holding her near him. It was a long time since she'd felt close to anyone. And it seemed so natural with Eddie. So easy, so safe, so right. Yet she said, 'I can't do this with you again.'

'It was only a kiss.'

'We both know it was more,' she said quietly.

He sighed. It was a long-drawn-out sound.

'I know.'

Daisy had made a decision, and it was the only right and proper one. She was married to his brother and this had to stop. But if it was the right decision, why did she feel so sad inside?

After a while, Eddie said, 'Let's go eat, shall we?'

They were subdued as they made themselves presentable. He put on his socks and shoes. Daisy tried to brush her hair but the sea breeze made it impossible. It wasn't long before the joy of the afternoon took over again and they were giggling as they strolled arm in arm near the fish stalls and up into the town.

'Posh food or fish and chips?'

'D'you really need to ask?' Daisy said.

Inside the small cafe they sat at an oilcloth-covered table, browsing through the menu. They were lucky to get seats, a table for two in the corner.

Eddie had cod and she had Dutch eel, her favourite.

'It's lovely to be served by someone else,' Daisy said, stirring a cup of thick brown tea exactly the way she liked it. The young waitress brought their meals.

'Looks good,' said Eddie. Daisy had to agree. The fish was one of the largest portions she had ever seen, the chips golden brown. Smothering the food with salt and vinegar, they ate like starving children.

'That's got to be one of the best meals I've ever tasted,' Daisy said, wiping her lips with a paper tissue.

'Are you happy, Dais?'

Across the table she grabbed his hand and squeezed it.

'You know I am.'

He left a big tip for the waitress. They walked around the town, hand in hand. She had to stop him buying her things. Everything he saw her looking at in shop windows he wanted her to have. But it wouldn't have seemed right. She told him so.

'I don't mind you forking out for the meal and day out, but no presents, Eddie.'

'Do you feel guilty at bein' with me, then?'

'No,' she said. 'Kenny would rather I was enjoyin' meself with you than bein' stuck at home miserable. Besides, 'e knows I'll be waitin' when 'e gets out.'

'Sure,' Eddie said quietly.

He put the hood up on the MG before they started for home. A cold wind had swept in from the sea and there was rain in the air. After driving lazily back through sleepy villages they arrived in Gosport as the cafe was closing. She'd had a wonderful day.

As Eddie pulled up, he said, 'You don't know what today has meant to me, Daisy.'

She looked into his eyes, too choked to answer.

After a while he leaned across and opened the car door for her, then drove off to garage it.

Vera was looking like the cat that got the cream when Daisy walked in. 'What did I tell you?' she said. 'There's a lovely side to 'im.'

'Don't know what you mean, Vera. We're friends. That's all.'

'More fool you then,' she said, stomping off upstairs. Then she yelled back down, 'Phone's been ringin' all day for you.'

As if on cue the phone rang then. She guessed it was Moira. She wasn't wrong.

'Dais, there's been some trouble.' She sounded bombed out. She started gabbling away.

'Slowly, love. Speak more slowly.'

'They killed him. There was his guts all over the carpet. Roy . . .' Daisy heard muffled voices and unidentifiable noises. Then Violet came on the phone.

'Hallo, Daisy.' All nice and calm, like Moira hadn't even spoken to her.

'What's the matter with Moira? She said . . .'

'I heard what she said, dear. You mustn't take too much notice of her. She's not herself. How are you, dear?' Daisy thought she was going daft. One minute Moira's acting like it's life or death, the next Violet is as cool as a fuckin' cucumber.

'I'm all right,' Daisy said, 'but—'

'That's good, Daisy. We'll have to meet up again soon. Perhaps when Moira's a little more like her old self. There's someone at the front door. I'd better go, dear.' Daisy stood there with the receiver in her hand. Violet had hung up.

Violet was fobbing her off. No one had knocked on her door. She'd have heard it. What the fuck was going on?

'Daisy, Daisy.' Like a whirlwind Susie came rushing into her bedroom.

'Steady on,' Daisy said. She was just about to pour a saucepan of warm water over her head to rinse off the Amami shampoo, and nearly missed. 'What's up?'

'We're gonna get married.'

Daisy set down the pan on the draining board and threw a towel, turban style, over her hair. She'd changed out of her decent clothes and was in her old white bra, which had been washed so many times it was a dingy grey, and a pair of Kenny's pyjama bottoms tied tightly to stop them falling down.

'How did that come about?' Daisy gave her a wet cuddle. Susie was all excited, jumping up and down like a kid.

'Si asked me an' I said yes.'

'Does that mean you're engaged, then?' Susie stopped jumping about and looked thoughtful.

'S'pose so. But we can't afford a ring or nothin' yet. That don't matter anyway, does it?' Daisy shook her head. It made her heart glad to see the girl so happy.

'Si's parents okay with it?'

'Yes,' she said proudly. Her face was flushed and the joy was pouring out of her. 'It wouldn't 'ave 'appened if it hadn't been for you.'

'Don't be so bloody soft. He loves you, Suze. That ain't got nothin' to do with me.'

Daisy towelled herself where the water was dripping down her neck.

'Take that off an' let me finish it before the water gets cold,' Susie said. Obediently Daisy shook her hair free of the towel and bent over the sink again. Susie lifted the pan and poured the cooling water over her head. Daisy watched it run down the plughole then made a grab for the towel. Suddenly, Susie went quiet.

'What's the matter?' Daisy asked.

'I need permission to get married.'

'Oh fuck.' Daisy stopped fiddling with her hair and turned to her. 'I'd forgotten about that,' she said. Then added brightly, 'We'll just 'ave to go an' see your mum an' get her to sign the necessary forms, won't we?'

'She won't do it.'

'Don't be silly. When she sees how 'appy you are, of course she will.'

'It ain't that.'

'What, then?'

'There's no way I'm goin' anywhere near that scumbag of a bloke.' Susie grabbed hold of her. 'Daisy, I couldn't.' Daisy saw real fear in her eyes.

'All right, love,' she said. 'Calm down. That may not be necessary. We could write to your mum.'

Susie was shaking her head. 'If I write a letter, he'd be spiteful enough to tear it up because I ran away. She wouldn't know no different.'

'Phone 'er first.'

'Phone? That was the first thing to be taken away when the bills wasn't paid.'

Daisy sighed. 'We'll work it out. Don't worry.'

Susie grabbed hold of Daisy and put her arms about her, burying her face in her damp neck.

'You don't understand,' she said in a muffled voice. 'Mum just sits there all day, waitin' for the next hit or half bottle of whisky, whichever he doles out first after 'e's made 'er . . .'

'Don't upset yourself. That's not your problem,' Daisy interrupted. 'To get the papers signed is the main thing.' She didn't want any more graphic descriptions of Susie's home life.

'But how we gonna do that? I can't wait another two years until I'm eighteen. I just can't.' She started crying again. Daisy got hold of Susie and shook her. She pulled away, a look of shock on her face.

'Listen, an' stop it! We've got this far. Right?' Susie nodded dismally. 'Leave it with me.'

What the fuck had she said that for? Because she couldn't bear to have things go wrong for Suze now. Why didn't she keep her trap shut?

'You'll sort it? Thank you. Oh, thank you.' And there she was again, jigging about, throwing her arms around Daisy.

Daisy shook her off.

'Leave me be. Let me finish doin' me 'air. I've had enough excitement for one fuckin' day.' Susie pulled a face at her but slipped towards the door. Daisy heard her go downstairs, whether to the cafe or her own room, she didn't care. She had enough to think about. She took a dry towel and began rubbing at her scalp. How the fuck was she going to sort this out?

She was sitting in bed, a library book to hand, but scribbling a few of her thoughts down like she sometimes did, when she heard the street door slam. Actually, she'd been waiting and hoping that Eddie was going to come home tonight.

Daisy got out of bed and slipped on her new dressing gown. It felt a whole lot better than her old blue coat. Quietly, so as not to wake Susie or Vera, she crept downstairs.

Eddie was sitting on a stool, his head bent over the *Daily Mirror* which was spread out on the counter. His jacket was slung over a chair, his tie was loosened, his hair ruffled, and the kettle was purring away nicely on the gas. He looked up and saw her and a big grin spread over his face.

'What you reading? That Profumo scandal's getting heated nicely, ain't it?' Daisy said.

'Na,' he said. 'Don't care about that. You seen this?' He pointed to the paper. Daisy went and stood behind him, reading over his shoulder. Cigarette smoke clung to his clothes, his hair. There'd been a gangland killing in London, almost a disembowelment, in the Rainbow Club

'Fuckin' 'ell,' Daisy said. It was the same club she'd been in at New Year with Roy, Violet and Moira. She quickly scanned the item. No mention of names. Not much information there at all really except the horrific discovery of the murder victim.

'Anything the matter, Dais?' He turned to her. She wasn't about to tell Eddie she'd been in that club. Then she thought of Moira's phone call, her talk of 'guts all over the carpet', and the phone being taken off her by Violet. But surely there was no connection?

'Bad business that,' she said, thinking quickly. He was staring hard at her. 'Who would do a terrible thing like that?'

'Sometimes, Dais,' he said, shaking his head, 'you act like you was born yesterday. That sort of stuff goes on all over the place. All the time. The only difference is, this killin' made the headlines. Someone has to be brought to book for this. This is one killing the coppers won't let be swept beneath the table.' He swung round on the stool so he was facing her. Daisy was now standing between his outstretched legs. 'Gangs are rife. It's better to work on your own as much as possible.' He put his hands on her waist. She didn't pull away. The kettle was coming up to the boil and she'd be able to make her escape then.

'Ain't it hard to work on your own if gangs already control

areas?' She pointed to the article on the counter. 'Like what happened 'ere. This guy has obviously stepped out of line so he's been dealt with.'

'Well, he didn't have his head screwed on right. He should have kept one step ahead all the time. That's what you got to do.'

'I'm not arguin' with you, Eddie. I know you sails pretty close to the wind.'

'Who, me?' He laughed, a real belly-laugh. 'Don't you worry about me.'

'What makes you think I do?' The whistle had started up on the kettle. But Daisy was remembering DS Vinnie Endersby. A couple of days ago she'd met him in the market. She was buying kippers from Tom Bradley's fish stall. Endersby was walking along with a woman constable. There were usually a few coppers about checking for stolen stuff on the stalls. When he came face to face with Daisy he told the constable to walk ahead, that he'd catch her up.

'Morning, Daisy.'

She felt flustered, but couldn't understand why. She wondered if she felt guilty about some past misdeed, then chided herself for being so foolish.

'Hello.' Her voice had suddenly developed a sort of croak. He was unsettling her.

'How's Eddie?' His eyes seemed to see right inside her.

'Fine, I suppose.' She handed over a pound note and took the newspaper-wrapped parcel of fish.

'He's not at the cafe, then?'

'I never said that,' Daisy had snapped. 'I don't ask him for progress reports.' He'd smiled at the sharpness of her tone, but Daisy knew he'd been assessing her words for hidden meanings.

'Eddie and I go back a long way,' he said. He chewed on his bottom lip with his upper teeth. Daisy saw they were very white.

'And I'm married to his brother,' she replied. She smiled a thank you at Tom and put her change in her purse.

'Ah, Kenny.' His words were slow, thoughtful. 'One brother in Winchester, the other only one step ahead of the law.' His eyes roved over the seafood, and the fish decorated with parsley.

'Funny the way a fishing net has a way of gathering the bigger fish along with the tiddlers, isn't it?'

Daisy put her purchase in her wicker shopping basket. 'Dunno. I don't go fishin'. Not like you coppers. I run a cafe.' And with that she moved swiftly away. But she could hear him laughing behind her as she walked.

'You sortin' that kettle or shall I?'

The bloody thing was singing its heart out. Daisy smiled at Eddie. Then she folded the newspaper and tossed it in the plastic swing-bin reserved for rubbish.

'Actually, Eddie Lane, it's because I know you like taking a few risks that I need your help.' She went to the stove, pulled off the whistle and started on the job of making tea.

Later, when she was alone in bed, she thought how once again she'd needed to ask Eddie for help. And how once again he'd readily agreed.

CHAPTER 18

8 June 1963

Susie danced down the yard where Daisy was swilling out the dustbins. She was waving a letter.

'Look, Dais! I can't believe it!'

She thrust the envelope at Daisy, who wiped her hands on an old bit of rag she had tied around herself to protect her jeans and took out the single sheet of cheap paper. The writing was a scrawl but Daisy could just make it out. Susie's mum said she wasn't to worry about getting married. The registrar at Fareham had all the necessary information plus Susie's birth certificate. And her plans should all go ahead without a hitch. Her mother went on to say she was sorry she wouldn't be there but she wished Susie a better life. Nothing else. Just a short, sweet note.

'Ain't you sorry she won't be at your weddin'?'

Susie shook her blonde curls. 'Nope.'

Daisy hoped, some day, mother and daughter might be able to reconcile, find themselves some common ground, but she feared it would be a long time in the future.

'It's like a miracle, ain't it?' Susie's eyes were shining like glow-worms on a pitch black summer's night.

Ain't no fuckin' miracle, thought Daisy, that's Eddie Lane's doing.

'You did this, didn't you?'

Daisy shook her head.

'Not me. But I know who did.'

They stared at each other. And Daisy knew Susie realised that Eddie, in his own way, was trying to ask her forgiveness.

After a while Daisy asked, 'What does Si think?'

'Doesn't know. I came to you first.'

'You'd better get round to The World's Stores then and tell him, hadn't you?' Susie's eyes lit up. The cafe wasn't due to open for a while. She had time.

'Thanks, Daisy.' She rushed off in a flurry of Woolworth's scent and rose-patterned flounces, leaving Daisy to swill out the scummy bin bottoms with her own particular perfume of Jeyes fluid.

'Thanks, Suze,' she said to the empty backyard.

After she'd finished, she went upstairs and knocked on Eddie's door. She didn't know whether he'd be there or not. No one answered. She pushed open the door and peeked inside. The room was tidy and clean, the curtains open so the early sun shone into the room making tiny dust motes dance on shafts of light.

He was sprawled on the bed, his eyes closed. Naked.

Daisy stood quite still, admiring his hard, muscled body. His generous penis gave a slight twitch against his thigh. His handsome face was turned towards her, his eyes with their dark lashes still closed, his breathing even and deep. Then he opened his eyes, gave a couple of sleepy blinks. He reached out one of his hands towards her.

'Come in here with me, Daisy?' His voice was sleep-dark.

The room was warm, stuffy with the scent of cologne and maleness, not un-nice at all. Daisy stayed where she was, feasting her eyes on him.

'No. You've got nothin' on.'

'I have.'

She looked at him in disbelief. He hadn't even bothered to pull the sheet over himself. All he was wearing was a big grin.

'Not,' she said.

'Have.'

'What?'

He held up his other arm and jiggled his gold watch. 'I've got my watch on.'

'Shitbag,' she said. She moved to the bed and quickly threw the sheet over him, although it pained her to cover his beautiful maleness. Feeling safer now, she sat down on the bed.

'A letter came for Suze this morning from her mum. You sorted it, didn't you?' He yawned, pulled himself up to a sitting position and repositioned a pillow upright against the headboard. He leaned back on it.

'Might have,' he said. 'But then, your wish is my command.'

'Should I ask how you managed it?' He ran a hand through his hair. It stuck up in dark wavy peaks. A man shouldn't have such silky hair, she thought. She wondered what it would feel like if she moved her fingers through it. He was looking at the bedside table.

'Didn't you bring me up a cuppa?'

'No. Didn't know if you was 'ere or not, did I?'

He pulled a face at her.

'You don't want to know how I sorted things out, Dais. Let's just say that fuckin' pervert ain't gonna be messin' around with any young girls again.' His voice was hard now. He was frowning as he remembered, as if he was being transported to some dark place.

'Eddie Lane! You likes 'em young yerself!'

He leaned towards her. His head was very close to hers. She could smell his breath, not mint-fresh because he'd not long woken, but clean, vital, male.

'At least I wait until they're wearin' bloody gymslips. And Daisy Lane, if you asked any bloke how he'd like his women, he'd say the same.' He looked into her eyes. 'That's if he was honest. Ninety-five per cent of blokes likes to have had plenty of experience themselves but would much prefer the girl they end up with to be a pure young miss. They like to be the first, see?'

'I see,' said Daisy. 'An what 'appens to all the females they've 'ad their experience with?'

He laughed. 'You're so fuckin' sharp you'll cut yourself one of these days. But I'm goin' to tell you one thing. That fuckin' bastard what messed up Susie's life was still fuckin' about with kids. An' they was little kids. One looked like a miniature Suze. Only a baby. You should have seen that place where they was livin'. Not in that flat that Suze told us about but a filthy squat near Kingsland Market. Door all broken in, no fuckin' light, only tilley lamps. It fuckin' stunk of shit and piss an' . . .' He shook his head. 'I can't abide filth,' he said.

Daisy put her hand on his arm, and saw the disgust in his eyes.

'Four of 'em there. Him, 'er an two kids. I saw these photos.'

He shook off her hand and turned his head away. 'Poor little fuckers. He wouldn't 'ave let me in but 'e thought I was after some of those photos. Kids, Dais. And him.' He was silent except for a sigh. She couldn't speak. What could she say that wouldn't sound trite?

'People mostly ask for everything they gets,' he continued. 'But I can't bear anyone touching little kids. Innocent little mites.' He went silent for a while, then said, 'Afterwards I took both them kids where he won't get at 'em again. No one will.'

Daisy looked at him, concern in her face. 'Oh, don't you worry. They're safe. Safer than they've ever been before. I took 'em round to St Columba's and handed 'em in to a little nun no bigger than you. Gave her a wad of money an' told 'er what had happened. They don't say nothin', them nuns. Just gets on with the job in hand. I'm sorry, shouldn't have unburdened myself like this.'

'You wouldn't be in this if I hadn't asked you for help, would you?' Daisy leaned over and touched his face. Running her hand up his cheek and then into his hair. Smoothing it back from his face. It was softer than Kibbles' fur, softer than silk. She dropped her hand away. 'I knew you'd make it come good for Suze.' So many questions she wanted to ask. So many answers she didn't want to hear.

He gave a small laugh of resignation.

'Yeah, well, I didn't make it come good for that fuckin' pervert. In fact he can't come again, ever.' At first, Daisy didn't understand the meaning of his words. When she caught on, her mouth hung open.

'Catching flies, Dais?' He grinned at her.

'Eddie, you didn't?'

'Sorry to disappoint you but I fuckin' did. Made him lay his tackle on the table an' used a meat cleaver on 'im.'

'Eddie, you didn't!' she repeated.

'Okay, I didn't.' And he laughed. She breathed a sigh of relief. Then she reckoned she was being premature in thinking it was all a joke. Would he have done something like that? Surely not. But deep down Daisy knew he was capable of it. If justice needed to be meted out, Eddie could do it. She shuddered.

'Power, Dais. That's what you need to stay one step ahead of the game. Power will get you money. Money brings respect.'

'You're in a thoughtful mood today. And fear? How do you feel about bein' feared?'

'Fear has to start the ball rolling. The rest comes later.' She didn't like him speaking like this. It was self-preservation talk, with no thought for others.

'Eddie, what about love? Don't love come into things?'

'If I can't 'ave what I want, then I settle for what I can get. You know what I mean.' He stared hard at her, like he was trying to look deep inside her. She said nothing.

So he gave her a lovely big smile and threw back the sheet, exposing his body once more.

'And if this don't entice you to get into this fuckin' bed with me and you ain't getting me a cup of tea neither, then buzz off so's I can get some more kip.'

Daisy left.

It was going to be a July wedding.

Suze was so excited, she was getting on Daisy's nerves.

She was getting on Vera's wick as well.

'Si's mum says this, Si's mum says that. Si's dad says. She's like a fuckin' parrot,' said Vera. 'When are we gonna meet this marvellous couple so we can judge for ourselves?'

'Tomorrow morning. They're comin' round to find out what's happening about the reception.'

'What reception?' Vera glared at her. 'Oh, that reception. I suppose we got to give the poor little bugger something, ain't we?'

'Got no-one else to do it,' Daisy said. 'Si's mum and dad . . .'

'Now you're at it. Si's mum an' dad . . .'

Daisy ignored her. 'They've made it plain that they'll provide the dress, the bridesmaid dresses, flowers and transport. Also a honeymoon in Devon.'

'Fuckin' 'ell. They made of money?'

'Na, just ordinary people who've worked hard an' put a bit by.'

'I've got some money to chip in with.'

'Thanks. I knew I could rely on you.' Daisy sniffed.

'Well, I know you're a bit strapped for cash.'

Eddie had already offered to pay for everything. Daisy had refused. 'I'm not taking your fuckin' blood money to pay for a new start for Suze,' she'd told him.

'Suit yourself,' he'd shrugged, knowing full well that she was worried about where his money came from. Vera 'earned' hers, that was honest toil. Eddie's money was something different. His physical help she knew she'd always accept.

Last night he'd slipped a note beneath her bedroom door.

The bloke who ran the Co-op Hall in Queen's Road owed Eddie a favour. So the hall was theirs for the night of the reception. A band was going to be provided. Another mate, a pub landlord from Pompey, was going to provide two barrels of Watney's Ale. Some other Pompey pub landlords had, according to Eddie, insisted on providing spirits, Babychams, sherry, wines, crisps, nibbles and lemonade.

Daisy told Eddie she was going to do the food. She ordered stuff from The World's Stores and they were going to close the cafe for a couple of days to spend the time cooking and baking – Vera, herself and Susie.

Daisy was as excited as if it was her own wedding. But sad as well. She wanted Kenny to be there. She really missed the daft sod. But they wouldn't let him come home for a wedding. A funeral, yes. Didn't make sense to Daisy.

'And how am I going to explain myself?' asked Vera.

They were waiting for Si's parents to arrive, and of course she was tarted up to the nines. Not that Daisy would have had her any other way. In her eyes she was her best friend, a bloody good mate. If they didn't like her, they could fuckin' lump it.

'Just say, in your posh voice, "I'm Auntie Vera". That should do it.'

Vera was wearing a red silk dress some sailor had brought home specially from Thailand. It had a flared ruffle round the middle which showed her nipped-in waist to perfection. She was wearing it with black fishnet stockings and red high heels. She had on enough Californian Poppy to drown the smell of Daisy's Jeyes fluid in the hallway. And eyelashes an inch long.

'False,' she'd said proudly.

'I'd never 'ave guessed. Only one's danglin' down a bit, like a hangin' caterpillar. You better go an' fix it.'

She came back minutes later with the lash in the right place, only now she'd put on her red hat with the fuckin' feather in it, the same colour as her bright lipstick.

'Red 'at, no drawers?'

For an answer she dug Daisy in the ribs. And it hurt.

Half an hour later Si's family was sitting in the cafe, drinking tea and eating wedges of Violet's sponge cake. Daisy was happy with the way things were going, everyone getting pally. Except Vera wasn't prattling on like she usually did. Daisy wondered why. She put it down to Vera being on her best behaviour.

Si's mum was a bit overbearing but in a motherly sort of way, Daisy thought. They'd come in a light green Ford Prefect. Daisy could see it, parked right outside the window. It looked like it had been polished especially for today.

Mr Leadbetter was a bit shorter than his wife. Very quiet. Probably a bit henpecked, Daisy thought. He'd got freckles and red hair, and in ten years Si was going to be the spitting image of him, even down to the glasses he wore perched on the end of his freckled nose.

'Daisy,' said Vera, in a strange voice, 'I'm going out to make some cheese and onion sandwiches for everyone.' She added in a tiny whisper to her, 'I gotta talk to you.'

'Go on then, *Auntie* Vera.'

She was cross because they'd already made enough sandwiches to feed an army.

'What's the matter?' Daisy asked, when they got to the scullery. 'Can't you see I'm tryin' to create a good impression for Suze?'

'Won't work,' Vera said flatly.

Her fuckin' eyelash had come unstuck again. Daisy decided not to tell her. Let 'em think she's an eccentric aunt.

'Why?'

'Si's dad is one of my regulars.'

'What? Fuckin' 'ell!'

'Every Thursday night for the past four years. He picks me up at the ferry. I call 'im Rufus. Rufus the Red, see?' All Daisy could do was nod. She was too stunned to say anything.

'Last week he introduced me to his friend. He's nice too. Likes me to wear my long leather coat. Nothin' on underneath, mind. He picks me up an' off we go to Fort Gilkicker where there's never no-one about. He takes off all his clothes and I dresses him in a doggie waistcoat. Made big enough to fit 'im of course. I puts a collar round his neck. Then I takes him for a walk on a lead along the beach. He gets on all fours an' does his business. He looks ever so funny, walkin' with his arse in the air an' his old man wigglin' and swingin' in the wind. It gets very parky down there when the wind's blowin'. I 'as to keep yankin' the chain and callin', "There's a good dog. Come on, Rover. Good boy, walkies." He's a lovely chap. No trouble.'

'Who, Si's dad?'

'No, 'is friend. But Si's dad is a lovely man as well. Good payer.'

'I won't be able to look him in the eye again,' Daisy said.

'What about me? How can I be Auntie Vera? He can't look at me, let alone talk about weddings.'

From the cafe Daisy heard the sound of Si's mum laughing. She blessed Suze for keeping things going in there.

'This is gonna be Suze's big day. And nothin's going to spoil it, not even them fuckin' false eyelashes. Sort that one once and for all, will you?' Vera looked at Daisy and blinked, and the lash drooped further. She raised two talon-shaped red nails and delicately plucked off the offending lash, then held it between her finger and thumb like it was a spider.

'When we go back in there we're goin' to talk nicely as though you've only just met him. See?'

'I suppose that's the best thing,' Vera said. 'I don't want to lose such a good paying customer.'

'Well you wouldn't, would you?' God give me strength, thought Daisy. 'Hardly likely he'll say anythin'. Won't want his wife to find out nothin', will he?'

Vera shook her head. 'What if he doesn't turn up on Thursday?'

'I'm sure you'll find a way of makin' sure he does.'

*

182

Eddie walked along Commercial Road in Portsmouth feeling like he owned the place. One day, he thought, perhaps he really might. The sun was shining. The market was bustling, stallholders calling out their spiels. The air was thick with the smells of fruit, cheese and veg, vying for supremacy against the sharper, tangier scents of soaps and perfumes. There wasn't a cloud in the sky and many of the stalls were uncovered. Brightly coloured clothing was hanging on metal rails, lighting up the drab paving stones of Charlotte Street as he crossed through on his way to Queen Street and the ferry, near The Hard.

Eddie was well aware he was being given the once over by women, and twice over by the more adventurous ones. He smiled at them but he was more concerned with the Woolworth's bag full of pills he was carrying. He swung it along in his left hand as though he hadn't a care in the world, as though he'd just popped into the store and bought a few boxes of sweets.

This was a new line for him. The stuff was just off a boat at Langstone harbour. It had come via the channel and France from Pulheim in Germany. From Langstone it had been collected, to end up in a two-up, two-down terraced house in Somerstown.

Not that he'd try this stuff himself. He'd leave that to others. A couple of lines at parties was his limit. But he could take that or leave it. Mostly he left it. He liked a clear head. He just couldn't bear not to be one hundred per cent in control of any situation. These tiny white manufactured circles of magic were new on the market. Eddie absentmindedly glanced in the bag and smiled.

A young blonde, trying to pacify a kiddie in a pushchair, looked up as he passed. For devilment, he winked at her. She blushed. He paused a few steps ahead, to glance back. She was looking after him. As she was short-haired, blonde and slim and he liked them like that, he gave her one of his special smiles, before he turned again and walked on. Probably made her day, he thought. Give her something to think about before she gets home with the screaming kiddie, bags of shopping to unpack and then the old man's dinner to cook. Little did she know he was a fuckin' walking pharmaceutical factory. A couple of these, he thought, shaking the bag, and he could have really made her day.

The terraced house had stunk of stale cabbage, sweat and old farts. Martin Kelly wouldn't live long enough to tell anyone who'd had it away with the latest consignment of happy pills.

Eddie had to do him over because, for one thing, Kelly had been reluctant to let Eddie into the house. And besides, if he hadn't done him, Kelly's boss would have. For letting the pills go AWOL. Either way, Martin Kelly was a dead man. So he'd really saved someone else a job, hadn't he?

In exactly forty minutes the pills would be off his hands. Moneywise he was in clover because he'd already been paid for 'em. And he was handing them over in broad daylight, too. The beauty of it was that all the pills were in Quality Street boxes.

Eddie had kept his promise to Daisy. No business took place on cafe premises. It was merely a place to hang his hat.

She was smart, was Daisy, knew what he was about but never asked no questions. But she'd be pleased when he told her about his proposed wedding present to Si and Suze.

When they got back from their honeymoon there'd be a letter asking them to collect the keys to a prefab at Clayhall. Their first proper home. And the favour owed him by the bent local councillor paid back in full.

They'd be like two fuckin' little lovebirds in the prefab. Living on easy street. Hot water from a back boiler. Bathroom and separate toilet. Living room, kitchen with a cooker, clothes boiler and fridge all built in. And best of all, two bedrooms so they could start producing little copper nobs like Si. Eddie had to admit he was a little jealous. Suze and Si had found each other and were ideally suited. It was fuckin' heartwarming that there was some happy endings in this cruel world.

If only, he thought, he could make Daisy happy. She'd certainly been bright-eyed and bushy-tailed enough that day in Littlehampton.

She wouldn't take anything from him, that was the trouble. And it pissed him off to see how thin she'd got lately. Kenny was playing her up. He could see it in her face when she came back from visiting him. Daft sod, his brother was. Hadn't he told him to keep his fuckin' head down in prison? Still, two thirds of Kenny's sentence had gone. He hoped the time would soon pass for him.

Then Kenny could come out and start making it up to Daisy for all the grief he was giving her.

Not that it wouldn't pain him to see the both of them acting all lovey-dovey. But if it made Daisy happy then that was all he cared about.

If only she'd let him, he could make her a whole lot happier than Kenny ever would. And that day, on the beach, when she'd kissed him. He'd really believed, just for a moment, that she'd known it too.

Perhaps he'd buy her some fish and chips later from the Devonia in Stoke Road. Lovely grub they cooked. Almost as good as the food Daisy and him had in Littlehampton. Daisy was very partial to a bit of Dutch eel. Yes, he could do that. She'd like it.

Maybe that mate of hers, that Moira, would cheer her up if she went up there again? Hadn't seen each other in a while, though they chatted on the phone a lot. He knew he wouldn't like to have to pay Moira's phone bill, the amount of times she phoned Daisy.

He walked briskly down Queen Street, past the naval barracks, then the Sally Army place and onwards towards the Dockyard gates. To his left was the expanse of water the ferry boats crossed to Gosport. There was a boat in. He ran along the road built on iron pilings over the mudflats and joined the queue of people moving on to the squat boat. Handed in his ticket then climbed up the stairs to sit on the top deck. He didn't like sitting inside, out of the wind, because the smokers were in there, fouling up the air and leaving their trodden-in fag butts all over the floor.

It was pleasant in the warm wind and the sun. The air smelled clean and sweet and sea-fresh. Yachts, destroyers and work boats were in his view as the Round Tower of Portsmouth faded and Gosport's bus rank came into sight. Gosport was changing, and for the better he reckoned. Across the horizon the Isle of Wight spanned the sea, while on the other side the chalk hills flanking Paulsgrove stood guard.

The engine slowed and the boat turned, causing waves to pound the sides of the craft. As the ferry bloke threw the rope neatly over the bollard to secure the boat so the people could disembark, Eddie looked towards the boatyards.

He remembered that dark, wet night the girl's life had ended. It was months ago now, and there'd been no local gossip of what the coppers were doing about it. Not that he was worried about being implicated. Even the landlord had stated Eddie had left the Nelson Arms before the girl. And Vera, bless her, had corroborated the fact he'd been indoors before she'd got home. Vinnie Endersby could assume what he wanted. If there was no proof, there was nothing to tie him to the girl's death. It had all gone very quiet, like everything was cooking slowly on a back burner.

That had been a tragedy. Whore she might have been but she didn't deserve to die. Unlike Martin Kelly. He was a scumbag who wouldn't be missed.

Eddie had a lot of respect for Vinnie. Gone on to university after school, he had. He'd heard he'd married some posh bint after he'd joined the force in London. Heard the fancy piece had given Vinnie the fuckin' runaround with one of his superiors. Vinnie was still with her, so perhaps he'd reckoned a transfer back home might give his ailing marriage a shot in the arm.

He looked towards the Gosport landing stage. Scruffy town. Full of dogshit, an' pubs overflowin' with matelots the local lads liked to beat up at weekends. Slags with open legs, open arms and open purses. There was money to be made from any situation if you screwed your loaf. But it was a warm-hearted town as well. The folks who lived in the dirty little terraces looked out for each other. Most of them lived uncomplicated lives, paid their bills, sent their kiddies to school clean and tidy, aspired to move one day to the upper part of Alverstoke where the real money was. He'd have a house there one day. Eddie Lane would live in Alverstoke, he vowed. Then he'd say, 'Fuck the lot of you, I've arrived.'

'Wotcha, Stan,' he said, stepping off the ferry and walking up the wooden pontoon to where a fat bloke in sandals, too-tight shorts and a baggy red tee-shirt was waiting. He handed over the bag of Quality Street boxes.

'I 'opes you likes soft centres,' he said.

CHAPTER 19

3 July 1963

Rain slashing against the windows woke Daisy. Her heart plummeted until she got out of bed, slipped on her dressing gown and looked out across the harbour. The ferry boats, like rain-slicked beetles, scurried across the water, but the streets below where the rubbish had been washed down the drains were shiny and new-looking. Over in Portsmouth Daisy could see sky the colour of topaz. Her spirits lifted. In an hour the sun would be shining for Susie's wedding day.

She opened the door and padded down to the kitchen, then into the cafe, smiling with satisfaction at the counter piled high with plates and dishes of prepared food. The sweet smells of vanilla, lemon and strawberry mingled with the richer flavours of quiches, cooked ham, eggs and chicken. Yesterday she, Susie and Vera had excelled themselves.

First she'd have a cup of tea, then get dressed and make a start on the sandwiches. Before the kettle had boiled, she heard the clip-clop of Vera's mules on the stairs.

'Thought I heard you get up,' Vera said. Daisy marvelled anew at how clean and scrubbed Vera looked without her make-up. She'd once asked her the secret of her flawless skin. She told Daisy she never went to sleep without taking off all her slap. Except when she went to bed with men. Only that wasn't to sleep, was it?

'I came down because I knew you'd start washing the salad stuff,' she added. 'Thought you'd had enough after yesterday.'

'I'm a bit tired,' Daisy admitted, 'but no worse than anyone else. I'm excited as hell, though. Daft, innit? It ain't my wedding day.'

'Na. But I knows what you mean. Suze is a member of the family, ain't she? She belongs to us.'

'S'pose so.' Daisy wondered where she stood in that scheme of things. She was beginning to feel like someone's old granny, hard-worked and used up. Even more so when Vera slapped a cup of tea in front of her that had slopped in the saucer.

'Shall I start buttering the bread?'

'Drink yer tea first,' Daisy said. 'I'm goin' to put some clothes on. There's a lot of running around to be done today.'

'Right,' said Vera. 'I'll run upstairs and sling somethin' on as well.' As she clip-clopped past and up the stairs again, Daisy yelled, 'What about yer tea?'

'I'll 'ave it in a minute. You know I can't drink it scaldin' 'ot.'

Later, they worked side by side, Kibbles sitting on a stool, waiting for tid-bits.

'You know if it rains on yer wedding day, it's bad luck?'

'Bloody Job's comforter, you are,' Daisy said. 'Anyway, don't you think them two poor buggers 'ave 'ad enough bad luck?'

'I'm only sayin'.'

'Well don't. An' it's stopped rainin'.'

'Is that lazy sod goin' to shift 'imself?' Vera thrust her chin in the direction of the stairs. 'We need to get this lot round the Co-op Hall as soon as possible.'

'Eddie said he'd collect the van at nine.'

'Did 'e get them trestle tables?'

'Yes. And they're set up. Stop worryin'. You're like an ol' hen, cluckin' about. He even covered the tables with sheets, like you said. The 'all's ready. The beer's ready. All the booze is on a separate table.'

'Who's servin' the drinks? Can't 'ave everyone 'elpin' them-selves. They'll be fuckin' paralytic in 'alf an hour.'

'Two of Eddie's boys are takin' care of that. An' another one will be at the door so we don't get no gatecrashers.'

Vera sniffed. 'Well, trouble does seem to follow Eddie around like a mongrel dog. It's good 'e's takin' no chances.'

'He's makin' sure nothin' goes wrong today for Suze.'

Vera sniffed again, louder this time, and said, 'Not for Suze. For you.'

'Well, it don't matter who it's fuckin' for as long as everythin' goes all right.'

'Ooh! Tetchy, tetchy.' Daisy glared at her. Vera pulled her lips into a straight line, put her head down and looked at her friend from beneath her pencilled brows. Daisy couldn't be angry. So she laughed instead.

Just then Eddie came in. He was dressed for action in light-coloured slacks and a black polo-neck shirt. He was whistling 'Wheel of Fortune'. Daisy knew it was that because he always whistled his favourite song when he was happy, but his whistling was a bit like his singing, not quite on key. He went straight to the pot and poured himself a cup of tea. He looked enquiringly at both women, who declined the offer of more tea. Then he tickled Kibbles under his chin and the cat started purring and rubbing himself against Eddie's hand as though Eddie was the only person who mattered in the whole wide world.

Vera looked at Daisy and raised her eyes heavenwards as though to say, 'What d'you expect? Blokes always stick together.'

Eddie grinned at Daisy. 'Everythin' all right, Dais?' he asked. 'I want today to be just right for you.'

'See?' said Vera, looking at her with a smarmy expression on her face.

They both started laughing. Eddie looked at each of them in turn, bewildered. Daisy could see he was on a short fuse.

'What have I bloody done now?' They couldn't speak for laughing so he said huffily, 'I'm off to pick up the van. I'll have me tea later.' He stomped off. They were still giggling as the street door slammed.

By the time nine o'clock came all three were loading covered food into a black Thames van.

'Wait 'til you see the hall, Vera. You'll be amazed,' said Eddie. He was inside the van, stacking stuff, said he didn't trust them not to let it slide about when he started driving.

'I'll be fuckin' amazed if I ever get into the front seat of that thing. Ain't it high off the ground?'

'No, you got short legs,' he said.

'Well, give us a bunk up then.' Vera tried to lift her leg onto the step, only her tight skirt wouldn't allow it. Daisy had tried to tell her earlier that very high heels, a pencil-tight skirt and a red shirt cinched into her waist might be a bit restricting with all the rushing around they had to do. But talking to Vera was like talking to a brick wall. Might meet one of me clients, she'd said. Of course she would never speak to any of them outside 'shop' hours but it wouldn't do for anyone to see her less than perfect.

'Don't think so, Vera,' Eddie said. 'I'll pass on the bunk up. You ain't my type.' But he lifted her bodily into the front of the van where she collapsed in a giggling heap before sliding along on the seat.

'You ain't 'alf strong, Eddie,' she simpered, fluttering her heavily mascara'd eyelashes at him. Daisy swore she saw him colour up.

'Shouldn't 'ave been too difficult for you to climb up, Vera. I've 'eard you can get into any position.'

'Shut up, you.' But she said it in a playful tone. Daisy clambered up and slammed the door shut. Eddie got into the driving seat and off they went.

Queen's Road wasn't all that far. Eddie jumped out of the van first, then made a big thing of opening the double wooden doors to the hall. He pushed them both inside.

'Cor, bugger me!' gasped Vera.

'Oh, Eddie,' Daisy exclaimed. 'It's lovely!'

The hall was decorated with streamers and tinsel, twists of crepe paper and round red paper balls. Plenty of colour, everywhere.

'Up on the stage is the bride and groom's table and the rest of the immediate relatives.' Eddie pointed to the table set ready with glasses and cutlery.

'That's us,' said Vera, importantly.

To one side of the hall was a long table, covered with a white sheet and empty save for paper serviettes and piles of cutlery and plates.

'That's for the food,' he said. 'The bar's the other side of the room, near the barrels.' Overflowing with bottles of drink and glasses of all sizes was another table. There were even slices of lemon, ready cut in a dish, and a jar of glace cherries. Small round pub tables were dotted about the hall complete with padded bar stools.

'Me and the boys did it last night. Cal used to be in catering so 'e knew exactly where everything should go. We thought the band should be over there.' He waved his arm. Their eyes followed. 'An' dancin' in the middle of the floor.'

'But where did all the stuff come from?' asked Vera. Daisy could see she was impressed with everything. So was she.

'Pubs I do business with insisted on donating stuff,' said Eddie. 'Like the hangings?'

'Yes,' said Vera, 'but shouldn't it be pale colours for a weddin'?' Then she looked at Daisy, questioningly. Eddie coloured up.

'Nobody won't notice they're Christmas decorations, will they?'

'I think the red, green and white might give it away a bit,' said Vera. 'But not to worry. You've done us proud.'

Daisy went over and kissed him on the cheek. She had to stand on tip-toe to do so.

'It's fuckin' smashin',' she said. 'Suze will be so happy. This is the day she'll remember for the rest of her life.'

Everything was crisp and clean, glasses shining, cutlery gleaming and the floor without a scrap of rubbish left behind.

'You've really worked 'ard,' Daisy said. 'Thank you, Eddie.'

He looked down into her eyes. 'I did it 'cause I wanted to, for you,' he said. Then more gruffly, 'Come on. Let's get the bloody stuff out the van.'

By the time they got back to the cafe the flowers had arrived. Susie was now upstairs getting ready.

'Look at that bouquet,' whispered Vera. The scent filled the place. Red roses. And white rose button-holes for the men, with white rose sprays for the women. 'Red for love. White roses for peace.' Her fingers were touching the petals and there was a look of wonder on her face.

'What are you, some kind of fuckin' oracle? How come you know the meanin' of flowers?'

Vera looked at Daisy scornfully. 'Travellin' folks told me. I just never forgot.'

Daisy smiled at her. They were both silent. Daisy guessed Vera was thinking about what might have been. She was thinking about her own wedding day to Kenny and wishing he could have been there with them today.

Although they had plenty of time before the cars were due to arrive, the hours were flying by.

'I'm glad it's a late weddin'. At least after the ceremony we'll be able to go on to the 'all an' start celebratin' straight away,' Daisy said.

Eventually Susie was ready.

Daisy could have cried, there and then. Susie's dress was creamy white, with tiny pearl buttons right up to the high neckline. She wore white satin shoes with little heels and a veil that didn't swamp her heart shaped-face. Not one scrap of make-up. She said she wanted to be as pure as she could be for Si. She looked anxious: anxious, yet beautiful. A child.

'Very virginal,' said Vera. Daisy could have thumped her for that. Susie looked suddenly crestfallen.

'Now I feel sick,' she said.

Daisy glared at Vera. 'That's your fault. Why don't you go and put your own glad-rags on?' Vera took the hint and stomped off.

'She didn't mean anything by that. It's that you do look so fresh, so clean, so lovely, Suze.'

'It's just we ain't . . . we ain't . . . done it.' Her face was scarlet.

Daisy was glad Vera wasn't there to come out with some stupid quip. Not that she would deliberately hurt anyone, least of all Susie. 'I wanted everythin' to be right,' Susie whispered.

'An' it will. It will be unique. Because you love each other.'

Daisy tried to change the subject, didn't want the girl suddenly bursting into tears. If Susie cried, she knew fuckin' well *she* would cry an' all.

'Vera's done a lovely job on your hair.' A French pleat with tiny tendrils of hair escaping.

'You've both been so good to me,' Susie insisted. 'I'll never be able to repay you.'

'For God's sake.' Daisy was embarrassed now. 'Shut up. I don't want to start blubberin'. I'm off to get meself dressed.'

Daisy had to hold back the tears again at the sight of Susie getting into the first car with Eddie. All the people in the street were looking and whispering, and the staff from Murphy's was standing out on the pavement near the new dustbins they had on special offer, smiling and waving. And other people, passers-by, were cheering and shouting out, 'Good luck.' Daisy was quite overwhelmed by it all.

They were married at Fareham.

Si had his unruly mop of red hair plastered down and he looked so happy, like a fuckin' dog with two tails. Daisy swore even Eddie's eyes glistened. She saw Si's dad take Vera's arm as they came out of the register office.

'Come on, Auntie Vera,' she heard him say, 'I'm gonna get you a large gin an' tonic.'

'I don't mind if I do,' Vera replied, linking arms with him and Si's mum, who was dressed like the Queen, big hat an' all.

Eventually the dewy-eyed couple were sitting in state at the top table in the Co-op Hall. The room was packed. Daisy had catered for about one hundred and fifty people and there were all sorts sitting down there. Old people, little kids running around with their hair all messed up.

'Kids make occasions like this, don't they?' Vera said.

There were friends from The World's Stores, a few special customers from the cafe. Si seemed to have countless relatives, all ready for a good old-fashioned knees-up.

'I think I'm about ready for a brandy,' Daisy said to Eddie. He went off to get her one and they just had time to sit in their special places before Si's dad, flanked by Vera one side and his wife the other, started banging on the side of a beer mug with a spoon.

'Unaccustomed as I am—'

'Get on with it,' yelled someone at the back of the hall.

Everyone was giggling. He gave a speech, helped along by all the beers he'd already consumed. He laughed at his own jokes, which no one else understood but they laughed along with him anyway. Susie wanted Daisy to say a few words, but she couldn't. She knew if she tried, she'd end up in tears. She gave Eddie a pleading look. Bless him, he stood up, squeezing her hand, and made all the right noises, wishing the couple a long and happy life together, lots of children and saying how well they were suited and things like that. Daisy's heart was overflowing.

She thought how distinguished Eddie looked. He was going to be one of those blokes that got even better looking with age. He was wearing that orangey cologne that she liked. She could see all the women wishing they were her, sitting next to him, and thinking they wouldn't mind a piece of him. Then he was asking everyone to give a hand to Daisy. To me? she thought. To clap for me? She managed to say thank you, then raise her glass at his words. One gulp and her large brandy had disappeared.

The wedding couple had the first dance amidst cheers and good-natured banter.

'Come on, Dais, our turn now,' said Eddie as the floor began to fill with couples. He scooped her towards him then led her into the crowd. His arms went around her and the music seemed to vibrate through his body as he danced, perfectly in rhythm, and she saw how his eyes caught the light as he stared down at her. He pinned her body to his and desire rippled through her. Daisy felt as though they were flowing into each other.

'You want to be with me, don't you?' Eddie's voice was low, throaty, he bent his head and slid his lips along Daisy's cheek. Of course she wanted him. Her arms went up and around his neck of their own accord and all Daisy could think was that she wanted Eddie. She wished she could make love with him, wished she could have him, just once, inside her. 'We're cut from the same mould, Dais. So alike, I know what you're thinkin'.'

She felt the electric charge rush through her body. She met his amused eyes then quickly looked away.

The dance ended and Daisy pushed Eddie towards one of Si's sisters who wasn't dancing. Daisy went to Cal who was minding the drinks bar and got another large brandy. She watched the celebrations. She'd already done her hostessing bit of greeting people and making them feel welcome. Everything was going well and she could relax now. She thought of Kenny and how she missed him. She thought of Eddie, and walked out of the door and into the night.

*

Glass in hand, Daisy walked down Queen's Road and along the alleyway, round by the allotments and into Forton Road to the recreation ground.

Not far. About seven, ten minutes' walk away. The air was warm and the scent of flowers from the poky gardens strong. There was only a very slight breeze.

Making her way over the uncut grass, she approached the swings and made for the wooden spider. With her foot, she set it slowly revolving. Sipping her drink, she sat on the wooden slats, and cried.

Yet, if she'd had to, she couldn't have told anyone the reason for her tears. She hardly ever cried. Daisy was the one who made the best of things, made herself see the light at the end of dark tunnels. And yet here she was, sobbing her heart out. For a long while she sat there, thinking about things. Eddie. Kenny. Sipping at her drink. Until the glass was empty and the darkness had almost swallowed her up.

Daisy didn't understand Kenny any more. That last visit had been a nightmare. It was as if she couldn't do anything right. Then to cap it all, as she was leaving, Kenny had grabbed hold of her promising everything was going to be all right from now on.

'Penny for 'em, Dais?'

She jumped, hadn't heard him come up.

'How did you know I was 'ere?'

'I can't lie. I watched you leave. Gave you time to be on your own.'

'You been 'ere long?'

He nodded. 'Waitin' 'til I felt it was the right time to approach you.' He sat down next to her. 'Want to share?'

'Nothin' much to say.' He put his arm around her. She hadn't realised until then that her new red trouser suit didn't have much warmth in it. Although the night wasn't cold, she'd got chilled. 'I just got to thinkin', about Kenny, about 'ow good you've been to me. How I wished me mum could 'ave been 'ere . . .' And then she was sobbing into his silk shirt and she knew she'd get mascara all over it. But Eddie wouldn't mind. He let her cry. Finally, she sniffed.

'Sorry. Must be the fuckin' brandy.'

'Don't worry,' he said, producing a clean white handkerchief and wiping her face. He could be so fuckin' nice when he wanted, she thought. And then she looked away. Because it hurt her heart to look at him.

Daisy didn't want to go back to the hall. She wanted to go home, wash her face and change her clothes. Perhaps put on the dress of Moira's that Violet had given her.

'You just want to get into your "dolling up" gear,' he said, chivvying her along as they walked, arm in arm. She was feeling better now and ready for anything. Thanks to him.

Before they got in she could hear the phone ringing.

It was Violet. 'Thank God I've got hold of you.' From her tone of voice Daisy knew at once there was a problem.

'What's the matter?'

'It's Moira. She tried to kill Roy. Then had a go at killing herself.'

'No! Fuckin' 'ell! Is she okay?' Daisy's head was whirling. Surely she couldn't be hearing right?

'We think so. Here's Roy.' There was the muffled noise of the phone being passed over, then his voice, measured, low.

'Sorry, Daisy. We just never saw it coming. Or maybe we ignored the fact it might. She slit her wrists in the bath.' Daisy had the fleeting image of a blood-filled bath and Moira white as a sheet, waiting to die . . .

'I have a great favour to ask.'

'Anythin',' Daisy said. She could imagine his strong face tortured with anguish, Violet hovering at his side, in the hallway of their terraced home.

'Moira's in hospital. She'll get over this, maybe. With scars on her wrists. But it's the scars inside her head that won't heal. Not unless we can get her off all the shit. She'll do it again. I've arranged for her to go to Spain, Daisy. A clinic. I've got a house out there so Mum'll go as well to be near her.'

'What can I do?' Daisy thought of the Moira she'd known in Winchester, the way she'd smiled when she'd produced plasters for Daisy's heel.

'Mum sets great store by you. After she gets back, would you allow Moira to stay with you? Perhaps give a hand in the cafe? She'd be away from access to the drugs. Won't be for a while, of course.'

Daisy didn't hesitate. 'Yes. Not a problem.'

'I wouldn't expect you to do this for nothing.'

'I don't want bloody paying . . .'

'You don't know what I'm proposing yet,' he warned. 'I'll give you a wage that you can pay Moira with. She'll believe she's earning her keep. It'll give her confidence. That won't put a strain on your finances, and she'll get better all the quicker thinking she's worth something. I'd like to pay you for your trouble, too.'

'I said I don't want your money. Not to help my friend would be—' Daisy wasn't allowed to finish her sentence.

'All right, you win. But listen, Daisy, I know I can trust you to say nothing. But I always pay my debts. So for now, I'll owe you.'

'Fine.' Then Daisy remembered: Violet said Moira had tried to kill him. 'What did she do to you?' Obviously she hadn't hurt him, else he wouldn't be speaking now, would he?

He gave a brittle laugh. 'Almost a carbon copy of the Ruth Ellis tragedy. She shot at me as I came out the club with Elaine. She's one of the hostesses I employ. Luckily Moira'd had no practice, else I wouldn't be here now. The irony of it is, she used my own fucking gun on me.'

Daisy put the phone down.

Eddie came down the stairs.

'You look as white as a ghost. Your hands are shaking. What's goin' on?' She gave him the best grin she could manage.

'Nothin' much,' she said. 'My friend Moira's coming to stay.'

CHAPTER 20

8 August 1963

'Visitor for Lane.'

Kenny walked ahead of the screw down the corridor lit by wire-covered electric lights. No wonder prisoners got depressed, he thought. No soddin' windows. And if they'd only paint the walls in more cheerful colours instead of all these bloody shitty greens and browns and creams. The metallic noises of cons and keepers about their prison business reverberated in the dank air. His footsteps echoed in the confined space between the claustrophobic walls, seeming to keep time with the keys jangling from the screw's belt. Kenny was told to pause, while yet another barred door was unlocked and he was walked through, then the door was locked behind him.

'Wait here,' he was told. He sat down on a wooden bench. And breathed in the stale air. Another guard eyed him. They all looked the fuckin' same, he thought. Like mean-faced bastard bluebottles, the kind that wouldn't leave the fuckin' food alone when him and Eddie used to take jam sarnies out to Walpole Park when they were kids. Always around, never letting up. Just like the guards. Today they'd been bragging about how soon it would be before the train robbers were caught. More than a million pounds had been stolen from a mail train, just this morning. All the cons were talking about it, wishing they had a stake in it. Amazing how something like that could lift the prisoners' spirits though. He hoped the mail robbers would never get caught. Never have to come inside where the fuckin' paint was depressing and there weren't enough windows or fresh air.

He'd been looking forward to Daisy's visit, just as he couldn't wait for her letters to arrive. He loved her small, round handwriting. She kept him up to date with all the news: chatty bits about Vera and that poxy cat of hers, and Suze and how her and Si were trying for a baby already. They wanted a large family. It was like another world, out there in the Gosport cafe. He'd never set eyes on Suze or her new husband, but to Daisy they were very special people. He'd been told about her new friend Moira coming to stay for a while. She'd be helping in the cafe, now that Susie wanted to play at being a housewife and wouldn't be working so much.

There was more he could write in his letters to her, but he didn't have the gift of words like she did. Always scribbling things and reading stuff, she was. Eddie was like that too. Deep. He wondered if Eddie still wrote poetry like when he was a lad. Lovely stuff it was too. Eddie liked the ships in the harbour at Portsmouth. The old ones, galleons and warships, like the *Victory*. Eddie had told him that the *Victory* was England's flagship. Kenny wasn't really listening, didn't much care about history and that old crap. But he listened to Eddie's poetry. He'd write about Nelson and the Battle of the Nile and Trafalgar an' all that stuff. Kenny consoled himself with the thought that even though it took him a great deal of pen-chewing to come up with half a page, Daisy knew he cared about her.

But now that bad feeling had come back.

The one where he desperately needed to see Daisy, yet now she was here, he didn't want to go in to her, didn't care to sit near her – his Daisy, all clean and sweet-smelling. Not when he was dirt through and through, worse than dog-shit, contaminated by what Big Eric had put him through, and even filthier for levelling the score against his abuser. And then lying about it at the enquiry.

Eric had been in no condition to talk, he'd been operated on but it had been touch and go. Afterwards he'd been wired up with machines keeping him barely ticking over. Then he'd been carted away from the prison and there'd been no more rumours since.

Kenny had been questioned until he thought he'd confess just to stop the fucking questioning.

'There was no-one in the kitchen when I left to see what the noise was outside.' Over and over again he'd said those words.

'No, sir. There was no bad feelings between us.' These words, too, he'd stressed.

Other cons had been questioned. Shaking heads had confirmed Kenny's words.

'No, sir. Don't know anything. No, sir. I never heard any rumours. Is that a fact, sir?'

But whenever Kenny closed his eyes he could see Eric on the floor of the kitchen, his face mashed beyond recognition where the spikes had torn into the skin. God, how he hated himself for what he'd let himself become in prison.

He doubted Eddie ever had nightmares about the punishments he doled out. But Eddie, for all his brutality, was kind to those he cared about.

Like the time they were going to Privett Park to watch a football match. To get there they had to walk through a newly built housing estate. There were flats, houses and old people's bungalows all mixed together in a sort of grassy, open-plan design. In an alley they'd come across three boys, bigger than him and Eddie, who was about twelve at the time. Quite tall for his age, even then.

These kids were chucking stones at a small cat. Black and white, it was. It couldn't stand, let alone run away. One of its back legs was all twisted, one eye closed, and there was blood on its head. The boys were laughing, taking bets on who could do it in first.

Eddie gave out one roar and ran straight at them. He head-butted one, punched another in the face and when the third one started running, he gave chase. When he got back, all breathless and shaking, he didn't say a word. Simply took off his grey school jumper, picked up the bewildered animal and wrapped it up. Then he marched to one of the old people's bungalows. When an old man answered the door, Eddie spoke to him and showed him the cat. The man called his missus. She took the cat off Eddie. When he came back all he said was, 'It'll be all right now.'

Only it wasn't. Pappy locked Eddie in the coal hole because he'd lost his school jumper. Eddie wouldn't let him tell Pappy the truth about how his jumper came to be missing. Said it wouldn't have made any difference to the old fucker anyway. Kenny admired Eddie for that.

He knew how scared Eddie was in the coal hole.

Pappy stopped hitting Eddie shortly after that. Just before Eddie's thirteenth birthday, it was. Eddie had bunked off school one time too many. The head sent a letter through the post. Pappy was laying into Eddie with his leather belt, calling him a bastard and such names. Stupid really, when he only had to look in a mirror. Alike as two peas in a pod, him and Eddie.

Kenny remembered screaming out to Pappy to leave him alone. And then Pappy turned, swinging the belt. It caught Kenny on the arm, not enough to wound him through his clothes but it was enough to infuriate Eddie. He yelled at Pappy.

'No! Don't go on belting us because you don't know how to fuckin' love us.' And he jumped forward, wrenching the belt from Pappy's hand. Too astonished to say anything, Pappy just stood there, then he hunkered down, cowering, his hands over his face, trying to protect himself, the way Eddie and Kenny had done, many times. Kenny could taste the old man's fear, even now, after all these years. Taste it and smell it. Eddie had brought the belt up high and slashed at him for a change. Just the once.

'I'm wise to you, old man. You'll never beat it out of me that I'm so much like you. That's your problem, not mine. But I'll 'ave the upper hand, you bastard. I'll defy you to your fuckin' dying day. The boot'll be on the other foot when you're dependent on me. And you will be dependent on me. You'll need me before I need you, you fucker.' Then Eddie threw the belt at him and, as it landed on the floor, he stood over Pappy and said, 'No more. Understand?'

Pappy never hit on either of them again after that. Just seemed to drink himself into oblivion, night after night, shrivelling into himself like an old dried apple.

'Come on, Lane.' The guard broke into Kenny's thoughts. In a daze he walked into the visiting room.

She was already there, sitting waiting. His Daisy. Other tables and chairs held cons and visitors, children. The buzz of dialogue interspersed with children's chatter sounded like a hive of bees. Her face broke into a welcoming smile and she got up to kiss him.

He knew she'd been searched on the way in, like a criminal, and she'd be searched again on the way out. Didn't seem right. Couldn't they tell she was an honest person? Look at her, he thought. Dressed in white trousers and a white blouse. Even a white bag and shoes. Like an angel.

'Hallo, Kenny.' She smelled like a field of fresh corn on a hot day, all warm and wholesome. He sat just looking at her, drinking her in. She shouldn't have to come to this fuckin' place. It was all his fault. She had no business in this depraved shithole with all the other losers visiting their fuckin' cons.

'Eddie looking after you?'

He saw her frown. 'I can look after meself.'

'I'm only askin'. He ain't all bad.'

'So you keep sayin'. I know that.' She treated him to one of her special smiles, put out her hand to touch him. He shrank back in his chair, trying to move as far away from her as possible. One minute it was Daisy sitting there smiling at him, the next, she'd been transformed into Eric's smashed face, leering like a fuckin' Frankenstein.

'Kenny, what's the matter?' He couldn't tell her. She'd think he was round the bend, or on something. But it was all right now, Daisy was back again. He wondered why this was happening, why this thing should play on his mind. That he'd done it in retaliation now seemed quite irrelevant. No, not irrelevant, but was being raped by Big Eric enough for him to destroy the man's face?

'Nothin',' he said.

'There is.' She was staring at him. Like she was seeing him for the first time.

'There's nothin' the fuckin' matter.' He saw her flinch. That was the first time he'd ever sworn at her in anger.

'Kenny, I know it's 'ard bein' in 'ere . . .'

'You know fuck all,' he said. But she was ignoring his words, trying to pacify him.

'It'll be better when you're home, and you'll like the caff—'

'Did anyone ever ask if I wanted to spend me time in a poxy fuckin' greasy caff? No they fuckin' didn't.'

'But . . .' She couldn't finish the sentence. Her eyes were brimming with tears. He should apologise. He couldn't.

'Why d'yer come in 'ere all tarted up? I don't want the other blokes remembering and 'avin' a wank 'cause of you.' He'd hurt her, but he couldn't stop. 'I s'pose you'll be off with Vera soon, 'angin' round street corners? If you ain't already . . .' She stood up, the chair scraping as she moved.

'I'm not listening to this—' He stopped her before she could continue.

'No? If you're mouthin' off at me, I'm the one goin'.' He signalled to the guard who started over towards them.

'Kenny?' Daisy sat down again. Her sudden anger seemed to have evaporated. It was his fault and he felt the guilt surface again. He couldn't fuckin' deal with any more guilt. He walked away from her and met the guard.

'Take me back to the cell,' he said. Without a backward glance he left, with the screw legging it behind him, jangling his fuckin' keys.

Walking along the corridor he knew he was to blame. She'd be crying now. He'd made her look small in a room full of cons and visitors. He shouldn't have done that. He hated himself. He was making Daisy pay for what he'd done to Big Eric.

Back in the cell, Casanova asked, 'Everything all right, mate?'

'Why don't you shut yer fuckin' gob.'

Moira had been at the cafe about a month. She was sleeping in Susie's old room.

When Daisy met her at the train station she'd been shocked by her changed appearance. She'd assumed Roy or Charles would bring her down in the car, but Violet told her that Moira wanted to travel on her own.

Daisy might have ignored the woman in the A-line dress and white boots if she hadn't recognised the stiffly lacquered platinum hair in its dated style. For a start she'd put on a lot of weight.

Her heavy make-up was immaculate, though stuck in a time warp because the fashion now was for softer eyes, pale lips. The knee-high boots were to die for, but the dress was a big mistake, making her appear frumpy. And her eyes, for all that liner, mascara and shadow, were as dead as a fish on a slab. Daisy thought Moira was pleased to see her, but it was difficult to tell because she seemed in a world of her own. I'll need to give her time, thought Daisy, remembering the ordeal she'd been through. She hoped that later she'd maybe tell her what had provoked the attack on Roy.

Daisy couldn't believe how nervous Moira had become.

'Get him away from me,' she cried at the first sighting of Vera's Kibbles, who loved to meet new people and normally had the run of the place. The cat seldom left the building except through windows at night. 'He might hurt me.'

'Whoever 'eard of a daft lump like Kibbles 'urting anyone?' Daisy moaned to Eddie. They were in the yard, where she was taking a break from whitewashing the lavatory. The sun was beating down. Eddie, who caught the sun easily, looked fit and tanned. And thoroughly at ease with himself.

'C'mon, Dais. Screw yer fuckin' loaf. Cats ain't stupid. Ain't you seen how he stays away from her of his own accord?' Daisy thought for a moment.

'You're right. He sometimes slept on Susie's bed. Now Moira's sleeping in there, 'e won't go in that room.'

'Too right. The poxy thing comes in to me. Pulled my Crombie off the hanger on the back of the door. Must 'ave kept jumping up to do that, the swine. I found him curled up asleep on it. Bloody hairs everywhere. I don't mind him on the bed, but not on my clothes.' Daisy laughed. She had an image of Eddie Lane asleep with Kibbles coiled against him, Eddie doing business in some dark club with Kibbles' grey fur clinging to his Crombie.

'Could ruin your street cred, that,' she said. 'Don't worry. I won't split on you, that you're kind to cats.'

He glowered at her. 'I know the woman's had some problems. It sticks out a mile. Besides, you said she'd been in 'ospital. But the sooner she leaves 'ere, the happier I'll be. She's weird.'

Daisy turned back to her distempering. She thought how good it was being with Eddie and being able to voice her thoughts without fear of him suddenly turning on her. Kenny frightened her sometimes. She hated having to watch every word she said to him when she visited the prison. Daisy slapped the brush on the bricks. There was more distemper on her than on the walls, but the spiders and woodlice were running hell for leather and at least it would smell sweeter when she'd finished, especially as she'd already had a go at the pan and pissy floor with bleach and Ajax. Why on earth some people couldn't use a lavatory properly was beyond her. Blokes seemed to wave their willies in every direction except the bowl.

She'd put newspapers down to save the mess she was making but that had been a fuckin' waste of time, she thought. She seemed to be treading white stuff everywhere.

'Moira's a quiet person,' she said, bending to fill the brush with more distemper. It dripped down her arm as she raised it and slapped the stuff on the small area of wall.

'Quiet? She don't open her fuckin' mouth.'

'To tell the truth, I was a bit worried you might make a pass at 'er. An' 'er ol' man wouldn't like that one little bit.'

'Pass at that?' Eddie looked amazed. 'I wouldn't touch 'er with that brush you're 'olding.'

'Don't be nasty.'

'I like a bit of rough, maybe. But that one's round the fuckin' twist.'

Daisy stopped slapping the wall, threw the brush in the bucket and looked at him. He'd already offered to help, but she'd refused. The two of them in that confined space was more than she could handle. So he was sitting on the wall, swinging his long legs and keeping her company while she, supposedly, got on with it.

'She gives me the willies. Always creepin' about. No wonder 'er old man sent her down 'ere. I wouldn't have 'er in the house, either.' He pointed to the lavatory's inside roof. 'You gonna do the ceiling? You ought.'

'You tellin' me the right way to do this?' She bent down, dipped her fingers in the distemper and flicked them at him. She missed, but whitewash splattered the wall. 'If so, don't. Or you'll get some more of that.'

'I'll get you back,' he warned, grinning.

'You didn't know Moira before,' Daisy said. She thought of the high-breasted woman in the tight sweaters and five-inch heels. 'She's 'ad shock therapy an' stuff. Medicated to the eyeballs now. But at least she's not doin' 'ard drugs no more. She ain't been back from that 'ome in Spain all that long. From what Violet was sayin', they was pretty 'ard on 'er there.'

'Got money then? Her old man?' Daisy saw the sudden gleam in his eye. Steady on, Dais, she thought. Better box clever here.

'Would I be paying her to work if there was money?' Trouble from Roy Kemp was not on Daisy's agenda. She'd realised he was a fuckin' big fish in the London gangland pond. Daisy watched Eddie thinking. He puffed out his cheeks, then blew out the air.

'S'pose not,' he said. 'Just try and keep her away from me, that's all.'

'Moira don't really like bein' around a lot of people. She's nervous of the customers, so she won't even move round the bleedin' counter to pick up the dirty crocks. She don't smile, nor nothin'. But she's a fuckin' godsend at washin' up. She's willin' to scrape dishes and scrub pots all day long. It makes 'er 'appy. I've 'eard 'er singin' to 'erself.' Daisy held her hands up to Eddie. 'In fact, 'cause she likes washin' up an' I don't go near the sink so much no more, me nails have grown.' She showed him her white-spattered nails that she'd painted a pearlised pink. 'Ain't they nice an' long?'

He laughed. 'Daft bitch,' he said, and made an unsuccessful grab at her hand.

'I tried to get 'er to come round the market with me, but she wasn't 'avin' any. I thought it might liven 'er up a bit. An' I asked 'er what she did alone in 'er room, thinkin' she might like to borrow some books or somethin', but she said, "sleep".'

Eddie shrugged. Daisy sat on the wall beside him, her face turned up to the sun. It felt good, warm. Like it was recharging her spent batteries.

'I used to like sittin' on Suze's bed. Having a natter. It's different now.'

'You still got Vera,' he said. 'And you got me.'

'Thanks,' she said. 'I'm glad you're 'ere.'

'Really?'

She nodded. Then tried for a different subject, this one was leading up the same old sexual path. It was like a contest between her and him. Each time battle commenced Daisy felt her resolve to conquer her feelings being chipped away a little bit more.

'You know, I never go into her room. She likes her privacy so I stays out.'

'So?'

'She's always washin' stuff. The beddin', the curtains, 'er clothes. Washes so much Vera says she never got no room on the line for 'er knickers.'

'I never thought Vera—'

'Shut up,' Daisy said, twisting down to the whitewash and skipping away after having another flick at him. This time it got him fair and square on the forehead, with some bits settling in his hair. She started laughing. The look on his face was ever so funny.

'You cow.' He jumped from the wall and wrestled her down to the warm earth. Daisy knew they'd get covered in whitewash and clay soil and probably a lot more besides. But she didn't care.

'I wish it could always be like this, us laughin' an' it bein' all nice,' she said.

He stared into her eyes. She could see desire there, tinged with sadness.

'It could be, Daisy,' he said. 'If only you'd let it.'

CHAPTER 21

30 September 1963

'Daisy, Dais!' She awoke to Vera shaking her shoulder and repeating her name. Daisy blinked, then gagged at the thick stench of cigarette smoke surrounding Vera. She was in full, but smudged make-up. Daisy guessed she'd only just come home. There were two large tufts of cotton wool sticking out from her ears.

'What's the matter? What you got them in for?' She sat up in bed and began rubbing her eyes. She looked at the clock. 'You know what time it is? 'Alf past three.' Daisy answered herself. Then she became aware of the noise. 'What's that racket?'

'One bloody question at a time, please. That racket is Madam Moira. I been in about twenty minutes an' it ain't let up yet. Drivin' me fuckin' crazy. That's why I got these earplugs in. You gotta go down an' stop it.' Sure enough the moaning and sobbing was enough to drive a sane person mad. Sighing, Daisy got out of bed and slipped on her dressing gown, Vera grumbling as she followed her down the stairs.

'I don't know 'ow you can sleep through such a noise. It's a bloody good job Eddie ain't 'ere, he'd go in there an' knock her block off.'

'Shut up, Vera. I can 'ardly think.'

'Don't forget you got that salesman in the next room,' Vera carried on. 'The bed an' breakfast from Manchester. What's 'e thinkin' with all that noise goin' on, I'd like to know?'

Outside Moira's room Daisy rattled the doorknob. Then looked at Vera.

'You can go back upstairs now.' Vera's mouth went into a thin, determined line. 'Go on, shoo!' Muttering something Daisy couldn't hear and didn't want to know, she swung on her high heels and stomped back up the stairs, making enough noise to waken the dead, let alone the bloody salesman. From the back, her cotton wool tufts stuck out like the ears of a toy rabbit.

'Moira,' whispered Daisy, as forcefully as she dared. 'Shut up an' open the door.'

There was no answer but she was sure the crying had lessened.

'I can 'elp. But only if you open the door.' There was no movement from within. She tried again. There was a spare key on the rack in Daisy's room, but she didn't want to use it. To enter that way could make Moira feel she had no privacy at all. 'There's a good girl. Come on. It's only Daisy. You know you can say anythin' to me.' She waited. After a while she heard footsteps then the bolt sliding back. Moira opened the door.

Daisy pushed it wide and slipped in quick in case she changed her mind and shut the bloody thing again. Moira was fully dressed in the shapeless green dress she'd been wearing all day. Even had her white boots on. Her hair was all over the place. She might have been a mess but the room was spotless, from the bed cover, which had only a few wrinkles where she'd been lying, to the sparkling curtains. Jars and make-up were laid out in evenly spaced rows on the dressing table. No creases showed on the armchair cushion covers, no dust on any surface. Nothing was out of place at all, not even a book lying open.

'Gawd, look at your poor swollen face.' Daisy put her arm about her and led her back to the bed. At least she was quiet now. Moira sat right on the edge of the bed like she was scared to mess it up, her hands lying lightly in her lap, her palms uppermost. The scars on her wrists were jagged, clearly visible. Since Daisy had entered the room, she'd not uttered a word.

I can't be having this, Daisy thought. How can I help when I don't know what the fuck's going on? Moira's presence in the place was disturbing Vera and Eddie, though until tonight, Daisy could honestly say she hadn't been any real bother. She sat down next to her and picked up one of her hands. It was ice cold. For a while they sat in silence. Finally Daisy spoke.

'How can I 'elp if you won't say?'

Moira had been staring vacantly into that dark place that seemed to swallow her up. But for a brief moment, when she turned to Daisy and their eyes connected, she saw the old Moira again.

'Is it Roy?'

Behind most women's grief is a man who has wronged them. Since Moira'd been with Daisy, Roy had visited only once. Even then he hadn't actually come along himself. Merely sent the car so she could meet him at some posh Portsmouth restaurant. Business in the area, Violet had explained on the phone to Daisy. She'd got more words out of Violet than she ever had from Moira. And she got fuck all from Violet except news of what she was cooking for tea. Daisy now had enough recipes to open a high-class restaurant.

Moira's tears started to well up again. Daisy squeezed her hand, hoping the heat from her touch would warm her friend, not that it was cold in the room.

'Hush,' she said, as though talking to a child. 'You'll feel better if you talk.'

'I wanted to kill him.' A strange thing to say, but it was a start.

'Who?' She knew very well who Moira was talking about but she needed to draw her out.

'Roy, of course.'

'But why?'

'I took the gun he keeps loaded from the bedside drawer. That drawer is always locked but I stole the key from his keyring.'

'But why did you want the gun, darlin'?' Daisy stroked the hair back from her face with her other hand. Moira's eyes were nearly swollen closed with all the crying. Daisy remembered she had once asked if Roy owned a gun and Moira had said no. Daisy wondered if Moira had lied about other things.

'I'd been following him. Just like Ruth followed David.' Here we go again, Daisy thought, her obsession with Ruth Ellis. This was beginning to feel like something she'd read in a novel. Except for the seriousness of Moira's tone which made Daisy think she could just possibly, this time, be telling the truth.

'I knew he'd be with her, Elaine, you see.'

Was she now getting Ruth Ellis and herself mixed up in some weird fantasy of her own invention?

'Let's get you undressed,' said Daisy. She moved towards

Moira, intending to help her with her clothes. 'Then I'll make us a nice cup of tea and we can talk some more before you sleep.'

'No!' she shouted. 'Leave me alone!' Daisy thought about the salesman next door who had paid good money for a bed for the night.

'Okay, okay. You stay as you bloody well are. Keep them clothes on 'til they start minging, if that's what you want.' Moira quietened, then after a while spoke again.

'It started just before the killing in the club. That poor man. Roy did it. I saw it, Daisy.'

Daisy's brain was going into overdrive. What was she on about now? From Elaine and Roy to clubs . . . The killing in the club? What fuckin' club? Fear drew icy fingers down her back. Fuckin' 'ell. The killing in the club! The Rainbow. The one in the paper. Eddie and Daisy had read about it. Even discussed it. Was Roy Kemp involved in some way? Moira was off again. Now it seemed she wouldn't shut up.

'It was right in front of me. He stuck this big hook thing in him and twisted it. Half his guts came out when he pulled out the hook, in a big sucking noise. The bloke was screaming. It was a terrible sound, Daisy. And all that blood and the stench . . . And Roy, cool as you like, like he was scooping vegetables from a cooking pot . . . When it was over, I got took 'ome by Violet. But Roy stayed with her, with Elaine . . .'

'Hush,' Daisy said. 'Thinkin' about this ain't doin' you any good.' Too fuckin' right it wasn't. It had sent her round the twist. And she'd been fragile enough to begin with. But that gang killing had been so gruesome when it had been reported in the paper even Eddie had been shocked. And Daisy always thought he was pretty unshockable.

If this was all true, no wonder Roy wanted his demented wife out of the way. One word in the wrong ear from her and he could be looking at a long spell inside.

'Did this 'appen in the club you took me to?' she asked, for something to say.

Moira seemed to be collecting her thoughts. Like they was scattered about and they had to be in some sort of order or she might say the unsuitable thing.

'Yes.'

Daisy let out a big sigh. 'And you saw Roy kill this man?'

'Roy said he needed to toe the line.'

Toe the fuckin' line! The geezer was six feet under with his toes turned up now.

'But you didn't try to kill Roy for that?'

Moira looked more confused than ever.

'Why would I do that?'

Oh God, thought Daisy. So the fact that her husband was killing people was part and parcel of her life with him, was it? No wonder Moira was doo-lally. No wonder she'd tried to blot everything out with drink and drugs. Poor cow.

Now Daisy had that part of the story reasonably straight, she had another try. Moira was looking into space again. Daisy gently shook her shoulder.

'Moira. Look at me. Tell me why you tried to shoot Roy.'

'Because of Elaine.'

Jealousy. Okay, thought Daisy. I'll go along with the jealousy theme. 'And you've been following 'em?'

Moira nodded. 'He changed towards me.'

I'm not surprised, Daisy thought, if you act like this. But that was unfair of her and she knew it. Look how Kenny's strange behaviour had affected her. And he was locked up away from bloody women.

'Daisy, I love him so much.' She started crying again. 'But he has to pay for the way he's hurting me. And he will.' Tears were streaming down her face but she let them fall, not even using her hand to check the flow.

'Stop it!' The severity of Daisy's voice actually made her flinch, but it seemed to stem the tears. Now Moira was sniffing and shaking. Couldn't have any more tears left inside her, surely? 'They were together when you tried to shoot him?' Moira nodded. 'You didn't 'urt anyone?'

'I didn't know how to use the gun properly. It was heavy.'

Daisy sighed. 'Okay, I believe you,' she said.

So this was the unabridged version of Violet and Roy's short telephone explanation, was it? No mention of Elaine. No mention of a club killing. What did they think Daisy was? A fucking mushroom to be left in the dark and shat on?

'Then what?'

'I went home and locked myself in the bathroom, I think.'

'What do you mean, you think?'

'Oh, Daisy. I didn't want to die but I didn't know what else to do. I just wanted him to love me like he used to. To look at me like I was his own special little girl. Not that silly cow Elaine. Every time he didn't come back at nights I knew he was with her. Every time he was later home than he said he would be, it was because of her. I could imagine him touching her. Kissing her. Oh, Daisy, it hurt me so much. I kept thinking about it until it went round and round in my head and so I took some more stuff and then some more. Then I ran a bath I think and I got the cutthroat razor that Roy uses because he says it gives a closer shave and I . . .'

God help me, Daisy thought. Oh God, help me, because I don't know what I can do to help you, Moira. Daisy dropped her head in her hands. God give me strength, she begged.

She got up, pulled back the covers and swung Moira as best she could into the bed. Clothes, boots and all. Then she tucked her in so tight she would have had to have been a fuckin' contortionist to get out. When Daisy was satisfied she couldn't move, she said, 'Listen to me. Don't you dare start cryin' again. I'm going downstairs to make us both a cup of strong tea. Then I'm coming back. Don't try and get out of bed. Don't touch the door. Understand?' Moira looked at Daisy like a whipped kiddie, but she nodded.

Breathing a sigh of relief, Daisy went downstairs.

If only Eddie was here. He'd know what to do. And then she was glad he wasn't around. One whiff of gangs and scandal and Eddie would be poking his nose in like a dog after a bitch in heat. And where would that get him?

One thing Daisy didn't want was for Eddie to be too far on the wrong side of the law. Oh, she knew he had all sorts of scams going. But for now he was keeping his promise that the cafe would remain a trouble-free zone. And if the cafe was clean he couldn't be up to much, could he? Though you never knew with Eddie Lane. Like the time he'd asked Daisy if there was money around

Moira and Daisy had denied it. But he'd seen the posh car they'd gone to London in, and the quality of Moira's clothes.

Daisy only hoped he'd assumed by her negative reply that Moira's husband had cut her off without a penny. Or else he would realise she was warning him off. Daisy just didn't want Eddie getting involved. It wasn't that he couldn't handle himself. It was because, because ... Was it because she cared about him? She pushed the thoughts from her mind, and lit the gas beneath the kettle.

Why hadn't Violet told her the whole story? They'd spoken several times on the phone since then. She always seemed chatty enough, kind, motherly even. But of course her loyalties would lie with her beloved son, wouldn't they?

And what about Roy Kemp? Was Daisy really only doing a favour for a friend by having Moira here? Did he and Violet genuinely feel she was to be trusted to care for Moira? Daisy never dreamed when she first met Moira that day in Winchester that she was married to someone like Roy Kemp, a killer, a thug. But that was none of Daisy's business, was it? She didn't want to know about guns and gangland killings. As long as things don't interfere with me and mine and the cafe, she thought, which was Kenny's future. As long as Roy Kemp wasn't taking the piss ...

She set out mugs and filled them with strong tea, putting enough sugar in Moira's to give her a bit of a lift after her shocking night. Night? Daisy looked at the clock. It was fuckin' morning now, daylight almost.

When Daisy got back to Moira, she was asleep, her breathing regular. She looked like a plump, contented matron cuddled under the blankets. Whoever would have thought they'd just had all that fuss and bother? Daisy tip-toed out and took the tea up to her own room.

Sitting in bed she drank both mugs of the strong liquid and then turned off the bedside lamp. In an hour or so the alarm would go and she'd have to get up again to cook breakfast for the salesman. She wasn't looking forward to explaining the night's noise. Though she'd listened at his door on the way up and it all seemed normal. Normal? That's a fuckin' laugh, Daisy thought.

Then another thought struck her.

What if Roy Kemp really was taking the piss, using her to look after Moira while he was out screwing?

Na. He could have left her in Spain, couldn't he? That would have solved the problem.

Moira wanted to be with Daisy. And like he said, Roy valued Daisy's friendship with her. Okay. It was better to be on the right side of Roy Kemp. She'd read about what could happen if you fell foul of him. On the other hand, if he was using her, taking her for a fool . . . He wouldn't get away with it, she'd make sure of that.

When the alarm went off Moira was asleep. Daisy looked in her room throughout the morning and she was still sleeping. She slept all day.

When she finally padded downstairs she was wearing the same green dress and boots.

'What time d'you call this, madam?' Daisy said. Then she laughed, so Moira would know she was teasing. Moira sat on a stool, staring into space. Daisy made her a ham sandwich. Moira ate it automatically, like she just needed fuel. So Daisy prepared her some more food and left her to eat while she mopped the stairs, corridor, cafe floor and passage. When Daisy returned she sluiced away the filthy water and washed her hands to get rid of the disinfectant smell.

Moira was still sitting where Daisy had left her.

'We're going out tomorrow,' Daisy said. 'Vera's looking after the place.' There was no response so she added, 'An' you're going to change your clothes. I'm sick of seein' that poxy green dress.' Moira blinked. 'Go back to bed now. You must be nice and fresh for tomorrow because we're taking a picnic.' Moira looked at Daisy, though it was more like looking right through her. Then, obediently, she trotted upstairs. Daisy heard her door close, then crept up to listen outside. Thank God all was quiet.

She went next door to clean the room. The salesman had left that morning without uttering a word of complaint. As she stripped the bed to wash his sheets she found a ten shilling note under the pillow. Couldn't have been that dissatisfied, could he?

*

215

The next morning Moira was up before Daisy was.

'Gawd, you gave me a fright,' Daisy said. 'What you sittin' in the dark for?' She was wearing a different A-line dress with the white boots, a rose-patterned one that made her look like a bloody flower garden. Daisy was a bit sick of rose-printed material. She'd seen enough roses on Susie's clothes. Moira's hair was pretty and she'd made an effort with her make-up – heavily lined eyes and technicolour red lipstick, but perfectly applied.

'Where we goin'?' Moira suddenly asked.

I'm making headway, Daisy thought. She's coming out of it at last.

'We're off to the seaside to get a bit of colour in our cheeks.' Daisy watched Moira's reaction and saw panic steal over her face. 'It's time you went out. Me, too.' Moira looked scared stiff. 'Don't worry. We'll be together.'

Thank God it was a nice day, with a clear blue sky and still a bit of heat in the sun. Working in the cafe all day Daisy didn't know where the summer had gone. She'd already made up a bit of a picnic with pork pies, boiled eggs, a flask of tea and some packets of crisps.

'Go an' put your coat on,' Daisy said. 'It could get cold later.'

It wasn't long before they were walking through the upper part of the town towards the boating lake. Daisy had brought bread for the swans, thought Moira might like to feed them. She had this notion that if Moira got fresh air, good food and plenty of exercise it might help her to recuperate. On the wooden bridge spanning the lake they threw crumbled bread.

'Don't they make a fuss?' Daisy said. To tell the truth, as the swans flapped and squawked and viciously pecked each other to get at the food, Daisy was petrified. Moira seemed oblivious to the warring birds.

They walked to the engineering works by Alver Bridge

'This used to be the old workhouse,' Daisy said, pointing to the rounded red brick exterior. She was watching Moira to make sure she wasn't getting tired. At the end of Park Road they walked through part of the old railway line to the beach.

They sat on the pebbles at Stokes Bay and threw stones into the water.

'Can I have some tea?'

Daisy wanted to cry, remembering how full of life Moira had been, pushing Daisy into the bus station at Winchester so they could buy tea there and Daisy could put a plaster on her heel. It seemed such a long time ago. Now she was pleased if Moira had enough get up and go to ask for a drink.

It was nice on the beach, so clear they could see the town of Ryde on the Isle of Wight. The air was filled with the smells of the sea. Moira was running her hands through the pebbles, looking for cockle shells. Gulls soared above their heads, riding the breeze and calling to each other.

They ate as much as they wanted and Daisy gathered up the remains of the food to leave on the green for the foxes who scavenged at dusk. She asked Moira if she wanted to paddle in the water but she didn't seem keen on that idea. She looked tired now and Daisy had to help her to her feet. She been planning to take her into Stanley Park and explain some of the local history of the place to her, but decided she'd had enough for one day.

Moira went to bed immediately they got home.

'I don't think she's getting better,' Daisy said to Vera. 'After that outburst I think she's worse than before.'

'Eddie wants to see the back of her,' Vera said.

'Well, Eddie can want,' Daisy replied.

'I bet she's the reason he stays away so much.' She didn't look up but went on filing her nails.

'That's up to him.' Daisy thought she was probably right. Funny, but she missed him, only she wasn't going to tell Vera that and have her say, 'I told you so.'

Eddie came back a couple of days later. He was sitting on top of the counter, swinging his legs and clicking his heels against the wooden side. Daisy was wiping the tops down.

'If you can't 'elp, don't 'inder me,' Daisy said, running the cloth one side of him then having to step round the front of him to rub the other side. They'd shut up early because of the rain. It was belting down. Daisy reckoned they were in for a night of it.

'Let me go,' Daisy said. As she'd moved across him he'd encircled her with his arms.

'When's she goin'?'

'Who?' Daisy knew full well who he meant.

'She's been moanin' all day.'

'Singin',' Daisy said.

'I know fuckin' moanin' when I 'ear it. She wasn't singing.'

'Perhaps she's like you and can't sing very well.' He was a bit too close for comfort. She could feel her heart pounding. She wondered if he could hear it. Must be able to, she thought. They were that close his breath was sweet and warm on her cheek. For some reason she remembered him lying asleep in bed, naked, the sheet tangled in his feet.

'Kiss me, Dais. You know you want to.'

'I bloody don't,' Daisy said, doing her best to twist away from him. But she did want to kiss him. And he soddin' well knew it.

'You do,' he insisted.

'Not,' she answered. He dropped his grip, stared at her, let out a sigh. He jumped down from the counter and snatched up his jacket from a stool.

'Fuck you,' he said.

Daisy heard the street door slam as he went out into the rain. With a heavy heart she finished cleaning and mopping up. And after that there were potatoes waiting to be peeled.

CHAPTER 22

9 October 1963

Vera came swanning into the cafe. It was nine o'clock at night and she was breathless. Like she'd been running.

'Hallo,' Daisy said. 'Goin' somewhere?'

'What you sittin' there for?' Vera always seemed to answer a question with another question. Daisy was seated on one chair with her feet up on another, a cup of tea on the table beside her. Until Vera came in she'd been contentedly listening to 'The Night Has A Thousand Eyes' sung by Bobby Vee on the jukebox. She was very tired and her feet hurt.

Susie, who was back at work part time, had only just left on the back of Si's new Lambretta scooter. Si had got promoted and was now working full time in The World's Stores. Susie had got fed up being on her own all day in the prefab and had decided to come back to the cafe. Thank God.

'I was just thinkin',' Daisy said.

'You're too deep. You think too much.'

'Come runnin' 'ome to tell me that, did you?'

Vera looked sheepish. She started treading from one black patent high-heeled shoe to the other. Then the dam burst and her words rushed out in a flood.

'Daisy? You know I been thinkin' about givin' up the game and how I been savin' me money? And 'ow I'm fed up with bein' mistaken for Pompey Lil when I'm standin' down the ferry? An' 'ow me feet 'urt, as well as yours?'

'Shut up an' get on with it,' Daisy said. 'I'll be asleep in a minute.'

'Me dream's gonna come true.'

'Yes?'

'I does an estate agent from the town. Lovely chap 'e is. Been doin' 'im for years. We always 'as a different bed to do it in. He 'as all the keys to the furnished properties, see? An' he's a real good payer.' She'd gone off at a tangent again, bless her.

'Yes, Vera?'

'He always knew what I wanted and at last it's come up.'

'If you've been doin' him for years it must 'ave come up more than once.' For the first time Daisy noticed Vera's hat was on the wrong way round. The feather was sticking up at the front. 'Where did you get dressed?'

Vera looked at Daisy like she was daft. 'In a car. Why?'

Daisy got up and led her to the mirror. 'Just look at yourself.'

'Cor, bugger me,' she said. 'Ain't that a silly thing for me to 'ave done? See, I told you I was gettin' too old for this game.'

Daisy shook her head. 'So, love, what's your news?' Daisy trotted back to her two chairs, leaving Vera to take off her hat. She came and pulled up another chair beside Daisy and sat down. Her face broke into a big smile.

'I got me shop. With livin' accommodation above it.'

'A shop?'

'Yes.'

Daisy leaned towards her and threw her arms about her. Then they both got up and danced around, hugging each other, laughing and making silly, happy, screaming noises to The Four Seasons belting out 'Sherry'. What Daisy didn't show was that deep down she was sad, yet hating herself for it. Vera and she had sat many nights talking about what they wanted from life and at last it looked as though Vera's dreams of opening a massage parlour were coming true. Perhaps, Daisy admitted, she was even a bit jealous. Not that she wasn't excited for her, she was. At last they collapsed on to the chairs again.

'Will the council agree to a massage parlour in the High Street?'

''Course. Nigel from Plannin' sorted it.'

'Nigel bein' another nice friend?'

Vera giggled like a little girl.

'Harry Summers can get 'is 'ands on the equipment.'

'Yours? Or stuff for the shop?'

'Well, he's 'ad 'is 'ands on my equipment plenty of times.' Daisy laughed. It was good to see her friend so happy. Vera was that excited it was infectious.

'Cyril Arnold is goin' to set me up with the cubicles. He says I can 'ave the materials at cost an' the labour for free.'

'You got it all worked out. When's it goin' to 'appen?'

'In a little while. The shop's vacant but the family ain't moved out the flat. But they're exchanging contracts this week on a house.'

'Buyin' or rentin', are you?'

'Buyin'. I'm gettin' signed up in the mornin' an' plonkin' the deposit down in cash. Oh, Dais. Imagine me, a proper business-woman!'

'Silly cow,' Daisy said. 'What else 'ave you been all these years? I don't know anyone with a sharper 'ead for makin' money than you.'

'But it's gonna be all above board now. I'll get a couple of girls to work for me. Get them certificated, just so they know where their 'ands should go to do the most good. All the pressure points an' such . . .'

Daisy began to laugh. 'I really am so very, very, happy for you.'

But Vera wasn't listening.

'Me own flat 'as a bathroom. Imagine, Dais, a real bathroom. You know . . .' She stopped in mid-flow and put her hand on Daisy's arm. 'Oh, Dais. I am a selfish cow.' Her eyes searched deep into Daisy's. There was genuine sadness in her voice. 'I'll be leavin' you. You'll be all alone.'

Daisy put on a brave smile.

'It were always on the cards that you'd do this some day. Besides, you'll only be round the fuckin' corner. An' Kenny'll be 'ome, an' Eddie's 'ere, most of the time anyway. Suze works 'ere. Moira's . . .'

Vera wrinkled her nose. 'You know I can't take to 'er.'

'Well, you won't 'ave to for much longer, will you? I'm worried about 'er, Vera. She's been stuck in 'er room for days.'

'She a law unto 'erself that one,' said Vera.

'I've been leavin' cups of tea outside 'er door and plates of sarnies, but they was 'ardly touched. I can 'ear 'er movin' about so I know she's in there. I wish Eddie was 'ere, he'd soon sort it. I was goin' to phone Violet about 'er. Do you reckon I should call in the doctor?'

Vera shrugged and then shook her head. 'She'll come out when she's ready an' 'er not eatin' won't hurt. She's too fat, an' 'ave you seen the size of her titties? Do you want me to sort out the jukebox?' she asked.

'Yeah, pull the plug. I've 'ad enough for today. I'm going to bed,' Daisy said. 'To dream about you and your parlour. Gosport won't know what's bloody hit it.'

'Did you wash the stairs down?' Vera asked, switching off the lights. They walked along the passage together.

'Cheeky cow! 'Course I did. There was a funny smell upstairs, so I did the lot, top floor outside our rooms an' all, with Zoflora. Hyacinth,' Daisy added.

''Spect it's Eddie's cheesy socks. Men are such dirty buggers.'

'Eddie's not,' Daisy said indignantly. 'You know how bloody fastidious he is.'

'It's worse now,' she said, as they reached the first floor. All the doors were shut. Eddie kept his locked most of the time but Daisy had a key. It was no good knocking. She knew he was out.

'We gotta have a look,' Vera said. 'It's like rottin' fish, only worse.'

They tried Eddie's door.

'It's worse now than it was before I scrubbed down,' Daisy said. 'I'll get the key.' She ran up to her room and fetched the key-ring that held the complete set of house and cafe keys.

Vera took the bunch of keys from her hand and fitted the correct one into Eddie's lock. She knew the keys better than Daisy, having lived at the place longer.

Apart from a few cat's hairs on Eddie's counterpane, the room was immaculate. In fact, the moment the door was opened Daisy could smell his orange-scented cologne. Gave her a warm glow that did, before she was brought up sharply by Vera.

'He's got some lovely gear.' She had the wardrobe door open and was rifling through. 'These shoes must 'ave cost a fuckin' fortune. Italian leather. There ain't nothin' in 'ere that smells bad, Dais.'

Eddie wouldn't like too much prying but Daisy bent and peered beneath the bed, though she knew as soon as she put her head down the air was going to be cleaner there. Opening the door had brought the smell in. A suitcase lay beneath the bed but it was locked.

'We're wastin' our time in 'ere,' Daisy said.

Vera was looking out of the window. Apart from the lean-to down in the yard, making a kind of step to his bedroom, it was almost a sheer drop to the ground. She pointed to the window frame left open.

'How can you say 'e ain't got an 'eart of gold when he leaves 'is window open for my Kibbles?'

Daisy grabbed her arm.

'C'mon, you daft cow. He won't 'ave an 'eart of gold if 'e comes in an' finds us pokin' about.'

'What about madam's room?' asked Vera.

'She's a private person,' Daisy said. 'Besides, everythin' in her room has been washed senseless. An' I told yer she ain't been out of there in fuckin' days.'

'Fuckin' private or not, I'm goin' in there.' Vera banged on the door.

'Let me,' Daisy said. 'Moira, are you awake?'

'She ought to be. All the noise we're makin'.'

'Moira? It's Daisy. Open up, love. Please?'

She heard movement and then the door opened a few inches and Moira stared out at them like a frightened fawn with eyes as big as dinner plates. As the door opened the smell came out too.

'Let's see what you got in 'ere,' said Vera, pushing her way in. Then the stench hit them. 'Fuckin' 'ell. I can't breathe.' Moira slid over to the bed and sat quite still on the edge, her hands clasped in her lap. Daisy pulled her apron up over her mouth and tried to breathe through that. Vera had got her hanky out to cover her nose and mouth.

'What's that?' said Vera. 'That fuckin' buzzin' noise? It's comin' from the wardrobe.' Daisy heard it, too.

Vera went over and opened the door, then stepped back smartish as a cloud of flies flew into the room.

Daisy heard the sound of paper being crumpled.

'Jesus Christ,' Vera said, bending down and peering. 'It's in 'ere.'

Vera jumped back up as though she'd been bitten. She turned to Daisy.

'Fuckin,' fuckin', fuckin' 'ell.'

'What is it?' Daisy cried.

'Well, it's ever so small but I think it's a little dead baby, Dais. All covered in maggots ... It's movin' ...'

'Christ Almighty!' Daisy had to think quick. 'It'll be the maggots making it move. Get 'er out of 'ere.' She slammed the wardrobe door shut.

Amazingly, Vera said nothing. She went over to Moira and took her arm, lifting her firmly but gently to a standing position.

'Come on, dear,' she said softly, 'you don't want to be stayin' in 'ere.' Daisy had never heard her talk like that to Moira before, all kind like. 'Let's go in the spare room. Pretend we're a bed an' breakfast, eh?' Moira allowed herself to be led out by Vera.

Daisy locked the bedroom door and kicked the runner up against it to try to keep some of the smell from seeping through. Too late for that, she thought. It seemed to have oozed everywhere. She heard Vera coaxing Moira into bed. She came out, leaving the light on.

'Just a moment,' Daisy said before Vera closed the door. Moira was tucked in tightly, lying there with her blonde hair and frightened eyes. As she looked at her, Daisy felt the guilt rise.

'I'm so sorry, Moira,' she said, sitting down beside her. 'I failed you, didn't I?' She stroked her hair. Never expecting a reply, she was surprised when Moira whispered,

'Roy would have so wanted that child. I couldn't kill Roy. I did try. An' I had to pay him back for sleepin' with ... that slag. He hurt me so much, Daisy. So I killed his baby.'

That knocked the wind out of Daisy's sails. Her breath sort of folded in on her.

'You knew you were going to do this from the very beginning, didn't you?'

Moira nodded. Her eyes were wide, unblinking. 'When I found I was pregnant, I kept it secret.'

'Wearin' those shapeless clothes?' More nodding.

'But Roy wanted a baby ... you told me.'

'A baby. Not me.' Her eyes bored into Daisy's.

'I tried takin' hot baths with gin to shift it. But with Violet around most of the time it was difficult. Then I tried taking

Pennyroyal pills. Nothing happened and the weeks were passing by. Then I came here. I used a coat hanger . . . Pulled it out straight and stuck it inside . . . Made myself bleed. Kept on doing it 'til it all came away.' She's round the bend, Daisy thought, shuddering. Right round the fuckin' twist.

'You could have bled to death poking wire up there. Didn't you think about that?' Daisy was getting angry. Poor little baby. 'How far gone were you?'

'Five months.'

'And no one suspected?' Moira shook her head.

'But the pain you must have endured? The blood?' Then Daisy remembered. 'There was lots of blood, wasn't there? That's why you've been washing . . .' Moira stared at her, then nodded. 'Fuckin' 'ell, it's all fallin' into place now.'

'Paid Roy back for hurting me,' said Moira. And then she smiled! Fuckin' *smiled*, like she'd achieved something great. Daisy felt the bile begin to rise in her throat. She swallowed. It wouldn't do to show how sickened she was.

'I didn't know what to do with the baby. It was lying there covered in this waxy stuff and strands of blood. Almost perfect. Tiny fingers, tiny toes, pretty face. But quite quite dead. A little boy like Roy wanted. I wrapped it up and put it out of sight. Tried to forget about it.'

'No more,' Daisy said. 'Don't tell me no more . . .' She paused. 'You got money, Moira, why didn't you get rid of it properly? There's people you can pay in London, an' I don't mean back-street abortionists.'

'Violet knows everyone, Specially them kind of people. She'd have found out, told Roy. I couldn't take that chance.'

'But you could have killed yourself, bled to death. And Roy don't know nothin'. How can that hurt him?'

'I know. But if I want, I can inflict pain on him, any time, with the true facts.' Her eyes were wild.

Automatically Daisy put her arms around Moira and held her tight. All kinds of jumbled emotions were running through her mind, but most of all she felt compassion, and such grief for this poor demented woman brought to this state by jealousy.

'It's going to be all right,' Daisy finally said, but her words were drowned by Moira.

'I didn't know what to do, Daisy. There was loads of blood and stuff and it hurt, Daisy. It hurt so much. I was scared. I tried not to make a noise. I been washing stuff so no one would know but I couldn't put the baby in the dustbin, could I? You'd find it. So I wrapped it up, and that horrible stuff that came out afterwards.'

'Close your eyes,' Daisy whispered. She was trying to think of the best course of action. Moira needed medical attention. The child needed removing. 'Try to sleep. I'm goin' to make it better.'

Moira closed her eyes. Daisy didn't know whether she was asleep but Moira began breathing deeply. Eventually Daisy rose from the bed, satisfied she wasn't going to move, then she locked Moira in.

Vera was still waiting in the hall. They looked at each other, both trying not to breathe in the foul air. Daisy knew Vera had heard every word.

'Go down an' make us a cup of tea,' Daisy said eventually. As she turned Daisy grabbed her shoulder. 'Thanks for everythin'. Thanks, love.' She saw the tears in Vera's eyes. She followed her downstairs.

'You gonna call the police?'

Daisy shook her head.

'Coppers'll take her away, put her in a loony bin. But the damage will 'ave been done. It'll be all over the *Evening News*. No customers will come in 'ere. Everythin' I've worked for, for Kenny, will 'ave been for nothin'. I've got a better idea. The most important thing is to arrange care for that poor soul up there.'

She went along the passage to the phone.

Violet answered.

'Get me Roy, please.'

'He's busy, Daisy my love. The boys are upstairs in a meeti—'

'Fuckin' do as you're told, Violet.' Daisy didn't mean to be so sharp but she wasn't phoning for a chat.

She heard the phone being picked up off the table. When Roy came on the line, she quickly told him what they'd found.

'The way I see it, Roy, you got a simple choice. Either you get down 'ere quicker than fuckin' shit can fly an' sort this. Or I'm over the road to the cop shop. An' somehow, I don't think you'll want me to do that, will you? I might just say something you won't want me to. You better be 'ere within two hours.' Daisy never gave him a chance to say more, or ask questions. She hung up.

Daisy was shaking, sweat sticking her clothes to her skin. But most of all she was horrified at what that poor girl upstairs had gone through on her own.

In her own mind Moira felt justified in killing the kiddie because it was the only way she could pay back her husband for cheating on her. It must have made sense in her head, but Daisy was buggered if it made sense in hers.

Vera came out into the passage and thrust a mug of black tar at her.

'Drink this.'

'Thanks.' She took a big soothing gulp and followed Vera back into the cafe. They perched on stools. 'Her man'll be 'ere,' Daisy said.

'I don't know what to say,' Vera began. 'But at least we know why she was wearin' those baggy clothes. Did you 'ave an inkling she was pregnant?' Daisy shook her head.

'I wish Eddie was 'ere,' Vera said.

'Thank God 'e's not.' Daisy made a swift decision to share the secret. 'Her man is someone big in the underworld.' Vera's mouth dropped open. 'I know you'll keep this quiet, else I wouldn't tell you, but I need your help.'

'You got it,' she said. That's what Daisy loved about her. Always ready to help in a crisis.

'If Eddie was 'ere 'e'd try somethin' silly, just to protect me. Of course, 'e'd think 'e was doin' the right thing but . . .' She thought about the London killing. No way did she want Eddie hurt. 'Moira's bloke makes Eddie's scams look like nursery playtime. Eddie'd only get 'imself into somethin' he couldn't get out of. This is why it's important you help me.'

'Why don't you just call the cops, Dais?'

'Trust me, Vera. I know what I'm doin'. Her man will sort this out without the coppers. We don't want them involved. Them big gangsters, like the Krays, the Richardsons and Roy Kemp, keep the coppers on the right side of them. The police get involved only when they 'as to, when innocent people gets hurt. But mostly they knows the gangsters look after their own and sort their own troubles without the ordinary man in the street getting hurt. They say the Krays actually keeps the streets of London safer. But I promise you, if Roy don't get 'ere in two hours, allowin' for night traffic it shouldn't take no longer in his fuckin' flash car, I'll go straight over to South Street cop shop and talk to that Vinnie bloke. I promise. Two more hours, Vera?' She nodded her head.

'All right. What can I do for you?'

'Get outside. If or when Eddie comes 'ome, do anythin' you can to stall 'im from settin' foot in 'ere until everythin's sorted. Understand?'

''Ow can I do that?'

'Use your 'ead. You can tell 'im I've been taken up the War Memorial Hospital. Tell 'im Kenny's escaped an' wants to meet 'im somewhere. I don't care what you say to him but keep 'im away from this place.'

'All right,' she said. 'Story of my life, ain't it? Waitin' around on street corners for some bloke.'

'You can drink your tea first.'

'Thanks very much, ta!'

It took Roy Kemp an hour and a half. He stood in the hallway and damn near filled the place with his bulk. Two men were with him, stonefaced and dressed in suits. But Daisy didn't take much notice of his lackeys. Why worry about the monkeys when you got the organ grinder? She took him into the cafe and shut the door on his men.

'I appreciate this, Daisy,' he said. 'Keeping things quiet.'

'Thought you might. Did you know she was pregnant?' He shook his head. And sighed. 'I swear on Violet's life.'

That was good enough for Daisy. She believed him, but she wasn't going to let him intimidate her. He might have towered above her, but she reckoned she had the upper hand.

'I want you to clean up your mess. I don't want no comebacks on me or the cafe. You know what I mean?' He nodded, and was about to speak, but she didn't give him a chance. 'That girl upstairs needs proper takin' care of. She's not right in the 'ead. I made a promise to her she'd be looked after. If I find out she ain't . . .' This time he did manage to speak.

'Already she's booked on a flight back out to Spain with Mum, tomorrow morning. I think I ought to explain . . .'

'I don't want to 'ear it. I don't want to see nothin', know nothin'. That means I don't say nothin', either.' Daisy could see by his face they had a perfect understanding. 'I want another promise from you. That tiny scrap upstairs in the wardrobe? I want it to 'ave a decent farewell. None of your fuckin' carrier bag in the Thames.' Daisy put her hand up on his shoulder and stared into his face. She was surprised to see his eyes wet with tears.

'You got my word on that.' Then he said softly, 'Moira knew how much I wanted a kiddie.' Daisy dropped her hand and had to look away from him.

'You played away from 'ome. She did 'er version of Ruth Ellis. When she failed to kill you and found herself pregnant, she killed the one thing you wanted. She did it to get back at you.'

Daisy looked at his face. Yes, she decided, they understood each other very well. He surprised her by adding, 'No wonder Mum sets such store by you. You're just like her.'

Daisy gave him the two keys to the two rooms.

'I'm goin' out,' she said. 'This place is empty. I'll make sure it stays that way. How long do you need?'

'Couple of hours? Maybe less.'

'Okay.' She went and shrugged herself into her old coat hanging in the scullery. 'There's not many folks about this early in the mornin'. But I trust you'll be discreet?' She opened the street door.

'Daisy, I owe you,' he said.

She saw Vera up on the corner where she had a good view of the streets leading to the cafe. She was hopping up and down with the cold. After five minutes Daisy was hopping up and down too.

'You do this for a livin'?' she asked. 'Now I know 'ow cold you gets, I don't fancy it.'

'Cheeky bitch,' Vera said, blowing on her hands. 'Though if you joined me, we could do threesomes.'

'I got a big enough job keeping Eddie's 'ands off me, let alone inviting some bloke I don't know.'

'Good pay. Plenty of overtime,' she said. Then, more seriously, 'Everythin' bein' taken care of?'

Daisy nodded. 'You don't want to know.'

'Too right,' Vera replied.

'All we got to do is keep a lookout for Eddie an' keep him away for the next couple of hours.'

They took turns keeping watch and looking in the shop windows of the High Street, not that there was much to look at as the street lights had gone off ages ago. They also had to keep an eye open for the odd copper doing a bit of patrolling. Didn't want no questions asked, did they?

Daisy's feet were numb with cold and she wished her head was as well. She couldn't get the horror of it out of her mind. But she knew Roy would keep his promise, and she was sure Vera and she would never speak of this night again. It would stay a secret between them, forever.

'The car's leavin', listen.' Vera was right. As they walked back they could hear it purring into the distance. It had also started to rain. As Daisy opened the door, she breathed a sigh of relief as well as a fresh, piney smell.

'I don't know what to do,' Vera shuddered. 'All of a sudden I got the heebie-jeebies.'

'Don't you fuckin' fall to pieces on me now it's all over. I need you, you silly cow.'

'What's that smell?' Vera said, wrinkling her nose.

'Fuckin' better than it was before.'

The floor was still wet. Not only had the passage and stairs been washed, but the walls as well. Roy had got the monkeys working.

The keys had been left in the locks. Daisy pushed open the door to the spare room. Her heart was pounding. Everything was clean and polished. There was nothing on the bed except the blankets, folded neatly. The window was open. Without a word to each other, they went along to what had been Moira's room.

'I can't go in,' Daisy said. There were butterflies in her stomach. What would she find in there?

'Well, I bloody can,' said Vera. 'Five minutes ago I lost me bottle and now it's your turn to lose yours.' She opened the door. 'Look at this, Dais They've washed an' polished everythin'. And taken all her clobber.'

'What about the wardrobe?' Daisy said.

Vera went over and opened it. Then swung the door wide.

'It's wet inside where they cleaned it. There's even fresh drawer paper in the bottom. Smell's gone,' she said. 'Everythin's gone.'

'I don't care,' Daisy said. 'I can live with the rest of the stuff in the room but that wardrobe's got to go.'

'How you gonna do that?'

'Billy, the rag man, can 'ave it. That'll make 'is day.'

'What's that note?' asked Vera. On the pile of blankets was a piece of folded paper.

'I must 'ave missed it, bein' so unnerved,' Daisy said. She took it and opened it out. Just three letters: I.O.U.

Downstairs the street door slammed. Daisy pushed the note into her pocket.

'Take your coat off,' she hissed. She shrugged herself out of hers and they closed the door just as Eddie bounded up the stairs.

'Ain't you two in bed yet?' His hair was glossy with rain, his face slightly ruddy and damp. He'd obviously been running to avoid the worst of the heavy downpour and was slightly out of breath. Daisy wanted him to cuddle her.

''Course we're in bed,' said Vera. 'We're really two ghostly apparitions who 'ave cleaned the place from top to bottom.' Then she waved her arms about like a demented scarecrow. 'Whoooo!'

Eddie glared at her, then sniffed.

'Smells nice. New disinfectant?'

'Zoflora,' Daisy said.

'Jeyes Fluid,' said Vera in the same breath.

Eddie looked from her to Daisy then back again to Vera.

'You two get bloody dafter,' he said, going in and shutting his door behind him.

'Cup of tea?' Vera asked.

'Why not?' Daisy replied.

CHAPTER 23

20 October 1963

Kenny shook Casanova's hand. He felt awkward. Wanted to say so much to him. 'Don't come back to this shit'ole,' he finally said.

While he was happy for Casanova because he was leaving today, he was sad he was losing his mate. This bloke who had been like a fuckin' rock to him. But Casanova's leaving meant he had something good to look forward to, this cell to himself for a while. So it wasn't all bad.

'Come on, Kenny, you'll soon be out yourself. I'll do what you says, try to keep me nose clean.' Casanova gave him a grin that stretched from ear to ear. 'But I do like all the fuckin' paraphernalia of weddings. An' if the women likes to be married, who am I to argue?' He put his hands out, palms uppermost, and shrugged. 'They reckon marriage gives a relationship permanence.'

'Don't see 'ow. Not when you don't divorce any of 'em.'

'But that's the beauty of it, me old mate.' Casanova shook his head. 'They don't know that, do they?'

Kenny laughed. Casanova put his hand on Kenny's shoulder.

'I'll miss you, you old fart. But not so much I'd rather stay 'ere when I got a nice bit of fanny waitin' outside the gate for me.' He winked, then bent down and picked up a brown carrier bag off the floor. 'Cheerio, mate.'

Kenny watched him walk away with his possessions and the guards, their footsteps echoing along the corridor. A good bloke, he thought, a damn good bloke.

He'd be on his own now, at least for a bit. He'd put in for a single cell, but no fuckin' chance of that. Mostly it was three to a cell, so he'd been lucky so far, just sharing with Casanova.

By nine-thirty he was in the kitchens washing up. He didn't

mind the mountains of greasy trays, plates and mugs, or even the food-baked-on cooking utensils. Dunking and scrubbing gave him a chance to let his mind wander. He picked up another tray and held it under the running hot water. He supposed it was a good thing he didn't mind washing up. It was just a taster of what he'd have to do when he got out and was sharing the chores in the cafe.

And it wasn't long before he'd be out. He couldn't wait to be shot of this place. Fancy the possibility of him actually owning the cafe!

Some solicitor bloke had been to see him, told him there was a good chance he was the legal heir to Bert's estate. He laughed. Bert didn't have a fuckin' estate. But he did have a cafe and now it might even belong to Kenny. And Daisy, of course.

Legal heir. What a lot of fuckin' twaddle to tell him that he wasn't Pappy's boy, and that his mum had dropped her knickers for Bert. Fuckin' turn-up for the books, that was. It had been a right shock. But after a bit, when he got used to the idea, it wasn't so bad. And the property must be worth a few bob.

It also explained why him and Eddie were like chalk and cheese. He wondered if Eddie knew he was only his half-brother. Wouldn't have made no difference to Eddie. He would still have stuck up for him.

When he got out, he was gonna make it up to Daisy. She'd been fuckin' good to him and he'd been a prick to her. It was because of her he had a business to go home to. And a bit of money stashed away, by all accounts. Daisy was one in a fuckin' million.

How would he feel if Eddie and Daisy had been messing about? He half expected something to happen. He wasn't fuckin' stupid, and he'd been so awful to her. All he really wanted was for her to be happy.

It was gonna be good on his own. The cell would be a sanctuary, especially at nights when the fuckin' noise was at its worst. And the lights were always on. Noise and lights, metal clankin' against metal, yells and sobs and swearing. But you got used to it. Even the smell of sweat and urine you accepted in the end.

In the exercise yard, though, he'd take great gulpfuls of air to clean out his lungs. When he got home he'd breathe fresh air all the time. Go out when he wanted, come in when he wanted, and never return to prison. Not like some of the tossers in here, in and out all their lives. Like Big Eric.

Things had gone very quiet on that score. According to the prison grapevine the enquiry hadn't been resolved. But as time went by and nothing happened, Kenny's fears lessened.

He wanted to get out and make it up to Daisy for the way he'd treated her. Especially on those visits.

It had been confusing, the rapes, the nightmares, the unreal experiences when he felt as though he wasn't really there. But he knew damn well he was. And when he'd seen Eric's bloody face everywhere, even when his eyes had been closed, he believed he was losing his mind.

Eddie wouldn't have let it bother him. But then he wasn't Eddie, was he?

The buzzer sounded. Kenny dunked the last plate and stacked it. He pulled the plug, watched as the dirty water swirled away down the plughole, rinsed the sink and wiped the drainer. Then he joined the crocodile of other workers leaving the kitchen.

'Daisy's not herself these days. Anything wrong?'

Eddie folded the newspaper he'd been reading while lying on his bed and gave Vera a smile. She'd been about to walk by but now she stepped inside his room. If anyone knew what was the matter it would be Vera.

''Spect she's been workin' too hard.' Eddie could tell by Vera's eyes she was hiding something. Fair enough, she didn't want to tell him she didn't have to. Bloody women always stuck together.

'By the way. I nearly forgot. A young lad about sixteen came 'ere this mornin' lookin' for you. He was in a bit of a state. Never seen the kid before. Didn't say what 'e wanted. Luckily Daisy's been out all day. Otherwise she'd 'ave been worryin' about that an' all.' Eddie shook his head. Let Vera think what she wanted.

'None of my business,' he said. 'But you'd reckon she'd be 'appier now Moira's gone.' That was a hasty exit, he thought. Still, now the witch was gone he could spend a bit more time at the cafe. He liked being around Daisy better than being over at Cal's. Sounded like Cal's sister's boy Mikey, the lad looking for him. A surge of anger rose in him. Warnings had been given to the boys about coming to the cafe. That lad was a stupid fucker.

Cal had a comfortable enough gaff, though. Nice prefab. Pleasant nights he'd spent there, few games of cards with the lads. In a way he envied Cal. Happy-go-lucky Cal, satisfied with his lot. Looking after his sister's lad, just the two of them. More contented than Eddie would ever be until he got what he wanted. And what did he want? He wanted the fuckin' lot.

'Daisy's depressed about Kenny, that I do know.' Vera had come over to the bed and was sitting on the edge. Font of wisdom, was Vera. Was that a few strands of grey at the front of her scalp? Better not draw her attention to it. She was a generous sort, was Vera. And if he couldn't get close to Daisy then it was a good thing Vera was around. Got on like a house on fire, them two did.

'Every time she comes back from a visit she's as miserable as sin. Ain't right. And now I'm up to me eyes in me new venture.' He saw her puff up with pleasure at the thought. 'I ain't got the time to 'elp 'er out so much 'ere.' She fingered the newspaper, then opened it and started to read.

'Look at this,' she exclaimed. 'Poor little lad.' Eddie didn't want to look. He'd already read it. Heard it on the radio, too. 'Thirteen years old and dead because of some drug.'

'You can't stop kids experimenting, Vera.'

'No. But if I ever found out who was dealin' to kids I'd chop off their balls an' feed 'em to the dogs.'

She was reading the paper in earnest now, moving her finger along the lines.

'They say it's called Ecstasy,' said Vera. 'Poor little fucker. Died of a brain haemorrhage. Climbed out his bedroom window to meet 'is mate, then they went off to a party in a barn at Titchfield. Got 'old of this fuckin' shit and now 'e's dead. It's his parents I feel sorry for. Thinkin' their kiddie was safe an' sound in bed. Can you imagine what they're goin' through?'

Eddie didn't want to imagine anything. After all, the possibility the drug had come from him was negligible, wasn't it? He thought about the screw of paper containing five tablets he'd saved from the last big haul, tucked safely in his Crombie top pocket.

But he wasn't the only supplier. Life was fuckin' hard enough without worrying about consequences.

'You finished readin' my paper?' he asked. 'If you ain't you can have it for half price.'

'Cheeky bugger,' she said, throwing the newspaper at him and flouncing out on a wave of Californian Poppy. He heard her clatter down the stairs on her ridiculous heels and the street door slam.

He got off the bed and checked himself in the mirror. Combed his hair, removed a stray tabby cat hair from his new green sweater.

'Bloody cat,' he said affectionately, leaving his room.

He knocked on Daisy's door. 'It's Eddie.'

'Come in, I'm decent,' she called.

'That's what I was afraid of,' he said, pushing open the door. She was standing by the window staring down into the street. After a while she turned and faced him.

She was dressed in the smart two-piece of some black woven material he'd seen her in earlier. It was creased, like she'd been lying around in it. That wasn't like Daisy, he thought. She usually got changed into jeans or cropped trousers when she came back. Her black shoes had been kicked off and were on the floor instead of put away in the wardrobe. She'd been crying.

'What's up?' he asked. His heart went out to her. It hurt him to see her so distressed.

'Nothin'. Everythin'. Sometimes Kenny don't say much when I visit. Sometimes 'e can't stop findin' fault. I wonder why 'e bothers sending me a fuckin' visitin' order.' Now she was looking up at him and he saw the shadows beneath her eyes. She went and sat on the bed and he followed, sitting down beside her. She was wanting some kind of reassurance from him. He wasn't sure he could give it.

'Sometimes it's 'ard being inside and seeing the person you love visit. Then they're goin' home and you can't go with them. It's difficult, Daisy.' He took her hand. It was small, warm and rough to the touch. Her nails she'd been so proud of and had painted pink were short again and unpolished.

'He's so different, Eddie. He's 'ard. Where's my kind, daft Kenny gone?'

The tears she'd been keeping at bay welled over. She leaned across and took a tissue from the bedside table and dabbed at her eyes. She moved back against him and started crying in earnest. He could smell her hair, freshly shampooed for the visit to his brother. It was scented and clean.

'Where's 'e gone, Eddie?' came her muffled voice. He didn't try to stop her sobbing. She needed to get the emotion out. At last she quietened and her tears subsided. And still he held her, until finally she pulled away from him and looked up into his eyes.

'Will you take me away for a while, Eddie?'

He thought he'd misheard at first. Then his heart leapt. That he was only a substitute, a stopgap to ease her pain, didn't matter. She'd actually asked to be with *him*.

'I'd do anything for you, Dais, anything.'

She wiped her face with the back of her hand and sniffed.

'I could close the caff for a few days.'

'That'd be a turn-up for the books, closing the caff.'

'Where could we go?'

He could see the sudden glitter in her eyes, hear the new sound of excitement in her voice. 'Abroad?'

'Oh, no,' she said. 'Though I have got meself a passport now, just in case I need it, you know?' She gave him a weak smile.

'That's right,' he said. 'Be like the boy scouts, always be prepared. Where do you fancy going? And when?' He could see her thinking. He was practically shaking with excitement. He would have her to himself for a while, make her laugh, make her forget the bad things that were causing her sadness. And love her like she ought to be loved.

'Tomorrow. I want to go tomorrow.'

'That's short notice.'

'I can get Vera to let Suze know she can 'ave a paid 'oliday. An' Vera will cancel the order from The World's Stores an' see to anythin' else that needs seein' to. She won't mind . . .' He was thinking quickly. Could he go off at such short notice?

'Hold on, where we going?' He could see her pondering his question. Her forehead creased into frown lines.

'Devon. That's where Si and Suze went on their honeymoon. They said it was lovely there.'

'When you're on your honeymoon, anywhere's lovely, Dais. Even a tent pitched on the fuckin' ferry gardens. But if you want Devon, you shall 'ave Devon.' Now he could see her awash with happiness.

'Can we go in the MG?'

'If that's what you want.' It was then he remembered about Cal's boy. Better pop along and see what's up, he thought. And tell the stupid young sod that if he ever set one foot even outside the cafe again, he'd fuckin' kill him.

'Tell you what. You sort yourself out. Be ready for nine sharp, in the morning. I got a bit of business to attend to. But whatever 'appens . . .' he got up from her side and standing, feet slightly apart, made a low sweeping bow, 'my car will be at your disposal, madam.' Daisy laughed at him.

'See,' he said, 'I can make you smile.' He bent down and kissed her lightly on the forehead, then left.

He decided the walk out to Clayhall would do him good. It was a clear night, the stars in the sky shining like jewels on black velvet. Daisy should have a black velvet dress, he thought. And jewellery that glittered at her throat and wrists.

He walked down Mumby Road towards the ferry. At the public toilets he was forced to take a quick slash. Eddie hated public urinals, couldn't stand the stench in them. He hated touching doors and handles that had been taken hold of by countless unknown hands. Sometimes he tried to use his elbows or a foot to open or close a door. He tried to remember the name of the celebrity who had developed a phobia about germs. Howard Hughes, that was him. Ex-lover of some of the most beautiful women in the world.

'All right, Eddie?'

Eddie turned at the sound of his name.

'Doin' a bit of cottaging, Vinnie? Didn't think it was quite your style.'

Vinnie Endersby came and stood at the trough.

'Could ask the same about you, Eddie. Only I know you like the women too much.'

238

Deep down Eddie respected Vinnie. He'd come from nothing and chosen to make a career out of a job that didn't endear him to people. Coppers were scum. Yet Vinnie was doing well enough for himself.

Eddie turned on the brass tap and let the cold water run down over his wrists. Afterwards he wiped his hands on his handkerchief. Vinnie unbuttoned his fly and turned his back on Eddie.

'Well, I certainly don't fancy you, mate,' laughed Eddie. 'Bet you still don't know what to do with that.' He shrugged towards Vinnie's groin.

'It may not get as much wear as yours but I'm careful where it goes. Unlike some.'

'Meanin' me?'

'If the cap fits, Eddie.'

'So what if I like a bit of rough now and again? It all comes to the same end in this rich tapestry of life, don't it, Vin?'

'And the poor slags? Do they sometimes come to the same end?'

'Watch it, mate. I could fuckin' take you when we was at school together and I could take you now.'

'That what you said to the slag in the boatyard, Eddie?' Vinnie stepped back and buttoned himself.

Eddie shoved his hands in his Crombie pockets and leant his body forward.

'What you on about, Vin? You got a fuckin' vivid imagination, mate. But then you always did come out top in English essays at school, didn't you?'

Vinnie laughed. 'And you know what, me old mucker?' he said. 'You never was quite clever enough to catch me up, was you? I'll always be one step ahead, Eddie. You may think you've come out on top this time, but—'

'But nothin', Vin. And nothin' on me is what you got.' Eddie took his hands from his jacket pockets and felt in his inside pocket for his comb. He raked it through his hair with all the nonchalance of a man who had not a worry in the world.

Vinnie smiled at him.

He'd turned into a good-looking bastard, even with those odd eyes, thought Eddie. And the bastard hadn't told a livin' soul about what he'd witnessed all them years ago, of the puppy his father had killed. Eddie had trusted him once. But Vinnie was a copper now. And he had a few problems of his own, so he'd heard.

'Got a little boy, ain't you, Vin?'

Vinnie smiled. 'The jungle telegraph in Gosport spreads tales faster than the *Evening News*.'

'What d'you expect? Local boy comes back home with high-profile job, pretty wife – not my type, but pretty in that ice-cold, Grace Kelly way. Got a kiddie an' a nice house – an' plenty of baggage by the looks of them shadows under your eyes and that 'angdog expression of yours.'

'My hangdog expression comes from knowing it was you that killed that girl.'

'Knowing?' Eddie laughed. 'You know fuck all. If you had any proof, you'd take me in. But that ain't gonna happen, Vin. Anyway, I'd love to stand in these delightful surroundings and go on chatting, but I got business to attend to. Nice to have you back in dear old Gosport. Be 'appy, Vin. Be 'appy.'

Eddie slid his comb back into his pocket and sauntered out into the darkness. Vinnie's throaty laugh followed him.

'You too, Eddie, you too.'

When Eddie arrived at Cal's prefab on the Clayhall Estate it was in total darkness. Only a street lamp on the road illuminated the flag-stoned path. He banged on the side door. After a while, hesitantly, a curtain was drawn back.

'Open the door, you little shit,' mouthed Eddie with a grin. A frightened Mikey started blurting out words as soon as he was through the door.

'Me and Cal walked into the pub on The Hard in Portsmouth . . .'

'Slow down, Mikey. I'm here now.' Eddie guessed something was very wrong. Where the fuck was Cal? And why hadn't the little fucker put the lights on? The lad was scared shitless, he could see that.

'For a fuckin' start lets 'ave some light on the subject.' Eddie flicked the switch. Mikey looked awful. He'd been crying. His eyes were like piss holes in the snow.

'They was waitin' for us. Must 'ave staked the place out, because they couldn't 'ave known what time we was going there to collect your money.'

Mikey was twisting his hands together like he was washing them.

'That's why collection times vary,' said Eddie in a calm voice. He needed to put Mikey at his ease, else he'd never get to the bottom of his garbled shit.

'The place were cleared of customers,' gabbled Mikey. Until tonight, Eddie thought the sixteen-year-old was shaping up nicely. He'd been doing Cal a favour, taking the lad off the streets where he could have got into trouble. Cal kept an eye on him. But he'd fuckin' slipped up here, hadn't he?

'They glassed Cal.'

Eddie stared at Mikey. He was shaking. The lad hadn't learned to take the rough with the smooth.

'Where's Cal now?' Eddie kept his voice even. Didn't pay to show his feelings in front of this kid. But Cal was not just one of the boys. He was the closest to a mate Eddie had ever had.

'That's just it, Mr Lane—'

Eddie didn't let him finish.

'What did they do to you?' What had the little fucker said to 'em?

'Well, nothin'. I wet meself but they just laughed. Three big buggers they was. Not from round 'ere. I could tell by their accents.'

'But they must 'ave said somethin'.'

'One said, "Don't worry, sonny. You're the messenger. You're gonna tell Eddie Lane that he's bein' watched an' his days are numbered."' Eddie shrugged. He was being warned off by some fucker. But they had to catch him first, didn't they?

'I didn't ask what he meant, Mr Lane. An' all the time Cal was screamin'.'

'It ain't nothin' for you to worry about.'

There was a moment's silence. Already the atmosphere had changed in the prefab. A couple of nights ago when the boys had been playing cards there had been music, laughter, ribbing each other about stuff. Blokes talking dirty, putting the world to rights after a few whiskies. Now the place was cold as the grave, like good times had never happened there.

Eddie walked into the living room and switched on the standard lamp in the corner.

'Let's brighten the place up a bit. You're sure they didn't 'urt you? Make you talk about anything?' He sat himself down on the sofa. The place stank of cigarette smoke.

Mikey had perched himself on the arm of a chair. He shook his head.

'Didn't need to ask questions. Seemed they already 'ad all the answers.'

'Well, thank God you're all right. You are, aren't you?' Of course he wasn't all right. He was a dangerous fuckin' wreck. But Eddie had to show concern, didn't he?

'Now you're here I don't feel so frightened.'

'What did you do when Cal got hurt?' Where the fuck is he? In hospital?

'They wouldn't let me go to 'im. He was still screamin'. So one of 'em, a blond ugly mush, stuck a needle in 'im. Told 'im that'd shut 'im up for a bit. Pretty soon Cal was out of it. They bundled 'im up an' had to drag 'im out. They pushed us into a car parked behind the pub, then drove off, one drivin' and four of us squashed in the back. It didn't take long to get to Southsea Common. They slowed down there and shoved Cal out into the road. I went to get out but they said, "Not you, sonny." Then, while Cal was lyin' in the road, they revved the car up an' reversed over him. I was beggin' them to let me out. I wanted them to stop, but they just laughed. I could feel Cal's body under the wheels, when they . . . They laughed when I vomited in the car, said the car wasn't theirs. I'd be leavin' the owner a present. Then they ran over 'im again. Fuckin' backwards an' forwards until they was sure he'd be just like roadkill. All the time they was treatin' it like some big joke.'

'You need a drink.'

Eddie got up and went into the kitchen. He felt sick. Cal had got it, had he? Well he'd be buggered if he was going to be the next on the list. From the cupboard he got the bottle of scotch and poured Mikey a small one. He took it in and placed the glass in the lad's shaking hand.

'Drink this back,' he said. Mikey didn't need any urging. Eddie returned to the sofa.

'They let me out of the car near Clarence Pier. I ran all the way back to the ferry, stoppin' every so often to spew up. When I got over this side in Gosport, I took a taxi 'ere. I been 'ere since last night. I thought they might come after me. Or the cops might come. But they'd emptied Cal's pockets, took his stuff, so he didn't have nothin' on him to show who 'e was. This morning I came down to Bert's, but you wasn't there. Some black-haired tart took the message. I knew you'd get 'ere eventually. What am I gonna do?'

'You ain't gonna do nothing.'

Eddie rose from the battered sofa again and, picking up Mikey's glass, went back into the kitchen. Sixteen years old and already a fuckin' liability. And what right did he have going to the cafe when he'd told him to stay away?

Eddie poured whisky into the glass. The first had been just a taster. Eddie took all the pills from his top pocket and with the back of a teaspoon crushed them into powder. He put the powder in the whisky and stirred it. Then he topped up the glass. He looked at the bottle. Ten-year-old malt. What a pity to spoil it.

The boy had been crying again when Eddie returned to the living room. He handed Mikey the glass.

'I'm gonna take care of everything. Feelin' better now?'

The boy shook his head.

'You'll forget all about it when you've had this,' Eddie said. 'Knock it back.' Mikey did as he was told.

'I won't tell anyone, Mr Lane.'

'I know you won't,' said Eddie. He saw Mikey begin to relax as the drug hit him. Rapid eye movements would follow. As his nervous system speeded up he'd feel his confidence returning. But the mood enhancement wouldn't last. The swelling of the brain would see to that, until the haemorrhage ended it all.

''Bye, Mikey,' he said, and let himself out the metal back door, closing it behind him.

CHAPTER 24

21 October 1963

Eddie was waiting outside the cafe at nine. He'd polished the car, the hood was down and the autumn sun was shining on the bodywork and chrome. He thumped the centre panel of the wooden sports steering wheel. After the noise of the horn had subsided, he looked up at the sound of a sash window sliding up.

'Great,' Daisy yelled. 'I was goin' to ask if we could 'ave the top down. Be straight out.' She had a smile on her face that stretched from ear to ear. He was going to make Daisy love him if it was the last thing he ever did. And she'd be happy doing so, or his name wasn't Eddie Lane. He waved back at her.

The window slid shut. Two seconds later she was walking out the street door carrying a small holdall which she placed on the floor at the rear of the two-seater car.

'Got your dollin'-up clothes in there?' He leaned across and opened the door for her.

As she was climbing in she said, 'You always call 'em that, don't you? Would you mind if we stopped somewhere while I do a bit of shoppin'? I ain't 'ad nothin' new for ages an' I thought I'd treat meself.'

'You always look fine to me.' He stared at her flowered print shift dress and the kitten-heeled pumps which made her legs look long. Over the dress she had a belted shortie fawn raincoat. 'And today you look specially nice.'

'Get off with you,' she said. But he could tell by the blush that now covered her cheeks she was pleased to be complimented. He guessed she didn't get many compliments.

'You smell nice, too. Different.' He wrinkled his nose trying to place the perfume.

'It's some of Vera's Californian Poppy. D'you like it on me?'

'It's okay. But that scent belongs to Vera. You deserve a special smell all of your own. Then people'll know who's coming before you get there.'

'You're daft, you are,' she said. But an idea had formed in his mind.

'We ready for the off, then?'

'As I'll ever be.'

North Street was alive with shoppers. Murphy's was doing well. Eddie looked at the small fruit trees with their roots tied in wet paper. It was that time of the year. Summer was over and the season for planting shrubs and trees had begun. People were fingering the tree branches, deciding what would suit them best in whatever garden space they had. He wondered if he would like a garden, getting his hands dirty in the earth, helping to make things grow? Maybe one day he'd find out. He turned the key in the ignition and they were off.

Every so often he couldn't resist taking a glance at Daisy. Sometimes she'd return his smiles. Sometimes he'd catch her unawares, and think she looked kind of lost and lonely. But he was the luckiest man on earth and he felt more relaxed and happy than in ages.

'Want to stop in Southampton?' he shouted above the traffic sounds and throaty roar of the MG's engine. Daisy's hair was being blown about her face by the wind, accelerated by the speed of the small car. She nodded enthusiastically.

'We could go to the market,' she shouted back at him. The market wasn't what Eddie had in mind as a shopping centre, but if that was what she wanted first, fair enough.

He just wanted to buy her something nice. Anything. Everything.

Eventually they parked in the Kingsland Market car park near the traders' vans. He pulled the hood up and fastened it in place.

'Can't be too careful,' he said, locking her holdall in the small boot. 'There's a lot of thieves and undesirables about 'ere.'

Daisy put her hand in his as they walked through to the covered market. He liked that. But it was shortlived as she began flitting from stall to stall looking for bargains, exclaiming joyfully as she picked up brightly coloured clothing and tried on cut-price shoes.

'You're like a kid,' he said. But he too was caught up in her excitement. She bought a tie-waist broderie anglaise blouse but wouldn't let him pay for it. The place was crowded with shoppers, and traders barking their wares.

They stopped at the book stall and thumbed through a few dog-eared second-hand copies of novels. Eddie bought an Ian Fleming novel, *Doctor No*, and Daisy settled on a biography of Gloria Swanson

'Bags I read that after you,' he said. She grinned. Then surprised him by saying, 'You reckon we'll have much time to read, then?'

He put his arm around her waist and, feeling the warmth of her response, winked at her. She giggled and handed him the bag to carry.

Knowing she spent most of her days hard at work, he was content for her to wander through the many stalls, happy to just tag along.

Eventually he was able to steer her across the road and through the park to the centre of the city. Outside Elle he stopped. It was a woman's shop with clothes classy enough to suit what he had in mind. The stuff in the window was top notch.

'Shall we?' He pointed to the door. 'I want to buy you some gear for night time.'

'Nighties?' She was teasing him but he rose to the bait.

'If you like. But I was thinkin' of something slinky, in black. I love blondes in black an' you're a special blonde who deserves special treatment. So I don't want no crap about me not paying.' He practically pushed her through the door. She went around glaring at the price tags. He kept nodding his head, telling her the prices were fine. He loved the way she reverently fingered the materials with a rapt expression on her face. It was a good feeling, buying stuff for someone you really cared about, making them happy. He'd never done that before, for any woman. And knowing Daisy, he guessed it was a first for her, too.

She settled on two black dresses and disappeared into a curtained cubicle with an assistant who looked to Eddie as though she had a poker up her arse. Or needed one, he thought.

When Daisy emerged, he gasped.

'Don't 'ave to ask if you like it,' she said. It set off her slim figure a treat. He made her do a twirl.

'It's pricey.' She looked at him shyly.

'It's yours,' he said. 'Sort yourself out some tops and pants and stuff for day wear and we'll have that other black dress as well. You wouldn't have taken it to try on if you didn't like it.' He thought for a moment. 'Only if you want, of course. Oh, and some underwear. Whatever. Shoes to match, Dais. I'll be about ten minutes.' He turned to the assistant. 'Wrap whatever she wants. I'll pay cash.' To Daisy he said, 'No arguments. You never let me buy you nothing except that dressing gown. I'm makin' up for it now, okay?' She nodded. As he left the shop, he smiled to himself at leaving her with a bewildered expression on her face. Nice to get me own way with her, for once, he thought.

Eddie ran up the street and through the throng of shoppers like a dog with two tails. He ran past a chemist's shop, almost colliding with a woman with a prescription in her hand. He thought about Mikey. He hadn't wanted to harm the little fucker but sooner or later the boy would have told the filth everything. He had to look after number one, didn't he? Why was everything so fuckin' complicated?

A while later Daisy was excitedly jumping up and down outside the shop and he was trying to take the packages and bags from her.

'I'll look as smart as you do now,' she said. He stood quite still and stared at her.

'Daisy, you could dress in a sack an' you'd look wonderful to me.' She stared at him.

'You really care about me, don't you, Eddie?' All around them people shopped and pushed past, with bags and pushchairs and packages.

But Eddie just nodded. He was in a special place, one where nothing mattered. Nothing except Daisy.

For the first time in his life he was stuck for a quick comeback. Nervously he said, 'You hungry? Let's get back to the car. I know a little place in the forest.'

He held her hand and in his other one all the bags. They didn't speak on the way back to the car. He couldn't say anything because he didn't know what to say, didn't want to break the spell. It was like they were in a special cocoon and to speak, to examine it, would destroy its fragility. He sensed Daisy had discovered something as well. Good or bad, he didn't want to know, not just yet.

He didn't put the soft top down. Her nearness, in the confined space of the small vehicle, was exactly what he craved.

The autumn colours of the New Forest dazzled his senses. The greens, the reds, the oranges, the browns of the leaves. Leaves ready to drift to earth as winter claimed its treasures. To Eddie, the winter meant new birth, a promise of things to come. But like Daisy, he revelled in the summer months when flowers, trees and bushes were like fat trollops, overblown, blowsy and bursting at the seams with colour and scent.

As they neared Cadnum roundabout Daisy surprised him by gently laying her hand on his knee. He turned his head and looked at her. She broke the silence.

''Ave we really got time to be truly together?'

Eddie felt the emotion rise. Yet everything was very calm. So calm he wanted to stop the car, gather her to him and cry into her hair. At last, at long last, she had feelings for him.

He just nodded, too full to speak, then covered her hand with one of his. Down the narrow forest roads, hemmed in by trees, he drove, only removing his hand from hers when he needed to change gear.

At last he turned into a gravelled driveway to a pub with Tudor timbers and white walls. Smoke drifted from its chimneys. He pulled up.

'Lunch?' She nodded. He went round, his shoes crunching on the gravel, and opened the door for her. Together they entered the low-ceilinged bar, their feet sinking in the red plush carpet. Smells of food assailed them, mixing with the scent of polish from the gleaming tables and wooden bar top. Polished brasswear winked from tops of shelving and horse brasses hung on beams. Eddie motioned Daisy to a table laid with serviettes and cutlery. He walked to the bar, where he ordered Daisy a brandy and lime, and a half of shandy for himself. He took two menus back to the table.

'What do you fancy?' he asked, moving her drink towards her.

'Steak,' she said without hesitation.

'Two steaks it shall be.' He smiled at her. He could feel things were different between them now, but he was walking on eggshells with her.

'It's nice 'ere. Can we stay the night?' she asked.

His heart started thumping.

Before he had a chance to reply, the woman from behind the bar came to take their order. He had to make himself take deep breaths but even so he found himself stuttering. Come on, Eddie boy, he thought, get a grip of yourself. Isn't this what you've been aiming for, a night with the woman you love? And she wants *you*.

He looked at Daisy. She was clearly enjoying his discomfort. When the woman had gone, tearing the page from her order pad to hand in at the serving window, he said, 'If that's what you really want, Dais.' He stared into her eyes but couldn't read a thing there. Except her warm smile.

Then he got up and went back to the bar, where he chatted briefly with the barmaid. She went out the back to return, moments later, with an elderly woman with iron-grey hair.

'A room? No trouble. Honeymoon couple, are you?' Eddie nodded vigorously. The woman turned to the back of the bar where shelves of bottles winked their translucent colours in the light and took a key from a rack near the bar hatch. 'Finish your lunch first,' she said, handing him an old-fashioned key. 'Janice here will show you where to go afterwards, won't you, Jan?'

''Course,' smiled the barmaid. 'Breakfast is from seven 'til nine. Settle everything before you leave.'

Eddie thanked her, looked at the number on the weighty key, four, took it back to the table and laid it on a serviette in front of Daisy.

'Your wish is my command,' he said.

'An' I told you before when you said that, you're daft, you are.' He could see she was nervous now. But not as nervous as he was.

They ate in silence. Neither of them managing to finish. When they laid down their knives and forks, Daisy took the initiative.

'Let's go upstairs,' she said, reaching across the table and laying her hand over his.

*

249

'What a lovely room,' said Daisy, walking to the window that looked out over a duck pond at the rear of the property. He saw there were two swans on the water. He took in the beamed ceilings and grey-washed walls, the wall lights with orange satin-fringed shades.

'It'll do, Janice,' he told the barmaid. She blushed at his use of her name, before closing the bedroom door and leaving them alone.

'Well?' he said to Daisy.

'She fancied you.'

He laughed, easing the tension. 'Are you jealous, Daisy Lane?'

''Course not,' came the tart reply. All the same, he was glad she'd noticed. He watched Daisy walk to the en suite bathroom and open the door.

'Oh, Eddie,' she cried. 'Just look 'ow lovely it all is. There's a fuckin' shower an' all. An' look at the thickness of these towels.' She picked a towel from the heated towel rail and held it against her cheek with a rapt expression on her face. 'An' warm,' she said. Eddie simply stood and watched her, delighting in her happiness, smiling as though she were a child he loved indulging. Then he looked at the bed.

It was an enormous ornate brass bedstead, covered with a frilled, flower-patterned quilt he just knew was going to be filled with the softest duck-down feathers.

He felt shy. It wasn't like before, when he'd been with her and taken her for the hell of it.

'I'm just goin' to the car to bring up the stuff,' he said abruptly.

All the way down the stairs and through the bar and out to the gravel parking area he worried. Worried that it wouldn't work out the way he wanted it to.

From the boot he extracted her holdall and his own leather zip bag, plus the shopping. Then he locked the car and stood listening to the breeze, rustling the remaining leaves on the trees.

A thin sun was bravely trying its best, but the late afternoon dampness was already overtaking its brightness, dulling the gloss on the leaves of the rhododendron bushes that grew thickly about the shrubby gardens. Everything was remarkably green here, he thought.

Then he told himself not to be so silly, to get back upstairs. Why should he be scared of Daisy? He took a deep breath and strode back into the pub.

When he reached the room, Daisy had kicked off her shoes and was lying on the bed, one hand propping her head, her body turned towards the door and him.

'I don't ever want to leave this room,' she said. He set the stuff he'd brought on a chair, then went and sat on the bed beside her. He took from his inside pocket two small bags bearing expensive shop logos.

'When you were in the shop tryin' on clothes I went shoppin' as well.' He opened one of the bags and presented her with a small black jeweller's box. He unfastened the clip then handed it to Daisy so she could lift the top and see what he'd bought her. His heart was thudding. Suppose she didn't like it? He'd never seen her wear jewellery apart from her plain wedding ring and sometimes the cat brooch Moira had given her. What if she wouldn't accept it?

He watched her eyes light up as she saw the wide gold bangle. For a while she just stared at it. Then she lifted it from the black velvet base on which it lay.

'It's gold.' Her voice sounded full of wonder.

'Yes.' Oh God, he thought. Is this where I've spoiled everything?

She sat up and handed it to him. His heart sank. She was giving it back.

'Clip it on for me.' He took her small hand and fastened the bangle around her slim wrist. When it was secure she shook her wrist and looked at it. Her eyes were soft and moist.

'It's beautiful,' she said. 'Thank you.' Now his heart was bursting with pride. It was going to be all right, it really was. He grinned at her and handed her the second small bag.

Like a child she shook the bag, then looked at him. He knew it wouldn't rattle.

'Open it,' he said. This time she didn't even try to hide her delight.

'Oh, Eddie! Chanel No. 5. Fuckin' 'ell, that's what Marilyn Monroe used to wear in bed. Just that perfume an' nothin' else.' She twisted the glass stopper and put her finger to the top of the bottle. Then to her nose, taking a long sniff, transferring it at last to the pulse spot on her wrist. 'It smells just heavenly. Thank you, thank you, thank you.'

'Well, I don't want you smelling like Vera. Not that what she wears ain't nice enough, but you're different.'

'Do you know you mustn't leave perfume on a dressin' table because it loses its potency?' She was babbling.

'Is that so?' She shook her wrist and smiled at the bangle.

'This is so special.' Tears came to her eyes. 'You never bought me nothin' before.'

'Only 'cause you wouldn't let me. Only that poxy dressing gown.'

'And now I've had all these presents in one day when I ain't had any presents from no one for ages. C'm'ere, you.' His throat was dry, but he thought she might want him to kiss her so he bent towards her.

'No. Take your clothes off,' she ordered. He straightened up as he realised the implication of her words. He got off the bed, began tearing at his jacket, his tie. He was down to his shirt when she said, 'Slowly. Very slowly. You've a fuckin' lovely body on you an' I want to savour every moment.' His head was spinning Not one woman had said anything like that to him before. He knew women fancied him. And those he'd taken had even said afterwards they'd enjoyed him.

But this was a new experience. He began methodically to unbutton his silk shirt. He couldn't look at Daisy. Four buttons and then the gold cufflinks with the black onyx 'E'. He slipped the shirt over his body, it slithered against his skin, then he was free of it. Making it into a ball, he tossed it on the chair where it missed and fell to the floor. He didn't want to think about picking it up. He managed now to look at Daisy's face, wondering what was going on inside her head. Her eyes gave nothing away.

Without bending, he used his feet to slide the leather slip-ons from his feet. He felt the sweat begin to break out on his forehead and neck as he bent to take off first one sock then the other. Each sock he left where it had fallen.

'Gettin' interestin',' said Daisy.

He unzipped his fly and pulled his belt free from the hasp at his waist. Then stood quite still, awaiting instructions.

'Slowly,' she said. In all this while she hadn't moved from where she sat on the bed. His breath was becoming shallow, his cock straining against the fibre of his trousers. He never wore underpants. The moment he began easing his trousers down over his erection, he would be on full view to her. It was too late to be embarrassed.

'Come on,' she said softly. He did as he was told and freed himself. 'Very nice,' she said. 'Very nice indeed.'

He stepped out of his trousers, leaving them on the floor. He wasn't breathing properly. He couldn't. His head was whirling but his body and senses seemed to have a life of their own and he thanked God for that.

'Now undress me,' she commanded, and slid from the bed to stand close to him, so close the scent of the Chanel No. 5 mixed with her own musky fragrance was inflaming him. Fuckin' 'ell, he thought, this is torture of the sweetest kind.

His hands were shaking as he fumbled at her clothes. All he wanted was to tear the fuckin' things from her and enter her, so great was his need. But he knew he wouldn't do that. It was excruciatingly painful pleasure as each garment – dress, stockings, panties, suspender belt and bra – came off. Her small taut breasts were revealed, her triangle of pubic hair that he wanted to grasp to his face with his hands, pushing her small buttocks so he could taste every part of her, her white skin, her slim legs he wanted to feel around him.

'You're so little,' he said in awe of her nakedness. She pushed him back on to the bed. He struggled to sit up, to make a grab for her.

'No. Lay down,' she said.

So he did, in the centre of the bed, his penis hard, standing proudly.

Daisy straddled him. He could feel the dampness of her vagina open on his thigh. She was grasping his penis with both hands. He moaned. God, this was the most difficult thing he'd ever had to do, holding himself back, when the heat of her sex and the smell of her was excruciating torture.

'Fuckin' 'ell, Daisy.'

Her fingers played lightly over his engorged tip. She smoothed a little of the milky cum on her index finger and pressed it to her lips.

'Slowly,' he admonished. 'Please, slowly.' She eased herself backwards and, bending forward, took him in her mouth. Her tongue was like sparks of fire shooting to that special pleasure spot behind the head of his penis. He gasped again and had to hold his breath to contain himself. Her tongue circled and licked as she tried to take the whole of him, up to his scrotum, into the warm, wet recesses of her mouth.

'Daisy,' he groaned, arching his back and gripping the eiderdown.

Then she let him go and he breathed a sigh of relief. Which was, at the same time, a yearning to be inside her and thrusting. She slithered up the full length of him and lay, her body resting on her elbows. She looked into his eyes, and he saw the tenderness there. He felt tears rise.

What the fuckin' 'ell was happening to him? He blinked the wetness away and she lowered her head, her lips and mouth swollen with desire. She kissed first one eye, then the other, then the tip of his nose, finally coming to rest, warmly, firmly, on his mouth. One kiss and her mouth opened. Her small tongue snaked inside his open lips. But not for long.

She pulled away, sat back, eased herself forward and guided his straining cock inside her. She was now astride him and every soft, warm, wet ridge of her was his. She eased her legs down at his sides and began the dance of skin against skin. She was weightless on top of him. He felt he was going to explode.

'We're joined completely now, Daisy,' he whispered. It was hard not to let go and spoil it for her.

She let herself be eased onto her back so she was beneath him. Now there really was no going back. He could feel her moving too, extracting the pleasure as he slid in and out of her. He never knew he could be this gentle. She was matching him movement for movement, clinging, drawing him into her, perfectly in tune with his rhythm. Her legs rose and encircled his buttocks, and then there was nothing but one glorious thrust after another until that final loss of control as he spent into her, and was immersed in a whiteness that meant total abandonment and oblivion. He called her name, then collapsed, his head on the pillow, the softness of her hair and warmth of her skin to the side of his face. He breathed evenly, until he spasmed, then shuddered, finally to sink in that joined, warm abyss of sex.

Slowly his senses returned. Daisy lay unmoving beneath him. He was shrinking but didn't want to slip from her. He remembered the gratifying moment he had come. She had called his name. He knew why she'd cried out, had felt her.

He pushed himself up on one elbow. Gazed down at her.

'You came with me, didn't you?'

'Is that so fuckin' bad?' she asked sleepily, opening her eyes but putting both her arms around him so he was clasped tightly to her. She'd been thinking her own private thoughts, he reckoned. He felt the excitement begin to bubble up inside him as he marvelled at the wonder of them making love. For that was what it had been, not fucking. Well, yes, that too, but they had *made love* together. And he loved her. Fuckin' loved her!

That was an alien feeling. Frightening.

'We can't go back to bein' what we were.'

'No,' she replied softly.

He moved away, wriggling inside the bed. She was still lying on the quilt. He made a tent of the sheet.

'Get in 'ere with me.'

She scrambled inside the sheet and lay facing him. He put his arms around her and kissed her gently on the lips. She held him.

'You feel the same, don't you? I can tell. You love me, don't you?'

She gave a long sigh. But to him it was the final acceptance. He thought about his life so far.

'It's a fuckin' mess, Dais.'

'I tried not to even like you,' she said. Her face was inches from his, her breath warm on his face. The smell of sex mixed with her perfume in the small space intoxicated him.

'I know you did,' he answered. 'An' I tried hard not to let you get under my skin. Only it didn't work. Can you feel me lovin' you?' He could hear both their hearts beating.

She smiled and gave a wry smile.

'Yes.' Her eyes held his. 'I fuckin' love you an' all.' Daisy snuggled her face into his neck. 'I don't want to go back. I want to stay in this room forever.' Her muffled words were said with such emotion, such force, that he knew she meant it.

'For once in his fuckin' life, Eddie Lane don't know what to do,' he said.

'You'll fix it. You fix everythin', Eddie,' she said. 'You fixed me.'

'What?'

She looked at him. 'I feel like I've loved you for a long time but been fighting against it. I knew, deep down, it was inevitable. You know when I tied you up that time because of Suze?' She didn't wait for an answer. 'It was the hardest thing in the world for me to walk out that door without havin' a taste of you first. But I had to do it, to teach you a lesson, didn't I?'

'Suze wasn't nothin'—'

She didn't let him finish. 'I know that.'

'I've never felt anythin' in my life before for any woman,' he said. 'There's very few people I do care about. You, Kenny . . .' He thought about Pappy. Yeah, and that old bastard, he thought. But that would be a story to unfold on another day.

'I care about Kenny,' she said.

'I know you do. But it'll be all right. I'll make it all right. I promise.' His desire for her rose again. She felt it too, for she put her hand down and encircled him.

'Is that lovin' or fuckin'?' she asked.

'Come 'ere and find out,' he said.

CHAPTER 25

21 October 1963

Today he'd been made to drag out kitchen equipment and clean behind cupboards, shelving and heavy work surfaces. Kenny was tired, and sick of being made to do stuff he didn't want to. It's not, he thought, the same as hard work on a building site in the fresh air. The banter with other blokes, the sun on your back when your shirt was off in summer, friendly noises of site sounds and passing traffic. Carrying a hod filled with bricks up a ladder day after day toned every part of your body. Kenny firmly believed in 'if you didn't use it, you'd lose it'. The dreary hard work in here wore a bloke out more quickly than constant physical labour.

His cell door was open. On the bed that had belonged to Casanova was the same pile of stuff on the rolled-down mattress that was there before he'd gone to eat his evening meal.

So he had a cell mate already, did he? His solitude hadn't lasted fuckin' long. 'Bout time the bastard showed himself. Caught up in the infernal red tape that every known movement in prison entailed, no doubt. He didn't even want to be nosy and examine the crap on the bed. He could tell there wasn't no personal stuff, just the same kind of toilet crap they all bought at the prison shop. But he'd find out who it belonged to soon enough.

Kenny lay on his bed, his eyes closed.

'Hello, Golden Boy. 'Eard you was on your own. Didn't want my little playmate to get lonely, did I? So Daddy's come to give him some company.'

Kenny shot to a sitting position. God, he was hearing that fuckin' voice in his dreams again.

Only this wasn't a dream . . .

'What . . .'

257

'What am I doin' 'ere? Is that what you wants to know, my pretty boy? I just told you.'

Kenny couldn't speak. He stared at the grotesque face in front of him. If he'd hit the target an inch higher Eric would have lost the sight in one eye. As it was, the livid scar ran from below his eyelid to where his cheek, nose and mouth had taken most of the impact from the meat tenderiser.

Eric's nose had been sort of put back together. But his top lip where it met his left cheek was curled in a grimace, and his cheek was pitted from where the metal spikes had torn his skin.

'You'll get used to me looks, sweetie. But then, I never was a great beauty, was I?'

Kenny's heart was thumping loud enough for the whole fuckin' prison to hear. Sweat had started running down his back. How the fuck could he cope with sharing a cell with this cunt?

'You're out of 'ospital, then?' He tried hard not to let Big Eric see how frightened he was.

'Been out for a while. Recuperation, they called it, at that fuckin' place they sent me. Trauma to my system, they said I 'ad. Me fallin' so heavily, like, in the kitchen that day. Still, you don't know nothin' about that 'cause you wasn't there, was you?'

Kenny's whole body felt like fuckin' jelly.

Eric moved closer, bending down to him, his breath washing over Kenny like a foul wind.

'I ain't forgot you, cunt. I've 'ad plenty of time to think about my Golden Boy. Even managed to get the promise of a cell share when your mate Casanova shipped out. 'Cause I got mates among the staff, see? I does 'em favours and they does 'em back. I'm gonna be closer to you than any bastard's ever been before.'

Kenny flinched as one of Eric's big hands shot downwards and squeezed his balls. Kenny backed up, until he felt the edge of the metal bed frame and could go no further. Eric's grip tightened and he went on rubbing at him through his overalls. He felt his body shame him by responding. Eric laughed. 'You like that, don't you, you fucker?'

Then he stepped away. Allowing Kenny freedom to move, to breathe.

All the while, Eric laughed to himself as he went about the

important business of settling into his new home. The sound of his laughter eclipsed all other noises in the cell, the prison and Kenny's mind.

Kenny collapsed on the bunk. He couldn't handle being locked in with Eric. He fuckin' couldn't.

Why did they let the bastard share his cell? Easy. The screws didn't know fuck all about what had happened between the two of them, did they? Not a fuckin' thing. Didn't know the truth because the truth had never been told.

That black blanket of depression dropped over him like a fuckin' shroud. He sat immobile now, too frightened even to cry.

Oh, it was gonna happen again. He knew it. And because Eric was bigger than him and had the advantage of surprise on his side, all Kenny could do was wait. It was gonna drive him round the fuckin' twist.

If he could only hang with it until he got his release date. Two-year sentence. Sixteen months, with time off for good behaviour. Wasn't much longer and he'd be away from this shithole. And Eric.

And now Eric had stopped fiddling with his gear, was coming closer, his big powerful hands snaking out. Kenny turned away, though there was no fuckin' place for him to hide. One hand grabbed the back of Kenny's head. Something was being stuffed in his mouth. He struggled, kicking out with his legs, his arms flailing, no longer on the bed. No fuckin' use. He couldn't breathe. A sock? Kenny couldn't cry out.

'We're gonna play games, Golden Boy.'

Eric had gripped both his hands and wrenched them behind him. Now he was lashing something round his wrists. Effectively he was bound and gagged. He tried for another kick back at Eric. Eric hit him on the side of his head. Kenny's neck jerked and dazed, he sagged, to be caught by Eric and slammed unceremoniously against the bunks.

'This is where the fun starts.' Eric slipped something over his head.

Kenny couldn't see. Was it a pillowcase? Then he felt something else follow, lighter, thinner. A cord? He tried to twist away but it cut into his neck. So difficult to breathe. How the fuck had Eric accomplished this?

Kenny knew he was strung up to the top bunk. Whatever was so tightly round his neck was also secured above him. Then he felt his overalls being tugged from his body.

Eric's hands were on him. His thick voice whispered in Kenny's ear, through the fabric.

'We're gonna 'ave a bit of fun. Like cons do in 'ere. Sex games, they call it. I got to make up for lost time, and lost fun, ain't I?'

God forgive me, thought Kenny. Look after Dais. I ain't never gonna be able to make it up to 'er now.

'I know who you are, and what you are, Eddie Lane,' Daisy whispered.

Yet she felt secure with him, cherished even. Her heart hurt just glancing at him. He looked like all the fuckin' cliches of trashy romance heroes rolled into one. His profile when he was driving the car for instance. She'd sneak a look and her mouth would slip into a involuntary smile. He was hers. This good-looking bastard loved her. He'd catch her staring, turn, and instantly they'd be grinning at each other like a couple of fuckin' conspirators. Which in a way, they were, she thought.

In that wonderful room they'd made love, talked and made love some more. Around three in the morning Daisy fell asleep, sated.

Very early Eddie went downstairs to ask if they could stay longer. He came back bearing a tray of coffee and breakfast.

'I didn't know I could be so 'ungry,' Daisy said. They'd demolished every morsel. Eddie put the tray outside the door. Hung a Do Not Disturb sign on the outside door knob and got back into bed. They made love again. Slept, talked.

That first time, when Daisy had made love to him, she'd amazed herself by taking control. Not something she'd ever done before. But she wanted to show him she needed him as much as he wanted her. Was that so wrong? Now he was making love to her. Kissing her body all over. Doing things to her that were new, exciting. Vera had been right. Eddie was a man. Darling Kenny was just a boy.

Eddie gently shook her shoulder to stop her dozing all day. His hair was damp from the shower and he smelled gorgeous.

'You look scrumptious,' she said, stretching. He had on a dark suit and a bow tie.

'You,' he said. 'Get up. Put on the classy black dress. We're goin' out.'

'Where?' Daisy wasn't sure she wanted to leave the safety of the room.

'You'll find out when we get there.'

'Yes, sir,' she said, saluting. 'I love it when you take charge.' She crawled out from under the quilt, and went into the bathroom, revelling in the luxury of the shower, the warm, fluffy towels. When she emerged, the room was empty. Looking out the window she saw Eddie down below with the bonnet of the MG up.

After dressing in her lovely new clothes, complete with perfume and bangle which she resolved never to take off, she felt like a million dollars. She slipped into new black high heels and surveyed herself in the full-length oval mirror. She couldn't believe it was her. Where had Daisy Lane from Bert's Cafe gone?

The door opened and Eddie breezed in.

'Fuckin' 'ell,' he said. 'Dais, you scrub up a treat.' He came and stood beside her. 'Don't we look nice together?' And they did. They complemented each other perfectly and Daisy wasn't ashamed to think it.

When they were in the car Daisy asked, 'Where we goin'?'

'Bournemouth.'

The forest cast dark shapes across the darkened roads. The only lights were beams from the MG and other lone vehicles they passed. Daisy snuggled against him, content. Soon the expanse of heathland gave way to isolated cottages until they merged into villages and then the sea became visible. Daisy didn't think she could ever live in a place where she couldn't see the sea when she wanted to.

Eddie drove along the seafront then into a quiet residential street. He parked in a side road. After locking the car they walked along the pavement towards a huge house almost hidden from view, behind a high wooden fence and tall trees. El Trocadero, stated a brass nameplate on the door.

'What's this place?' Daisy asked.

Eddie had rung the door bell. 'You'll see.'

After a short while the door was opened by a girl, slim and tall with a cloud of silvery hair to her shoulders. Even her strapless dress was silver, clinging to her body like a second skin, except the top part which was too small and she was falling out of it.

'Hello, Mr Lane,' she purred. 'How lovely to see you.' He got a genuine smile and Daisy got a false one. I've got your number, cow, Daisy thought.

'Evening, Patsy,' Eddie said.

'Go on in. You know the way.' The place was softly lit and smelled of the flowers that sat on tables and every conceivable surface. Lilies. The overpowering scent filled the place, reminding Daisy of a giant cemetery. Eddie held her hand as they walked down a thickly carpeted hallway. Patsy was still with them. Daisy hadn't forgotten she'd said Eddie knew the way, so why was she so close to Eddie, even at times brushing against him?

'Cow,' Daisy said so quietly that only Eddie could hear. He squeezed her hand. Then she clamped her mouth shut in surprise. For they were in a large room with gaming tables. Daisy had never seen anything like it, except in films. The decor was velvet red. Even the walls were of heavily flocked vermilion wallpaper.

'Look at those chandeliers,' she said. She couldn't stop the wonderment creeping into her voice, even though old fart-face Patsy was still hanging around.

'Daisy Lane comes to El Trocadero and admires the chandeliers,' smiled Eddie. 'That's what I love about you.' He bent and kissed her on the forehead.

'Yeah, an' when you've been 'ere in the past I can see who's bin admirin' you,' Daisy snapped.

'Daisy Lane, I do believe you're jealous.'

And she realised she fuckin' was. It was not an emotion she'd experienced before so she didn't know how to deal with it. She wasn't about to show her jealousy to anyone though. Well, she might, she thought, if fart-face Patsy didn't clear off soon.

Patsy led them through the players, all dressed in their finery.

They were engrossed, sitting at the tables, drinks at their elbows. Around the outside of the room there was a raised dais for dining. Patsy was stuck like a fuckin' fly paper to Eddie.

Tables with flickering candles were laid up for meals, set with shining cutlery and real linen serviettes. Everything shone, from the tablewear to the brass on the gaming tables, and, specially, the jewellery glittering around the throats and wrists of the punters, thought Daisy.

'Don't be daft.'

Daisy finally answered his question about jealousy as they were directed to a table for two in an alcove. 'Don't be daft,' she repeated.

Eddie pulled out her chair. As she sat down she was struck by the similarity of this place and the club in London. Daisy almost told Eddie so. Then decided this special time with Eddie was not the time to dwell on things past. The future was what mattered now.

Patsy took two menus from a side table and handed them to Eddie. He passed one to Daisy. He nodded to Patsy and she slid away like a perfumed snake.

'It's in French.'

'The top one is steak.'

'That's all right, then. I'll 'ave whatever you're 'aving as long as it's steak.'

He grinned at her. Then the grin faded. His eyes found Daisy's.

'There's a lot we need to sort out, Dais.'

'Steak.'

'Not dinner. You and me.' A waitress dressed in black and white appeared and took their order, including wine, which, for a man who seldom drank, Eddie seemed to know a great deal about. Patsy came back. She touched Eddie lightly on the shoulder and handed him a package which he slipped inside his jacket pocket without opening. He didn't look at Daisy or acknowledge what had just taken place.

The meal was unquestionably one of the best Daisy had ever tasted. Eddie seemed to know his way around, all right, she thought.

'Don't serve this up in the caff, do I?' she said.

Eddie reached across and covered one of her hands with his own. She liked the firm, warm touch of his skin on hers. He indicated the wine. His own glass he left empty.

'No bad 'abits?' Daisy joked. She sipped the fragrant red liquid.

'You know I'm not a drinker.' His smiling face had turned serious again. He wanted to talk, but was she ready to listen? All she'd ever wanted was this fairytale. Being serious could spoil things. Daisy decided to have her say.

'I know you ain't no fuckin' angel, Eddie Lane. Because I asked you not to bring your life home to the caff, and you agreed, it don't make me think you're whiter than white. But to me, Eddie, it's what you do, like a job. An' I don't want to know. You're my Eddie. It's 'ow you treats me what counts, not how you are with other people.'

Daisy paused while the waitress cleared the table. Dismissing a sweet from the trolley, Eddie ordered coffee. When the waitress had gone, he said, 'You're one in a fuckin' million, Daisy. But what happens next?'

She knew exactly what he meant.

'The cafe's a new start for Kenny. I've done the buildin' up an' there's money in the bank for 'im.' Eddie would know she'd made her choice. That she was ready to be with him. To leave Kenny.

'Bert's estate cleared yet?'

She nodded. 'Last week I had a phone call.'

'Pappy ain't Kenny's father?'

Daisy shook her head.

'I thought not,' Eddie said.

The coffee arrived and Daisy poured. She stirred in two spoons of sugar for Eddie and passed him the cup of black liquid.

'How do you feel about that?'

'It was on the cards,' he said. There was noise all around them but once more they seemed to be in their special cocoon, Daisy thought.

'Daisy, I have to explain something.'

She sat back on her chair and waited. As she'd stated quite firmly she wanted to know nothing of his business dealings, this must be something personal.

'All my life I've wanted to be somebody. But right now I'm not

264

the man I want to be. I've money, some property – but until yesterday, I weren't happy. You've changed all that.' Daisy leaned forward. Opened her mouth to protest but he waved her back.

'I know if I can't trust you, I can't trust nobody. Under my bed at 'ome is a locked suitcase. Beneath the suitcase is a loose floorboard. Under there, between the joists, you'll find a box. There are deeds, money. Clean money. Some of the property is rented out. The money's paid into Lloyds on the corner of North Street. Everythin' there is above board. Should anything 'appen to me, you'll be able to draw on my account. It's for you, Daisy.' His words were sinking into her. Now she knew just for how long he'd loved her, that this state of affairs hadn't come about overnight.

'What about Kenny?'

He shrugged. 'You'll take care of him.' Then his eyes clouded. She knew there was more to come.

'I don't know where our mother is, or even if she's still alive. There's an older brother. I haven't traced him. They cleared out years ago. But my father, Pappy, is still in Gosport.' Daisy let the shock wash over her. 'Kenny knows nothin'. He just hated Pappy for the way he'd treated our mum and us. But I pay for Pappy's upkeep in The Cedars, in Alverstoke. I need you to promise that as long as 'e's livin', 'e'll be looked after.'

Daisy nodded but asked, 'Why? If 'e was so awful to you?'

'Mind games, Dais. He beat me because he didn't know how to love, thought it would be a sign of weakness to show he cared. Only I sussed him out. I was just like him, you see. And he knew it. So I took the beatings. Sometimes I provoked him, took Kenny's beatings as well. But he couldn't break me. And I told him I'd have the last laugh. He thought he could drown his feelings in a bottle after that. Now he's senile, dependent on me and he can't do a fuckin' thing about it. There's money set aside for that.'

'Why are you frightening me like this, Eddie?'

'I'm just tellin' you like it is. You're the one person I trust. I loved you, Daisy, from the moment I fell into your bed at Henry Street. An' I've gone on wantin' you.'

Daisy got up from her chair, leaned across the table and kissed him, a kiss that was meant to convey love for him. She could feel his body trembling, like he was relieved his secrets were out in the open at last.

'You think there's trouble ahead, don't you?' Pain lay in his eyes, was etched on his face.

'What goes around, comes around. Trust nobody, Dais. Trust nobody.'

Then he looked at the remains of the coffee and grinned at her, that lovely smile that could melt hearts. 'Life's a gamble, Daisy. We ought to try it out.' He looked over at the gaming tables.

Glad his mood had lightened somewhat, Daisy said, 'I ain't never . . .'

'Now's your chance.' He opened his wallet and presented her with a couple of very large notes. He threw another note on the table as a tip. Patsy was there like a wraith at a haunting.

'Everything all right, Mr Lane?'

He took the two notes back from Daisy and gave them to Patsy.

'Fine. Patsy, be a good girl and change these into chips, will you?'

Daisy could tell she didn't like being talked down to. Patsy tottered away to the cash desk.

Eddie steered Daisy towards the gaming tables.

'What do you want to try?'

'I've no idea.' She was overwhelmed. There seemed to be an awful lot of jewellery and expensive suits about. Her eyes darted everywhere. The players seemed so serious, their faces, eyes, betraying nothing. Fans whirred amidst the chandeliers above, doing their best to clear the heavy pall of cigar and cigarette smoke that lay like a blanket in the room. Despite that, Daisy loved the heady atmosphere of underlying excitement.

Patsy had returned. She handed the chips to Eddie who thanked her and passed them to Daisy. Patsy had a look on her face that Daisy wanted to smack right off.

'Roulette? No, blackjack, I think.'

Punters were nodding at Eddie. He was well known there. Several women gave him the once over then came back for a second look after dismissing Daisy.

At the crescent-shaped table with six seats Eddie bade her sit in the vacant chair. The croupier smiled at Daisy. Even his glittery waistcoat looked like it cost a fuckin' fortune, she thought.

'You can use either money or chips here,' Eddie said. 'Twenty-One's the game.'

'I'll use the chips.' Use them? Daisy lost everything so quickly you wouldn't believe it. She was distraught.

'Oh, Eddie,' she said. 'I'm no good at this. I've wasted all that lovely money.' He laughed. She thought of the way Vera worked to earn that much. How that amount of money would have given a boost to Si and Suze in their new home. And how many hours Daisy herself had to put in, standing on her feet all day, for much less.

'Want to try somethin' else?'

'No. What I'd really like to do is go back to our room. I don't have to share you there.'

Eddie gave her a look of such tenderness that she thought she might cry.

'Come on, then.' He grabbed her hand and said a few farewells. Patsy walked them to the door.

'Goodbye, Mr Lane. Come again, soon.' Yeah, Daisy thought, she could see her thinking *and preferably without me.* Cow!

Outside a drizzle threatened to turn to full-blown rain. They hurried to the car. Once inside Daisy snuggled against him. It seemed so normal, so natural to be close to Eddie. They drove back the way they'd come, back to their haven in the forest. With the rain beating a tattoo on the soft top of the car, the headlights penetrating the darkness, Daisy felt complete.

Eddie let them in with the provided night key and they were as silent as they could be on the creaky carpeted stairs. Why do old houses come into their own at nights, wondered Daisy, with sounds you never notice during the day?

Once in their room they fell into each other's arms.

Daisy never knew what love-making was until Eddie. Well, she'd never had any experience. She'd wanted to please him. Now he took his time in pleasing her, with his hands, his lips, his tongue, his lovely cock.

In the morning, they breakfasted downstairs in the dining room.

Then Eddie paid up and they left. Daisy knew that their room would forever remain a blessed memory in her heart.

They stopped along the way for lunch and to wander around the villages. After the storm of the previous night the sky was blue. But a winter chill had come upon the countryside. They reached the tiny hamlet of Bere around six in the evening.

It was little more than a street leading to the sea with guest houses, tea shops and hotels. Eddie booked them in at a hotel overlooking the picturesque harbour with its grey stone beach, lobster pots and fishing boats. Above the beach was a wooded headland, where later they walked hand in hand amongst the trees.

In the fading light Daisy could see the grey cliffs and the white-crested waves as they scudded against the rocks.

'That would make a lovely photo,' Eddie said.

'Pity we don't 'ave a camera,' Daisy said. 'But you're so right. Do you know, I don't 'ave a photograph of you.'

'You don't need one, Dais,' he said, drawing her into the warmth of his chunky-knit sweater and jeans. 'You got me.'

'If only all our days could be like this.'

'Could be, Dais. I'd 'ave to straighten a few things out, but it could always be like this. Maybe not in Gosport, but abroad, certainly.'

'You really mean that?' He nodded.

'I'd like that,' Daisy said. 'Abroad. Where it's warm. I'd thought our days together was numbered.'

'Dais, we could do anythin' we wanted. But we'd 'ave to move away to do it.'

'I ain't askin' no questions. But I want to be with you. Let's do it, please?'

The last rays of the sun were glinting on the waves, making the sea twinkle and glisten as it flowed gently over the stones.

'I ain't never been so happy in all my life,' Daisy said.

'Me neither, Dais.'

'It'll be a wrench going back to cookin' bacon and swilling floors.' Daisy laughed.

'You don't even 'ave to open the caff if you don't want to.'

'I will,' she said. 'And I'll tell Kenny, face to face. I'm already hatin' myself.'

'We could wait until he comes home an' tell 'im together. It won't be long'

'Na. I owe 'im the truth as soon as possible.'

A fishing boat had landed after a day at sea and the gulls were going daft, zooming about and calling to each other, telling about the good catch. A couple of manky cats had also appeared for a feast of fish from the good-natured fishermen who threw scraps on the cobbles.

The night hours were spent in making plans and love.

Next morning Daisy was woken up by Eddie presenting her with a gift in a brown paper bag. He smelled of the outdoors. Daisy guessed he'd got up very early. He made her drink her coffee first, coffee that he'd brought up on a tray with toast and orange juice. There was also a tiny vase with a single stem of Michaelmas daisies.

'They was all I could find,' he said. 'Pinched that sprig from a garden near the shop. Can't buy flowers 'ere. But I know their name's "Daisy", just like yours. Now open the present.' Daisy fumbled at the box until she'd opened it.

'A camera! I ain't never owned a camera before!'

'Now you can snap away all you wants.'

'Thank you, thank you,' she said. 'We're goin' straight out so I can take pictures of you.'

'Better get dressed first, then.' Daisy threw a pillow at him and that resulted in them falling back into bed again. Daisy decided then that there was something else they needed to do before getting up and leaving the room.

'You're insatiable, Daisy Lane.'

'Only with you,' she said. 'We've got a lot of lovemaking to catch up on, ain't we?'

For an answer Eddie was already slipping out of his clothes.

After a huge breakfast down in the bar they walked along a cliff top to a cove. 'I want to take a picture of you with that in the background,' Daisy said, waving her arm towards the open sea and the grassy edge of the cliff. Eddie complied with her wishes by striking a pose with his arms spread out. 'Back a bit, back a bit,' she cried, trying to get the picture of him straight in the camera's viewfinder. She wanted a picture of all of him, not with chopped-off bits of legs and head.

'I'll be over the fuckin' edge in a minute,' he grumbled. 'An' take your finger off the lens. All you'll get is a picture of a finger.' Daisy snapped him anyway.

The morning air was crisp and sweet, the smell of the sea fresh and clean. A light breeze ruffled Eddie's hair. Daisy sighed. This surely must be heaven because she had never felt like this before, so happy, so full of life. So in love with a man who loved her like no man had ever loved her. Nor, she knew, would ever love her.

An elderly couple walking a black Labrador were approaching. Daisy ran up to them over the grassy turf.

'Would you take a photograph of the two of us together, please.' Without waiting for a reply she thrust the camera at the man.

'Of course.' Daisy ran back to Eddie and slipped her arm through his. Looking up at him, laughing into his smiling face.

The dog ran around them barking and playing but eventually the man got them in focus. Standing arm in arm with their backs to the sea they were snapped. Then Eddie insisted on another one with him looking down at Daisy and loving her.

They never did get to Devon.

But it didn't matter.

Eddie was all Daisy wanted.

It was a filthy, rainy day when they decided they couldn't put off the return to their other lives any longer, a far cry from the sunshine that had first lit their adventure. Now, Daisy thought, it was like winter had suddenly come upon them with a vengeance.

Outside the cafe she didn't even want to get out of the car and open the front door. Everything looked dingier than ever.

'Thank you for the 'appiest days of my life,' she said.

'There will be more to come, Dais,' Eddie promised.

She watched the rain sweeping empty crisp bags and sweet wrappers along the gutter and dragging them swirling down the drain. Before the water fouled their freshness they looked like bright sailing ships floating gracefully.

Eddie unlocked the door. Someone was in residence because there were no evening newspapers or letters on the mat and the smell of disinfectant was fresh.

The cafe kitchen was empty, clean and cold, just as she'd left it. As she climbed the stairs, Kibbles wandered down to greet her. Daisy bent to make a fuss of him. He was purring, his fur warm to her touch.

'Vera's still here, then,' said Eddie, knowing she'd go nowhere without her beloved tabby cat.

At that moment Vera's head poked over the banister. One look at her face and Daisy knew something was up. She came down to meet them.

'Thank God you're back. The police have been 'ere. Kenny was found 'anged in his cell.'

CHAPTER 26

7 November 1963

Daisy stood in the front row of Portchester Crematorium trying to sing 'There Is A Green Hill Far Away'. It may not have been appropriate but it was Kenny's favourite hymn. Tears ran unchecked down her face for the man she'd married and betrayed. 'We may not know, we cannot tell the sins he had to bear'. My Kenny, my happy-go-lucky boy with the ready smile who'd changed beyond recognition inside that fuckin' prison, she thought.

Eddie had been by her side from the moment Vera told them the news.

'What 'appened to my Kenny?' Daisy kept asking him.

Eddie put his arm across her shoulders. 'He couldn't cope.'

'It's my fault, isn't it?'

'That's ridiculous.'

'No. It's a kind of judgement because for the first time in my life I was truly happy.'

'Stop it, Daisy. This is doin' you no good. Kenny didn't hang himself because of us. You know that's the truth.'

His words were meant to drag her from her grief, but she knew it was her fault. And her punishment.

When eventually Kenny's body was released by the authorities, both Eddie and Vera were surprised Daisy insisted on a cremation.

'Kenny was afraid of the dark an' 'e didn't like the cold. Why should I put 'im somewhere 'e wouldn't want to be?'

The large sunny hall smelled of flowers and incense. Living things, people and hope. The sunshine outside kept up this pretence by sending a bright beam across Kenny's coffin as it waited to go through the curtains to the furnace.

Now the coffin began slowly to slide from view. Eddie cleared his throat. Daisy knew he was shedding tears for his lost soul of a brother.

The short service drew to a close. Daisy left with Eddie following close behind and walked ahead down the glass-sided corridor to wait and greet the mourners as they emerged. The courtyard was filled with flowers.

Vera came out first. Red-eyed, she hugged Daisy and kissed Eddie on the cheek.

'Look after 'er,' she said.

Susie, Si, and his parents were there. They had never known Kenny but had come to support Daisy. She was pleased by their show of respect. Some of Kenny's old friends shook her hand. Word had got about locally, the sad event splashed all over the *Evening News*. It had even made the national press. Some of the prison and police officials had turned up, too.

Vinnie Endersby shook Eddie's hand, then turned to Daisy.

'Kenny was a good kid. There wasn't any real harm in him. I'm so sorry for the pair of you. If you need anything or feel I can help, you know where to find me.' His eyes met Daisy's. He really means what he's saying, she thought. Eddie nodded his head.

'Thanks, Vin,' he said.

He'd been a tower of strength to Daisy, keeping his own emotions in check. She'd been waiting for him to cave in, show his true feelings. A few tears, a faraway look in his eyes and a voice that he could barely keep steady were the only outward signs of the great pain she knew Eddie was concealing.

How did Daisy feel about Kenny taking his own life? Cheated. Bewildered. Angry. Incredulous that something had chucked him over the edge so that the only way out was death.

Did she think he was a coward? No, she didn't. It took great courage to tear yourself away from hope. Kenny had lived with hopes and dreams. Knowing him as she did, it had to be something monumental to have tipped him over into the chasm.

The final three people coming towards her made her gasp. Sitting at the front of the hall, she hadn't a clue who was in there behind her. But she realised now that Kenny had had a fair few people to mourn him.

Roy Kemp, holding on to Violet's arm, and another bloke, also dressed in black, came towards her. Roy barely glanced at Eddie but the nearer he came the more she saw the genuine pity in his eyes.

'My dear, I'm so very, very sorry,' said Violet. Daisy waited for her to gabble on as she normally did but she was unusually quiet. The other man took her arm and Daisy watched as they walked out into the gardens beyond the courtyard towards the car park.

Roy put his hands on Daisy's shoulders. He bent down so he could whisper in her ear. His cologne was spicy. It made her think fleetingly of the sea.

'I offer my sincere condolences, Daisy. Can we go somewhere private after you've done your duty here? To talk?' He leaned away to gauge her reaction. She searched his eyes but they betrayed nothing. She could feel Eddie, agitated, at her side. She turned to him, saw his lips set in a hard, thin line. His eyes narrowed, glittering in the cold sunlight.

'Eddie,' she said, 'this is Moira's husband. Roy, Eddie, Kenny's brother.' The two men nodded, a weighing-up affair. She sensed Eddie relax slightly as he realised who the man was.

They shook hands, but like cats deliberating their chances before going in for the kill. Much of a muchness in height; Roy, older, had a slight edge on Eddie, an edge that said, 'Don't fuckin' mess with me. I know who and what you are.' As briefly as their hands touched, Daisy swore she felt something flare between them, but not good, malevolent. Neither spoke.

'There's an open invitation across the road at the Seabird. Shall we go there?' The food there was good and Daisy had arranged a free bar for the mourners.

Roy shook his head. She turned to Eddie.

'Please go on ahead and host everyone for me. I'll be along shortly.'

'You'll be all right?'

She nodded. Their eyes locked briefly then he walked away. He didn't look back.

'How about a ride up to the top of the hill?'

'Suits me,' Daisy said.

274

In the car park was his familiar Humber complete with Charles the chauffeur. The door was opened for her by Roy. She clambered inside and Roy got in after her. Neither spoke until the car had passed through the crematorium gates and was on its way up the winding road to the chalk hills of Portsdown.

'How's Moira?'

'She's fine. In a villa in Marbella. She has a live-in nurse and companion. You can visit any time you want.' Daisy nodded.

'But Moira's not the talking point, Daisy.' She turned in her comfortable seat to stare into his face. He looked tired beneath his year-round tan. 'You are one very strong lady. I respect you, Daisy. So I'll get to the point quickly. You and I had a score to settle. I always settle my debts. If I didn't, my reputation would suffer. And if that happened, any two-bit fuckin' toerag would reckon on takin' me for a cunt. And I can't have that, can I?'

'What's your reputation got to do with me?'

'I owed you.'

'Owe me,' she corrected.

There was a half smile on his face.

The car had come to a halt on a gravel look-out area, a favourite parking place for couples at night. During the day, especially in the summer months, kids rode up there on bikes and young mothers pushed buggies to picnic with their offspring. Now it was deserted. There was a panoramic view of the harbour mouth and Portchester Castle. To the back of them was Nelson's monument, standing guard over the *Victory* moored in the distance at the Dockyard. Trees were bare of leaves now and fields brown, ploughed and left to overwinter.

'No. I've paid my debt. We're even, lady. It's important you remember it.'

'You'd better explain,' Daisy said. 'I've got a pub full of people to see.'

'Okay.' He turned from her and pressed the button in the car's upholstery. The bar swung out and he poured two brandies, one with a dash of lime, which he handed to her. She swallowed half straight away. As the spirit warmed her throat, raw energy seemed to seep into her bones and brain.

'Before I let you anywhere near Moira, I checked you out. You were honest, reliable and like Mum said, "a nice girl". Daisy, you did good by me.'

'I did nothin' for you. Moira was my one concern. But my, you are interested in self-preservation, ain't you?'

'It pays. Keeps me on top, lets me find out what I need to know. Kenny was a pretty boy? Yes?' Daisy nodded. She wondered where Kenny came into this scheme of things. And yes, Kenny was a looker. Perhaps she'd never have described him as pretty. Roy continued.

'His first time inside, a pretty boy like that, where even straight men set themselves up as "wives" just to survive—'

'You mean ... '

'He wasn't queer. I mean Kenny was raped. Repeatedly.'

Daisy felt sick, felt the tartness of the brandy rise at the back of her throat. She swallowed, allowed the meaning of his horrible words to sink in until she understood perfectly their implications.

'Why didn't 'e tell me?' she asked finally, quietly.

'How the fuck could he?'

Of course he couldn't. He would be ashamed. Ashamed she'd think him less of a man. Ashamed of what Eddie might think if word got to him. And now Kenny's mood changes held meaning for her. God, what he must have gone through, she thought. Her gentle Kenny. How physically and mentally hurt he must have been. And he'd kept the secret to himself so as not to hurt her.

'He fought back, Daisy. And for a while he was left alone.'

'What about the prison officers? Didn't 'e say somethin'?'

'Grasses and nonces don't last long inside. Cons rule. There's a pecking order in prison. The guvnor lets the cons sort themselves out as long as it's safe for all concerned. An' what the guards don't know, don't get sorted. An easy life. A well-run establishment. That's the aim of the authorities.' He paused, swigged back his drink and Daisy followed suit. She was trying to get her head around these facts. That this was the truth she had no doubt. There was no reason for Roy Kemp to lie to her. Daisy believed he respected her, just as she respected him. She surprised herself by accepting another brandy.

'Kenny made an enemy who was bigger and stronger than him.

By the time I started makin' it my business to find out your business, it was too late.'

'Kenny 'ad topped himself?'

'Don't you ever believe that, Daisy. Your Kenny handled himself well. But not well enough. When Kenny's cell mate left, the bastard called Big Eric got himself transferred to Kenny's cell. Kenny didn't kill himself. But you can rest assured the geezer that hurt Kenny is on a life support machine.' Daisy took the brandy and downed it. Roy took the remains of the drink from her hand and set it on the drinks cabinet. 'If I'd known sooner what was goin' on, I could have saved your old man, like you saved Moira for me.' Daisy let the truth sink in. She couldn't cry. She was numb.

'The fucker won't prey on anyone else. The last words he heard was, "This is for Kenny." They'll pull the plug on the machine an' that'll be the end of him.'

'My I.O.U. paid in full?'

'Best in the circumstances, don't you think?'

'Thank you,' she whispered. She stared, unseeing, out of the car's window. Then she turned and looked at him. His gypsy dark eyes were cold. 'Let's go,' she said. 'This don't go no further. An' you're a good friend, Roy.'

He knocked on the glass that separated them from Charles. The car started up, heading back down the road to Portchester.

'When you get used to the idea of what's really happened and sort yourself out, I might have a proposition for you. Ever thought of selling the cafe?'

'Ain't mine to sell.'

'Don't be too sure of that. What was Kenny's comes to you.' Daisy was stunned. After the news of Kenny's death she hadn't thought of the cafe or who now owned it.

'I never wanted it for me,' she said. 'That place was Kenny's new start in life.'

'Ain't gonna need it now. And I'm sure you got other plans,' he said. 'So if you want to unload any time, I'll give a more than fair price. Could be useful to me, a prime position like that. Think about it, Daisy. Could be profitable for the both of us.'

The car was turning the roundabout now and pulling into the

car park of the Seabird. Within seconds they'd stopped and
Charles had her door open. She nodded her head towards Roy.

'I'll send Charles in with you to collect Violet. I wish you luck,
Daisy. I've a feeling you'll need as much as you can get.'

Daisy slipped out the car and walked towards the pub.

She saw Eddie was watching from the lounge window.

'Don't you know I'm worried about you?' Vera slammed her red
felt hat on her head and skewered it with her pearly-headed hat
pin. She did it so ferociously it almost bit into her head. She
winced, then scowled at Daisy. 'See what you made me do?'

'I'm all right.'

'Since the cremation you got fuckin' worse instead of better.'
She paused for a moment, thinking she might have overstepped the
mark – after all, cremating a husband took time to adjust to, didn't
it? Daisy was still staring out of Vera's bedroom window, only not
for much longer would it be Vera's bedroom. Vera had already
shed enough tears about leaving, in the privacy of this room. It was
time to look forward now, she thought.

'I'll be all right when you've gone and you ain't naggin' at me
no more an' you've taken that fuckin' fleabag away.'

Vera clamped her lips into a thin line. She started at Daisy, then
at Kibbles trying his best to eat his way out of the wicker carrying
basket. Only he wasn't doing very well, just making a lot of noise
and some very suspicious growling sounds.

Vera took no notice of him, nor of Daisy and her harsh words.
She knew Daisy loved Kibbles, no matter what she said about him.

'This the last of you an' him?' Daisy nodded towards the basket.

'Yes,' said Vera.

Today she was moving into the flat above her massage parlour,
Heavenly Bodies. She'd worked hard getting it just the way she
wanted. The flat was entirely self-contained, with another entrance
at the back leading to Beach Street. The front entrance to the flat
was right next to the double doors of the parlour on the High
Street.

This was her first real home of her own. Now she owned a

business as well, with three pretty young girls who knew all the ins and outs of massage techniques.

There was lovely Samantha, who liked to be called Sam. She was blonde and sassy with generous curves. Margo had that great fall of dark hair that hung loose like a blackout curtain, shining like polished mahogany. Then there was Kirsty. A big girl with a big heart and other large attributes. Men liked big girls, Vera knew that. And she'd no doubt in her mind that her main source of income would come from the men. To this end, the private cubicles at the far end of the parlour had very firm beds, just in case one or two of the customers had a reaction to any of the special oils used, she assured Daisy.

'It's a soddin' brothel masqueradin' as a legit business,' said Daisy. 'An you're the fuckin' madam.'

'It's a registered business, Dais. Approved by the authorities. Look, it says so on my business cards.' She took a black card from a bundle secured by an elastic band from her capacious mock-alligator handbag. She shoved it under Daisy's nose.

Daisy peered at it.

'It just says Authority Approved. It don't say what fuckin' authority.'

'It don't 'ave to,' said Vera, snatching the card back. 'An' if you're goin' to poke fuckin' fun at me ...' She tucked the card down the front of her blouse and eyed Daisy. 'Later, I'm going to open another place specially for lezzies an' one for pansies,' she said. Daisy put her arms around her.

'You're my best friend an' I'm goin' to miss you so much.' Vera put her arms around Daisy.

'There, there,' she said. 'I'm only round the corner.'

'I know,' cried Daisy. 'But I'm gonna miss Kibbles as well.'

'I don't know why you don't get a couple of girls in and reopen the caff,' said Vera. 'It'll give you somethin' to take your mind off things.'

Vera was now stuffing bras and knickers into a brown paper carrier bag with string handles. She'd emptied the drawer and was discarding those items she didn't intend to take with her. Where does all this fuckin' rubbish come from? she thought.

'I ain't ready to be nice to people yet,' said Daisy.

Vera sniffed. 'You can say that again.'

Daisy ignored her, then added, 'Anyway, Eddie's windin' down 'is interests an' then we're goin' away.'

There was no doubting Eddie's love for her, thought Vera. It was just that she was a shadow of her former self. And there wasn't much of Daisy to begin with. It was like a light had been switched off inside her.

'Have it your way,' said Vera. She opened another drawer. 'I don't know why I put my 'at on. Oh yes. I was goin', wasn't I? So Eddie's givin' up the bad life for you, is 'e?'

Daisy nodded. Vera shut the drawer with a snap.

'Eddie ought to give up the fists as well. Young Iris from Forton Road is in hospital with her jaw wired up. Told 'em, well, as best she could tell 'em, she fell down the back stone steps. Eddie gave 'er somethin' to remind her that freebies ain't allowed. Even if it is her fuckin' boyfriend. By all accounts Eddie nearly killed—'

'I don't want to know,' snapped Daisy. 'He ain't like that with me. It's his business, not mine. An' it certainly ain't none of your business.'

'I'm only sayin',' said Vera. 'An' they do say love is blind.'

'Vera, live your life an' let me live mine.'

Well, thought Vera, I don't have to stay here to be spoken to like that. She slung on her red coat, searched for her hat and remembered it was on her head. Then she stomped towards the bedroom door and down the stairs.

Vera wasn't really angry with Daisy. How could she be? Daisy was following her heart. Bad boy though he was, Eddie was a pussy cat around Daisy. Vera stopped at the street door and turned. Daisy had run after her and was holding the wicker basket by its handle.

'You ain't leavin' this smelly bugger with me.'

Vera's heart melted. 'No, I ain't. He's my little man. You get a fuckin' cat of your own.' She snatched at the basket. Kibbles glared out between the wicker bars.

'You goin' to Suze's tonight?'

'Yeah. Got some dear little bootees and mittens for her. Bought them off Albie's Baby Stall. I got white. Can't buy pink or blue until you know for sure, can you?'

'She's got it all now, ain't she?' Daisy said. 'Nice 'ome, man who loves 'er, baby on the way. I'll come with you, if you like. We can go together.'

'Yeah, Dais. Be nice, that.' Thank God Daisy was cheering herself up a bit, thought Vera. For days after Kenny died, she'd shut herself away and the only person she'd speak to was Eddie. She wouldn't reopen the cafe. Mind you, the poor cow's had more than her fair share of hard knocks, thought Vera, and everyone has a breaking point. But now the place belonged to Daisy and it was such a shame to let all her hard work go to waste. Vera decided a bit of street chat might do her good.

'One of the girls told me the lad that overdosed at Clayhall 'ad done it deliberately.'

'Why?'

'Because that same night 'e'd seen 'is uncle knocked down an' killed. In Southsea.'

''Ow do they know that?'

'Accordin' to a nosy neighbour, the two of them went out together. Cal, the uncle, remember he used to come in 'ere sometimes?'

Daisy shook her head.

'Anyway, his body, what was left of it, was found an' a sailor goin' back to the dockyard said 'e saw a kid runnin' 'ell for leather towards the ferry boats.'

'So?'

'They reckon the kid took it bad. Stuffed 'imself full of crap. Idolised his uncle, he did.'

'Well, Vera. Thanks a lot. That's fuckin' cheered me up no end. Got anythin' else nice to tell me?'

'There's no fuckin' pleasin' you today, is there, madam.' Vera opened the street door. 'No fuckin' pleasin' you at all. Come round later an' I'll make a cuppa before we go to Suze's.'

CHAPTER 27

22 November 1963

Eddie opened the bedroom door, stepped in and threw the flight tickets on the bed along with his hat and his Crombie.

'Tomorrow, from Gatwick, we fly to Kos.'

Daisy was sitting in front of the mirror brushing out pincurls. She was going along to meet Suze and Si and other guests for the official opening of Vera's Heavenly Bodies. Eddie would go along later, after he'd done a bit of last-minute business. Daisy looked up. Her eyes met his in the mirror and her face split into a huge smile.

'Where's that?' she asked, nodding towards the bed and the tickets. He loved surprising her. But this time it was special, a new beginning for the pair of them. In a place Daisy could only have dreamed about. He gave her a wink, thought again of the secret he was keeping. The secret that this time tomorrow would be shared by Daisy.

'Greek islands,' he said.

'Eddie?' Her voice held more than a tinge of excitement. Then her eyes clouded. 'When we comin' back?'

'Never, as far as I'm concerned.' She rose from the stool. The fitted black lace slip was moulded to her body. Her pale legs were bare but her toenails were painted red to match her fingernails which, now she wasn't working in the cafe, had grown long again. Later, Eddie knew, when she went round to Vera's, she would have applied to her mouth exactly the same shade of lip colour. Pouting and stretching those perfect lips until she had it just right, then blotting and putting on a second coat. Eddie knew everything about Daisy and his heart felt as though it would burst with happiness each time he saw her concentrating on performing some mundane task or other.

'You mean . . . ?'

'Yes. It's all over. I got one visit to make tonight while you're at Vera's. But I'll meet you round there. Then it's you, me and the sun. Only we might have to wait a bit for the really hot weather as it's the rainy season in Greece now. But their winter won't be as gloomy and cold as ours, Dais.' He walked over and put his hands on her shoulders. Smiled at her reflection in the mirror.

'Remember when we was in that room in the pub in the New Forest?' He saw a smile play at her lips as she thought of it. She nodded. He could smell the subtle tones of Chanel No. 5 rising with the heat from her body. 'Remember how you said you never wanted to leave that room?'

'Yes.' One of his hands moved down to her breast and caressed the firm contours. Her nipple rose to greet him. She leaned into his hand. He sighed, moved away as he felt his body respond. Later, he thought. With his Daisy, he never wanted to rush.

'That was because we'd found somethin' in that room to keep forever. Us,' she said.

Eddie felt tears prick his eyelids. God, how he loved her.

'Daisy, that special something is there in Kos waiting for us. And this time we'll be able to keep it forever.' He shuddered involuntarily. It was like someone was walking over his grave. 'I really thought when we came home that I'd lost you again.'

'I was crazy for a while,' she admitted. 'But you'd shown me a glimpse of what life could be like. Not in fuckin' casinos or hotels, but just you an' me, together.'

He shifted from one foot to the other. He was so nervous. He had a question to ask her. He, Eddie Lane, was fuckin' nervous of a woman. His Daisy, an' all. What if she didn't want to? She could have any man she wanted. She'd the cafe. Some money. What if she said no? But it had been on his mind a long time. Here goes, he thought.

'Dais. Will you marry me?' There, he'd asked her. It had all come out in a rush. And now he was shitting himself waiting for her answer.

Emotions he couldn't read flitted across her face. She was thinking about it. What was there to think, for fuck's sake? Either yes or no. He couldn't bear the wait. At last she spoke.

'Could I have a beach weddin'? Like you see in films? With the warm wind blowin' and—' She didn't get time to finish before he swept her up in his arms. She clung to him, her arms snaking around his neck. And he wished it was tomorrow already and they were out of this fucking dump.

'I'll take it as a yes then?' He smiled into her eyes.

'An' we don't have to come back 'ere?'

He shook his head.

'This cafe will still be 'ere, still belong to you. Stuff in the bank can be sorted anywhere, any time. I need to take some papers along to Lloyds in the morning . . .'

'Don't we need proper luggage for Greece? It's such short notice.'

'We can buy whatever we want when we get there. Travel light, Dais.'

She kissed him, a long, lingering kiss that reminded him of how much he liked being kissed by her. He wanted to lift her on to the dressing table, put his hands on that lovely milky spot between her legs, bury his face . . . Later, Eddie Boy, he thought. Later. Get the business out the way first. He disengaged himself, gave her a light peck on the tip of her nose, breathed in the smell of her.

'Go on. Clear off then,' she said reluctantly. 'Let me finish gettin' ready.'

He stepped away from her and flicked at his suit with the back of his hands to dislodge any particles of her make-up left from the clinch. Grabbing his Crombie and hat once again, he started whistling 'Wheel of Fortune' as he ran lightly down the stairs. He slammed the street door behind him.

After tonight he was going to be the right sort of man for Daisy, make her proud of him. Hey, maybe they could have kiddies, like Suze and Si? He knew he'd make a good dad. He wouldn't fuck about at it like Pappy had done, or knock his kids about. And he'd treat Daisy like the princess she was. Not beat her like his father had done to his long-suffering mother.

The dark and drizzle wrapped itself around Eddie like an old overcoat. Murphy's was shut, the windows filled with kitchen paraphernalia ready for tomorrow's punters. He pulled his coat collar up, crossed the street and walked past the Seahorse pub. Music, mixed with the stench of beer and fags, issued forth into the street as the frosted glass doors swung open. He side-stepped neatly as a couple coming out nearly bumped into him.

'Sorry, mate,' said the bloke. The girl on his arm giggled. He could smell her cheap perfume.

At the end of Seahorse Street he walked by Ratsey and Lapthorne's, the sail-makers. Forton Creek washed up here. There was a mist on the muddy water. He could smell the silt. When him and Kenny was kids they'd go down near the ferry and squelch about in the mud, calling to the people crossing to the pontoon as they waited for the boats to take them to Portsmouth. The people would throw coins into the mud and him and Kenny would dive down, searching in the filth for the precious treasure. All the kids did it. Mudlarks, they were called. Kids don't do that now, he thought. Certainly him and Kenny never would again. His heart was heavy thinking about Kenny. In the past he'd always managed to get the silly sod out of trouble, always managed to keep him safe. But this time he hadn't been there for him. If only they hadn't gone together to rob that place. If only it had been him banged up and not Kenny. He was the oldest, he should have looked after Kenny better. He breathed deeply of the mud, seeing in his mind Kenny, skinny legs green with the seaweedy stuff, blond hair darkened by the slime, triumphantly holding up a penny he'd dived into the stinking blackness for. But most of all he remembered Kenny's gap-toothed grin as he shouted proudly, 'I got it, Eddie. I got it.'

He heard the sound of a car engine and stopped by the bollards near St George's barracks to let it pass. It was raining harder now. He hated the fuckin' rain. Still, it might not be raining yet in Greece. They had a lot of rain in the winter, though, he knew that. And a hell of a lot of sun in summer. Daisy was going to love it. He imagined her lying on a beach towel, reading a book or scribbling away and getting more tanned by the minute. God, he loved her. He looked at his watch. Seven-fifteen. Perhaps by this time tomorrow him and Dais would be waiting for a taxi to take them to their hotel in Kos. They'd make love then go in search of a taverna where he'd buy real Greek food and she'd never have to eat a chip again in her life. He'd hire a car. He'd take her up into the mountains. Then he'd take her to that little village called Asfendiou and give her the fuckin' surprise of her life.

Once, he'd asked her what she wrote about. Just poems and notes about her life, she'd said. And told him he could read it all if he wanted. He'd shaken his head. They were her own private thoughts. She'd told him she respected him for that.

A Hants and Dorset bus was coming down the road towards him. The rain was shining like spears in the yellow glare from its headlights.

Would he miss Gosport? Would he, fuck. After Cal's death the first thing he'd done was to tell Bri and Pat they were no longer needed. He'd given them a healthy screw. Bri had shaken his hand and asked him if he was really happy. Eddie nearly told him he was so fuckin' happy he didn't even get them terrible headaches no more, another thing to thank Daisy for, but he'd been touched by Bri's concern. Then they'd buggered off to Scotland. Bri had his head screwed on all right but he reckoned Pat would go straight back on the bottle again, what with all them fuckin' distilleries up there. Bri had met a girl, was making a go of it by all accounts.

He heard car doors slam as he approached the White Swan. Mucky Duck more like. A repeat performance going on in there like the one at the Seahorse. More noise, more fumes, perhaps a fight later. Heavy footsteps echoed behind him. Sounded like boots, cadets returning to St Vincent, a stone's throw away. Plenty of sailors about, picking fights with the locals, the locals head-bashing the skates.

'Hello, Eddie.'

Eddie recognised the voice before the big bloke stepped up close and he could see him. To his left another big bastard was practically rubbing shoulders with him. The fucker at his back was almost kissing his neck.

'Well, well. Roy Kemp. And what's your pleasure with me?'

'Cool fucker, I'll give you that. We're goin' to the same place so we'll walk together, shall we?'

'Don't see as I've a lot of choice with these goons breathin' down me neck.'

'Eddie, Eddie, don't call them names. My friends might take offence.'

The quartet had reached the open gate of the Georgian house. Eddie made to pass it but Roy shouldered him inside to the long stretch of dark pathway leading up to the steps at the front door. When they'd climbed the flight of steps one of the goons kicked the door and it opened easily. Eddie was pushed, stumbling, inside.

Fear crawled over him, pulling at his skin like fish hooks. He'd known dread earlier this evening while waiting for Daisy's answer. This was a different fear, all-consuming. In the living room a couple of girls were smoking fags and drinking tea, slouched in front of the television. They were watching a re-run of the President Kennedy assassination, killed in front of his wife as his car drove through Dallas in Texas. Eddie shuddered. He'd heard it earlier on the wireless. Mowed down in his prime, poor sod.

'Get the fuck out of here,' said Roy. He didn't even raise his voice.

''Ere, who are you tellin'?'

The slag saw Eddie. Her face went white. She got up and switched off the television. Skinny cow and her hair needed a good wash, he thought.

'Get dressed and get out,' Roy snapped. 'Who else is in here?'

'Bella and Angie.' The girl speaking had already reached the stairs. The air inside the place reeked of old mouldy house, fags and stale sex. 'Scotch Fiona's washin' some clothes.'

'I don't need a fuckin' resume of their lives, just tell 'em they got two minutes to clear out of this shithole. I want you cunts out. Now.'

'Angie's got a bloke in . . .'

'Tell her to give him a wank but get him OUT.' He turned to Eddie. 'Mr Lane, would you accompany us to the cellar?'

Eddie knew he had no choice. A flight of stairs led down to the back kitchen. From the kitchen, a door led to another, smaller room. Eddie was herded in here.

'Used to be a "bottle and jug" when this old place belonged to Hobbs, the brewers,' said Roy. 'Got an alley named after him in the town. Still, I expect you're familiar with all the history, you bein' a local man.'

'Called Beer Alley, is it?' Eddie was determined not to let this bastard see how afraid of him he was.

'I do like a man who can joke in the face of adversity,' said Roy. 'Fuckin' sit down.'

Eddie pulled out a chair and sat down. Then he rose again.

'Mind if I takes me hat and coat off, mate?' He did just that. Laying them carefully on the table. Roy shook his head in obvious amazement as he watched his movements. Then he barked at the other two.

'You cleared this house?' They disappeared like kids being shouted at by their dad. Eddie heard their footsteps up the uncarpeted stairs, the sound of raised female voices, the lower grumble of men's. Eddie sat back on the chair. His eyes met Roy's. Roy's gaze was cold. He put his hand in his inside pocket and pulled out an envelope. He waved it in front of Eddie's face.

'Not doing a collection tonight?'

'Na. Looks like you've done it instead,' said Eddie.

'You think I ought to?' Roy put the money on the table on top of Eddie's coat then went back to his pocket, this time taking out a packet of Players cigarettes. He offered the pack to Eddie, who shook his head. Roy lit a cigarette from a gold cigarette lighter, breathed smoke in Eddie's direction.

'Somebody's gotta take whores' money,' said Eddie.

'Not your whores, though, are they? You don't smoke. You don't drink. No bad habits apart from moving in on my territory.'

Eddie sighed. 'Had to be someone's.'

So this was it, he thought. Payback time. He'd heard the doors slam upstairs, listened as the silence took over the old house, noticed the bolt being drawn noisily across the back door. Now the goons were clomping down to this cellar room. In they came. The blond one had a brick in his hand. Gosport brick. Red.

It wasn't so musty in here as up in the living room. A worn carpet, stained. The ceiling was very low. Eddie had known that, sooner or later, he'd have to get caught out in his dealings. The old wheel of fortune had circled back at him. The wonder was it had lasted this long. As if reading his mind, Roy Kemp spoke.

'I've been watching you for a few months now. Earnings from this area shouldn't disappear, Eddie. My box number in Clapham hasn't had as much money paid into it as it should. You been feathering your nest with my money, and if you hadn't been looking after Daisy, I'd have sorted you long ago.'

Now the door had been closed. The four of them practically filled the small room. Eddie looked about him. A little window and two goons at the door. Not a fucking chance he could escape.

'You know I'm good then?' said Eddie. He lifted one leg and draped it across his other knee.

'Eddie, Eddie, Eddie. What am I going to do with you?'

'If you wanted, you could use me.' It was a long shot, decided Eddie, but anything was worth a try.

'How would I hold my head up, if I let a toerag like you rob me eyes blind and then come back for me fuckin' eyelashes? Even you can see that ain't a feasible request, Eddie.'

Eddie thought about the death of the London snout in this bloke's club. Eddie knew who Roy Kemp was all right. A fuckin' big boy like the Kray twins and Eddie and Charlie Richardson. Just his luck, he thought, to take what wasn't his away from a fuckin' big London name.

Eddie thought how he'd rather be any place but here.

Thought about the girl in the boatyard. Thought about Mikey. And all the others . . . Jesus Christ, it was like his whole fuckin' life was flashing past. He smiled to himself. At least Vinnie Endersby hadn't been the one to come out on top again. Close, though, very close. He'd felt Vinnie's net closing in. But Eddie had foiled him this one last time, even if it was at the hands of Roy Kemp.

'Daisy?'

'She knows nothing,' said Roy. 'She knows me only as Moira's old man. Knows I can pull a few strings here and there. Why do you think you've lasted so long?'

'You an' her . . .'

'Don't you just hate yourself for even wondering? Na. My old mother thinks the world of that girl. You'd have been snuffed out a long time ago if Daisy hadn't been so useful to me. I owe her no favours now. And you? You're surplus to requirements, as they say. I can't have you slicing off profits from my girls, my drugs, my clubs and pubs, can I? Not because I can't afford it. It ain't the money, Eddie. It's the shame. Surely you can see that?' Yeah, he could see it.

'Will you grant me one favour?'

Roy laughed. 'As long as it ain't to let you go.' He went on laughing. It was the sound of a man totally in control. Eddie shivered.

'Afterwards – I don't want Daisy to see me . . .'

'We wasn't going to leave you around, Eddie Boy.'

'An' you'll tell her? Not just leave her waitin' for me?'

Roy examined the nails of his long-fingered hands. Eddie could see him thinking deeply. Then he nodded. 'She deserves that.'

Eddie knew he could trust this man to make it easy for his Daisy.

'Get the brick,' said Roy. The blond placed it squarely on the carpet near the fireplace.

'Lay flat on the carpet, Eddie. And bite on the brick.'

This was it, then. The end of Eddie Lane. But his Daisy would be provided for. Daisy was his last thought as he opened his mouth, then clamped his teeth along the top edge of the brick. And they brought their boots down on his head.

Daisy was humming 'Wheel of Fortune'. Eddie's got me at it now, the bastard, she thought. Tomorrow she'd be sleeping in a different bed with her Eddie, in a place that held no memories for either of them.

White sand, herbs and olive trees, the smell of spices in the air. She looked at the holdall. Just a few necessary things. Toiletries. She'd buy everything when they got there. Just like he said. Eddie could choose my new bikini, she thought. Perhaps she'd be wearing it when she told him . . . She looked at the clock. It was nearly midnight.

She'd had a good time round Vera's. She wasn't surprised Eddie hadn't shown up. Sometimes he was a law unto himself. Vera would make a go of that place, no doubt about it. She laughed, thinking of Si. He wouldn't let Suze out of his sight. She had quite a little bump there now. No doubt the kiddie would be the spitting image of Si, just like the rest of his family.

Then came a knocking at the street door. Eddie had a key. So did Vera. But Vera was in her own place now, wasn't she? She opened her window and looked down. The rain stung her cheeks. She recognised the car before she saw the man.

'Be down in two ticks,' she shouted.

Roy was on the doorstep.

'Can I come in?'

'Sure,' she said. 'Is it Moira? What's happened now?' He shook his head as he stepped into the hallway. The rain had darkened the shoulders of his overcoat. She saw then he was wetter than she'd first thought, dripping on the lino, like he'd been out in the rain a long time. Momentarily she wondered why. He'd just got out the car, hadn't he? 'You're a long way from 'ome.'

'Business,' he said. 'Can we sit down?'

She led the way into the cafe, switching on the electric light, going automatically towards the kettle. A fear gripped her heart.

And she knew then that business was Eddie.

'Where is 'e?'

They stared at each other. All the colour in the cafe seemed to drain to a winter grey, a cold, cold winter grey. Daisy shivered. Roy walked towards the tables and pulled two stools out. He sat on one, motioned towards Daisy to sit on the other.

'Come and sit,' he said.

'I don't want to fuckin' sit down. Where's my Eddie? It is Eddie, ain't it?'

He nodded.

'Where is he?'

'It won't do you no good to know. He didn't want that.'

'He's fuckin' dead, ain't 'e?'

The silence seemed to Daisy to go on interminably. Why didn't Roy shake his head? Why didn't Roy tell her Eddie was all right? Why didn't . . .

'He was a good bloke.'

'You killed 'im.' Daisy couldn't believe this was happening. 'How can you say he was a good bloke if you killed him?'

'I had to, Daisy. He made me look a fool and that's not good for business.' And all at once she realised Eddie was gone. Everything was gone, her whole future snatched away by this man.

She flew at him, spitting and swearing, kicking.

'You bastard, you bloody fuckin' bastard . . .' She really lost it. But the strange thing was, he let her beat on him. Just stood there and let her lay into him, until she fell, exhausted, on the floor, sobbing with heaving breaths that racked her body.

Then he picked her up in his arms, like she was a kid, and sat her down on the stool. For a fleeting moment she thought she could smell Eddie's cologne on him. She sat there like a wet dishrag and he went and got her a glass of water from the tap. He handed her the glass, then pulled the other stool up close in front of her and sat down.

'Was it quick?' He nodded. Daisy didn't drink the water but set it down on the floor at her feet.

'Why did you do it?'

'Daisy, he played a big boy's game. He knew the score. He went with dignity.'

She thought of when Eddie tried to tell her things and she didn't want to listen.

'You knew I loved him.'

He sighed.

'It was business. I don't owe you a thing.'

She thought of the way he had avenged Kenny's killer. It was true. He owed her nothing. Roy's face was impassive.

And they both knew she wouldn't involve the police. After all, hadn't Roy simply taken another scumbag off the streets? This was justice meted out the Roy Kemp way, the survival of the criminal fraternity's fittest.

'Eddie wanted me to tell you.'

'And now you 'ave. So get the fuck out of 'ere.' He looked at her. Put out a hand to touch her. She shrugged him away.

'You'll be all right?' Daisy shook her head at him. Even managed a small laugh.

'As if you fuckin' care.'

He frowned. Then got up and walked towards the hallway, his wet shoes making soft scraping noises on the scuffed lino.

'For what it's worth,' he said, 'I'm sorry.'

She heard the street door slam. He hadn't even fuckin' looked back.

She picked up the glass of water and threw it. It shattered against the wall, the water running down the paintwork in rivulets.

'Roy fuckin' Kemp, I owe you one,' she shouted.

She wanted to cry. It was a pointless exercise. She went upstairs to the room Eddie used before he started sleeping with her in her bed. As soon as she pushed open the door she could smell remnants of him in the air. His clothes hung in the wardrobe, waiting for his return. His hairbrush was on the dressing table, waiting for him to brush his silky hair. She pulled out the dark hairs clinging to the bristles and tucked them next to her skin inside her bra. The room was clean, practically empty of his presence. He'd used it as a dressing room.

She stood at the window, looking down at the roof of the shed and the lavatory, all shining in the rain.

She remembered flicking paint at him on a bright summer day, his smile, the way his hair had shone blue-black in the sunlight. She wondered how long it would take before she wouldn't be able to recall his features. That's what happened, didn't it? No matter how much you loved a person, after a while their face blurred into nothingness, leaving just that awful, awful ache in the heart.

And then she was pushing the bed aside, picking up the suitcase. It wasn't locked. She lifted the lid. Inside were Pompey football programmes, well fingered, smelling like old cardboard, the edges ragged. Stuff he thought was important enough to keep. A child's drawing of two stick people, one with crayoned yellow hair. A larger figure with black hair holding stick-fingered hands. Kenny's name scrawled in the corner in big round letters. This was the side of Eddie people never knew, the sentimental, caring side. There were photos of the two boys. Two scruffy kids sitting on a wall. Two smiling faces. Two kids who wouldn't laugh any more but were captured forever, there on that bit of card. She felt tears rise. She couldn't cry now. Wouldn't. She pushed the case to one side. She'd go through it when she was calmer.

She knelt on the boards, saw the barely visible marks where she should be able to lift the wood.

Inside the hole were a few dusty wood curls. Her fingers

searched either side of the sawdust-covered joist. And there it was! The box Eddie said she should look in. She shook away the thought that in the morning before they left they would have been going through this box together. Tying loose ends, before their new life commenced.

The first thing she saw was banknotes, held together with elastic bands. She picked out a bundle and flicked through. This was a great deal of money. Never in her wildest dreams had she envisaged money like this. And hadn't Eddie said there was more in the bank? She felt around beneath the bundles and came up with a long envelope tied with red solicitor's ribbon.

Inside were property deeds.

The thick papers felt sticky. She opened one batch. A house in Western Way, Alverstoke. The neatly folded pages showed the names of owners through the ages. Plans of work done, receipts for thatching and roofing repairs. People would kill to live in that exclusive part of town, she thought. Eddie owned a house there? And yet he had stayed with Daisy?

Another deed was in a language she didn't understand, until she saw the address. Asfendiou, Kos. Greece. She guessed then that he would have taken her first to a hotel and in the morning would have driven to this house and he'd have said, 'It's yours.' Just like that. 'It's yours.' That's how well she knew her Eddie.

She sat back on the floor, and stretched her legs. There were other deeds to houses in the town. These must be the places that were rented out. She folded up the papers and returned them to the big brown envelope. Again she delved through the money. Her fingers found a narrow object.

As she raised the small lacquered box, memories came flooding back. With shaking hands and thudding heart she snapped open the clasp.

Her mother's brooches.

They were all her mother had to leave her. But why were they here? Amongst Eddie's stuff? Daisy took up the gold and ivory brooch and turned it in her hand, remembering it shining on her mother's old grey coat. Then she saw the piece of white notepaper tucked down the side of the box. Returning the brooch alongside the small diamond half-moon one, she unfolded the note. Her hands were shaking worse than ever now.

> If you are reading this, alone, I'm sorry.
> I've tried many times to tell you of my
> secrets. This is my guiltiest secret.
> Kenny told me about the jewellery and
> I went that afternoon to steal it. Your
> mother was asleep. She was still asleep
> when I left. The brooches were in my
> pocket when I met you for the first time.
> I fell in love with you in that instant.
> I couldn't sell the brooches, as I'd
> planned. They belonged to you. So I've
> kept them for you.
> Forgive me. I love you. Eddie

Daisy put all the stuff back in the box. She breathed a sigh of relief. Years of wondering about the whereabouts of her jewellery were ended with Eddie's confession. Would he ever have told her to her face?

She thought of the secrets she'd been forced to keep from him.

She'd never have revealed the truth about Kenny's death, would never have wanted Eddie hurt by knowing how his brother had lived and died in prison. Roy Kemp's intervention? That too she would have kept secret. Why? Because she'd promised. A promise to Daisy was sacred.

Taking the box up to her room, she set it on the dressing table. Then she went back down to Eddie's room and took his shirt, the one he'd had on earlier and had changed for a clean one. She could smell him on it.

She went back upstairs and got into bed, the side Eddie slept. The musky scent of him, his orangey cologne, was heightened by her body heat as she curled, foetus-like, around his silk shirt.

For a long time she stayed like that, thinking, wondering, wanting and hurting.

The flight tickets were on the dressing table. She knew she'd go to the bank in the morning. What then? She'd survive. She was a strong lady, wasn't she?

She stared at the photograph in the brass frame, of her and Eddie, taken on the cliff top. They were happy then, just discovering each other. Short and sweet it had all been. She sighed.

Maybe she'd come back to Gosport. Maybe she'd be like Vera and shower all her love on a cat. But one fuckin' thing she knew for certain.

Roy Kemp, she vowed.

I fuckin' owe you.